CW01082870

# PRAISE FOR HEIDI CHIAVAROLI

"Chiavaroli delights with this homage to Louisa May Alcott's *Little Women*, featuring a time-slip narrative of two women connected across centuries."
    PUBLISHERS WEEKLY on *The Orchard House*

"Beautifully written, this God honoring and compelling story is Heidi Chiavaroli's best yet."
    CATHY GOHLKE, Bestselling, Christy Hall of Fame and Carol Award-winning author on *Hope Beyond the Waves*

"*Hope Beyond the Waves* tugged at my heart from page one, and I was totally immersed in the seemingly insurmountable challenges of both the past and present day characters. Kudos to Heidi Chiavaroli for pouring out this beautifully raw and moving story about finding love and hope in the most unexpected of places."
    MELANIE DOBSON, Carol Award-winning author of *Catching the Wind*

"*The Hidden Side* is a beautiful tale that captures the timeless struggles of the human heart."
    JULIE CANTRELL, *New York Times* Bestselling author of *Perennials*

"First novelist Chiavaroli's historical tapestry will provide a satisfying summer read for fans of Kristy Cambron and Lisa Wingate."
    *LIBRARY JOURNAL* on *Freedom's Ring*

# The Way Back

## LIGHTS OF ACADIA

HEIDI CHIAVAROLI

HOPE CREEK PUBLISHERS

Visit Heidi Chiavaroli at heidichiavaroli.com

Copyright © 2024 by Heidi Chiavaroli

All rights reserved.

Hope Creek Publishers LLC

Cover Design by Hannah Linder at https://hannahlinderdesigns.com

Edited by Melissa Jagears

No part of this book may be reproduced in any form or by any electronic or mechanical means, including information storage and retrieval systems, without written permission from the author, except for the use of brief quotations in a book review.

Scripture quotations are taken from the New International Version and the King James Version.

*The Way Back* is a work of fiction. Where real people, events, establishments, organizations, or locales appear, they are used fictitiously. All other elements of the novel are drawn from the author's imagination.

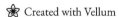 Created with Vellum

# Also by Heidi Chiavaroli

The Orchard House

The Tea Chest

The Hidden Side

Freedom's Ring

The Edge of Mercy

Hope Beyond the Waves

## The Orchard House Bed and Breakfast Series

Where Grace Appears

Where Hope Begins

Where Love Grows

Where Memories Await

Where Dreams Reside

Where Faith Belongs

Where Promises Remain

## Lights of Acadia Series

The Way Back

*To the faithful readers who anxiously await the release of every book I write.*
*You know who you are.*
*Thank you.*

# *Prologue*

The memory is never far. To let it flit away like a fearful sparrow instead of holding it close like the persistent, weary ghost it's become would be to forget my penance for the life I took.

Maddie.

I still remember the slight dip in her cheek when she smiled at me at the top of the cliff, nerves fringing the stretch of her mouth. I remember the smell of salty air, mixing with the *Banana Boat* coconut sunscreen on our tanned skin. Sunlight glinted off her necklace—a sterling silver pendant picturing a sparrow.

I wore an identical one. Engraved on the back were our initials and the words *Best Friends*. I'd picked them out because the sparrows reminded me of a card Nana had sent me for my ninth birthday. I used to repeat the scripture verse written beneath the bird's silhouette over and over in my head to lull me to sleep, to distract me from the sounds of drunken laughter and men and noises I didn't completely understand coming from my mother's bedroom.

*Are not two sparrows sold for a penny? Yet not one of them will fall to the ground outside your Father's care.*

Even though I didn't comprehend them, something about the words comforted.

Strands of brown hair brushed Maddie's face and she squeezed my hand. "Sure we want to do this?"

I dragged in a breath, nodded, and pressed her hand back. I looked over the ledge and down into the Pacific waters below where two of the hottest guys from San Simeon High called up to us, urging us to jump. I'd had a crush on Jason since the sixth grade, when he'd sat next to me on the bus the morning after my mom showed up at the school, drunk, black mascara and lipstick smudged along her face, too much of her bra exposed, stumbling and slurring my name in the parent pick-up line—a perfect advertisement for what you *don't* want to be when you grow up. I still remember the whoosh and sink of the brown bus seat as Jason sat beside me and, without provocation said, "My mom's a loser, too." The insult felt more like camaraderie, and I thought maybe I fell in love with him then and there.

"On three?" Below us, the waves pounded against the rocks. We'd have to jump out far enough to miss them. We were crazy with thoughts of invincibility. We were young, ready for the rest of our lives, ready for anything.

"I don't know, Laney . . ."

I squeezed her hand. "Together, right? It'll be over in seconds."

She nodded, her bottom lip visibly trembling.

I began counting. "One . . ."

In a minute it'd be over. We'd be in the water and Jason would circle me with those strong arms of his, nothing but water and swimsuit between us.

"Two . . ." Maddie joined in with me now.

Soon we'd be laughing and trying to spot dolphins on California's coast. Later we'd celebrate the end of summer with Maddie's parents at Sierra Mar restaurant.

"Three!" We ran, our bare feet pounding smooth granite, the wind on our faces. It felt like flying. Freedom.

As we neared the edge, I noticed our footsteps weren't quite synchronized. I thought of letting Maddie's hand go so we could better balance ourselves, but she held tight and we soared out from the cliff together.

My stomach lurched as we fell, fast, toward the guys beneath us. Maddie released my hand and I remember being grateful. My hair flew upward, my arms flailing as I hit the water at an awkward angle, my foot bent out from the rest of my body. It stung at first, cold prickly needles replaced by soothing water, soaking through my suit and cutoffs. Then the water swelled over my head and a few seconds later, I burst above the surface, laughing. Relieved.

I looked for Maddie, sure this moment was the highlight of our eight years of friendship. A swell in the water lifted me up, then down, and I lost sight of where she may have fallen.

As anticipated, Jason swam to me, his large hand ran along my waist, cupping my hip. "You are so hot, Laney. I knew you wouldn't chicken—" His words broke off as his friend, Aaron, called out to us, his voice carrying over the bob of the waves.

"Where is she?"

My treading limbs grew weak in the water. Jason started with fast strokes toward Aaron's voice, and I willed my legs to kick after him. Maddie hadn't come up from the surface yet. Maybe she wanted to give us a scare like that time at the Fourth of July parade. While searching for prime seats, Maddie had gotten separated from us. After an hour of trying to find her, she finally showed up on the Statue of Liberty float, throwing well-aimed bubblegum at our faces.

Yes, that had to be it. Maddie would surface any second.

With each stroke though, my confidence waned. She wouldn't be under the surface this long. She *couldn't* be under this long.

"She hit the water, right? Aaron—she hit the water!" I screamed the words, searched the rocks at the base of the cliff, my breaths ragged and shallow even as I pictured the bloodied and bruised body of my friend, splayed on the rocks.

3

Aaron stared at me dumbly, a wet lock of hair like a snake along his forehead. "Right here. She was right here."

I inhaled the deepest breath I could beneath my tears and dove under, heard Jason call for me too late. I forced my eyes open against the salt, dove deeper into the darkness, swam away from the rays of sunshine, grasped for anything of my friend's—a clump of hair, an arm, a piece of the bathing suit she bought just yesterday—but nothing. I stayed down until my lungs nearly burst, forcing me to break the surface.

"Jason! Jason—where is she?" My voice was hysterical. But Jason and Aaron were both underwater, doing as I had done moments earlier.

I went under many more times, screaming Maddie's name beneath the water. She hadn't wanted to jump. Not at first. I'd pressured her into it. And for what? For the split-second admiration of a boy?

We didn't find Maddie's body that day. The Coast Guard found her washed up on shore the day after. The casket was closed for her funeral. I tried not to imagine Maddie's bloated body, the necklace claiming we were best friends snug against her blue skin.

The necklace that now sits at the bottom of my jewelry box, shouting accusations up at me whenever I glimpse the drawn feather of a wing. The one calling me out on my empty promise to look out for her. Making me question God over his broken assurance to care for my friend, a fallen sparrow.

Six years later, I still half expect Maddie to find me in the restaurant where I work and tell me she's sorry, the joke has gone on too long.

But she doesn't come. Someone else does. And as soon as I see him, I know that I will never be able to escape that day.

It will always, always haunt me.

# Chapter One

*My daughter was beautiful and bright, but she seemed to*
*illuminate the truth that I could never be the mother she needed.*
*After her birth, I sank deeper into my addictions.*
*~ Locked Light* by Miriam Jacobs

## LANEY

When I step out of my therapist's office into bright sunshine, it is with the kind of optimistic enthusiasm a child feels on the first day of summer.

The possibilities are endless.

My life is just beginning, stretching before me in a myriad of paths that are mine for the choosing.

I *am* healing.

If only the seed of this enthusiasm would take root and land on fertile soil. But I know from experience it is destined for rock or a patch of weeds. It will not last.

Every time I go home, try out a new, positive outlook with my mother, I get crushed. It's inevitable she will say something to suck every corner of hope out of my windblown sails.

But this time—this time is different. This time, I vow not to let that happen. I vow to escape.

I walk down the sidewalk, and when I reach the spot where I've parked my car up against the curb, I keep walking. Eventually I reach a small bench tucked up against a box of golden petunias.

The scars on my forearms stretch taut when I tie my hair up into a messy bun before sitting and reaching into my purse for my phone. My fingers brush against my rehab journal and then to the envelope inside—a card, like a dozen others, from a grandmother I've never met. A grandmother I very much long to meet.

I tap in the code to open my phone and search for one-way flights to Maine. Memorial Day weekend is approaching and prices are expensive, but if I don't book now, I'll chicken out.

I know myself. I've been in this place before.

I mentally seek out Dr. Shelley's words to coax my thoughts back to rights. To blow that seed of hope past rocky soil onto tilled earth.

*It's time, Laney. Time to decide how you're going to move forward. Time to decide what you want from your past and for your future.*

Leaving home, leaving the place where the memories chase and haunt—that is what I want. That is what all my time journaling has revealed.

The first time I cut myself was two months after Maddie died. It was an accident, in the shower while shaving. The burn of it took my mind off my guilt, off the pain of living without my best friend. It was numbing relief. Like menthol on a muscle ache— cool, and then burning so thoroughly it took my thoughts off all else. Eleven months ago, though, I made a cut too deep. I panicked, thinking I had ended my life with one swipe. In the haze of it all, I called 9-1-1, exposing my long-held secret and getting the help I needed. Rehab. Therapy. Help for which I am grateful.

But Mom's recent book success has threatened my stability. What she included in her memoir was the ultimate betrayal. It causes me to wake at night reliving memories both known and unknown, scratching at itching, burning arms. My tight skin calling for me to relieve the pressure of the fear and the pain.

I remember seeing Jason's father in the grocery store yesterday. He spoke to the clerk behind me while I pulled my hat tighter on my head and prayed he didn't notice me.

He didn't. Just kept talking to the clerk about his son finally moving back home.

If I ran into Jason's dad at the grocery store, what were the chances I'd eventually run into Jason himself?

That couldn't happen.

Reason enough to book a flight to the other side of the country.

I choose a flight that leaves the next evening, type in my information, and let my finger hover over the *Book Flight* button.

I'm not running, I'm searching. Trying to find answers in the deluge that Mom's book has left in its wake. Trying to find the last stretch of healing on this long, arduous journey of living without my best friend.

With resolve, I press the yellow button, confirming my flight.

And, perhaps, my future.

*Bar Harbor, Maine*
*Nine Days Later*

I SWIPE at a bead of sweat on my brow, unsure if it's due to the mile walk from my motel or the shear anxiety of meeting the grandmother I have never met. I push back my shoulders, forcing determination into my stride. I'd spent the last week settling into the rhythm of Maine. I found a job at a local restaurant, read a dozen tourist guides. There is nothing left to do but search out the woman behind the cards.

My grandmother.

The mailbox at the end of the driveway stands white and quaint, with an abundance of pink impatiens planted at its base. The distant crash of waves does nothing to calm the queasiness in my stomach.

I dig out the envelope my grandmother sent four years back from the side of my backpack and note the return address. They are the same numbers that are on the mailbox.

I slip the card from the envelope. The lighthouse on the front is the same as the one to my left. It doesn't at all match the description Mom wrote about in *Locked Light*, the memoir she published three months ago. She said it was a looming dark tower, when in fact, it is quite stout and bright with whitewash.

Imagine, a *memoir*. My mother, who barely graduated high school and whose daily reading didn't go beyond the two lines written on her prescription bottles, had written an entire book.

And somehow, she'd pulled it off. *Locked Light* was a runaway bestseller. In it, Mom told all, including the one thing I had asked her explicitly *not* to tell.

I blink, looking up at the beacon facing the vast waters of the Gulf of Maine. The light appears sturdy and solid, seeming to whisper of mysteries begging to be unearthed. The yellow caution tape crossed over the doorway whispers of secrets.

I glance back at the matching lighthouse on the card, Nana's scrawled words on the front.

*You are the light of the world. A town built on a hill cannot be hidden. Neither do people light a lamp and put it under a bowl.*
*Matthew 5:14-15*

I open the card, knowing what I will find and looking to the words now for the courage I need.

*Dear Laney,*

*I know these last couple of years have been hard for you. If I had a different relationship with your mother, and I suppose, if I'm honest, with you, I would have flown out there by now. You don't know me except through these cards and letters, but Laney, say the word and I will be on the first plane out.*

*I'm sure it's the fantasy of an old woman that you might want me to come see you. I haven't been part of your life for all these twenty-one years. Still, please know, there is always a room in my house for you should you ever decide to show up for a visit. I say that not to put any guilt on you, but because I mean it. Laney, it doesn't matter that we haven't met. You are precious to me, dear girl.*

*Nana*

I sniff and close the card, again staring at the drawing of the lighthouse. Mom wrote of the inside of the light in detail. Does my grandmother's lighthouse actually match the description in Mom's book, or will I find that also ingenuine?

I readjust my bag over my shoulder and walk up the drive.

*One step at a time.*

Dr. Shelley's words. We've agreed to keep up our appointments on Zoom. That, and the fear of running into Jason, might be the only thing keeping me from booking a flight back home.

I suck in a breath as The Beacon Bed and Breakfast comes into view off to the right—a large white farmhouse with a wraparound porch. To the left, across a patch of well-worn grass, is the footbridge to the lighthouse.

From the look of the worn grass, many come and go to the lighthouse. I should probably ring the doorbell before visiting it, but something inside me longs to see it now, for myself. To form an opinion of the lighthouse before I form an opinion of my grandmother.

I start across the footbridge.

"Hey!"

I startle, jumping back at the near bark of the voice. When I turn, I see a fit older woman with ashy hair at the bottom of Nana's back porch steps. I open my mouth, but no sound comes out.

"If you're thinking about going to the lighthouse, don't try to go inside, all right?" She breathes out a gust of air that fans a few strands of hair near her eyes. She walks closer, and I waver, half wanting to run back up the drive and never return.

The older woman gestures toward the lighthouse door. "That caution tape's there for a reason. I don't want anyone getting hurt, especially if you're out there by yourself."

I turn to fully meet her gaze and recognition flickers behind eyes that match the ocean beside us.

"Are you . . .?"

I lick my lips. Do I call her Nana? It's how she's signed her cards, but without a relationship outside of the one we have on paper, it feels presumptuous and fake, as if I'd be stealing something I don't have a right to.

"Laney?"

"You . . . you know me?"

All traces of severity vanish from my grandmother's face. "Your mother has sent me your school picture every year. Of course, the last one was six years ago, but you've only grown more beautiful. You have your mother's eyes." Her voice cracks on her last words.

Mom had sent my pictures to Nana? Why would she do so, when she continually refused to see her again?

"I'm so sorry I snapped at you, honey. There's been an endless stream of tourists lately, crossing my property, trying to get past the caution tape. It's not there for my convenience, that's for sure. It's dangerous in there."

I suck in a small breath. That's exactly how Mom had described it in her book.

Nana's eyes widen and she waves a hand through the air. "Not dangerous because it's a dungeon like your mother believes, dangerous because it's old and in need of repair. I think I'm going to have to have it torn down."

"Torn down? But it's a historical landmark. It'd be a crime to —" I stop short at the fact that I'm about to outright accuse Nana of committing a crime. Touchy subject. "Sorry." My gaze drops to the ground.

"Laney."

I meet her clear gaze, and it's so open and full of acceptance that I can't believe I ever doubted coming here.

"There's nothing to apologize for." She looks at the white-washed lighthouse. "I wish the Beacon wasn't attracting the worst kind of people, but she is. Not you, of course, but after that *Hello, America* interview . . ."

Mom's interview on the popular morning show had led to dozens of other interviews, creating a fan base that rivaled Matthew McConaughey's memoir.

Nana shakes her head. "Forgive me. That's not important right now. What's important is that I'm meeting my grand-daughter for the first time." Her smile matches the sun high in a robin's egg blue sky. All too soon, though, it wavers. "But if you've only come to see the light, I suppose it would be safe enough to go down on the rocks for a better view."

"No, Nana." The name is out before I can stop it. "I mean, I came to see you, too." Although I had traveled all the way across the country to do so, admitting it outright places me in a vulnerable position. I hadn't even told her I was coming.

"Oh, I'm so glad, dear girl. How long were you planning on being in town?"

I shrug. "I'm not really sure. But I did just get a waitressing job." If I had stayed in college, stayed with my business management degree, perhaps I'd have an official career—some sort of purpose to my life. Instead, I am as shifting as the sands on the beach below. Indecisive. Without goals. An underachiever.

At least Mom had pulled herself up by her bootstraps after a series of bad choices. She had forced good out of it, which was more than I could say for my own sordid history.

"Good." When she smiles, her weathered face looks ten years younger. "Where are you staying, honey?"

"The Acadia Gateway Motel. They said it'd be fine to stay for the summer."

"That will be an expensive summer. I have plenty of room here, and I'd be happy to have you for as long as you like."

My muscles tense, from the base of my neck all the way down to my toes. "Oh no, I couldn't impose. You don't even know me. I don't know you." Why did she think she could trust me when her own daughter had written such terrible things about her? Why would she think I could trust her?

She raises one eyebrow. "Do you believe what your mother wrote in that book? Is that why you don't want to stay with me?"

"No, of course not." But that's not true. "Or . . . I don't know."

"That book has cost me just about all my paying guests, so I'm not lying when I say I have the room. I don't see why you shouldn't stay with me, if you can get past the notion that I'm some sort of a prison warden."

"I'd want to pay rent, or at least help out."

She flings her hand through the air again as if I've suggested the most outlandish proposition. "I'm not worried about that."

My fingers itch to dig my phone out of my bag and dial Dr. Shelley's number. Would she agree this is the best way forward? Would my "new" start truly be new if it was under my grandmother's influence? What if Nana turned out to be just like my mother?

I think of Mom's overbearing, controlling ways. After Maddie died, she'd turned a corner and gotten clean, married a half-decent man who gave us a half-decent life. As much as I resented her for not being there for me while I was growing up, she'd wanted me once she'd cleaned herself up. And like a neglected dog hungry for attention, I'd stuck by her side.

But the recent success of her memoir had thrown our three-person family into chaos. Even Bill, who had somewhat supported Mom's writing endeavors grew weary of Mom's . . . enthusiasm. And though betrayal was nothing new to me, I still couldn't get over the fact that Mom had included in her book the story of me and Maddie jumping off the cliff. Even if my friend's death had given her a wake-up call, I'd explicitly asked her to keep Maddie out of her book.

She hadn't listened, and now the world knew of my part in my friend's death. If I'd ever thought I could forgive myself, it would be ten times harder now, with thousands of readers knowing what I'd done.

"Perhaps I can show you around before you make your decision?" My grandmother smiles, and I note that she has applied a tasteful amount of makeup.

I nod, readjust my bag over my shoulder and follow her up the back steps into the house.

She leads me into a small foyer with plentiful coat racks and then into a generous kitchen with a butcher-block island in the center, a dozen pans hanging above. Intricate woodwork embellishes the top and sides of a large, hooded gas stove. On the small table in the corner lay bank statements and an old-fashioned calculator, white tape spewing out the side. Nearby is a bright yellow book titled "Social Media Marketing for Beginners."

Nana rushes to the table and starts shoving the bank statements into a manilla folder. "What a mess. Why don't you go into that next room and take a look at the view?" She points to a room that adjoins the kitchen.

White wainscoting and wallpaper adorn the walls. Around the room sit small tables—where the guests eat their breakfasts no doubt—and windows that give a magnificent view of the lighthouse on the property.

The round tower is beautiful beyond imagination. Seeing it here, framed perfectly out the window, sunlight shining warm on its whitewashed sides, it's hard to imagine it as the prison my mother has portrayed.

I tear my gaze away, taking in the blue flowers on the wallpaper, the hutch with shell decorations and mugs featuring the names of Maine towns I read about in the guidebooks. Everything about this place seems to reach its arms out to welcome me. Such a far cry from my mother's sleek and modern home—all hard edges and no-nonsense convenience.

"Let me show you the guest rooms." Nana appears at the threshold, and I follow her past a cozy sitting room with a wood stove and up a narrow flight of stairs. The steps creak beneath my feet, worn with age. I imagine the people who have gone up and down, her many guests, and those who have kept the lighthouse before Nana.

The rooms are clean and fresh with subtle colors reminiscent of the flowers outside. One boasts a bay window with a lovely view of the lighthouse and the Atlantic. Another, the gorgeous Maine coastline. It strikes me how I'm not quaking at the sight of this ocean—a world away from the one in which I lost my best friend.

After Nana shows me the rest of the rooms, each quaint and clean and homey, she leads me back down the stairs.

"Would you like some tea or coffee?" she asks.

"Maybe water? If that's okay."

Nana pours me a glass and one for herself, then leads me out on the back porch, the view overlooking the shimmering Atlantic and the gleaming lighthouse. A gentle breeze carries the scent of briny sea and wild roses.

When she sits in one of the porch rockers, she grows thoughtful as she stares at me. Her bottom lip trembles. "I didn't think you'd ever come."

I force one corner of my mouth up into a half smile.

"I'd really like you to stay here so we could have a chance to get to know one another. I might not see you otherwise—that restaurant will keep you busy this time of year."

Her soft gaze and humble openness catch me off guard. The voice I've "heard" behind the gentle words written in my birthday cards matches this kind woman. A woman who seems nothing like the lady Mom wrote about.

Surely, it's all right to stay with my grandmother. Besides, there are guests here. I won't be completely alone with her. "Are you sure you have enough room?"

Her weathered face brightens. "Yes." Her smile dims. "People aren't exactly knocking down my door for reservations these days, I'm afraid. As long as this place stays in business, I'd love to have you."

"I would like that. And I meant what I said—I'm willing to pull my weight and pay rent. I'm not a bad cook, either." I don't want her to think I'm like my mother, that I expect things handed to me, that I expect to be waited on.

"We'll work all that out in time. But let me hear about you, dear girl. What brings you to Maine?"

I shrug, not ready to admit that I traveled across the country for the sole purpose of seeing her. Not ready to admit that Mom's recent success makes me feel like I live in her fancy fishbowl—one that doesn't reflect the truth of our lives. "I needed a change."

We sit in silence, the sturdy wind chime above us sounding out a calm, mellow tune.

Nana sips her water, and I notice delicate beads of perspiration at her temples.

I swallow. "Thank you for the birthday cards. They've . . . meant a lot."

More than I would ever admit. In the dark, lonely nights of my girlhood, they'd been like a lifeline to me. When the apartment was too cold, when the noises outside my door too scary, I'd huddle beneath my blankets and clutch a birthday card from my grandmother. I'd inhale the slight flowery scent and a small inkling of New England's sea. I'd recite the spiritual verses on them. I'd know that somewhere out there, someone thought about me.

I'd fall asleep pretending to count the hairs on my head, never getting to a number that, in my naïve youth, I believed God kept close to His heart. He knew. He cared.

And so did my grandmother. Despite what my mother told me.

Now, Nana places her glass down. "How is Miriam? And Bill?"

I nod, probably with too much vigor. "Well. Very well. Bill just got a promotion and they're adding on a pool house and outdoor bar. They're—"

I catch myself too late. This is my mother talking, trying to impress with the portrayal and accumulation of beautiful things. This is not what I want Nana to think of me. No matter how similar our looks, I am *not* Miriam Jacobs.

"Mom's happy," I finish. Because her home is grand, her car is new, her figure still perfect, her backhand decent, and her book is on the bestseller lists. I don't tell Nana about the excessive alcohol she drinks at night, the arguments I overhear between her and Bill behind closed doors. Arguments about money and the release of her memoir.

"I'm sorry her book is causing trouble for your business," I venture.

"That's not your fault, dear."

I clear my throat. It's on my tongue to ask if she's read what Mom's written about her, but I don't want to ruin the little progress we've made. Like a large novel, I am just in the first chapter of knowing Nana. If I read too fast or push too hard, the book might slam shut on me.

"I've thought about coming for a long time. With everything so crazy back home . . ."

Her foot taps out a soft rhythm on the porch floorboards. "You must be curious about me and this place after reading your mother's story."

It's not lost on me how she doesn't call it a memoir, but a *story*.

"I am."

I wonder if she would try to explain away what I read in Mom's book, make excuses. But she doesn't. Instead, she sits in silence, looking toward a few stray pedestrians taking photos of the lighthouse. They don't approach the caution tape and she doesn't move to intercept.

There's so much to say, and yet it all feels inappropriate somehow. I've only just met my grandmother, and yet she is a part of me, a part of my history.

"Nana—"

"Laney—"

We laugh.

"You first," I say.

"Laney, I didn't think I'd ever get the chance to meet you. I'm so glad you've come." She gathers a breath, and for one terrifying moment I fear she will cry. "I could not imagine a better surprise than seeing you in my yard."

A cool hand rests on the back of mine and I note the stretched, veiny skin—no thicker than tissue paper over bone—alongside the smoothness of my own. I try not to pull away, but my sleeve is inching up toward my scars. I give her an awkward pat then move away so I can tug my shirt cuffs down to my palms before folding my arms in front of me. "I . . . I hope that we'll have plenty of time to get to know each other before I . . ." Before I what? I didn't have much direction. Would I stay here forever?

"You'll stay with me, won't you?"

"Yes." But as soon as the word is out, I'm ashamed how my mind travels to an image of Mom as a teenager, locked in the lighthouse with nothing but the company of thundering waves below. I stand. "I should get going. I have a shift soon. Would checking out of the motel tomorrow morning be too soon?"

"No, that would be just fine."

And then she's wrapping her thin, yet surprisingly strong arms around me. I stand stiff, unsure what to do. Mom's not much of a hugger, and I've pushed everyone away since Maddie died.

I've gone on exactly two dates in the last six years, but try as I might, I'd only ever felt that special something with one guy. Unfortunately, the memory of my best friend's last day has never allowed me to reconnect with him.

I blink. How did one hug from my grandmother dredge up such thoughts?

With much effort, I lean in, no more than a centimeter. Just enough so she doesn't feel completely rebuffed. The hug is far from comfortable, but something about it feels . . . promising. It has been so long since I've hugged another human.

We part, and her gaze falls to my right arm, where my blouse sleeve has inched up. I tug my shirt back down, but know it is too late. Her wise old eyes noticed the bright pink horizontal scars.

I struggle to meet her gaze, wonder if she can see the doubt that lurks behind my eyes, the doubt I wish didn't exist—both about her, and her God. But I only see kindness.

"I'm grateful you've come."

Grateful. I feel the pressure of her fingers on my arm and remember the gratitude list I'd started during rehab. I should pick it up again.

When I walk back toward the motel, the ocean behind me seems to whisper of promise and new beginnings. The Pacific had never done that for me—all it did was grasp and take, raping me of any semblance of peace and normalcy.

I can only hope the Atlantic, a world away from California, will give me a second chance at living.

# Chapter Two

*Sometimes the sun shines and I can't feel it. Like its brightness isn't enough to reach that place inside me that needs the light. Or maybe the brightness is enough. Maybe it's the darkness within that drowns it out.*

~ *Locked Light* by Miriam Jacobs

## LANEY

I clear two glasses of wine from a corner table and pocket the credit card receipt to add to the drawer. A woman's tinkling laughter from behind me carries through the air and I turn to see my manager—a middle-aged woman named Natasha who has a penchant for beautiful floral dresses and gossip—making friendly conversation with an older couple as she seats them by the window.

"Yes, we did come here last summer. Bar Harbor is our home away from home." The woman sits in the chair Natasha holds out for her.

I perk up, but continue my task. I spray the table and wipe up a piece of spaghetti caked in congealed butter. Natasha hands the couple menus. "I thought I recognized you. We have so many tourists, it's nice to see a couple of familiar faces. Where are you staying?"

The woman's eyes light up. Her bleached blond hair doesn't quite match her mature face. "Oh, we stay at the Beacon Bed and Breakfast. You know, the one with the lighthouse?"

I hear Natasha titter. "We haven't been recommending that place since the book came out. Did you happen to see the interview with Miriam? It's horrific."

My heart is hammering. My skin is clammy, and I fight the urge to lower myself into one of the table seats. I want to tell Natasha to stop spreading rumors she knows nothing about, but I don't have the strength. Because really, I don't know all that much about what really happened all those years ago, either.

"Oh, we don't believe a word of that gossip, do we, Chris?"

Her companion, a man with hair as white as cotton, shakes his head. "No, ma'am. We've been coming to the Beacon for years and Charlotte Jacobs has always been the perfect host."

The woman places a hand on Natasha's arm. "You've not heard of Charlotte mistreating actual customers, have you?"

My heart lightens hearing this couple come to my nana's defense.

Natasha smiles. "No. I can't say that I have."

"Then we'll choose to believe what we've seen for fifteen years over a sensational story. Now, are you serving the seafood bisque today?"

I breathe out a long breath. Should I tell Natasha about my connection to the Beacon? Surely, my boss will find out who my grandmother is sooner or later.

My grandmother.

I think of the electric window candles lighting the inn at the end of the night, as they have the last two nights. The scent of cookies lingering in the kitchen.

There is no denying the feeling of safety Nana's home elicits, and although we hadn't talked of anything of import yet, I am learning bits and pieces. How she starts her day well before the sun comes up each morning, how she prides herself on flawless hair and makeup. How she hums while doing dishes and has a fondness for Elvis.

So far, there is only one thing that niggles about our time together. Yesterday morning, after Nana had come in from warning gawkers away from trying to enter the lighthouse, she'd huffed, the screen door shutting hard behind her. "It would be cheaper to tear down my poor light than repair it."

*My poor light.*

I couldn't keep those words from my head. Even now, as I greet the couple at the window table and recite the specials to them, it clings to the edges of my thoughts.

Surely, once the hype of Mom's book subsides, business would return for Nana. But if she got rid of the lighthouse—the main draw of the inn—would she ever recover?

I straighten and look out the restaurant window to Frenchman Bay, the same body of water that connects to Nana's property. This place is everything coastal and historic, from the four-masted schooner out on the water to the historic Bar Harbor Inn and Reading Room down the street. With Nana's bed and breakfast being outside of the downtown area, would she gain enough business without the lighthouse?

I take the drink orders of the couple who'd come to my grandmother's defense. When I'm walking to the bar to get their wine, I contemplate whether I should tell them I'm Charlotte's granddaughter. They must have checked in this morning because I didn't see them when I helped Nana serve breakfast. I might as well introduce myself now before—

"Laney?"

The baritone voice sounds so familiar. Not one of the other servers, though.

"Laney." It comes again, this time louder. The deepness of it

21

probes and picks at the scarred places I've been trying to bury for the last six years. My blood turns to ice.

It can't be.

I'm imagining things. No one from California is all the way out here except me. And even if one person from my old life happened to show up in Bar Harbor, of all people it wouldn't be *him*, the person I tried so hard to escape.

The bartender slides one glass of wine toward me, and I clutch the stem of the glass with enough force to shatter it. I turn from the bar as if my feet are weighed down with wet cement.

A small intake of breath passes my lips at the sight of him.

I'm caught unawares by how good he looks in his khakis and polo shirt, the slight shadow of stubble across his chiseled chin. I try not to think of all he's likely accomplished in the six years since high school, of all I haven't—the too-old college drop-out.

My face burns and I attempt to swallow down my emotion. "Jason."

"I can't believe you're actually here." He places his hand on my arm, and I'm shocked by the instant heat that burns my skin. A foreign longing rushes through me, and I attempt to tamp it down.

I pull away from the fingers that scorch the skin beneath my blouse. "What—what are you doing here?"

He rakes his fingers through his hair, a nervous gesture I remember all too well that pulls regret and desire through every ligament and muscle of my body.

"I'm here for business. Dad's business."

So, he'd followed in his father's footsteps, after all. He hadn't followed his dreams then. Why?

I glance down at the blood-red wine in my hand. "I have to get back to work. It was nice to see you." I grab the other glass of wine on the counter behind me and start toward the couple at the window.

"Wait." The word comes out almost desperate and I can't ignore it.

I stop, but don't turn.

"Could we talk sometime?"

Talk? About what? About Maddie? About how he seemed to have no problem moving on from that day while I seemed destined to be stuck in it forever? Or perhaps he caught Mom's *Hello, America* segment. Now, that would be a wonderful topic of conversation.

"I don't think that's a good idea."

He's in front of me now. "Just ten minutes, Laney. Can I meet you after your shift? Please? We can get ice cream or something."

My legs are as sturdy as the custard Nana made as an afternoon snack the day before. What harm will come to me if I agree?

But then I remember the last time I saw him, at Maddie's memorial. He'd given me a hug and the feel of his arms around me had churned my stomach. That was when I knew we were over. There was no way I could be with him after that day at the cliff. His touch, his presence, would always dredge up memories of the day we'd killed my best friend.

The scars on my forearms ache. I sink into the comfort of the pain, which I know from my time at rehab is not a sign of healthy progress.

"I'm sorry. I can't."

I walk to my table and paste on a smile for the couple. I take their orders—one lobster bake and one fish and chips—and head to the kitchen, exhaling slowly when I don't see Jason again. It is for the best.

But when I exit the kitchen, he's right there in front of me. "Can't, or won't?" He's close. So close I can smell the same *Giorgio Armani* cologne he wore in high school. The scent of ocean and woods and adventure—everything that seemed to make life worth living at the time, and everything that ruined my life forever.

I *can't* afford to be nice. I can't live through all the memories again, not without my therapist. Not without landing myself back in rehab. "Won't."

"It's ice cream, Laney. One cone. Mint chocolate chip still your favorite?"

I close my eyes. Our first date had been to get ice cream. How could memories be both precious and painful all at once? I force myself to meet his gaze, dark sapphire eyes deep and sincere. The last six years served him well. Broadened his shoulders, defined his muscles beneath his shirt. And yet the change is more than physical. Did that day still haunt him too? While I want to avoid reminders, maybe he sought healing in other ways—by seeking me out, perhaps?

"How did you know where to find me?"

"I just happen to be here for business."

*Even the hairs of your head are numbered . . .*

Was there something more than coincidence to our meeting?

I sigh and move to the table I'd been clearing earlier. I move the candle centerpiece to the middle as Natasha leads a group of four thirty-something ladies to one of my other tables.

"I have to get back to work."

"Please, Laney? Don't you think we should talk?"

I grind my teeth, scoop my notepad out of the apron around my waist. "Ten o'clock. Ten minutes. No ice cream."

He exhales. "Thank you. I'll meet you outside?"

I nod, not entirely sure I haven't just made the second worst decision of my life.

WHEN MY SHIFT ENDS, I dig my hands into the pockets of my sweatshirt on the way out the door. I see Jason waiting by the outdoor bar, the blue and gold lettering of his Berkeley sweatshirt reflecting the moonlight.

So, he'd gone to his family's alma mater. No doubt followed in his father's footsteps and majored in architecture.

He'd done what was expected of him.

He straightens at my arrival, gives me an easy smile. "I was scared you were going to sneak out the back."

"Considering the back is Frenchman Bay, I didn't have much in the way of getaway options."

His mouth strains at the edges. "Is it that horrible to see me again?"

I walk toward the street. "It's not you . . ." *Honesty, Laney.* That's what writing my thoughts down during rehab allowed me, what keeping things bottled up for four years had denied me. "And it is," I let out on a sigh.

"You never responded to my letter."

I remember holding it in my hands, my insides splitting open at the fact that he'd thought to write a letter when a text would have been so much easier. He'd poured his heart out on that lined paper, every sorrow and regret pressed between ink and white space. He'd asked me to forgive him, told me how he wished with all his soul he could take back that day.

And I hadn't responded.

"That wasn't right of me, Jason. I had a lot to get past, and I —I wasn't ready. I'm sorry."

There, pretend like I was past it *now.* That was one way to go about it.

"It's okay." We walk in silence. "So, what have you been up to? What brings you out east?"

"My grandmother lives here. I decided it was time to meet her." Then, so as not to be rude, "You?"

"The firm won a bid on the project design for Susan Sanderson's new home. Dad decided to send me out on my own. Finally. Guess I did my time."

Susan Sanderson, the famed actress? Couldn't pretend that wasn't impressive.

"So, Berkeley, huh?" I gesture to the sweatshirt he fills out all too well.

"Yup. That's always been the plan." But it hadn't. Not before that last day we shared together. He clears his throat, and I sense he's uncomfortable with the small lie. "Dad's plan, anyway. You went to school?"

I shrug, shrinking at the question. "A couple classes. Not really my thing."

"You? Miss Honor Society?"

"A lot changed after that day." My words seem to find their target since he turns quiet, and strangely, that bothers me.

We pass Jordan Pond's Ice Cream Shop. "You sure I can't buy you a cone?"

I shake my head. "I need to get home before Nana worries." In actuality, I have no idea if Nana is the worrying type. She doesn't strike me as one to wring her hands if I come home an hour past my shift.

"I'll see you to your car, then."

"I walked."

"Okay. I'll walk you home."

"There's no need—"

"Laney, I want to." He stares at me with an intensity that makes my heart pound like waves against the shore. The bob of his Adam's apple along the smooth skin of his neck draws me like a hummingbird to Nana's fuchsias.

I don't want to do this, to let my guard down, to feel anything that will make me vulnerable. I want to shut these feelings tight inside me, seal them away with hot wax until they harden so there's no chance of release.

Pain, I know. Pain is familiar. In a twisted way, sometimes pain is better.

And yet Jason's presence plucks at the rusted-over chords of my fragile heart. Beneath his gaze, I remember a time when I was carefree, invincible, filled with hope. It might as well have been a lifetime ago, for how foreign it feels. And yet for a moment, I remember. What's more, I long for it.

"Okay." So much for ten minutes.

We continue straight. The streets are sparse, the stars clear. In the distance, ocean waves shudder.

Jason fills the space with words about the past few months. His father's architectural firm, his impression of seeing the eastern seaboard for the first time, the hotel he's staying at here in downtown Bar Harbor, his desire to climb the Otter Cliffs.

When we turn left onto my grandmother's drive, I sense a change in him. He's nervous, grasping.

"I'd love to take you out to dinner while I'm in town."

I hold my tongue, vacillating.

"Or the Ocean Path. Maybe we could walk it together. Your next night off?"

While I can think of a million reasons to deny him, I find myself incapable of giving voice to any. When we reach Nana's house, the lighthouse is dark at the end of the stone-pillared walk and the waves crash over my unspoken words. Does he know the connection of the lighthouse to Mom's memoir? Does he think less of me and my family for it? Less of Nana, a woman he's never met? Suddenly, I am terrified to be so close to the ocean with Jason again.

"I'm not sure that's a good idea."

"Dinner and ice cream is always a good idea."

I turn to him, suck in a deep breath. "Can we not do this? Please?"

"Laney, I can't pretend like . . . like you don't matter. Like what happened between us didn't matter. Like she didn't matter."

I wince.

"I think we owe it to her," he says.

My chest bubbles. "Don't you dare bend this into some twisted way of honoring her memory."

"You think that little of me, huh?"

His wounded look is enough to make me check myself. It isn't right to wound others just because I am wounded. "I'm sorry."

He dips his head, juts out his bottom lip. "Please?"

I blow a breath upward, fanning the front of my hair. Seeing him is hard, but it's also easier than I thought it would be. "I guess dinner would be okay."

He smiles. The white of his teeth shines through the dark. "Really?"

I shrug, as if I haven't just willingly handed my heart over to be drawn and quartered. "Yeah."

He takes out his phone and confirms I haven't changed my number. When he says goodbye, he squeezes my forearm. It takes everything within me not to pull away, despite knowing he can't possibly feel the scars beneath my sleeves.

"I'm glad we ran into one another, Laney. Real glad."

And though I can't quite voice a "Me, too," there is something in the spaces and corners of my heart that whispers an agreement.

# Chapter Three

*I'm sorry, Dad. I need to go. I need to find her.*
~ Text from Jason Rutherford to his father five days earlier

## JASON

She is just as beautiful as I remember.

More so, maybe. Seeing her sitting across from me, the sun shining on her light hair is like poetry. I try to hide a laugh at such flowery thoughts. The guys on my pickup basketball team would never let me hear the end of it.

"Thanks for having dinner with me." After I picked her up, we walked to The Terrace Grille patio.

"Nice place." She wiggles her foot, moving the white tablecloth beneath us.

"Great view, anyway." I take a bite of clam chowder, the creamy sauce like a mouthful of New England.

She leans back and sighs, stares across the bay to the friendly mounds of the Porcupine Islands.

I clear my throat. "So, what's been happening with you these last few years?"

"Not much. A lot of rehab."

The chowder turns pasty in my mouth. Her answer is quick, too quick, and too filled with resentment. Maybe this wasn't a good idea. Who is this woman? She used to light up a room. Had Maddie's death leached every ounce of joy from her?

I stir a chunk of potato around in my soup. "I'm sorry." Sorry she was in rehab, sorry for my role in the tragedy, sorry that I was able to move past it in a way Laney evidently hadn't. In the end, I'm sorry for everything.

She shrugs. "What about you? Your dad's business is going well, I take it?"

Why do I feel guilty about that?

For the thousandth time in six years, I remember the day Maddie died. The sight of Laney and Maddie jumping off that cliff. What idiots we'd been. What an idiot *I'd* been. Full of myself, so certain I had everything under control. What if we'd done things differently that day? What if Aaron and I had never urged the girls to jump?

I lean back in my chair and gaze past Laney to the white gazebo near Bar Harbor Inn. How many nights had I found myself grateful it hadn't been Laney that died that day? Then more nights fighting the guilt that thought had ushered in?

"It's going well." I sip my soda. Dad sending me out here alone says a lot about the job he thinks I'm doing at Rutherford Designs. Even if I hadn't given him much of a choice in the matter, he could have shot me down. Could have sent one of the other associates to hold my hand. He hadn't.

"You like it?"

I pause. There was never a doubt I would join my father's business, but Laney's inquiry is like a pickaxe trying to dig up something buried long ago. Is she bringing up what I said that day on the beach two weeks before Maddie's death? For a girl acting like she couldn't care less to remember me, she remembers that?

I think back to that day, to two sandy towels on the beach beside one another, the thick crowd on the stretch of sand making it somehow more private.

When I'd confessed that I didn't want to join Dad's firm, she had rolled onto her side to face me. "What do you want to do?"

"You'll laugh."

Those deep brown eyes probed mine. "No, I won't."

I looked to the sky, where a faint moon grew brighter as the sun descended toward the horizon. "I always thought it'd be kind of neat to be an archaeologist."

She sat up. "No way."

"Stupid, right?"

"No. Why is it stupid?"

I shrugged. "Probably not a lot of jobs. Definitely not great pay."

She'd leaned down then, kissed my bottom lip gently before pulling away. "Jason, you'd be a *great* archeologist."

And for two brief weeks, that's what I'd planned. But Maddie's accident threw us all off course, and though my father hadn't pestered me with questions about what happened that deadly summer afternoon, I felt the lack of such a conversation hanging over us to this day. Wouldn't a good father demand to know the details of what happened? Wouldn't a good father ask me how I felt about it all?

I'd never told him I didn't want to be a part of his firm, that I wanted to be an archeologist. In light of what happened to Maddie, it hadn't seemed important. Mom had already crushed Dad when she left us—I refused to add to his pain.

Now, Laney's question hangs in the air. Did I like my job?

"I'm good at it."

She squints at me, the setting sun splashing off the glistening water and reflecting onto her sunglasses. Behind the plastic lenses, I can barely see her eyes.

"That's not what I asked." She crosses her arms over her chest. She is different. More direct.

"I like it. Most of the time."

She raises an eyebrow. "And the rest of the time?"

I exhale, the tension in my shoulders and neck releasing. "I put up with it to make Dad happy." There. Was that what she wanted to hear?

She curls her fingers around her water glass, then seems to change her mind about taking a drink and releases the glass. "How is he? Your dad?"

"Good. He finally met someone last year. I think that's why he was able to let me take this project on. She couldn't get away, and he didn't want to leave her behind."

Laney gives a close-mouthed nod.

"How about you? How's your mom? I think I caught her on some morning show recently."

Laney snorts.

"I guess not much has changed with you two?"

"Oh, it has actually." Her tone drips of bitterness and a weight akin to a bowling ball shifts inside my chest.

"Mom's off drugs but still deep in the bottle most of the time, but she snagged herself a man. A man with money who, for whatever reason, appears to actually love her."

"Oh."

"A regular old *Pretty Woman* story."

I remember the first time I saw Laney's mom all strung out in the parent pickup line, the farthest likeness from the woman I'd seen on the morning show. "I guess you're not too happy about her book."

I think about Dad's call last night regarding Miriam Jacobs. Not that it's a secret I have to keep from Laney, but she's only just agreed to talk with me. No need to ruin it with more outrageous news of her mom.

Laney takes off her glasses. "Crazy thing is, Mom plays the part of distinguished bestselling author scarily well." She shakes her head. "Whatever. I don't even know why I'm telling you this."

Does she need someone to talk to? Because I will move heaven and earth to be that person.

Silence envelops our small table. The waitress brings Laney's coconut shrimp wrap and my lobster macaroni and cheese.

"She would have wanted you to go to school, you know."

Her mouth tightens. Immediately, I regret the words.

Laney wipes her fingers, sticky with mango sauce, on the cloth napkin. "Don't pretend like you knew her better than I did." Her words are louder, more strident now.

I raise an eyebrow. "You don't think she would have wanted you to go on with your life after that day?"

"Does it matter?" She looks out at the pier, where a woman in a sunhat walks hand-in-hand with a man in Crocs and shorts. "She would have wanted to go on with her life, too. But she didn't get to."

"Laney, if I could change the course of that day, I would. I have, over and over in my head."

## LANEY

I CLENCH the napkin in my hand. The back of my pinky finger sticks to the cloth.

Did I truly think that suffering for the rest of my life would bring Maddie honor?

Jason is right. Living aimlessly would not honor Maddie's life. But how could I live happily ever after when I didn't deserve to?

I look at the table, where a single oyster cracker from his chowder hides beneath his plate. "I wish I had dreams about changing that day. But instead, I have dreams about her cold, life-less body, trapped beneath a rock out in the middle of the Pacific. It bothers me I never got to see her again. Aren't you bothered by that? Was she really in that casket, or did they just tell us they found her to give us some sort of peace? Do we even deserve that?

We gave up on her. She had to be so afraid. Can you imagine the panic, the pain? We're responsible for that."

"Laney—" He inches his hand toward mine, and I don't pull away when he strokes my knuckles with his thumb.

The waitress appears and I avoid her so she can't see my eyes as Jason takes care of the check. When he stands, I pull my sleeves down to my knuckles. My chest tightens. I'd only ever voiced such thoughts to Dr. Shelley, and now I regret every word. I regret my emotional display. It must be clear I'm a wreck—a shell of the girl I was six years ago.

We walk out of the restaurant the short distance to Jordan Pond Ice Cream and Fudge. The conversation has soured my appetite for sweets, but I force myself to order a small cone. Ice cream in hand, we stroll down Main Street alongside a myriad of tourists.

"Thanks, Laney."

A single drip of my mint chip ice cream slides down my waffle cone and I run my tongue along it to keep it from reaching my fingers. "For what?"

"For spending time with me."

A lump of emotion lodges in my throat. I've struggled to get past my own loneliness these last several years. To think that Jason is longing for companionship the same way I am fills a hole inside of me.

I breathe easier, taking in the summer sun that casts oranges and reds against the sky to our right. The night sings to us. Birds, tourists chatting as they pass, kids rolling down the hill in Agamont Park, cars navigating the pedestrian traffic.

"Any chance you want to see the site of Susan Sanderson's new house?"

"I was never awed by anyone in Hollywood." And if I had been, Mom's recent bout with fame would have cured me of it quick.

"Come on, Laney. Susan Sanderson. Even I remember how

crazy you were about that *Tiny Woman* movie—the one where she played the crotchety aunt, right?"

A giggle escapes me, and wonder of wonders, it feels beautiful. "I think you mean *Little Women*."

He shrugs. "Little, tiny, what's the difference? Besides, Susan won't be there. Right now, it's just a beautiful piece of land."

I raise an eyebrow. "You're on a first name basis with her?"

He grins. "Suse and I go way back."

I roll my eyes. "Isn't it private property?"

"I'm allowed to be on it, and you can tell me what you think of the plans. Always good to get extra opinions."

"Oh, all right."

He grins, and a burst of fireworks goes off in my chest. Good grief, he's handsome. More so than back when we were in high school. That chiseled jaw, those deep, probing eyes. When he smiles the dimple in his left cheek is like a comma, reminding me to pause and hold my breath to savor the moment. What would have happened to us if that day had never occurred? Would we have stayed together through college? Gotten married? Had kids?

We walk to his hotel where we slide into his rental, a sporty BMW. "It was a free upgrade," he explains, as if there's shame in having nice things. Yet, with my history, I'm touched he says it.

Ten minutes later we pull into a dirt drive that leads to an astounding overlook of the ocean. "Wow," I breathe as he parks the car and gets out, coming around to the passenger's side to open my door.

When he offers his hand, I take it. It's warm and big, calloused and familiar, and although I wouldn't mind hanging onto it for the rest of the night, I slip my fingers from his as soon as I am out of the car.

We walk toward the edge of a small hill that drops to a private beach, laden with massive rocks. The briny air tangles in my hair and a breath trembles into my lungs, my limbs quaking at being above the ocean, even at this small height.

"Want to sit?" Jason asks.

I back up a few steps and pick a spot on the grass. He lowers himself beside me.

We're silent for several long moments.

"How do you decide what to build?" I ask.

His mouth tightens into a thin line. "She wants unique, but classy. We'll present several drawings and narrow it down from there."

"This would be a great place for a lighthouse home."

"A lighthouse . . . that would be unique."

"If Suse likes the idea, you have to give me credit."

"Sure thing." He leans back on his arms, his hands planted firmly on the ground behind him. "Your grandmother's place is kind of amazing, huh? A real lighthouse."

I nod. "She plans to tell me some of its history, but I think it's hard for her. Hard to face the fact that she might lose it. Hard because of what Mom wrote."

"Why would she lose it?"

"It's falling apart. It was decommissioned over forty years ago when my grandfather bought it along with the keeper's house— now the inn. I think she's hanging onto it as a way to keep him alive."

Though I've only been there two days, I see how often she looks at the photographs of her and my grandfather. He died ten years ago, but she still wears her wedding ring.

Jason swallows and my eyes are again drawn to his Adam's apple. "It's a historic landmark. I can't imagine the townspeople will be happy with it being torn down."

I shrug. "Maybe I could look into running a fundraiser or something while I'm here, you know, in order to renovate it." I shift into a cross-legged position.

His eyes seem to want to pry me open. The sea air brushes the short strands of his hair, giving him an altogether alluring, tussled look.

"I could come by and take a look. I'd be happy to draw up some plans for renovating the lighthouse," he says.

"I don't think that's a good idea."

"Why not? I'm already in town. What harm would it do?"

"I'm not asking for your help, Jason. It's not even my place."

"Lane, let me do this. Let me do . . . something."

Does he think helping me out will make the past go away? Help me move on like he had? If only it were that easy.

If I remember anything from my time in therapy, it's that dwelling in the past is not helpful. And Jason is too strong a reminder of all that has happened. How can I break free of the history that's weighing me down if he's beside me, constantly reminding me of the past?

I shouldn't have burdened him with my unresolved issues. "Thank you, but it'd probably be best if you didn't."

He opens his mouth as if to protest, but then closes it and nods.

"I think it's time you take me home," I whisper.

He drives me back to Nana's in silence. When we reach the inn, he doesn't ask if he can get out, just quietly bids me goodbye when I push open the passenger door.

I ignore the pull to make our parting less awkward. But doing so would only encourage him to return. I don't think my heart can bear too much more time with him, reminding me of all the things that will never be.

# Chapter Four

*We never talk about Mom, that's what's wrong.*
~ Unsent text from Jason Rutherford to his father, three weeks
earlier

## JASON

I throw off the sheets of my hotel room bed and sit up, swiping at a thin sheen of sweat on my forehead. My heart slams against my chest, and I trudge over to the desk and unscrew a water bottle, taking a large swig.

The dream of Mom leaving is not a new one, but the night sweats that have accompanied them are new. In my dream, I'm twelve again, bristling against the soft, restrictive hands of my mother. I'm pushing her away.

And then, I have my wish. She's gone. All the way to Africa.

She's no longer grumbling good-naturedly over ironing the collared white shirts my dad wears to the office every day. She isn't in the kitchen making chicken marsala. Instead, Dad's shirts pile high on an empty chair, as wrinkled as the face of an old man.

Suppers become an endless array of take-out containers and awkward silence.

I rake my hands through my hair and trudge over to the desk where I've left my cell. I tap it on. No notifications. Who did I expect?

No one. No one at all.

The letter my mother wrote claimed that her leaving had nothing to do with me, which of course, made me think the opposite. She'd left us for some mission in Africa, her silence a chasm that said more than a letter ever could. Three months after Laney and I broke up, some of her belongings showed up on our doorstep in a large, crushed box with a short letter of condolence saying she died in a mudslide. That's when I knew it was really over. She would never return.

I run a hand over my mouth and sit heavily at the desk. I open my laptop and click on the first of two emails from my dad.

*To: jrutherford@rutherforddesigns.com*
*From: drutherford@rutherforddesigns.com*
*Subject: Sanderson Project*

*Jason,*
*I trust all is well in Maine. How did your meeting with Susan go? Please send drawings for my approval as soon as you can before sending them on to our client.*
*Also, Son, I wanted to let you know I proposed to Eva last night. She said yes. We're planning a simple ceremony in November.*
*Dad*
*Don Rutherford*
*CEO and Head Designer*
*Rutherford Designs, Inc.*
*www.rutherforddesigns.com*

I sigh. I'd seen this coming. I came home from college to find Eva practically living with Dad already.

It was time for me to fly the nest.

I think of Laney, sitting in the grass on Susan Sanderson's land, the wind blowing strands of light hair from the delicate features of her face. I shake my head. She isn't at all interested in me right now—and perhaps never will be.

I turn my attention to the second email, a chill racing up my spine as I take in the forwarded email address.

*To: jrutherford@rutherforddesigns.com*
*From: drutherford@rutherforddesigns.com*
*Subject: Fwd: Mount Desert Island Land*

*Could you take a look at this land while you're out east?*

*Begin Forwarded Message:*
*From: miriam@lockedlight.com*
*Subject: Re: Mount Desert Island Land*
*To: drutherford@rutherforddesigns.com*

*Dear Bill,*
*I'm so happy to hear you're willing to work on this project with me. I am about to close on the land and would love Jason to look at it since he's already in the area. What a fortuitous set of circumstances! I have some ideas for what I'm wanting on my Pinterest board below, if that is helpful. I am all about elegant and clean, something that speaks of new beginnings.*
*Much Appreciated,*
*Miriam Jacobs*
*NY Times Bestselling Author*
*Locked Light Now Available Everywhere!*

My gaze roams over the signature line and skims the Pinterest address along with the link to the land Miriam is buying.

Something that feels like new beginnings.

To symbolize a life apart from Laney? And yet, why would Miriam choose to settle in Acadia—a place that, according to her *Hello, America* segment, seemed to be the cause of painful memories?

I tap my socked foot on the floor. Laney definitely wouldn't want anything to do with me if I was tasked with designing her mother's dream home. But how can I turn down my father when I'm still trying to prove myself to him?

# Chapter Five

*That lighthouse will always symbolize the devastation of my childhood at the hands of my parents.*
*~ Locked Light by Miriam Jacobs*

## LANEY

I wake as the sun is rising. The vastness of the east coast ensures a breathtaking show, and I perch against the foot of my bed to watch the sun climb over the inky swell of the sea.

Unbidden, an image of Jason from last night comes to mind. The wind tussling his hair, revealing the blond strands touched by the sun.

I glance around the room—the Wisteria Room—and am once again awed at Nana's generosity. The bay window overlooks the lighthouse and the shimmering Atlantic. A queen bed, tasteful shades of purple and clean white. Fresh flowers from Nana's garden on the bureau, a cozy fireplace, and a sitting area with two chairs and a table.

It's a shame this room isn't booked in the middle of June, but I can't complain. It is lovely.

Could this have been my mother's bedroom? I try to picture her in the room as it is now, but can't. Certainly she would have ripped down the wallpaper at least.

I pull on jeans and a long-sleeve t-shirt and tie my hair back. I splash my face with water, run a brush through my hair, and brush my teeth before glancing in the bathroom mirror. Satisfied with my low-maintenance appearance, I head downstairs.

The scent of cinnamon and sugar meets me in the kitchen where Nana flips eggs.

"I thought I woke early enough to help you." I reach for the coffee and pour a mug.

"Morning, darling." Even this early in the morning, her short gray curls are neat, her makeup immaculate. "I'm up before five every day. Don't expect you up that early."

"Every day? Do you ever get a break?"

"Oh, more than I'd like to these days. And I don't mind getting up early. Guests keep these old legs moving and this place alive. I love every minute of it. Love it even more when there's more mouths to feed." She hands me a plate of eggs. "We'll have to wait for the coffee cake. It just came out of the oven." She gestures to the dining area in the room beside us. "Guests won't be down for another hour. Why don't we enjoy our breakfast first?"

I nod and lead the way to the place we've eaten for the last two mornings. I lower myself into a chair at a small table for two by the window. Outside, the lighthouse stands sentinel over the ocean, as if ruling the rising sun, the crashing waves.

"A bit warm for long sleeves, isn't it, honey?"

My skin warms. "I get cold easily."

She raises a brow, but I dig into my eggs, gesturing out the window with my fork. "I'm not sure this view could ever get old."

She smiles wistfully, following my gaze out the window to where visitors—not guests at the inn—are crossing the pedestrian footbridge. "It doesn't. I'm so blessed to have had it all these years." She sounds as if she's trying to convince herself it's okay for the final days of the business to be upon her.

"The lighthouse is quite a draw." I gesture to the tourists now taking pictures of one another. One of them stumbles backward, stomping on Nana's petunias.

She nods. "Though this is private property, I've never had the heart to enforce it with signs. A bed and breakfast plastered all over telling people to keep out isn't very welcoming." She gazes out the window and sighs. "It would be a shame if I have to sell it to someone who keeps it all to themselves."

"Where would you go? If you had to sell this place, I mean?"

She sips her coffee, places it carefully on the wooden table. "Oh, I haven't thought that far ahead, but there are some lovely communities for mature adults in the area." She laughs when I wrinkle my nose. It's hard to envision my spritely grandmother at an old folks' home. Hard to picture her anywhere but here.

"Or maybe I could find a place in Camden. That's about an hour south. My good friend Hannah owns a bed and breakfast there. It's a beautiful town."

I look out the window to the tall pines, the lighthouse, the coast meeting the sea. However beautiful Camden is, I'm not sure it can compete with *this*.

Nana sighs. "Although, I suppose if that were my first choice, I would have arranged it by now. Fact of the matter is, it pains me to think of giving up this place. I'm trying not to be anxious about potential lawsuits if someone gets hurt at the lighthouse, but I'm not going to lie—it's hard. I suppose I should board it up, but how depressing a sight would that be?"

I think of Jason's offer to draw up plans to renovate the lighthouse. "Would the town take it on? All the history that's there . . . and surely it's a draw for tourists."

She taps her fingers on the table. "I'm afraid I haven't put aside my pride to look into how to go about such a thing. I'm not on everyone's good side after Miriam's book released." She clears her throat and wipes her mouth with a napkin.

I think about what I heard at the restaurant. Nana isn't exaggerating.

I take a bite of the fluffy eggs, laced with cheese and bacon and topped with dill and chives. I groan. "This is so good, Nana."

"Cooking is one thing I know how to do."

"No arguing there."

We eat in silence for another minute before she speaks. "It's quiet this morning. Our guests are still upstairs and we have a few minutes. Would you like to see it closer?"

"The lighthouse?"

She nods.

"Yes, I'd love to."

We clear our dishes, and I follow her out the back porch across the dew-covered lawn and over the footbridge.

The yellow X of caution tape at the door mars the otherwise perfect picture. You can't *tell* it's dangerous from here. "What is it that needs fixing?"

The light in her eyes dims. "She's been hurting for some time, now. The stairs aren't safe anymore. The rails at the top need to be replaced. The light hasn't worked in a few years. It's an insurance hazard more than anything. It's not just the cost of knocking it down . . . " She blinks back tears.

I reach for her hand. It's the first physical contact I've initiated, and it feels right. "I'm sorry, Nana." My mind whirls. "Have you ever thought of a fundraiser?"

"I wouldn't know where to begin. And it would take an exorbitant amount of money." She looks to the ocean, to the waves rolling toward us. "I haven't been completely honest with you, Laney. It's not my idea to have the lighthouse torn down. There's been a push of late . . . a movement to demolish it for good."

"From Mom's fans."

Nana bites her lip. "I'm afraid so."

"But if you could keep it, you would, right?"

"In a heartbeat. It's been the main draw of this place for as long as we've been in business. It's the heart of the B&B. I can't imagine running the inn without it." Her smile vanishes. "But too many have cancelled their reservations in the last few months. Who knows? Perhaps it's time to let this place go. I've received some reasonable offers over the last year."

But I can see plain as pie that selling the place is the last thing she wants to do. With care, I reach out and caress the white-washed rock of the lighthouse. I press my palm into it and close my eyes, as if touching the stone beast will help me understand all its history. Will help me understand what happened between my mother and grandmother, the stuff that isn't written in Mom's book.

Though I badly want Nana to at least open the door to the light so I can peer in, she doesn't offer and I don't ask. We're walking back toward the inn when I ask the question I've been wondering the last two days instead. "Did Mom stay in the room I'm staying in when she was growing up?"

A soft smile curves Nana's mouth. "For a while. But when she was twelve she wanted her own space, a room without guests around. Since we needed the bedrooms and the guest house cottage for the business and since your mother loved the idea of the attic, we made a room for her up there. In fact, her things are still there. I—I haven't had the heart to give anything away." She opens the screen door.

"I understand why it might be hard to go up there."

"Oh, it's deplorable, really. A dust-filled mausoleum."

I press my lips together. "I could pack it away for you . . . if you want, I mean. Unless you have other things for me to do. Really, whatever you want. I appreciate you letting me stay here and—"

"Laney." She lays her hand on mine.

I love how my name sounds when she says it. Not in the child-ish, twisting beg Mom uses when she wants me to agree to a picture for her Instagram account. Or when she's rip-roaring hungover and needs me to get her ibuprofen and a glass of water. Or the way she says it when I've done something that displeases her, saturated with pity, as if it's immensely unfortunate for *me* that I've upset her.

The sound of my name is altogether different when Nana says it, a deep melody like that of the steel wind chimes hanging on her deck. As if she wants to assure me I have nothing to fear. "You could never be an intrusion. And I think that's a wonderful idea, not to mention very helpful."

My insides melt with relief. "Okay. I could start whenever you'd like. I'm off from the restaurant today, and I don't have any plans . . ."

"Today would be perfect. I can take you up after we serve breakfast, though I'm not sure I have boxes. I should probably ask your mother if she'd like to keep anything. I don't suppose you might use that fancy phone of yours to text her?"

I swallow. "Yes, of course I can." Though I'm assuming if my mother wanted her old possessions, she'd have made it known sometime in the past twenty-seven years. I bite my lip as I wash the breakfast table we used, readying it for guests. "Have you tried to talk to her at all?"

In my head, whatever happened between Mom and my grandparents is all Mom's fault. But what if that's not entirely accurate? What if Nana had been okay with Mom leaving without a word? What if she hadn't bothered pursuing a relationship with her daughter—with me—after their falling out?

But no. Nana has never missed a birthday. Surely, the cards alone speak of an effort to make amends, to be a part of my life.

Nana reaches for the plates in the cabinet she uses for the guests' breakfasts. She places them firmly on the counter. "Laney, the last thing I want is to cause a rift between you and your mother."

"I'm a grown woman. I'm old enough to know the truth." I glance out the window at the Atlantic. "Besides, there's already a rift between me and Mom. I guess I'm trying to understand her better."

At least, it feels noble to tell that to myself.

Nana opens a drawer, grabs silverware, and begins wrapping pieces in cloth napkins. "I called your mother many times. I hired a private detective after your grandfather died, and once, I showed up on Miriam's doorstep. She was pregnant with you then, but she refused to talk to me. The only thing she didn't seem to reject were my letters. I knew she opened them because I sometimes sent checks, which she always cashed, so I prayed she read my words as well."

Nana sent checks? Was it a way to make amends? A bribe? Or simply to make certain we were cared for because she truly did love my mother? "What happened?"

The corners of Nana's mouth turn downward. She gives a firm shake of her head. "That is a long story I don't think we need to get into right now. Besides, guests will be coming down to breakfast."

I nod. She doesn't volunteer to tell me the story at a later date, and I scold myself for being too presumptuous. We still barely know one another, and I'm all too eager to dig into her past.

After we serve our four guests and clean up the kitchen and the dining room, I follow my grandmother up the attic stairs.

"Now, I don't want you thinking less of me for the amount of dust you'll find up here."

Heat presses down upon us as we climb. When we reach the top, I see the wooden beams and floorboards of an attic to the left and a door to the right.

Nana opens the door.

The room is finished, painted a light gray, one side a steep, sloped ceiling. A nightstand sits beside a full-sized bed with a floral quilt, its edges aged from the sun. A no-nonsense bureau and a bookshelf complete the room. Nana opens the window and a refreshing gush of sea air sweeps through the room, stirring up the plentiful dust coating the furniture.

"I'm not sure it's fair to give you this task." Nana sneezes. She looks around the room, her mouth trembling.

"I'm not afraid of a little dust." I wink at her, but my gaze catches a spider in the corner, and I scrunch up my nose. "Maybe I should get some rags and a vacuum."

Nana nods. "Let me know if you need anything else. I'll bring up a fan from downstairs."

"I can get it." The last thing I need is Nana falling down the stairs trying to lug up a fan.

She claps her hands together. "Okay, then. Thank you, Laney. You're a real blessing."

A blessing. No one's ever called me that before.

She leaves, and I turn to the room, soaking in the silence. I back up and snap a picture with my phone, texting it to Mom.

> Guess where I am? We're going to clean out your old room. Is there anything you'd like me to save for you?

I try to instill enthusiasm and goodwill into the texted words, but I'm not sure I pull it off.

I stand in the middle of the room, aimless, before finally opening the drawer of the nightstand. A picture lies inside—a young woman sitting on the lap of a young man—and I reach for it.

I haven't seen any photos of my mother when she was a teenager, but this is undeniably her. She's smiling into the camera, her hair bleached blond from the sun. She wears pearls at her neck —unfitting for her simple blouse and jeans, and yet she pulls it off. It seems, perhaps, back then she could have pulled off anything. Her eyes are light and full of life. If I had known her, would I have understood her?

My gaze moves to the boy whose lap she sits upon. I don't recognize him. He has dark hair that curls at his ears and a serious gaze. I bring the picture closer, trying to make out any of my own features in him, but I can't glimpse—or even imagine—a likeness. I flip the picture over.

*July 4, 1997*

A few years before I was born, so this man likely is not my father. Still, what place had he held in Mom's life to be placed inside this drawer? Then again, Mom hadn't taken the picture when she'd left the inn, so more than likely I'm inserting meaning where there is none.

I return the picture to its home and move to the bookshelves, surprised at the vast array of novels. I hadn't thought Mom much of a reader, but these bookshelves tell another story. Along the top is a thick collection of V.C. Andrews' novels.

I pull the first one out. *Flowers in the Attic.* I'm familiar with the title but haven't read it. I flip it over and peruse the blurb. An image of my mother reading this story in her attic bedroom comes to life, the juxtaposition of her own memoir haunting alongside this tale of children locked in an attic.

I shiver, despite the heat. Maybe I'll read it this summer. Try to glimpse why this series enthralled my mother. I place it aside and run my fingers along the dusty paperback spines. Three books on quilting, comfortably dog-eared, and another hardcover on scrapbooking. Huh. Had Mom been crafty? On the second shelf sits an assortment of books on Europe, with a heavy emphasis on Italy. I slide them out.

My teenage mother seems to have varied interests. Had she actually been *interesting* once upon a time? Certainly, more than she is now. What changed her?

My phone jangles. I swipe right.

"Hi, Mom."

"She's put you to work, I see."

Of course, she would say it like that.

"I volunteered." Silence. "How's everything?"

"Did you see my post on Friday? My publisher called to tell me we sold a million copies."

I sigh. The book. Always, the book. "That's great."

"Bill took me to The French Laundry. Oh my goodness, the lobster was to die for. I wish you'd been here."

So she could take a picture to post on her socials, no doubt. Ever intent on cultivating an online mother-daughter facade that didn't exist, my mother seemed determined to prove to her fans that, despite her traumatic childhood, she at least had a beautiful relationship with *her* daughter.

Yeah, right.

I clear my throat. "I've been up close and personal with some great lobster here, myself." Mostly on the serving side, but she hadn't even asked about what I'd been up to, so why clarify?

"So . . . do you want anything from your old room?"

"Can't believe she's kept it like that all these years."

"Yeah." What more is there to say? *She's been waiting for you to come back? You broke her heart, you selfish*—I clear my throat again. "So, anything?" I open my mouth to mention the picture of her and the boy, but close it before the words eek out.

"I don't think so. Actually, I'm going to be taking a trip out there in a couple weeks. If you find anything interesting, set it aside for me, would you?"

I gulp, adrenaline rushing to my limbs at this threat to my peaceful world. "You're serious? You haven't visited all these years and now you decide to come?"

I should want Nana and Mom to reunite. And if I help them do so by simply being here, I should be grateful. And yet I don't want her here.

"I'm closing on a piece of land, if you must know." Her voice takes on a snooty, aloof quality. "This has nothing to do with your grandmother."

I scratch at the scars on my arms. She's *moving* here? Or at least planning to spend vacation time here right beneath Nana's nose? "You could have land anywhere you want in the country."

"I don't need to explain myself to *you*, Elaine."

I cringe at the use of my full name. She knows I hate it.

But she barely takes a breath, just rushes on with her precious

51

words. "I can buy land in my hometown if I want to and it's none of your concern."

None of my concern. Just like whatever happened between her and Nana all those years ago is none of my concern. Only the concern of anybody who read her book. But I don't want the book version.

"Fine," I grind out, more than ready for this conversation to end.

"I've actually reached out to Don Rutherford—I think you dated his son, Jason, for a bit in high school? Jason's going to work on the plans for the new house."

Why hadn't Jason mentioned this to me last night? There I'd been, telling him about the struggle Mom's book has brought to my grandmother's business and all along, he planned to design Mom a dream home?

Pressure builds in my chest. "I have to go."

"Keep in touch, darling." Mom's voice is syrupy sweet now. As if we didn't just exchange heated words seconds earlier.

I hang up and pace the dusty room. I pull up the sleeves of my shirt and dig my fingernail into one of the horizontal scars there. Press. Press harder.

With a frustrated groan, I remove my fingernail. An angry red crescent mars my white skin. I can't allow my mother to get to me. Better to go find some boxes to pack up her things.

Too bad the emotional baggage she's left me to carry can't be packaged up and shoved away as well.

# Chapter Six

*I tell myself that each cut lessens the pain within. I see myself bleed. I
know I'm alive. Somehow, that's comforting.*
~ Laney Jacobs' rehab journal

## LANEY

It's hot, and I didn't bring a hat. My long-sleeve shirt is
lightweight cotton, but sweat pours down my chest and
back, slicking my upper lip. I allow it all to further fuel my
irritation as I walk.

When I reach Jason's hotel, I search for his BMW in the
parking lot, but there's no sign of the flashy car.

I squelch a frustrated groan. He said a lot of sweet things last
night, but if he was really interested in healing whatever was
between us, he should have been honest about Mom's house.

I leave the hotel parking lot and walk farther downtown.
There's a Hannaford around the corner—surely, they'll be willing
to give me a few boxes. I walk down the sidewalk, taking in the ice
cream shops, restaurants, and small stores that make up down-

town Bar Harbor. I almost pass Back of Beyond Bookstore but catch a glimpse of a lighthouse display surrounded by a slew of books on the topic. I duck inside.

"Hello!" an Asian American girl about my age calls from the register as the bell above the door announces my presence.

I wince. If I'd known I would be one of only a few customers, I probably would have avoided entering. I hate the pressure to buy something.

"Hot one out there, today, isn't it?" she asks, fanning herself with bright purple fingernails that match the single strip in her dark hair.

Oh, great. A *conversational* clerk. I consider ducking back outside, but it's refreshingly cool in the store. Besides, I don't want to be rude.

"It is." I step toward the lighthouse display.

"I have some water back here if you'd like a bottle."

At her words, my mouth is ten times drier than it was a moment ago. I sweated a lot on the way here and didn't think to bring water. Then again, if I take a water from her, I will *definitely* have to buy something.

"I'm good, but thank you."

"Well, let me know if you need help finding anything."

She leaves me in peace to browse. The store smells just a tad musty, but also of paper and ink and salty sea air, as if the ocean has climbed through the windows to embed itself into the shelves, the worn wooden floor, and into the pages of each book.

The planks creak beneath my feet, much like the steps in Nana's house. I scan the lighthouse books. A couple I recognize from those on Mom's bookshelves in Nana's attic, but most are newer, with vivid pictures and friendly fonts. When I find one with an entire chapter on Nana's lighthouse, the Beacon, I take it to the checkout counter. No doubt Nana has any information I'd want about her lighthouse, but with how much I've already pestered her, why shouldn't I find what I can before peppering her with questions?

The girl nods at my choice of book and scans it. "Our bestselling book on the lighthouses in the area."

"It looks like a good one."

"I love lighthouses, don't you? So much history and mystery and romance and hope. If only . . ."

But her voice fades as I look at her bare arms. Black spots dance before my eyes and I grip the counter, trying to find breath.

Her arms.

They—they look like mine. Only, that's not true. For they're so much worse. Healed over and faded, but . . . bad. I want to tug her shirtsleeves down for her or throw a blanket over her skin. I'm embarrassed for her.

I force my gaze away.

"Hey, are you okay? You don't look so good."

But . . . but this girl is bubbly and outgoing. She seems well-adjusted. Then again, how well can you truly know someone in the space of a few minutes?

Oh, help. I'm going to be sick. "I just need to . . ."

I slide down the counter to the thin gray mat atop the wooden floor and place my head between my knees. What is wrong with me? Why am I reacting to the girl's scars as if they are my own?

I hardly realize she's come around the counter until she's kneeling beside me with a bottle of water, cap in hand. I take it with trembling fingers, consciously avoiding the pink lines on her arms. I'm being ridiculous. I have similar scars.

I gulp the water down until half the bottle is gone. "Thank you. Sorry about that." I move to stand.

"Whoa, there. Why don't you just take a breather for another minute? No one else is in the store. Here, I'll sit with you." She plops her thin frame a few feet beside me and leans against the counter. "Actually, it's good to have this view. I notice how much dust I'm missing down here."

I smile, but my stomach churns. I pray I won't be sick.

"You a local or tourist?"

"I'm visiting my grandmother."

"Nice. My grandmother lives in Colorado. I don't get to see her much."

If I had more energy, I might tell her this is my first time meeting Nana. Who am I kidding? I probably wouldn't.

I take another swig of water as the girl gives a monologue that could put a character in a Shakespearean play to shame. "I used to give tours on one of the boats. I learned a lot about the history of the island that way, but it was seasonal and I might love books even more than boating, so that's how I ended up here. Have you seen any lighthouses on the island yet?"

"Just the Beacon."

"Interesting history there. And it's gotten a lot more attention lately with that book out . . . what's it called? We have tons of copies, I should know . . ."

"*Locked Light*," I thrust out.

The girl snaps her fingers. "That's right. Have you read it?"

I nod, now sick for an entirely different reason.

"I haven't. Memoirs aren't my favorite, although my cousin tells me I have enough material to write my own. Actually, the book sounds horrible." She shrugs. "Guess I should read it before I judge, but I try to fill my mind with positive things, you know? Reading about a teenager getting locked in a lighthouse just doesn't do it for me these days. What did you think of it?"

I cap the water and shimmy my legs beneath myself. I can't talk about Mom's book with this near-stranger as if I'm at Tuesday night book club. "I'm feeling better, I think. Thank you."

I stand, and so does she. "Oh, good. I'm glad." But she doesn't move to go back around the counter. She points to my hand and at first, I think one of my sleeves must have crept up and she sees our commonality. I tug both my sleeves down. "You're a writer?"

"What?" I glance at my left hand. Oh. A smudge of ink trails from the bottom half of my pinky down the contour of my hand

—a curse of the left-handed writer. "Oh, that. I—not really. I just journal."

"You should come to our writers' group. Monday nights, right here."

Was the girl daft? Didn't she hear I'm not a writer? "I work most Monday nights."

Her face falls. "Oh, that's too bad. There's only a few of us. If there's a night that works better for you, I could talk with the other members about changing it."

Her dark eyes meet my gaze. Why is she so . . . forthcoming? Unafraid of being judged? Desperate? I couldn't decide, but in some odd way I find it refreshing. "My schedule's kind of all over the place now. Besides, I'm not really a writer." I repeat myself, whether to cement the truth in the girl's head, or my own, I'm not sure. My mom's the writer in the family, after all. Not me.

She gives me a tight-lipped smile, as if she doesn't believe me, then walks back around the counter to continue checking out my book. "Okay. If you ever change your mind, you know where to find me."

"Thanks."

"You feeling better?"

"Yes."

"That's nineteen ninety-nine. Would you like to donate a can of cat food to the pet shelter?"

I scrunch my nose.

"I know, odd request coming from a bookstore. But the owner loves cats."

I'm not a cat person, but the poor cats need to eat, and the girl did give me a bottle of water, so I agree.

"Twenty-one forty-nine."

I hand her the bills and she slips my book into a brown paper bag. "I hope you enjoy. Be careful, it's hot out there."

"Thank you." I walk toward the entrance, hesitate. There's still no one else in the bookstore. I could ask her about her scars. Maybe it could be a healthy thing for me.

HEIDI CHIAVAROLI

But no. I'm a coward. Besides, this woman doesn't need to deal with my problems on top of her own. Bad enough I near melted into a mess in front of her checkout counter.

I push through the store door, the bell announcing my departure and ringing with finality.

# Chapter Seven

*I'm sorry I urged you guys to jump that day, Mads. I wish I could take it back.*
~ Letter from Jason to Maddie found in a bottle washed up onshore two years after her death

## JASON

I'm cruising along Route 3 at a decent clip, but the sight of the woman on the side of the road, glistening with sweat, causes me to hit my brakes. I look in the rearview mirror to confirm my hunch. I'm right.

Not just any woman. Laney.

Broken-down cardboard boxes sit snug beneath her arms. A small brown bag hangs from her wrist, slapping her side with each step. I pull over and back up several feet, opening my passenger window.

A rush of warmth from outside tunnels into the air-conditioned car. I lean toward the open window, waiting for her to stop. She does.

"Need a lift?" I study the sweat beading on her upper lip. She's in a long-sleeve shirt, of all things, and her arms seem to melt into the cardboard she's carrying, but she shifts from foot to foot, appearing to vacillate at my offer. Come *on*, woman. "Is my help really that repulsive to you?"

She rolls her eyes and opens the back door to lay the boxes on the seat. I mentally pump a victory fist into the air as she slips into the passenger's seat and places the small brown bag on the floor.

"I take it you're headed back to your grandmother's?"

"Yes."

We sit in silence, but it's less than a mile to the Beacon, and I'm searching for something to say to bridge the rift between us.

"I stopped by your inn," she says after we've driven in silence for a solid minute.

"You did?"

"I didn't see your car."

"I wasn't there." Why I'm stating the obvious, I have no clue. Probably because I don't want to tell Laney what I *was* doing. "I was looking at some land for a new client."

"My mother's land?"

My hands fumble on the wheel when I turn into the driveway of the Beacon. My skin grows hot despite the chill of the air conditioner.

"You don't think you should have mentioned that last night?"

"Laney, I—"

"Don't even tell me you thought I knew, because I'm not buying that for a second."

"I didn't. Think you knew, I mean."

"Show it to me."

"What?"

"Show me my mom's land."

"Why?"

"Because I want to see it."

I blow out a long breath, put the BMW in reverse. "Fine." I turn right onto Route 3, silence filling the car. "The truth is that I knew your mom was talking to my dad about the land. I didn't want to mention it last night because we only just started talking again. I didn't know the land was so close, and I didn't know my dad would ask me to lead the project."

A small puff of air escapes her. She presses her lips together and turns toward the window.

God help me if she's going to cry.

"I understand. Why shouldn't you design my mother's dream house?" A hint of bitterness laces her tone, but I sense she really is trying to see things through my point-of-view.

"Thank you. I appreciate that." I drive another minute before making a quick decision. I turn into a hotel parking lot and turn the car around.

"Wait. What are you doing? I still want to see the land."

"How about we take the long way there? You have pressing plans for the afternoon?"

"I'm cleaning Nana's attic."

"You think she'll mind if I steal you away to see the sights?"

"She won't, but I might."

"Just a small detour. What do you say? I'm willing to bet you haven't toured anything on this island outside of Bar Harbor."

"That's not true. I walked the path near Nana's house."

"Well, humor me, then, because I haven't seen the real sights of Acadia—Sand Beach, Thunder Hole, the Otter Cliffs."

She groans. "Do you have any idea how many people will be on Park Loop Road today?"

"So, rubbing elbows with other tourists isn't your idea of fun?"

"Not in the slightest."

"What if we go later tonight?"

She wrinkles her nose, and though I know that means she hates the idea, the gesture is downright cute.

"Are you trying to wrangle another date out of me?"

"Maybe. Would that be so terrible?" I meet her gaze, but she looks away, staring at the empty parking space beside us.

"Jason, it's taken a lot for me to get to this place in my life. To find my way forward. I'm not sure if us hanging out is the healthiest thing for my mental state."

Talk about ripping the Band-Aid off. But she's being honest, which I respect, even if it feels like she's plunging a knife into my heart. I put the car in park and swallow, forcing myself to not react, to think before I speak.

I wet my lips. "The last thing I want to do is hurt you. If that means we don't see each other anymore . . . then I guess I'll try to live with that." I inhale, air expanding my stomach. "And if that means I tell my dad I can't work on your mom's house, then that's what I'll do."

She turns fast, her deep eyes searing mine. "What?"

"I don't want to hurt you any more than I already have, Laney. Now that I know how much it bothers you, I'll ask my dad to put another architect on the job."

My dad won't be happy, and while I'm not sure he'd fire me —I am his son, after all—I don't know what it might mean for our working relationship. But I know one thing: if me saying *no* to my father causes Laney even a little less hurt, I'll do it in a second.

## LANEY

I COULD DROWN in the rich hazel flecks of his indigo gaze. It pulls me in, like the undertow of a strong current.

One thing is as clear as those eyes, though: Jason Rutherford is not the boy that pressured me and Maddie off that cliff. He's a man, now. Maybe even a caring, considerate man. And that is both intensely alluring and intensely dangerous.

"You'd do that?" I whisper.

"Yes. In a heartbeat. In fact, consider it done."

I break whatever hold he has on me with those bottomless

pools to his soul. There's no denying the temptation of messing with Mom's plans, but is it right of me to do so?

I shake my head, lean back in the passenger's seat, the scent of Jason's woodsy cologne comforting and unnerving all at once. The air coming from the vents is cool, drying the sweat beneath my shirt and the back of my neck to a near chill. "I can't ask you to do that."

"You didn't ask, I'm telling you this is what I'm going to do."

I blink, fast.

"Can I ask you a question without you getting mad?" He slides his pointer finger down the curve of the steering wheel.

I nod.

"I'm wondering if maybe your mother wants to build a home here to make amends with your grandmother. Could that be a possibility?"

"Miriam Jacobs doesn't care about anyone but herself. And if she wanted to make amends with Nana, she wouldn't have written her stupid book. A book that is single-handedly ruining Nana's business."

"I'd think that kind of publicity would have helped your grandmother's inn."

I shrug. "I guess some are curious and book a room, but most of Mom's readers are showing their loyalty by boycotting the bed and breakfast."

"Maybe your grandmother could use it to her advantage— market it as the lighthouse from the bestselling memoir."

The thought disgusts me. "Nana has too much self-respect for that. Besides, it'd be like leaning into a lie for the sake of profit. I can't see her doing that."

"Wait. You think your Mom lied in her own memoir?"

I shrug. "I'm not sure. Mom's always been dramatic." I shake my head. "But I know the person Mom described in her book is not the Nana I'm coming to know. There's too big of a disconnect to ignore."

"People change. It happens."

"Yes," I whisper. Hadn't I acknowledged that very thing about the man next to me? I clear my throat, making my next decision quickly. "I'll go with you to the park tonight."

"You will?"

"And you'll show me my mom's land?"

"Of course. I can show you now, without Park Loop Road, if you want."

"I should get back to helping Nana."

"Okay. So, can I pick you up later?"

"Six?"

He nods, then puts the car in drive and heads back to Nana's. When he parks at the Beacon, he leans over to look up and out from under his windshield. "It'd be a shame to let it crumble. You sure you don't want me to look at it?"

But I'm afraid to get my hopes up. "No thank you, but thanks for the ride." I scoop up my brown bag from the floor and shimmy out of the car. Jason also gets out, grabbing the cardboard boxes from the back seat for me.

We meet around the front where he hands me the boxes. "I'm looking forward to being a tourist with you tonight."

I roll my eyes, but a smile tugs at my lips. "See ya." I sense his eyes on me as I enter the front door of the inn, and fluttering wings whisper across the lining of my stomach.

Should I allow him to make me feel this way? Hope is a powerful thing, for good—and for ill. I certainly don't need any more ill in my life. Most likely, it's best to crush any hope I'm feeling down into a powder and let it blow away in the sea breeze.

# Chapter Eight

*People say time heals all wounds, but if that's true, Mom would go home to see Nana. It's been twenty-five years. Isn't it time? If not for her, then maybe it's time for me.*
~ Laney Jacobs' rehab journal

### LANEY

T spend the rest of the day dusting and packing away Mom's things. I could probably make a fortune marketing her old lava lamps and Trapper Keepers and Steve Madison shoes in a Miriam Jacobs' yard sale, but I refuse to bring that kind of pain on Nana. I sort everything into three piles: Salvation Army, dump, and keep in case Mom wants.

In the keep pile, I put the picture of her and the handsome boy, as well as most of her books. I set aside the first book in the *Flowers in the Attic* series, curious to read it myself. Once I have filled one of the cardboard boxes with books, I carry it outside Mom's old room to the other part of the attic, full of pink insulation and boxes of Christmas decorations. I imagine the Beacon at Christmas and wonder if I might still be here.

I set the box down, my gaze snagging on an old box labeled *Bar Harbor history* atop another box labeled *Lillian*. Who's Lillian? And what's in this history box? Maybe I didn't need to buy that book at Back of Beyond, after all. Maybe Nana has some interesting reads on local history in her own attic.

Leaving Mom's old books aside, I lift the history box and carry it downstairs, the V.C. Andrews' book perched on top.

I find Nana on the back porch in a rocking chair, sipping tea and staring at the sapphire Atlantic. I set the box down on the chipped paint of the deck boards.

"There's a pitcher of sweet tea inside. Help yourself, honey."

When I come back outside with a cold glass, Nana is holding the *Flowers in the Attic* book. "She loved these. Mind you, I wasn't too keen on her reading them. Heard they were a bit racy."

This is the first glimpse I see into what Nana may have been like as a mother. No doubt, she ran on the conservative side and my mother, with her free-spirited ways, likely took up rebellion as a hobby. Were my grandparents unreasonably strict? Or was Mom simply a wild child, bucking against their reasonable expectations?

I don't tell Nana of my suspicions about the similarities between this book and Mom's memoir—right now, it's just a hunch. Instead, I lower myself onto the other rocking chair and gesture to the box at my feet. "I found this upstairs. Is it okay if I look through it?"

Nana twists her body to see the words on the box. "Oh my. It's been years since I've seen that box. Your grandfather was the history buff."

"I bought a book about the lighthouses in the area today. It had the Beacon in it, but I didn't see a whole lot of history surrounding it."

"Jack—your grandfather—was searching for all the names of the lighthouse keepers. The logs went missing right before we bought the place. He was always searching, though, right up until the day he died. Said he was going to write a book about what he found." She gives a small laugh. "Maybe that's where your mother inherited her desire to write."

"If he was going to write a book about lighthouses and their keepers, he must have found something interesting."

Nana shakes her head. "I'm sorry, dear. I don't remember much. I think he mentioned wanting to visit the grave of someone he read about, but that was around the time he started having heart problems."

Does it bother her that I want to revisit this part of her past?

"If I find something noteworthy, you might be able to use it as a point of interest, a way to market the bed and breakfast."

She sighs, reaches out a hand to cover my own. "Laney, I love this place and it breaks my heart to think of losing it. But I'm too old to keep up with such things. Facebook and Instacart and all of that."

I think she means Insta*gram*, but I don't correct her. Neither do I want to swoop in and tell her that I might be able to help with all of that. Because who knows if I'll find anything worth posting? Besides, I can only imagine all the trolls waiting to pounce on a new post from the Beacon. Many of Mom's readers view Nana as the jail-keeper to Mom's cell—the lighthouse. I have no idea if putting the Beacon out on social media would cause more harm than help.

*Could what Mom wrote be true?*

But the very thought feels like a betrayal to Nana. And haven't I, deep down, accepted that whether or not Mom's memoir is true, it's not the *entire* truth?

"I understand. Is it still okay if I search through the box?"

"Of course."

We sit in silence for several long moments, sipping our tea. It's sweet with a hint of lemon and I imagine the many times Nana's made it, tweaking sugar or tea or lemon to get to this point—the perfect batch. If only relationships and past hurts could be tweaked as easily.

I finish my drink and take our glasses to the kitchen where a soft, Celtic hymn plays in the background. I rinse the glasses and load them into the dishwasher before rejoining Nana. "That music is beautiful."

Nana cranes her head toward the door, listening for the music. I know when she recognizes it because her eyes light up.

"Of course. I forgot which one I put in. I'm still old-fashioned, using CDs. I can't bring myself to part with this one, though. My best friend Lillian gave it to me." Her smile dims. "She died from cancer almost twelve years ago."

I press my lips together. "You lost your best friend."

She nods. "It never gets easier, but Lillian rests, awaiting her part in God's new heaven and new earth."

I love the way Nana talks. Or maybe I just love that she doesn't need or require anything from me.

I lean down and lift the box. "I'll take this to my room. I made some good headway in the attic, but I think I'll keep it as a morning project, when it's still cool."

"Dear, you do as much or as little as you want, whenever you want. It's something I shouldn't have let go for so long."

"It's . . . insightful." I wink at Nana. "I'm going to go out with a friend after dinner—do you need anything before then?"

"Nothing, honey. Am I being too nosy if I ask who your friend is?"

My face heats. Best to be truthful. "I bumped into a guy I knew from California."

Nana raises one eyebrow. "That's quite a coincidence."

"I guess so." I avert my gaze, thinking about Mom hiring Jason's company to design her a house. Here, in Maine, on the same island where Nana lives. Should I tell her? And yet, what good would giving her such information accomplish?

"And does this friend have a name?"

Wow. She's quite the persistent little septuagenarian, isn't she? "Jason," I practically croak.

Her brow raises higher, all the way to her tasteful ashy bangs. "Jason?"

"He's a boy I know from back home," I repeat.

Her mouth twitches. "I see."

"It's . . . complicated."

She murmurs acknowledgment. Enough to keep me musing aloud.

"We were dating when my friend Maddie died. He was there."

"Oh, honey."

"I think he's changed since then. Do you think people can change?"

"I know they can. Trouble is, change is hard work. Not for the faint of heart, but sometimes God in his grace does the heavy lifting for us."

I smile.

"Feel free to invite him for dinner. We're having spaghetti and clams."

"Thanks, Nana. But I don't think I'm ready for that. Maybe another time?"

She nods, stands, and grips me in a firm embrace. "You mean the world to me, Laney-girl. Don't you ever doubt that."

I squeeze her thin frame, clinging longer than necessary but relishing the feel of her arms around me. She loves me without reserve—I know it, I feel it. "I'll be down in a bit to help you with dinner."

She nods. "Okay, sweet girl."

Sweet girl. I want to correct her. She read Mom's book, so she knows about what happened with Maddie. How then can she think me sweet? She glimpsed my arms that first day. Does she realize how I chose to deal with the many emotions pounding within me? The relief that a razor blade against tight skin could provide?

I walk upstairs with the box tight in my arms. I'm no longer that girl, that woman. I haven't self-harmed in more than a year. Many would consider me recovered, cured.

Why then, do I feel so far from healed?

ONCE IN MY ROOM, I gently close the door, exchange my long-sleeve shirt for a t-shirt, and settle myself on the floor with the box. If there's anything that can shed light on the inn or contribute to Nana keeping it, it could be here.

I open the box. On top is a black-and-white book titled *Lost Bar Harbor*. I flip through it, taking in the cottages of the Gilded Age, much of them lost in the Great Fire of 1947. I set it aside and pick up a black-and-white book about lighthouses in the Bar Harbor and Acadia region. A couple pages are dog-eared and I flip to them, finding the Beacon quickly.

Though there's no doubt that the photo is of the Beacon, it looks old and washed out in the photo. As if all the love and joy that Nana has brought to the place never existed in this leeched-of-character image.

Opposite the picture is a page about the lighthouse and I perk up.

*Beacon Lighthouse served as a guide to navigation for eighty years, from January 1, 1853 to August 18, 1933. Because information about lighthouses primarily comes from lighthouse keepers' logs, it's a mystery and a shame that the logs from the Beacon went missing in 1980. Though a substantial reward has been offered, the logs have not yet been returned.*
*What we do know is that a total of ten keepers and their families ran the lighthouse in its eighty-year period. The station was fully restored when it was converted to use as an inn in 1983.*

The page went on to talk of the first and last keepers, all that was recorded. A Frank Winslow was the first keeper. A Miles White the last. None of the names sound familiar. Nothing in the book indicates anything of interest—certainly nothing that would gain the attention of the town or potential guests.

I close the book, drumming my fingers on the cover. I wonder what happened to those logbooks? 1980. I didn't think my grandparents even owned the lighthouse yet. Had previous owners taken them in their move? I'd have to ask Nana if she remembers anything my grandfather may have told her.

I dig farther into the box, pulling out more history books and an envelope of old photographs. Some are discolored and stuck together. Most are of the lighthouse and the inn. I glimpse a picture of a little girl who looks like Mom, a striking woman who must be Nana holding her hand, the Atlantic and the Beacon shimmering behind them. They are smiling and they look happy, no doubt never guessing all that might be in store for their relationship in the future.

At the bottom is a photocopied black-and-white picture. A gravestone. But instead of a name it simply says THANKFUL,— the letters unevenly spaced as if whoever engraved the stone realized they'd have too much space at the end of the line and dragged out the marks to even it up. At the bottom of the page, in the white margin, is scrawled cursive handwriting in black ink.

*Thankful Phinney Burgess,*
*b. May 31, 1806 d. August 24, 1891*

So, Thankful was the name of the person on the gravestone . . . why then, the comma? And was Thankful one of the lighthouse keepers? I'd have to google the name.

I continue taking out the contents of the box—mostly books, lots of pictures. I glance at my phone. Almost five o'clock. I'd have to go downstairs and help Nana with dinner soon.

At the very bottom, I find an old leather-bound journal, pages slipping out of its binding, creased, and yellowed with age. My heart picks up speed. With care, I open to the first page, but it is illegible, the ink smeared from being stuck to the cover all these years. In an attic.

I groan. Who would have put such a wonderful piece of history in a hot attic for all these years? Surely not my grandfather.

I picture Nana packing up my grandfather's belongings after his death, perhaps books and mementos he'd left on his bureau or in an old desk. Carrying them up to the attic, where the painful memory of a runaway daughter lives. Not caring about their history, only knowing the pain that seeing them brings to her heart every day. Poor Nana.

Slowly, I turn to the second page, and although hard to read, I make it out with some effort.

*May 2, 1853*

> *Papa says that all of us have a little light inside.*
>
> *For some, it is buried deep and can barely be seen—like a candle struggling beneath too little oxygen. For others, it is as bright as the lights in the old north tower on a clear night.*
>
> *Papa doesn't say much about the darkness that's in each of us. I guess he likes to have a positive outlook and all that. But I know it's there, even if he doesn't say it. I know because I see it in me.*
>
> *But maybe it is not so bad focusing on the light. Because the more I try to see the light in other people—no matter how small and simmering it might be—the more it seems to grow.*
>
> *That's what I have been trying to do when I think on Mama and the anger I hold inside over us leaving little Rufus behind when we came to Matinicus Rock. Even now, I hesitate to write of my anger. It is not honoring to God, and yet I wonder if I keep it bottled up inside like a message one throws out to sea, if it will mold and fester and threaten to snuff out my own light?*
>
> *After Rufus's birth, Mama fell ill for so long that in many ways, Rufus became mine. If I didn't dream of my*

*little brother's face every night . . . the small hands he held out for me when I cooked up his eggs, his delighted face when he knocked down the tower of wooden blocks Papa made for him last Christmas . . . perhaps I would not miss him so and wonder how he fares.*

*Miranda will write of him soon. My oldest sister is more caring than me and Mama combined, so I trust she will look after him. But it does not change how I miss him.*

*I know the Rock can be dangerous and unpredictable. But with Papa and Benji tending the lights, there are more than enough hands between Mama, Lydia, Esther, Mahalia, and me to tend after a rambunctious little boy. Who knows when I will next see my little brother? He would love the rock birds— the odd-looking birds with bright beaks that remind us of clowns. I miss him so much it hurts.*

*Benji talks of going away. He wishes to live a life at sea. Papa has taken to letting him use the dory to go to Rockland and has begun training me in the care of the lamps in Benji's absence.*

*Though not common for a girl, the job suits me. It is cozy in the tall towers with Papa. As I clean the lamp bowls, trim the wicks, and refill all twenty-eight lamps—fourteen in each tower—with oil, securing their glass chimneys, I feel I am caring for each sailor that will pass our light station. That I am giving them a sacred message. A message that warns of the dangers of this rock of an island—how running aground on it could be deadly. But there is another message too, one that tells of safety in times of trouble. Of a warm fire and an adequate meal. Whatever is needed, the light sends its message.*

*I may not be able to care for my brother, so now, I care for the lights.*

I search for a name at the bottom of the entry, but there is none. Perhaps, by reading it through, I can discover who the author is. And yet, if this girl tended a lighthouse out on an island, what was the journal doing here, at the Beacon?

I scoop it up and open my bedroom door, smiling at guests— a couple—that I'd served at breakfast that morning.

I trot down the stairs, my feet light, and turn the corner into the kitchen. Nana is cutting white button mushrooms at the counter, and she looks up at my arrival.

"Nana, look what I found." I hold the journal out to her, watching her expression to see her reaction. Her mouth parts, but then her gaze is no longer on my hands but traveling elsewhere. Upward, toward my elbows.

The small smile of pleasant surprise disappears from her face. In its place is something more troubling. The lines along her mouth become heavier, darker. A look of pity and sadness over-takes her.

With horror, I look down, knowing what I will see but hoping beyond hope that I'm mistaken. That I didn't actually run down here in a t-shirt.

But no. There, with abundant afternoon sunlight splashing from the window onto my skin, are the ugly, dark pink scars. Scars I have carved out myself, to stay with me all my days on earth.

The journal slips from my hands and slaps the kitchen tile. I back away, slowly, as if any sudden movements will make this moment worse than it is already. Then I turn and go upstairs, my feet scuffing the worn carpet on the treads until I am safely in my bedroom with the door shut securely. While I want to throw myself onto the flowered bedspread and cry, more than that, I want a covering. Protection. Without taking off my t-shirt, I find the long-sleeve shirt I wore earlier and slip it over my head, relishing the feel of the cool fabric over my arms, a hiding place for my past.

I lay down face first on my bed, squeezing my eyes against my pillow. The guests I'd passed on the stairs. Did they also see? What would they think of the innkeeper's granddaughter flaunting such scars? Worse, had they read Mom's memoir? Did they know I was

Miriam Jacobs' daughter? Would they connect me to Maddie's death? Would they blab about my scars to anyone who would listen? Anyone with ears hungry for more of my mother's story?

The thought causes warm tears to squeeze from my eyelids. A soft knock sounds at my door but, although I know it is rude, I can't bring myself to tell my grandmother to "come in."

She knocks again. I murmur a sound that could be interpreted any number of ways.

The door creaks open. Out of the corner of my eye, I see Nana. She closes the door behind her, walks toward me with slow steps.

"When your mother hid herself away in her room and didn't answer my knocks, I respected her privacy. I didn't push. I often wondered if that was a grievous mistake. Laney, I won't make the same mistake with you. I love you. I cannot stand by while you push me away."

She sighs, lowers the journal to my nightstand. "'If a man owns a hundred sheep, and one of them wanders away, will he not leave the ninety-nine on the hills and go to look for the one that wandered off?'"

Birthday card verse, age 8.

"I'm sorry, Nana." I turn my face in my pillow, too ashamed to look at her.

She lowers herself onto my bed, places a gentle hand on my back. "We all have our scars, my dear girl. Hiding them doesn't change that they're there."

"They're so ugly." But my words don't portray the truth of what I mean. Yes, the scars are unflattering and shameful, but it's more than that—what they stand for is what's ugliest of all. What kind of a person mutilates herself?

"They are a part of your story. And while parts of your story might be painful, none of it is ugly. Because you, dear girl, could never be ugly."

Her words move over me like a cool breeze on a stifling day. Her hand travels in circles on my back, and I sink into her touch, something about the gesture reminiscent of a pleasant time in my childhood, although I can't pinpoint the time or moment.

Nana inhales, then exhales long and deep, as if she is pushing the past behind her with the force of air in her breaths. "Your past doesn't have to define you, honey."

A prickly feeling starts at the back of my throat and works its way up to my eyes. I swallow it down.

"After my friend Maddie left . . ." I notice the word I choose, realize it means I am far from healed, even six years later. I swallow, try again. "After Maddie *died*, everything hurt. If it wasn't for me, she would still be alive."

"Oh, darling."

I rush on before I can change my mind. "I thought about ending it all, but then I'd think about how disappointed Maddie would be in me. I'd think about those birthday cards you sent me. And I couldn't do it. But I had to do something. It started as a sort of punishment, and then I just did it to take away the pain inside."

"How long has it been?" Nana stops the circles on my back.

I flip over to face her. To face my shame. "Six years since Maddie died. A year since I last cut myself."

"I'm sorry about Maddie. But you not harming yourself for a year—that's a victory, Laney."

"I went to rehab. It helped. I don't think I'll ever cut myself again. But I hate my scars. They'll be with me forever, a constant reminder of Maddie, of my own failures."

"Or perhaps, someday they could be a reminder of your victory over this struggle."

I scrunch up my face.

Nana laughs. "You are a strong young woman. You have fought a hard battle, and you've won. I'm not saying it's over, and I'm not saying it will be easy, but I am so proud of you."

Fresh tears squeeze from my eyes. I'd never thought of it quite like that. Would thinking about the unsightly ridges that way help me move forward? "I can't imagine not caring that they're there. I can't imagine flaunting them."

"You are one of the humblest persons I've had the privilege of knowing. I don't think anyone could accuse you of flaunting your scars. Maybe, honey, they're just telling a story."

She's not wrong about that, I suppose. They do have quite a story. Not one I'm proud of, but one that's not yet over. "I—I'll try." Not that I'm ready to bare my arms to the world or anything, but the fact that I can glimpse and appreciate this perspective is a small triumph in itself.

"And I'm always here to listen, okay? About Maddie, about your arms, about rehab. About anything under the sun."

I nod. Nana reaches for the journal. "I see you found some of your grandfather's secrets."

"Secrets?"

"Maybe not secrets so much as research. I packed it all away after he died, too hurt to care much about any of it. Too hurt that he didn't share more about his work with me."

"You were hiding away your scars too, then."

Nana looks thoughtful, tilts her head to the side. "Yes, I suppose I was."

# Chapter Nine

*The light shines in the darkness, and the darkness has not overcome it.*

*John 1:5*

~ Verse on Laney's birthday card from Nana, Age 7

## LANEY

I'm scraping up the last of my spaghetti and clams, all garlicky and full of mushrooms and breadcrumbs and parsley, with a thick piece of sourdough bread when the doorbell rings. I go to the front room to open the door. Jason stands at the threshold in khaki shorts, a Bar Harbor t-shirt, and a deep blue hat that says *Acadia* on it.

"Wow," I say. "You do look like a tourist."

"I have my binoculars in the car, so I'm ready to go."

"I just need to say goodbye to my Nana." But I don't invite him in.

"Laney Jacobs, you invite that boy inside. Don't forget, now, we're in the business of hospitality."

Proud as a peacock, Jason struts past me with a wicked grin. "Yes, Laney. Let's not forget to be *hospitable.*"

I stick out my tongue at him.

He gives me a wink that seems to jump from the depths of his gaze straight into my chest, where it travels downward, lodging in my belly. I close the door behind me and find him staring at a framed picture of my grandparents in front of the lighthouse. Nana is young, her face smooth and beautiful. I can see the resemblance to my mother.

"We'd just bought the Beacon and the keeper's house. The realtor took the picture." Nana stands in the threshold of the kitchen, holds out her hand to Jason. "It's nice to meet you, young man. I'm Charlotte."

Jason clasps her hand. "Ma'am, pleasure to meet you. I'm Jason." He looks at the picture again. "When did you buy the lighthouse?"

"Oh, back in the early eighties. Jack retired from the Coast Guard, but he never could be without the sea." A wistful expression passes her face, as if she's remembering some private thought about my grandfather. "We loved the lighthouse right away."

"I can't imagine a neater place to live."

Nana smiles at him. It's apparent she likes Jason from the twinkle in her eyes. "Me neither."

"Laney said the lighthouse has some damage?"

I glare at him, but he ignores me.

"Like all old things, it does."

"I'd love to have a look sometime, if it's okay with you . . ." He looks at me. "And Laney."

Now, I'm shooting daggers. His mouth twitches.

"You're welcome to have a look anytime. I just don't want anyone in the lighthouse until I can get some professionals out here."

I don't tell Nana that Jason is a professional. Nana doesn't tell Jason that she doesn't have money for said professionals. The best thing I can think to do is get these two away from one another. Now.

"We should go before we lose daylight."

"It was nice meeting you, Mrs. Jacobs."

"You come back anytime, young man." She squeezes my hand. "You two enjoy yourselves."

After Jason opens the passenger door for me, I buckle my seatbelt. We head south toward Park Loop Road.

"Your grandmother loves that lighthouse, doesn't she?"

"And my grandfather. She . . . she really loved him, I think."

"You sound surprised."

I shrug, glimpse the tall trees out my window, the sunlight illuminating their leaves, transforming them to a thousand different shades of green. "I guess after reading Mom's memoir, after watching Mom and Bill in their marriage—I don't know, sometimes it seems easier to believe real love is a thing of fairytales."

He's silent for a moment, driving with his hands on ten and two, his face pensive, his jaw firm.

I shake my head. "Sorry to be a downer. It's a beautiful night and here I am being Eeyore."

"Eeyore, huh? You personally remind me more of Piglet—tiny and cuddly and pink."

"That's quite enough of that." I try not to giggle. "Besides, you should be scared for your life after the stunt you tried to pull with Nana."

"What stunt?"

"'*Oh, I'd love to have a look sometime.*' Could you be any more obvious?"

"What's so wrong with asking to look at the lighthouse? How many visitors does your grandmother get a year? I'm willing to bet all of them want to look at the lighthouse. It's cool. It's history. It's . . . symbolic."

"It's just—well, she gets a lot of trespassers poking around, and it's dangerous. Besides, you don't need to bother yourself with it. I don't want her suspecting we're trying to get into her business and help her."

His mouth turns downward, into a serious frown. "Huh, hadn't thought of it that way. *Helping* her. That would be terrible."

"Jason, I'm serious."

He pulls up to the Ranger station kiosk and pays the fee for a park pass, taping it to the lower left side of the windshield before driving deeper into Acadia.

"You ever think that maybe your grandmother's not the one who wouldn't want my help?"

"What's that supposed to mean?"

"I mean, maybe you don't want my help. Maybe it's your pride standing in the way of helping your grandmother."

I grit my teeth. A worming, niggling feeling tells me he's not wrong.

We meander along Park Loop Road, passing several pull-offs and overlooks. He tells me how Acadia is the only national park in the northeast, how it's the only national park created solely from donations of private land. The Rockefellers donated eleven thousand acres and the Vanderbilts donated money. We continue driving.

"Are we going to get out and see anything, or are we just doing a drive-by?"

"You're especially prickly tonight. I think you might be getting comfortable with me."

I don't answer.

He swipes a thin book from the dashboard and hands it to me. An Acadia National Park guidebook. "We don't have tons of time before it gets dark, so I planned a few stops to give us the best sights. Maybe another day you'll climb Beehive with me."

"Beehive, huh? Sounds tempting."

"You know, I remember you being a lot more adventurous back in high school."

I wince. "Yeah, well, I was also a lot more stupid in high school. Clearly."

Jason grows silent.

We pass Sieur de Monts Spring and the Beaver Dam Pond before winding around to a breathtaking view of the ocean. Jason pulls over and grabs his binoculars before getting out of the car. I follow.

Briny sea air winds around us. We step onto the large granite blocks overlooking Frenchman Bay. A few other tourists do the same. Jason searches the bay before fitting the binoculars to his face.

He lowers them, points. "There."

I see something like a house on a far-off island. He hands me the binoculars, but they are still looped around his neck, and I inch closer to use them.

He smells of spice and that familiar cologne and faintly of pine from the air freshener in the rental car. It's so uniquely him, so uniquely of this moment and this night, that I lean closer, inhale deeper.

"See it?" he asks.

I pull back from the binoculars, refocus, and raise them to my face again. "It's a lighthouse."

"Egg Rock Light. Built in 1875 in order to help ships navigate Frenchman Bay. There's a lot of rocks beneath the surface around here. The island's so small that they had to build the lighthouse beacon directly on top of the keeper's house."

I study the sparse rock, imagine the girl from the journal living on a similar rock, one many more miles out to sea.

"I guess during World War II, a German sub snuck past the lighthouse and dropped off two spies farther north. The spies had sixty thousand in cash and a bag of diamonds. They weren't caught until they reached New York City."

"You *are* a walking tour guide."

He shrugs. "It's interesting to me, you know? The land, the history."

I lower the binoculars but don't move away. "That's right. Archeology and all that, right?"

His gaze lands on me and I'm looking up at him, at those ocean-deep eyes that threaten to drown me. That old, familiar pull of attraction swirls in my belly. I guess I'm wrong about not being drawn to him any longer.

"You remember," he says.

"What happened to that dream?"

He breaks our connection, sighs deep. "After Maddie, I didn't feel like bristling against expectations. I decided to go with the safe route, keeping Dad happy."

"And what about you? Are *you* happy?" It was the first time I entertained the thought that he might not be. That maybe his life wasn't as picture-perfect as I'd thought.

"I'm happy to be here with you, right now."

"Not what I asked."

He shoves his hands in his pockets. "I don't regret going into business with Dad, going to school for architecture, if that's what you mean."

Vague, but I wouldn't push.

"Ready?"

I nod and we return to the car.

"We don't have time tonight, but there's a mansion around here. Highseas. A Princeton professor built it as a wedding gift for his European fiancée. Thirty-six rooms. Unfortunately, she came over on the *Titanic* and never made it to her palace on the sea."

"That's so sad."

"Sorry. I'm going overboard with my tour guide trivia." He drives a little farther and the road becomes crowded with cars parked on the side. "Here. Sand Beach, something a little more upbeat. You up for a walk?"

"Sure."

He pulls over once again and we cross the street, joining

others on the Ocean Trail, a narrow, dirt route with numerous off-paths that allow for majestic views of Newport Cove. He leads me off one of these private trails to a massive ledge overlooking the ocean and the beach.

My knees tremble and I back away, suddenly nauseous. "I can't. I'm sorry."

I should be able to look at the ocean. Jason isn't even near the edge. But I can't.

"I'm such a blockhead. Laney, I'm sorry. I wasn't thinking." He walks back toward me, back toward the path. "You must think I'm an insensitive jerk, bringing you here. I honestly wasn't even thinking about . . . you know."

I shake my head, lower myself to the large slab of rock I'm standing on at the edge of the path. It's far enough from the precipice that I feel safe. Safe enough. "I know you didn't. It's okay. I should be able to do this. I want to."

I can hardly believe that last statement is true, but it is. I told myself this would be a new beginning. An entirely different ocean, across the country from my history, from Mom. Nana is doing hard things in facing the destruction of her beloved business. She *has* done hard things in her life. Bearing the strain of an estranged daughter. Grieving a husband she loved. Now, trying to keep a struggling business alive.

I stand . . . well, if one can call squatting with legs bent like a bird and arms splayed for balance, standing, then that's what I'm doing. I take a tentative step forward, then sit back down on the rock. I've moved about six inches farther from the safety of the path.

Jason lowers himself beside me. He's all easy confidence and patience. It annoys me while I also find it insanely attractive. The security he exudes, the safety I feel with him beside me. As soon as the thought crosses my mind, though, I banish it out to sea. This is the sort of thinking that has made my mom weak over the years, thinking she needs a man to provide. And hasn't Bill done that? Given her everything she's wanted? Only recently with her book deal has she come to think of herself as self-sufficient, and it's causing marriage tension between her and my stepfather.

"I don't get you," I say.

"What?" His mouth hitches up into a half grin, but I guard my heart from its pull.

"I don't know what you want from me," I whisper.

He shifts on the giant ledge of rock, props one knee up to sling an arm over. "I want to spend time with you. Is that so hard to believe?"

I tug my sleeves down, hooking them securely at my palms with my fingers. Behind us, the sun is beginning its descent, casting shadows around us but illuminating the mountainous cliffs on the opposite side of the cove in brilliant rays of light.

Jason sniffs. "What you said about real love being only in fairytales . . . is that really what you think?"

I shrug. "I guess so."

"What about what we had?"

"At seventeen? That was more hormones than love."

"Not on my end." He speaks the words so quietly I scarcely hear them above the waves crashing on the rocks below. "I mean, don't get me wrong, there were plenty of hormones to go around, but Laney—I loved you. I . . . I still love you."

Whoa. This had gotten out of hand way too fast. "Don't say that."

"Why not?"

"Because you don't love me. Jason, you don't even know me. You're in love with the memory of who I was."

Who I can never be again.

"That's not true."

"Or maybe you're in love with who we both were back then. Before that jump. Before Maddie."

He stares at me and then at the curve of spotless sand in the distance that makes up Sand Beach. Tiny dots—people—are in the water, swimming and surfing. "I—I don't know. Maybe you're right."

My chest tightens. I like to be right. Why then, did his admission send me into a downward spiral? I nod, as if to solidify the end of our conversation.

He stands and holds his hand out to me. "Do you want to go closer?"

I slip my hand into his, and goodness if it doesn't feel like coming home. His fingers are slightly calloused and warm and large around my own. Something inside me melts as he helps me stand.

But as he leads me a step closer to the edge, any ideas of melting are forgotten. Despite the cool breeze that urges us away from the edge, sweat breaks out beneath my bra and at the base of my neck.

He stops, breathes deep, and I mirror the action. "You want to stop here?"

"Just a little closer." We're nowhere near the edge. It's perfectly safe. I have nothing to prove, unless of course, I have something to prove to myself.

With the gentlest of pressure, he guides me a few more steps. I can now see that the cliff doesn't drop straight to the water. There are several layers of rock below that jut out from us. My breathing relaxes.

It's beautiful.

The whitecaps of the waves swirl below us and for the first time in years, I appreciate the majestic nature of those waves. Of the sun and shadows weaving in and out of the movement of the water. How the waves travel in a million different directions, some thundering against the cliff, some out to sea, some to visit the beachgoers on the sand, all of it ruled by the moon and the wind in its unpredictable glory. It's impossible to describe, and yet it'd be a near sin not to try for the mere grace of it all.

Slowly, I release Jason's hand. I stretch my arms out at my sides as if I want to fly. I stand before it all, a sense of freedom stirring inside me.

Jason places his hand ever so lightly at my back, his fingers clutching my shirt. I almost ask him if he's scared I'll try to run and jump—a ridiculous thought, really. But perhaps not so ridiculous if he knew of the scars along my arms.

I have tried to jump. Maybe not off a cliff. But through a razorblade of escape.

After a long while, Jason slips his hand into mine again, and we stand, comfortable, soaking up the moment as the sun prepares to pull the blanket of the horizon over itself, to tuck its majestic, glowing rays in for the night.

"Do you believe in God?" I ask.

"I think so."

"Love your conviction."

He laughs softly. "I do believe in God. But I suppose I don't like to think on that belief much. Because if there's really a God and He's really good, then why did he let my mom leave? Why did he allow her to die in a mudslide? Why couldn't Maddie have hit the water at any other angle?"

I'm crying silent tears now. His questions meet my spirit so entirely that I fall a little more in love with him right then and there.

I swallow, lean into the pressure of his hand. An affirmation, an acknowledgement that he's not alone in his ponderings. "I didn't know your mom died. I'm so sorry."

Through my still-blurry vision, I see his mouth grow firm. "I guess in some way she's been dead to me a lot longer than six years. But, you know, now there's no hope for resolution."

My heart bends for his loss. At the same time, I imagine how I would feel if my own mother died. Do I have hope that we will one day find common ground? Or that I will at least find peace with who she's been as both a mother and a daughter?

"I'm so sorry," I repeat. "Six years ago?"

"About two months after Maddie."

I wince. "How awful." Not without some guilt, I acknowledge that Jason went through first Maddie's death, then his mother's, all while I ignored his texts and notes. "I'm sorry I wasn't there for you."

"You didn't know."

Because I'd cut him out of my life, just as I attempted to cut out anything having to do with Maddie. "You stay in touch with Aaron?" Maddie's on-again, off-again boyfriend who'd been with us that day.

"Did for a while. He ended up dropping out of college, creating some app that made him millions. He got married a year ago. Saw on Facebook he's expecting his first kid."

"That's nice."

I face the sea and inhale its brackish scent. It's so big. It can snatch life away at a moment's notice, but it can give life, too. The birds and loons seeking its surface and depth for their next feast. What if something—anything—good could come from my grief? What if coming here and starting over could peel back layers of good? Not that it could make Maddie's loss worth it, but what if new life could be birthed from death?

I remember the journal, the line about all of us having a little light in us. That's what I want to pull out from myself. To seek and search and find. I can only pray there is something inside worth fighting for.

Jason gently squeezes my hand, but he doesn't release my fingers. "We better go if you still want to see your mom's land before it gets dark."

I turn my head to look at him. The wind makes my ponytail slap against my back, and I can't help but feel like Rose on the *Titanic*, just a little. I feel strong, hopeful. And I want my next words to match the strength I feel. "You know what? I don't think I want to see Mom's land tonight."

Jason's eyebrows shoot up. "Really? You sure?"

"Yeah. I feel . . . peaceful right now. I don't want to ruin it."

Does he think I'm a nutcase? I was adamant that he take me to see Mom's land just a few hours ago. Now . . . now, I want this more. Peace.

But he nods, looks out to the ocean again, squeezes my hand. "Okay." He doesn't mention going back to the car, of seeing more sights on Park Loop Road, and I don't ask him to leave. We just stand there, hands entwined, while I mull over the possibility of new beginnings.

# Chapter Ten

*You, Lord, keep my lamp burning;*
*my God turns my darkness into light.*
*Psalm 18:28*
~ Verse on Laney's birthday card from Nana,
Age 11

## LANEY

My mind is whirling after my time with Jason, but Nana has already gone to bed, and after a shower, I do too. But I'm wide awake. All I can think about is the feel of Jason's hand in mine, of that brief glimpse of strength and victory wound tight with the grief of my past as I stood on that ledge of rock high above the Atlantic.

My gaze falls to the journal on my nightstand and I wince, remembering Nana placing it there after she saw my arms that afternoon.

I reach for it, craving distraction, and find where I left off.

*July 15, 1853*

    *Benji has left us.*

    *I cried all my tears this morning before breakfast as I watched the small dory waddle out to sea in the dim glow of early morning. Then I washed my face, donned a fresh dress, and went downstairs to make some eggs and gruel. Two brothers I have, and now both are lost to me.*

    *I try to be happy for Ben. The sea is in his blood, just as I am convinced this light is in mine. He will make a fine fisherman, but Papa is convinced once he fishes for a few months he is apt to come home.*

    *I hope so.*

    *Miranda writes that Rufus is growing as healthy as any boy his age should. He is fast as the dickens, she says. Last month, when they were in town, he wiggled away from her and nearly ran in front of a carriage. My heart stopped when Mama read that part aloud.*

    *After Mama finished the letter (which did have a happy outcome as Miranda was quick enough to scoop up Rufus and the driver was sure enough to halt the carriage), she placed the paper on her lap. "My, our little Rufus is quite the mischief-maker, isn't he? It's a blessing he's not on this rock. It's shame enough we've had to tie Mahala with a rope harness after she pranced around the catwalk of the north tower."*

    *The harness had been necessary. My little sister found herself in the most precarious of places—hanging from the catwalk railings of the lighthouse, beneath the fog bell, or too close to the breaking waves when the sea turned turbulent.*

    *I jabbed my embroidery with my needle a bit harder than necessary. "But if Rufus did get run over by a carriage, we'd be wishing we brought him here. There's more of us to look after him. Please, Mama, can't he come to the Rock? I'll watch over him myself."*

    *Mama's mouth turned downward. She looked older since*

*we'd left the mainland. No doubt her nerves attacked with a newfound ferocity. If she wasn't worried over Mahala's antics, she was fretting over Benji going out to sea or the next storm that might descend upon us.*

*"Your father and I have already discussed it. This Rock is no place for a small boy. I'm not even certain it's a place for your sisters, or even for us, Abbie. And with Benji leaving, your father will need your help with the lights. You won't have time to tend a small boy and your sisters are all I can handle."*

*I try to accept her reasoning. She is my Mama, and I've no right to question her. But when I slide into my cool bed at night, snuggling deeper near the soap stones we heat and place beneath our sheets on chilly nights, I long for Rufus's warm little body near mine, as we used to sleep. I lay a long time, shedding silent tears. And when I can't sleep any longer, I cast the covers aside, grab the lantern hanging from the post, and wrap my shawl around me.*

*I climb the tower and check the lights, glowing brightly in their holders.*

*Then, I slide onto the catwalk.*

*When we first arrived in early spring, Papa showed me how to go out onto the catwalk and scrape the glass free of ice so the light from the lamps could more easily shine through.*

*Now the night lays clear, the stars spackling the sky like fairy dust across a painter's canvas. On nights like these, still and quiet, and me being the closest person to the heavens for miles around, I can almost sense the breath of God. I feel it stirring within me, calling me toward something greater than myself.*

*It is a silly notion, perhaps, but I often feel closer to God on these lonely nights than stuffed in the church pew on Sunday mornings back on the mainland, suffocated by ladies' perfumes. I think about Reverend Hill's preaching of fire and brimstone as I sit against a hard-backed pew, of the ladies from Mama's social sect nodding their heads in approval at*

*his passionate words. Of course, they would forget them by
Tuesday afternoon, prefacing their tea and sweet cakes with, "I
don't mean to be a gossip, but..."*

*Sometimes, I am secretly happy that Papa is no longer a
captain. I like having him with us, and I like not being on the
mainland, pretending to be a proper young lady when all I
really want to do is run free and fly away with the wind.*

*Everything about this life agrees with me, save for missing
Rufus.*

I pause from my reading, soaking in the thought of this girl at
the top of her lighthouse. It makes me think about the Beacon,
the caution tape across the entrance. An insane urge to see it
whitewashed and glistening, caution tape gone with the wind, its
lamps lit for all to see, rises within me. Will I ever get the opportunity to walk its catwalk as this girl had done on Matinicus?

I blink, focusing back on the diary.

*August 22, 1853*

*I have been so busy helping Papa with the lamps that I
scarce have time to write. But I wanted to be sure to mark this
day down.*

*Papa returned from a trip to Rockland in the dory. I did
not know what to make of the wooden crate he pulled from its
depths and the foreign, cackling sounds coming from within.
Then I glimpsed white feathers.*

*"You brought us hens!" I exclaimed.*

*"I brought them with you in mind, Abbie-girl. How you
handled the inspector's visit last month was beyond
admirable."*

*I blushed beneath his praise. The inspector surprised us
with a call while Papa was selling his lobsters on the mainland. I took it upon myself to show him around. He inspected
the boathouse, the fog bell, and both towers, examining the*

*lamps and oil cans, as well as the windows. I even demon-
strated how I could light a lamp—how the lighthouse was in
capable hands while Papa and Benji were gone, no matter my
scant fifteen years.*

*Mama served him tea in the house, and over steaming
mugs, he admitted his doubt at being greeted by a young girl.
"But I was wrong, Mrs. Burgess. With you and your daughter, it appears Matinicus Light is shipshape, indeed."*

*I took the crate from Papa, peered between the slats at the
five beautiful hens.*

*"We'll have fresh eggs before long," Papa said.*

*I am eager to have eggs, but I must admit that cuddling
the one that allowed me close warmed my soul even more than
the thought of eggs.*

I sit up in my bed, the leather-bound journal on my lap.
Outside my window, the sound of the waves crashing against the
rocks below punctuates the silence.

I allow my gaze to travel the yellowed pages of the journal.
The entries have revealed the name of the author of this diary.

Abbie. Abbie Burgess. It sounds familiar.

I scoop up my phone and type *Abigail Burgess, Maine* into a
Google search. The first link that comes up is a Wikipedia link.
The preview states, *Abbie Burgess (1839-1892) was an American
lighthouse keeper known for her bravery in tending the Matinicus
Rock Light in Maine during a raging winter storm . . .*

My thumb hovers over the link. I skim the rest of the pages. A
Maine encyclopedia website, a New England Historical Society
website, all alluding to Abbie as a teenaged heroine and lighthouse
keeper.

This girl, Abbie Burgess, is legit. And I'm holding her
unknown diary in my hands.

I lower my thumb, but at the last second, swipe out of the
search and place my phone on the nightstand.

Though I could read about Abbie's adventures and life in two minutes' time in a post online, I find myself wanting to savor her journal, to experience her adventures entry by entry. Being here, at the Beacon Bed and Breakfast with Nana, reconnecting with Jason, is making me want to slow down and search for the secrets in life. Maybe the secrets of history. I'm already kicking myself a bit over knowing the year of her death. As if I've betrayed the girl who enjoys cuddling chickens, who very much misses her little brother, and who wrestles with angsty feelings toward her own mother, by skipping ahead in an unholy bout of Google curiosity.

And I don't want to read about any of it on a Wikipedia page. I want to read it through Abbie Burgess's eyes.

# Chapter Eleven

*I will come back, Don. I just need some time.*
~ Diane Rutherford's last letter to her husband

## JASON

I roll onto my side and punch my pillow. Unable to get comfortable, I grab my phone on the nightstand. Nothing from Laney. Don't know why I thought she'd text me after our time together tonight. Maybe because I'd let how I feel melt onto her like hot maple syrup, sticky and uncomfortable. Why couldn't I keep my mouth shut?

Then again, my being vulnerable had opened up the door to real conversation. She let me hold her hand.

I tap into our text thread and scroll up—way up, catching pieces of our texts over the years that I never could bring myself to delete.

I remember the first time I noticed Laney Jacobs. Aaron and I had been walking to the bus when we saw Miriam Jacobs stumbling out of her dented Nissan Altima at the place where parents who were picking up their kids lined up with their cars. We gawked, along with the rest of the middle school, at the show Miriam made. She was tall and thin with black circles beneath her eyes and her bra strap falling almost to her elbow, the lacy purple number showing at her armpits, where her cutoff t-shirt hung from her frame.

"Laney! Laney Jacobs, where are you? I have an appointment I can't be late for."

Aaron snickered. "To see her dealer, no doubt."

Mom had been gone four months without a word by that point. Something about her absence and the excuses I made for her put me on high alert. I studied my friends' moms—Aaron's parents were divorced, but he lived with his mother, who made us oatmeal raisin cookies after she came home from work. Seth's parents were together. His mom was busy starting a clothing line, so she was often distracted, but was still there to hug him after his basketball games. Told him to clean his room. Do his homework. All things he complained about, but all things I'd give my right arm to hear my mom tell me.

As a result of studying other mothers, I developed Spidey senses when it came to those who didn't quite make the cut. And those senses were tingling that day after school.

Head down and enormous backpack nearly toppling her, Laney had walked stiffly on the sidewalk toward her mother. She wore an Abercrombie and Fitch graphic t-shirt and flared jeans. She grabbed her mother by the arm and walked around to the driver's side door. Miriam kept ranting as if they were the only two people in the world.

"I was going to take the bus home, Mom. What are you doing here?"

"I have an appointment. You need to be there."

"Let's just go." Laney looked up and for one brief, horrifying second, our gazes caught. I forced a smile, but her face grew red, and she ducked into the back seat.

The next morning, I plopped down next to Laney on the bus.

"My mom's a loser, too."

Something about saying those words aloud shifted the relationship between me and my mom. Whatever relationship a twelve-year-old boy can have with his four-month-long absent mother, anyway. Up until that moment, I'd held out hope that Mom would be sitting on the porch waiting for me when I got home from school, a bright smile on her face, eager to hear about my day. But this—putting my mother in the same category as Laney's mom, this was something I could rally behind, something I could grow passionate about. Grow angry about.

Anger was a strong, active emotion. Not a weak, silent, meaningless *hope*.

Laney just stared at me, and for a minute I thought she'd shove me clear into the bus aisle, claim her mother *wasn't* a loser and who did I think I was anyway?

But she didn't do any of those things. She smiled. "Thanks." Then she looked out the bus window until we got to school.

Now, I scroll up to the very start of our texts. Though we'd hung out a lot in middle school, doing homework together and sitting on the morning bus with one another, we'd grown apart by high school. It was junior year when she'd approached me at my locker to ask if she could interview me for an article for the school newspaper. Our basketball team was going to the state championship, and I had been voted MVP that year.

Despite my then-girlfriend's disapproval over me spending time with Laney, I'd agreed to the interview, even asked her for ice cream—apparently my go-to date idea, even back then. I'd texted her the next day.

> JASON: Hey, Laney, it's Jason Rutherford. Are we still on for that ice cream interview on Saturday?

> LANEY: I don't know, Jay-Bear . . . are you sure that passes muster with Katie-Bear?

JASON: I broke up with her this afternoon.

LANEY: Wow. I hadn't heard. Figured that'd be the talk of the school.

JASON: Considering we haven't been to school since it happened, I'm assuming it will make headlines tomorrow.

. . .

JASON: So, ice cream or maybe dinner? Your choice.

LANEY: Am I some rebound or something, because I don't know if you remember, but I never was good at basketball, including picking up the rebounds.

JASON: Ouch. But also, clever.

No rebound. I just want to get to know you again.

LANEY: Since when?

JASON: Since you spoke to me at my locker yesterday. I miss talking with you. I was an idiot to not keep in touch.

LANEY: I'm not twelve anymore. You might be disappointed.

JASON: Maybe. But I'm willing to bet not. More likely you'll be the one who's disappointed.

. . .

JASON: What do you say? Ice cream? Dinner?

LANEY: Ice cream. But I'm buying my own cone.

We hung out nearly every day after that ice cream, but Laney wouldn't make it official for three more months. Three more months of getting caught up on all that happened in one another's lives the last several years, of forming a friendship, then, a few stolen kisses and one hot make-out session at the beach. When Maddie started dating Aaron, the four of us became inseparable. Prom, SATs, college applications, graduation—you name it, we did it together. But that was before that terrible day. When Maddie was still alive. When we thought we were invincible. When we thought our entire lives were before us. When death was a hazy something that might happen to us one day when we were old, wrinkled, and gray.

It took me a long time to work through all the losses in my life. Maddie, my mom, Laney. No one knows this, not even Dad, but I did some hard-core therapy while I was in college. Probably the only way I made it through college, even. I don't know why I'm such a pansy about letting people know. There's nothing to be ashamed about, and I'm glad I went. Guess I just didn't want anyone to know how much Mom's death bothered me. How much Maddie's death bothered me. Truth be told, the thing that bothered me the most, though, was Laney disappearing from my life. I suppose that makes me a less-than-stellar human, being broken up more about getting dumped than my mom dying or my friend jumping to her death at my urging.

No wonder I needed good therapy—and lots of it.

The words of our first text blur before me from staring at them too long. Did Laney remember that our first date had been ice cream? Was that why she'd been opposed to it at first a couple of days ago?

I force myself to put down the phone. She's not going to text me. She's still too busy pushing me away.

But then I remember standing at the top of that cliff, her small hand in mine.

We're different people, just like we were different when we

started dating junior year. We need to get to know one another again.

But in the end, no matter what we find, I know I'll still love her. Because last night, when I held her hand at the top of that cliff with nothing but wind and sea and forest around us, I felt it deep in my bones.

When it comes to Laney, I'm a goner.

I don't blame her for not believing my declaration of love. Because anyone can proclaim love—Mom told me she loved me the day before she left us. No, it's not just about words. It's the action behind the words that proves it.

And right now, a crazy urge to prove myself to Laney, to do something that shows her how I feel, surges within me.

And I have no intention of ignoring it.

# Chapter Twelve

*This is the message we have heard from him and proclaim to you,*
*that God is light, and in him is no darkness at all.*
*1 John 1:5*
~ Verse on Laney's birthday card from Nana,
Age 20

## LANEY

As the rain dwindles to a drizzle outside, Nana looks up at the mass of wet plaster and stonework, from ceiling to hardwood floor. A small puddle covers the mantel of the bedroom fireplace. "Well, this certainly wasn't in the plans."

We had both rushed upstairs to the Lavender Room after a couple in their thirties checked out that morning. "You might have a leak in that room," the man had said after handing Nana the keys.

"We *might* have a leak?" I dash into the hall closet to snatch some rag towels while Nana scurries downstairs to grab as many spare pans and mixing bowls as she can carry. She works efficiently, murmuring an occasional, "Oh, dear," but not showing any other outward signs of distress over the potential ruination of her most popular room.

After we soak up as much of the damage as we can and note the happy circumstance of sunlight on the far horizon, Nana calls the guests who had reserved the Lavender Room that night, offering them a full reimbursement or an opportunity to stay in another room. They choose another room, although they aren't pleased, my grandmother reports.

"Would you like me to call around for someone to fix the leak, or do you have a contractor?" I ask.

"I'll call Zack Garrison, although I saw his mother at the fish market the other day and she said he's up to his eyeballs in work."

I start on the dishes, glancing out at the slick lighthouse, imagining Abbie Burgess cautiously walking the top of the Matinicus Lighthouse catwalk to scrape the glass during a storm.

The last couple of days have been filled with double waitressing shifts and an endless summer crowd. Though I'd read the journal until my eyes grew heavy last night, I had not yet read of a storm. Abbie was sixteen, she'd taken a trip to the mainland to visit her friend Dorothy and had felt terribly out of place when prompted to don a corset, tight shoes, and an elegant dress imported from Paris. She spoke of the Rockland waterfront with its grand homes and widow's walks atop their roofs, of the smoke from the lime kilns that covered the roofs in a haze. She was able to visit four-year-old Rufus, who was lively and well, but, to her dismay, did not remember her.

I wept along with her entry and still remember the last lines, fresh in my mind since I reread them this morning.

> *As Papa steered the dory toward the Rock, I bid the mainland good riddance. True, I did not regret seeing Dorothy and Miranda and Rufus. Although some of my journey was painful, I've come to a greater realization about myself.*
> *The Rock is my home. The light is my home. Did the Lord*

*mold this passion within me or did my circumstances grow it?*
*Lydia would say I'm becoming a recluse and perhaps I am.*
*For how can I pursue marriage and homemaking and a*
*family of my own if it means leaving the lamps behind?*

My heart ached at the longing in Abbie's words. Did I ever feel so passionately about anything in my own life? Certainly not waitressing or school, not therapy or rehab.

A picture of my hand in Jason's on top of the granite ledge two evenings before flashes across my mind before it crumbles away. A moment of heady feelings is not the same as a passion of the soul.

"Well, I refuse to take you from your other clients, honey," I hear Nana saying in the other room. "Yes, yes, but I don't want any special favors, Zachary, you understand me?"

I stifle a giggle, listen to Nana say goodbye. A moment later, she walks into the kitchen, huffing.

"Was he too busy?" I ask, pretending I didn't hear her part of the conversation.

"That boy's too generous for his own good."

I smile. "Seems you have a lot of people in this town that love you. I don't think that's a bad thing."

"Not until you can't manage to pay your contractor a decent wage for his services."

"How do you know him?"

Nana lowers herself to the kitchen table. "Oh, I suppose how I know a lot of the year-rounders. The garden club, church, festivals. After Miriam left, Jack and I volunteered in the church nursery and youth groups." Her mouth hitches up in a quarter smile. "I remember thinking maybe they wouldn't let us volunteer, seeing as how we didn't know how to have a relationship with our own daughter, but they did."

"Nana, I hope you don't blame yourself. Mom can be . . . difficult."

"Oh, so can I, sweetie. So can I."

How could she sit there and act like Mom wasn't to blame for all this mess? Unless, of course, what Mom wrote about in her book was true. Did my grandfather, the man smiling in all those lovely old photos and who held a passion for history, have a side to him Nana didn't want to acknowledge, and I didn't want to believe? Could he have locked my mother in the lighthouse? Could Nana have allowed it?

Nana taps the table. "Anyway, Zack was one of the youngsters in the youth group. So much energy, that one. You might think someone wound him up every day and set him loose. But he took a shine to me and Jack. Started mowing our lawn when he was thirteen. Jack taught him everything he knew about cars and fixing things around the house. Now, I can't call him with a problem without him feeling like he must pay me special favors."

"You can use the help, can't you, Nana?"

"Those with skills should be paid accordingly. I didn't make Zack lemonade and cookies all his life to get a deal on his contracting services."

It's the first time Nana has spoken anything but sweetly to me. Not that her words are sharp, but there's an edge to them, a touchy spot I've struck with my question.

I'd been looking forward to sharing with her what I discovered two nights ago. That the journal of a famous Maine historical person has been right up in her attic for who knows how long.

Abbie's words are drawing me in and under, like a strong undercurrent. But it's one in which I want to be pulled away. I want to seek out what I can learn from this girl who lived more than a century earlier.

An hour later, Zack Garrison shows up on Nana's doorstep. He is nearly six feet tall with dirty blond hair and muscles that show beneath his t-shirt. Estimating age is not my strong suit, but based on what Nana told me and his appearance, I figure he must be in his mid-thirties. While not as boy-crazy as a teen, I'm not immune to an older man's good looks. And when he smiled at

Nana and assured her that he'd move her to the top of his client list . . . well, that about said it all.

"Zack, I'd like you to meet my granddaughter, Laney."

Zack holds his hand out to me, flashing me a smile that matches the striking brilliance of his green eyes. "Granddaughter, hey? Charlotte, that's great." He squeezes my hand. "Great to meet you, Laney."

"You, too."

Nana beams at me. "She showed up here a couple of weeks ago, and my goodness, if the Lord didn't know it was what my heart needed. Now, I know you're not here to chat, but how have you been? And your folks?"

"Good, good. All good."

"How about Miss New York? Any ring on her finger yet?"

Zack rolls his eyes. "Her name was Priscilla but she's back in New York. We decided to call it quits for a while."

"Oh honey, I'm sorry."

Zack claps his hands. "As much as I enjoy talking about my love life, I think you called me over for another purpose. Shall we?"

Nana looks adequately chastened. "It is so difficult to keep my nose where it belongs. Forgive me, honey."

"Forgiven." Zack starts for the stairs. "You said the Lavender Room?"

Twenty minutes later, he's promising Nana that the leak can be fixed in a day, and he can be back tomorrow to accomplish the job. "Can't have your best room down for long, right?"

Nana thanks him profusely, and after he leaves, she pours us each a cup of coffee.

"He loves you," I say.

"I don't know how I would have gotten by without folks like him. There's plenty of them around, too. People God places in our lives to help us along when we're feeling especially broken."

I press my lips together. "If the town's so supportive, why

won't you ask them for help with the lighthouse? It's a landmark, Nana. It must mean something to this community."

Nana taps her pink-painted fingernails on her mug. There's a picture of a moose on it with the words *Bar Harbor* in italics below. "I suppose I'm afraid."

I pause. I'm not used to grownups admitting fear. Okay, I'm a grownup. *I'm* not used to admitting fear.

"Afraid of what?"

"Afraid they'll think less of me for bringing all this bad publicity to the town."

"You mean Mom's book? But that isn't your fault—"

"Isn't it? Honey, I'm not saying your mother got all her facts straight in that memoir of hers, but there's a reason she wrote that book. And maybe, if I'd been a different sort of a mother, she wouldn't have felt the need to write it." Nana stands and bends to kiss my head. "I'm going to take my coffee out to the porch. Have a good night at work if I don't see you."

I glance at my phone. Nearly noon already. "Okay." I want to say more. To declare she is not to blame. But I know what it is to find twisted solace in holding onto guilt. Sometimes, there is nothing else to do, no way to pay for actions that cannot be reversed. The only payment is the torture of oneself. And yet, that doesn't seem in line with the little I know of Nana's faith.

I realize then that I've come here not just to find out about my grandmother, but to find out about the faith behind those cards she sent. Was it just sweet sentiment or was it authentic? Was it a faith that could maybe even heal me?

I wish I could be sure. Because if Nana's faith isn't enough to free her of the past, how can there ever be any hope for me?

# Chapter Thirteen

*I'm tired of writing about depressing things. Tired of writing about*
*darkness, so here's a try at something new.*
~ Laney Jacobs' rehab journal

## LANEY

One of the other waitresses at The Lobster Bar, Jenna, called out sick, so the restaurant is busier than usual. Over the last several days, Bar Harbor has come awake and alive; its streets burgeoning with tourists—women in sundresses, kids in hats and Crocs, and men in sunglasses and flip-flops. Many hold shopping bags, ice cream cones, or bags of fudge.

I scoop up drink orders from the bar, give meal orders to the kitchen, recite menu specials to dinner guests, and pacify over-tired children with crayons and coloring sheets.

Somewhere between bringing fried calamari to table nine and laughing with one of the chefs over an undercooked batch of rolls, I acknowledge a foreign sense of belonging. This place, with all its history, with Nana, with the massive Atlantic and the Beacon and that precious journal, with Jason and even that humble little bookstore down the street . . . this place is becoming home.

It's nearing ten and the restaurant finally slows. I'm grabbing two decaf coffees for a couple in their sixties seated outside at table fourteen.

That's when I spot her at the edge of the bar, scribbling furiously in a notebook.

The girl from the bookstore.

I stop in my tracks. Why am I surprised she's here? She works three blocks from The Lobster Bar, so her presence shouldn't be an anomaly.

She's writing so furiously that she doesn't notice me at first. So, I simply watch her in what I hope is a not-too-creepy, non-stalkerish way. A glass of root beer, slick with condensation, sits in front of her alongside her yellow legal pad, thick with black ink. She's in the middle of the notebook, the slightly crinkled, already-used pages curled around the top in what looks like an impressive stack of work. Her thick black hair with that purple stripe is tied in a no-nonsense ponytail at the back of her neck and in that moment, she reminds me of what a modern-day Jo March might look like while creating her next masterpiece.

Except for the ragged ridges of scars along the inside of her arms. Pretty sure Jo wouldn't have had those.

It's about ten seconds before she finally looks up. I envy how she can be so completely immersed in whatever world resides in that legal pad. What would it be like to lose myself in a world of my own creativity and passion? I wonder if Abbie Burgess lost track of time and space when she worked in the lighthouse towers of Matinicus Rock.

"Oh, hey!" The girl's face brightens. So, she *does* remember me. Then again, how could she not? I almost passed out on top of her checkout counter.

"Hey."

"I didn't know you worked here." She places her pen on top of the legal pad.

"For a few weeks now." I come to my senses. "I'm sorry, I have to deliver these." I hold up the two coffees in my hands. "I'll be back."

"Sure thing." And she picks up her pen to write again as if I haven't interrupted.

After delivering the coffee, I ring up table fourteen's bill, get change for another couple, and help the busboy clear and wipe down the remaining tables. When it's ten-thirty, I can consider myself clocked out for the night. I walk back to the bar, where the girl is still writing.

For half a second before I reach her, I consider slipping out of the restaurant. Going back to the Beacon, taking a long shower, and sliding beneath my cool sheets with nothing but the company of Abbie Burgess to distract my thoughts.

But the girl draws me. She reminds me of someone. Is it Maddie? Is it myself? Is it only the scars I'm obsessed with, much as I'm obsessed with my own?

Breathing deep, I slide onto a seat two down from her and ask Joey, the bartender, for a club soda.

The girl looks up. "Done with your shift?"

I nod.

She stretches, putting the tender, scarred flesh of her forearms up over her head for anyone to see. "Made good tips tonight, I bet. Summer's finally in full swing."

I did make good money. Over three hundred dollars. "Has the bookstore been busy?"

"Sure is. We do half of our annual sales in the months of July and August."

"Wow."

"Yeah. When winter comes and we're twiddling our thumbs, we try to remember how badly we wished for spare time in July."

I gesture to her legal pad. "What are you writing?" It seems a safe, logical question.

"Fantasy novel. Dwarfs and gremlins and a Little Match Girl-inspired heroine."

"Wow."

"It's better than it sounds. At least, I hope it is." She flips all the pages of the pad to the front and places her pen on top. "Give any more thought to our writing group?"

"No . . . I've been doing more reading than writing. I don't think I'm as easily inspired as you."

"Maybe that's your problem."

"What?"

"Thinking too much. I don't think when I write."

I scrunch up my face, open my mouth to tell her that would be impossible, but she must catch my expression.

"I'm serious. I mean, I know something in my brain must be thinking, but everything else in there, the part that deals with reality and worries and all that, just kind of disappears."

"Sounds like meditation."

She places a flat palm on the table. "That's it! It's like meditation. So cool." She shakes her head and sips the last of her root beer from her straw. The sound of dishes clinking from the kitchen echoes in the background. The scent of someone's late-order fish and chips teases my hunger. We've been so busy all night I haven't had a chance to eat, but I'd rather not ask the kitchen to prepare anything at this hour.

"How's the lighthouse book, if that's what you've been reading?"

"It's good." But I stop short of telling her about Abbie's journal. It feels too private, too sacred. I sip my soda, enjoying the fizz that works its way down the back of my throat. While I'm interested in her writing, there's really only one question I have for the girl. And here, in the dim lights, with the end of the night upon us, I dig up the courage to ask.

"I saw your arms." I nearly whisper the words, as if I'm drawing attention to something that isn't in plain sight.

She glances down at her scars. The skin that isn't marked is pale and smooth, and I wonder if she remembers, as I do, what they'd look like if she hadn't harmed herself. "Yeah. I told you my cousin said I should write a memoir? Well, these arms are one of the reasons she thinks so. I prefer fantasy."

She doesn't elaborate. I scour my mind for questions that might crack her open. Yet, why should I expect any answer when I have no intention of opening up myself?

I shift in my seat. What could I ask? *How old were you? Did you go to rehab? What hurt so bad inside you that you put a blade to your skin?*

But what comes out surprises even me. "My mom's the author of *Locked Light.*"

She blinks. "Wait. The girl locked in a lighthouse memoir?"

I nod, bite my lip hard.

"No way. Guess I'll have to read it now."

"Don't." It comes out loud. She squints at me as if I am a curiosity at the circus. "I mean, obviously you can read what you want, but I'm not sure it's worth your time."

"I take it you and your mom aren't real tight?"

I laugh. "I think that's a fair assessment."

Then she does something surprising. She runs the fingers of her right hand tenderly over the scars on her left arm. If I thought it alarming that she showed no qualms in wearing short sleeves, I find it doubly so that she's not only drawing attention to her scars, she's acting as if the feel of them does not cause inner turmoil or pain.

Countless times, I've vigorously scrubbed at my scars with a washcloth, as if I could rub away the pain and memories, as if I could erase the pain of my best friend's death.

"I learned about forgiveness through these scars." She stops running her fingers over her arm but continues staring at them. "Forgiving those who've hurt me and forgiving myself for hurting me."

"I'd read your memoir." I stir my paper straw around in the ice chunks at the bottom of my glass.

"Come to writing group. Maybe I'll tell you more."

She's trying to *bribe* me into going to her writing group?

Someone squeezes my shoulder from behind. "Hey, Laney."

My face warms as Jason sits beside me, a takeout container on the bar.

"Jason." I attempt to tame my thoughts. A moment ago, I wanted this girl to tell me everything about her scarred arms, now I don't want her to say anything. I don't want Jason to see her arms. "What are you doing out so late?"

"Couldn't sleep. Ordered some fish and chips. Figured you might be able to use a ride home if you walked?"

"I did." I gesture to the girl. "This is . . . oh my goodness, I still don't know your name."

The girl reaches across me to hold her hand out to Jason. "Kiran."

"Pretty name. I'm Jason."

Is he trying to make me jealous, because if so, it's working. I watch his gaze to see if he notices Kiran's arms, if I will be able to read something in his expression that will give a clue to how he perceives her. But as far as I can tell, he doesn't even notice.

"And I'm Laney." I hold my hand out to Kiran, more to stop her from touching Jason than to extend any manners.

She grips my hand in a firm shake, then peers around to Jason. "Laney was telling me how she might come to our writing group. Are you a writer, too?"

Jason holds up his hands. "Oh, no. Not me. I—" He glances at me. "You write?"

"I've considered writing . . . something."

"Oh. That's nice. Well, if you're in the middle of writing talk, I'll wait outside."

I push back the bar stool. "I was actually about to leave. I'll meet you out there in a minute?"

He nods, smiles at Kiran. "Nice to meet you."

"Nice to meet you, Jason!"

I watch him walk out the door.

"Is he your person?"

My back stiffens. "My . . . person?"

"You know, your lobster."

"My lobster?"

She rolls her eyes. "You know . . . your *lobster*."

Because that's so much clearer. "My *lobster*?"

"*Friends*? Phoebe says Ross and Rachel are lobsters because lobsters mate for life."

"Must have missed that episode." In truth, I don't think I'd ever watched an episode of *Friends* in my life.

"Okay, girl. Forget writing group. We need to have a *Friends* slumber party."

I laugh at how quickly she has adopted me into her life.

"So, is Jason your lobster?"

"No," I answer quickly, then think that maybe she's interested in Jason and change my mind. "Yes. Maybe. I don't know."

"Because if he's your lobster, you should definitely tell him about . . . " She again drags her fingers over her scars.

My face flames. I am one-hundred-percent positive I have not pulled up my sleeves in front of Kiran, either while waitressing tonight or in the bookstore. "How did you . . . "

"Pain spots pain," she says. "And, if you love him, you should let him know."

I push that suggestion aside. No way does Jason need to know. I've only just entertained the notion of letting him back into my life.

Kiran takes a five-dollar bill from her wallet and leaves it under her soda. "So, see you Monday night?"

I nod. I actually have the day off. And now that she knows my secret, there's a few things I must clear up, and it seems writing group will be my next chance to do so.

# Chapter Fourteen

*You have often expressed a desire to view the sea out upon the ocean when it was angry. Had you been here on the 19th of January, I surmise you would have been satisfied.*
~ Letter from Abbie Burgess to her friend Dorothy, 1856

*December 26, 1855*

*For the sake of Mama and my sisters, I put on a brave face, but this winter of tempests tries my faith like no other experience of my sixteen years. I half wish I had not found that old ledger up in the north tower this past summer. Or, that I had not read it. All the way back to 1829, keepers have written of "violent" or "bad" storms in the winter months. Several times a "severe gale." But it is the water-marked entry dated January 27, 1839 that I cannot keep from my mind.*

*The keeper wrote of a storm where several breakers rose nearly forty feet in the air and covered the entire Rock. The house was carried away. The Keeper and his family escaped in a dory and spent a night tossed about on a wild sea before being retrieved by a schooner.*

*When I asked Papa about the entry, he assured me I should not be alarmed.*

*"Only two storms proved severe enough to do damage, and only to the wooden towers and dwellings. The finest engineers in the Army designed this granite house and the towers at either end. We're safe, my dear."*

*I believe him, at least I want to. It seems that both my faith in God and faith in my Papa are being shaken simultaneously. The seas have been so unruly and the barometer readings consistently low. It would not be as worrisome if the supply boat had not missed both its September and October calls. Several snowstorms and one fierce gale storm kept Papa from going to the mainland for supplies. And now, here it is, end of December and we are barely living off our summer rations. Gone is the salt pork and salt beef. I scraped the bottom of the flour barrel this morning. Thank the Lord for my girls. They don't lay as consistently as they do in the summer, but every egg is helpful.*

*Mama takes to her bed often, leaving me with the tending of the home. Lydia, now fourteen, does her fair share but grumbles while doing it. She would rather be painting or creating needlework. She makes it plain she holds no strong affection for this Rock.*

*I cannot think about leaving the lights. They have wound themselves around my spirit, their friendly glow a reminder of the Lord's warmth in the darkness.*

*We have moved Papa and Mama's bedroom from the old wooden chamber of the home into the parlor. To keep Mama from fretting, Papa insisted it was to be near the warmth of the kitchen. I know his true concern—he is fearful the fierce waves will sweep away the wooden portion of the home. Much safer to move Mama into the granite dwelling.*

*Last week, yet another storm brewed gale-force winds. We carried extra wood from the shed and latched the wooden shutters on the windows. During our nighttime Bible reading, the roar of the wind and the waves made it hard to hear Papa's steady voice. The sound of ocean spray against the windows of Papa and Mama's old room caused goosebumps to break out upon my skin.*

*Papa cleared his throat, turned to the gospels, and read in his strong baritone. "And when he was entered into a ship, his disciples followed him. And, behold, there arose a great tempest in the sea, insomuch that the ship was covered with the waves: but he was asleep. And his disciples came to him, and awoke him, saying, Lord, save us: we perish. And he saith unto them, Why are ye fearful, O ye of little faith? Then he arose, and rebuked the winds and the sea; and there was a great calm." Papa looked up, his gaze first meeting mine and then Mama's and then Lydia, Esther, and Mahala's. "God is here with us tonight. Even if He does not choose to calm this storm, His presence is with us. It is enough. Sleep in peace, my family."*

*Papa insisted I not help him with the lamps, that I save my strength. I went upstairs to comfort Esther and Mahala until they fell into a restless sleep. Though the storm subsided within the week, the seas remained rough. Still, no supply boat, although the Lord did provide a splendid codfish for us on Christmas morn. Lydia mourned over the ginger cakes of Christmases past, of the turkeys and cranberries and mince pies, and secretly, I did too.*

*But Mama looked around the Christmas table, the delicious scent of fish overpowering the now-familiar smells of beans and chip biscuits. "It is times like these I am glad to be named Thankful. It is the Lord's way of reminding me, though I struggle, that there is so much to be thankful for. My family, this fish, the celebration of the Christ-child, and that God saved us from that storm."*

*We added our "Amens," and as I placed a bite of cod on my tongue, forcing myself to savor every precious morsel, I studied Mama. In that moment, I tried to see her as a person outside the confines of "Mother." I know how she struggles with her nerves. How it sometimes makes her physically weak, and how sometimes, I resent her for it. But here and now, I admire her outlook. I admire her. I vow to incorporate gratitude into my own life each and every day.*

*January 19, 1856*

    *Papa has gone for supplies. The barometer is finally steady and the ocean calm. After he bid goodbye to Mama and the girls, I accompanied him down to the dory. He was decidedly chipper, a spry spring in his step.*

    *"I'm certainly up for a good sail. Does it not feel like the spring thaw, Abbie-girl?"*

    *"Oh, that would be wonderful, Papa." But all I could think about was that 1839 ledger entry dated late January. "It will be better than all my Christmases combined to have both you and some supplies back on the Rock."*

    *He gathered me in a warm hug, and I inhaled the scent of him—wood and lamp oil and gruel and the slight dampness that never left us on the island. I closed my eyes and burrowed deeper into him.*

    *He squeezed me back. "I'm leaving the lights in good hands. Of this, I'm most confident. Keep them burning, Abbie-girl."*

    *I nodded fiercely. "I will, Papa. I promise."*

    *And now he is gone, nothing but a white fragment on the calm horizon.*

I stop reading and place Abbie's journal on my lap. Though I know what is to come next, something about Abbie's embrace with her father pulls out an emptiness from me that I haven't felt for a long while.

Not for the first time, I wonder if knowing who my true father is would make anything better. If my relationship with my mother was healthier, would I long for him—this figment of my imagination—as I sometimes do?

It should have been me and Mom against the world. Instead, she'd abandoned me for alcohol and men. In return, I fantasized about a near-perfect father waiting for me to appear in his life.

At the age of eleven, I confronted Mom, asking for the truth. She told me. There'd been too many men. She didn't know who my father was, and she didn't plan on finding out.

I close my eyes and remember the gentle kiss on the cheek Jason gave me when he dropped me off earlier. I wonder if Kiran is right, if Jason is my lobster. But even if he is, it's not fair to expect him to fill the holes inside me. I wouldn't think it right if he wanted me to fill his hollows.

I shake my head. There's nothing I can do to change the fact that my father either doesn't want me or, if Mom can be trusted, doesn't know I exist. I think of Abbie. Does her own father return? And if not, how does she deal with it? Is she able to claim a thankful attitude even in her grief?

Thankful. *Thankful*—of course! I'd completely forgotten about the picture of Thankful's grave. That's why Abbie's name sounded familiar when I first heard it. I'd recognized the Burgess name.

I slide onto the floor and shimmy out the box my grandfather had kept in the attic, pulling out the picture of Thankful Burgess's grave. She didn't die for many more years. Was this the grave my grandfather had planned to see before he got sick?

Though tempted to Google Thankful's name to see if I can find out more, I close the box, vowing to store it back upstairs tomorrow for the time being so as not to tempt myself. There will be plenty of time to Google after I finish Abbie's journal. After I see for myself how it all turns out.

I crawl beneath the covers, the distant sound of Nana's wind chimes on the porch persisting in a haunting call over the waters.

I think of Abbie's father gone far away, of him leaving her alone to tend the lights. It's not the same as my situation—not the same at all. But somehow, aligning myself with the girl on the Rock gives me a small amount of comfort.

I turn the page.

# Chapter Fifteen

*As the tide came, the sea rose higher and higher, till the only endurable places were the light towers.*
~ Letter from Abbie Burgess to her friend Dorothy, 1856

*January 25, 1856*

*I've relived the last week a thousand times, it seems, for I can scarce believe the turn of events, nor that I live to tell it.*

*Papa had only been gone several hours when ominous gray clouds billowed on the horizon. The flag on our pole whipped wildly in the wind, coming now from the northeast. Gulls called overhead, as if yelling at one another, warning of impending doom.*

*"Papa's in this storm!" Lydia cried, and I could have smacked her for causing the young ones to worry.*

*Mama groaned. "Dear Lord, protect him."*

*"He's surely almost to the mainland by now," I said. "Matinicus Rock sees the weather before Rockland does. He has time." Though I wasn't certain this was entirely true, it*

*sounded like fair logic. "Until then, we will pray for him and do as he would if he were here."*

*Mama claimed illness and I prepared her a tonic from the little we had left before she went to the parlor to lie down. Esther and Mahalia latched the shutters. Lydia brought in the flag. I closed up the sheds and moved my girls up higher on the Rock, in the protection of one of the towers.*

*I lit the lamps, for the storm ushered in the arrival of night several hours early. The wind flung breakers at the ledges of the Rock, creeping higher and higher. For the sake of my family, I fixed on a brave face. I made them each an egg and fried a few slices of cold cornmeal mush, forcing the food into my own belly, though it fought me on that account.*

*The days wore on with no sign of the storm letting up. The supply of oil for the lamps ran low and I wrestled with myself over keeping them lit throughout the dark days. In the end, I kept their bright lights glowing, following Papa's final instructions to me. If a sailor were caught in this storm, he would surely be dashed upon the Rock if not for the lights.*

*I prayed God would make the oil last as He did when the Maccabees were rededicating the Temple to the Lord. He'd made the oil last for eight days in order to light the menorah. Eight days, when there was only enough oil for one.*

*I knew the story from a Catholic girl I went to school with. I'd been entranced.*

*The Lord could perform such a miracle on the Rock now. I knew He could. But would He? Was Matinicus Light worthy of the same attention He'd given to His Temple?*

*Certainly not, but I knew that those Maccabees didn't twiddle their thumbs waiting for the lights to go out. They did the work of the Lord. And during this storm, that is what I vowed to do as well.*

*I slept during the day and put Lydia and Esther in charge of glimpsing the lights out the window. If the lamps went out for some reason, they were to wake me.*

*But they burned steadily onward. Mama burned also, hot
with fever, and I watered down the last of her tonic. Still, she
did not rise from her bed, comforting the young ones from a
distance as best she could.*

*On the morning of the fourth day, I woke to a great roar. I
sat up in bed, my heart hammering wildly, my throat tight
and tense at the thought of the breaker that had slammed
against our granite house. Would our dwelling stand beneath
the thrusting waves? When, oh when, would this storm end?*

*I pulled on my heaviest coat and ran up to the tower. The
lamps still glowed. I dared look below. The lights cast eerie
shadows against the giant swells offshore. With each successive
billow, they climbed higher and higher up the Rock. The wind
pushed the water to slap both rock and lighthouse tower,
sending me falling to my trembling knees.*

*"Save us, Father. Won't you calm the seas as you did that
long ago day on the Galilean Sea?"*

*The wind did not abate. The waters continued to rise. And
yet from somewhere outside myself, I knew a Presence that cast
itself over my weary spirit. It brought with it peace and calm,
hope and light. I remembered Papa's words.*

*"Even if He doesn't choose to calm this storm, His presence is
with us. It is enough."*

*"Thank you, Lord." I remembered my vow on Christmas
to be grateful in all circumstances. I stood on weak legs,
clasping the holy strength I knew within.*

*When I reached the kitchen, Mahala ran to me and clung
to my waist. "Are the waves going to eat us up, Abbie?"*

*I smoothed her hair, exchanged worried looks with Lydia
who mopped up the floor with a towel where the water came
beneath the door. "This house is sturdy as a rock. Remember
what Jesus tells us about the wise man who built his house on a
rock?"*

*From within my skirts, Mahala nodded her head. "The*

rains came. The floods came. The wind blew. But it did not fall, for it was built on the rock." She dried her tears.

"Seems to me a wise man might build a house on a rock, but likely not in the middle of the Atlantic," Lydia grumbled as she draped the towel near the wood stove.

I shook my head at her. She did not help matters.

It wasn't until we sat down to dinner, an egg for each of us and half a griddle cake a piece, that an immense breaker broke atop our roof with a sound so deafening it could only be compared to a cannon.

"Abbie!" Mama cried out in terror from her fitful rest and we all ran to her, clinging to one another, wondering if this was how it might end. Without Benji, without Papa. Just five women alone to perish on Matinicus Rock.

After a time, the pounding subsided. After again assuring my family the house was safe upon the rock, I stood, knowing what I must do—what had been on my heart to do since that tremendous explosion atop our roof. "I'm going to get the hens."

"No, Abbie! No. You will stay, you hear?" Mama sat up in bed, her feverish brow lit only by the faint light of the Betty lamp. I couldn't remember the last time she'd spoken so firmly to me.

"I must, Mama. I can't bear to think of the poor things out there, or worse, being swept out to sea. Besides, if Papa can't return soon, we'll likely starve without those eggs."

"Abbie, no." Mama's voice was quieter now, and I could tell she tried with all her might to keep calm so I could consider her earnestly. "You will be swept right out to sea, and we have no means to save you. Daughter, listen to me!"

But I was pulling on Papa's oilskins and my heaviest coat and seizing a basket amidst Mama's hysterical cries. The thought of parting with my hens without even an effort was not to be endured. I waited for the rollers to pass before I threw open the door and ran down the steps. Water swirled at my knees and once I slipped and fell, scrambling up lest a billow *come and take me out to sea with it. I pushed into the wind until, alas, I came to the coop. My hens toppled out when I opened the door, flapping frantically. I grabbed them and shoved them, one by one, into the basket.*

*Behind me came another roar and I grew desperate as two of my white-feathered friends sank into the water. I pulled them up, pushing them into the basket. One, two, three, four . . . where was my fifth girl? I glanced around, frantic, but I did not see her. The wind or the wave had swept her away before I even noticed. I closed the lid and started back as quick as my tired legs could carry me.*

*"Oh, look! Look there!" Mahala cried at the door, pointing out to sea. "The worst sea is coming!"*

*I pushed against the water, droplets coating my eyelashes but not enough to block out the sight and sound of a massive billowing wave, at least thirty feet in height, surging toward us. I remembered the journal entry from 1839 and dove inside, upsetting my squawking hens. "Close the door! Help me!" I raced to the sideboard and pushed it with all my might in front of the door, Lydia and Esther, Mahala, and even Mama, who had roused herself from bed, helping me do so.*

*The breaker struck just as we slid the sideboard into place. We braced ourselves, clinging to one another, white feathers and flapping hens flopping around us, all wondering once again, if this was the end.*

*After it appeared the house would not yet be swept away, Mama clung to me. "You stupid, stupid girl." But she said it tenderly, through her tears. "Do you realize it would have been my final undoing if you perished in that sea?"*

*My heart went out to her. "The Lord kept me safe, Mama. He will do the same for us. But I must check the lights."*

*She grabbed both sides of my sopping hair, looked straight into my eyes. "Your Papa would be proud of you, Abbie."*

*I blinked away tears, for she did not say what we were both*

125

*thinking. That even if we survive this treacherous storm, that perhaps Papa has not. That perhaps we may never be able to tell him of our time in this storm upon the Rock. I tried not to think of him alive and out of his mind with worry for us on the mainland, helpless to get to us.*

*"There's only four . . ." Esther counted the wet hens, who took to pecking at the braided rug and furniture.*

*"I lost one. The water was too deep." I'd named the lost hen Dorothy, after my best friend in Rockland.*

*The girls cried over the loss of Dorothy, but I swallowed down my own tears and opened the door to the tower, stepping into water up to my ankles. I froze at the sight of the vicious elements before me where the old wooden chamber once was. Pieces of wood and debris swirled in puddles at my feet. We had moved Mama none too soon.*

*I climbed the tower and refilled the oil, sparing as much as I could in case the storm continued for many more days. When a breaker passed, I slid out to the catwalk, grasping the slick, icy railing and scraping the ice off the frozen windows as best I could before the next breaker struck. Below me, the ocean swirled, slamming against the bottom of the tower. When I looked out, it felt as if the tower itself moved like a boat tossed on the waves, making me dizzy. Ice formed on my eyelashes in seconds. My fingers numbed beneath my thick gloves. The sound of an impending billow sent me back inside.*

*Once the billow passed, I returned to the catwalk, intent on finishing my job. I sang "It Came Upon a Midnight Clear" to encourage my efforts. When I finally slipped inside and closed the door, I'd never been more grateful for those happy lamps. If they should go out, what would we do?*

*I descended the stairs, weary and exhausted from the work and from constant hunger. What would Papa do if he were here?*

*I tended to the second tower and after I'd laid my wet clothing before the stove to dry, I addressed my family over a* meager dinner. "I think we should stay in the tower until the storm subsides."

Lydia laughed. "It stinks in there." The whale oil did smell, although I had long since grown accustomed to the scent.

Mama, feeling slightly better, managed to sit with us at the table but insisted she didn't want anything to eat. I wasn't entirely convinced she refused food because of her illness. I think she, like I, was scared we would run out altogether too soon. "We can't sleep up there. We will freeze to death."

"The lamps give off heat. It is actually quite cozy."

"Not everyone loves the lights like you do, sister." Lydia scraped the crumbs of her half-griddle cake from her plate.

I bit my lip. "The wooden chamber is gone. Washed away with one of those massive billows, likely the one that crashed upon us after I rescued the hens. This house is strong, yes, but the towers are stronger still. I think it would be safer if we bore it."

Alas, I convinced them. I heated soap stones on the stove to keep our feet warm. The girls helped me collect bedding and some food. With the family Bible and the hens, we climbed the tower together.

Though small compared to the kitchen, the lamp room did prove cozy enough. Once settled, I read the Bible—our Lord's words about not worrying, about Him providing for us.

Although bone weary, I slept fitfully, waking often to check the lamps. When I traveled to the second tower, I noted how the kitchen had flooded. When I returned to the north tower, Mama roused from her slumber. "I wish I could help you, daughter."

"The Lord is providing me with His strength."

Mama smiled softly. "My brave girl. So much faith." And then she was sleeping again.

The next day dawned brighter, and I snuffed out the lamps and gave them a thorough cleaning. I raised the flag at half-mast in hopes that some ship may see we were in distress.

*What a gift even a pint of flour or a half pound of salt pork would be!*

*Yesterday morning, the sun finally rose over the horizon, and we cheered. We made quick work of cleaning downstairs and I set my four girls back in their coop. I stared at the waves, still in chaos but not nearly as angry as we had seen. How quickly the ocean could change.*

*We split our two remaining eggs between the five of us for breakfast. Muscle pains started in my legs, as I'd gone without food for the last several meals to save for the younger ones and Mama, who was finally taking a few bites here and there. I thought about slaughtering one of our dear hens to have a bit of meat, but the thought caused my stomach to roil.*

*A bit longer. Surely, Papa would come.*

*When we sat at our breakfast table, Mama held out her thin hands on either side of her. "Let us thank the Lord for sparing us and for providing for us. Let us thank Him for our brave Abbie."*

*"Let us thank Him for giving us each strength to endure this trial," I added, feeling uncomfortable with being singled out.*

*"Yes. And let us pray for Papa's safe return soon!" Esther said.*

*"Amen!"*

*But still we wait. Papa has not yet come.*

# Chapter Sixteen

*I am the light of the world. Whoever follows me will never walk in darkness but will have the light of life.*

John 8:12
~ Verse on Laney's birthday card from Nana,
Age 14

## LANEY

The morning after seeing Kiran at the restaurant, I wake with a jolt, realizing I've slept straight through my alarm. And apparently through the intense banging on the roof. I squint at the time on my phone and groan. Nine o'clock. I promised myself I wouldn't lapse into old habits, that I would be as helpful to Nana as I was on the first day I arrived.

I'd stayed up well past one o'clock in the morning reading Abbie's journal. I'd dreamt of her in that great storm of 1856 . . . of her finding the strength to take care of both her family and the lamps.

What might it be like to believe in God as young Abbie did? To lean on Him through the storms of my past and present?

Abbie had been sixteen years old at the time of the last journal entry I read. An entire year younger than me and Maddie the day we jumped from that cliff. I couldn't begin to compare our maturity levels, realizing I fell hopelessly short of the brave young girl on Matinicus Rock.

But one thing is certain: I must share the contents of the journal with Nana. For some reason, my grandfather had thought this diary important, and I long to share Abbie's story with her, certain my grandmother will find it as inspiring as I do.

Taking the journal downstairs, I find Nana cleaning the breakfast dishes. I place the journal on the top shelf of a bookcase that sits in the sitting room adjoining the kitchen.

"I'm so sorry I slept in."

She turns and gives me a soft smile. "Honey, I've been handling breakfast service on my own for years." She winks. "Not that I don't appreciate the help, mind you."

"It won't happen again."

She turns the faucet off and dries her hands with a dish towel before placing her palms on either side of my face. "Laney, you seem intent on earning your time here. And I'm telling you, you have nothing to earn. I'm only grateful you're here. Grateful to know you. Really and truly."

I blink back tears. That might have been the nicest thing anyone's ever said to me. "I'm grateful to know you, too."

"There's some leftover apple pancakes keeping warm in the oven."

I slide them out of the still-warm oven and plate a portion before sitting at the island. I drizzle pure maple syrup on them and breathe deeply of the scents of Nana's kitchen—the baked pancakes and apples of course, and always the scent of the sea. I'm almost certain the ocean smells different on this side of the country.

I raise the first bite to my mouth and groan. "Oh, that's so good. Thank you, Nana. I'm sure to gain ten pounds before the summer's over, and I won't regret any of them."

She chuckles. "You could spare a bit of meat on those bones, I'd say. How was work last night?"

"Good. Jason brought me home."

She murmurs something that sounds like an "Mmm-hmm."

"Remember that journal I found in the box in the attic?"

"Yes."

"It's the journal of an Abbie Burgess. She lived on Matinicus Rock in the mid-1800s."

Nana nearly drops the dish in her hand. It clatters to the bottom of the sink. She turns, giving me her full attention. "Abbie Burgess?" Her tone is one of disbelief.

"Yes," I squeak.

She returns to her dishes. "Well, child, that would be something."

"So, you know who she is?"

"Of course, I do. This coast is filled with history and legends galore, Abbie Burgess chief among them."

Perhaps I'd done myself a disservice in not reading more about Abbie online. But no. There is value in living out her story through her eyes.

"Aren't you at all interested to read her journal then?"

Nana raises a thin gray brow at me. "Of course. But I find it hard to believe the journal of Abbie Burgess has been underneath my nose this entire time. More so, that Jack wouldn't have shared such a find with me."

"Maybe he didn't know or didn't read it."

"Uh-huh."

She doesn't need to believe me, she can read the journal for herself. "I'm not finished reading it, but I thought if you wanted to read it together . . . I don't know, maybe that's a stupid idea."

She's drying her hands on that dish cloth again. Turning to me. "It's *not* a stupid idea. I'd read anything that was important to you, Laney. Not to mention, it sounds fascinating." She throws

131

down the dish towel. "Now, where is this book? I have a couple of free hours later this afternoon and I'd love to start it."

I stand, tempted to wrap her in a hug even though I stop short of doing so. "You're the best. Will you just promise not to tell me any of the history you know about Abbie? I don't want to know until I finish the journal."

She studies me. "This means a lot to you, doesn't it?"

"I don't know why," I whisper. I tell myself Abbie is merely a distraction, a connection with the Maine coast I'm coming to love, but it's more than that. Is it her complicated feelings for her mother? Her immense bravery? Or her strong faith that I'm drawn to? Why does it matter, really? Perhaps by the end I'll find out.

I walk the few steps to the bookshelf and carefully hand the journal to Nana. She takes it, mirroring my care. "It certainly does look old."

I smile. "I think you'll enjoy it."

"I'm sure I will." She places the journal on the top of the hutch, allowing a lingering finger to graze over it before facing me. "Now, I have a couple of things I need to talk to you about."

"Okay." I lower myself to the chair and return to my pancakes.

Nana sits across from me. "First, my best friend is getting married."

"That's wonderful."

"It is. The wedding is next Saturday, a simple affair. Hannah has never been one for extravagance and it's her second marriage. I realize this is short notice for your work schedule, but she'd love for you to come. She's dying to see you and quite honestly, I can't wait for you to meet her."

"If it's important to you, I'll make it work," I say, echoing her sentiment from moments earlier regarding Abbie's journal.

Her gray-blue eyes sparkle. "Wonderful. It's in Camden, a couple of hours south of here. Hannah insists you bring a guest, if you'd like."

I scrunch my nose. "Aren't I *your* guest?"

"Well, yes, but honey, I can only keep up on that dance floor for so long."

I giggle. "I'll be okay, I promise."

"Why not invite Jason along? He'll still be in town, won't he?"

"Uh, I think so, but that's kind of a big step for us. We're not even officially dating."

"Maybe you could make it official, then."

"Nana!"

She shrugs. "Just a thought. Besides, it might be nice to ride down in that fancy BMW instead of your grandmother's old station wagon."

Couldn't argue there. "I'll see." I scrape the last of my pancakes, bits of apple and moist cake all covered in syrup onto my fork. "Was there something else you needed to talk to me about?"

"Yes." She taps her fingers on the butcher block of the island before meeting my gaze. "I spoke to your mother last night."

I slump in my seat, my skin growing hot, then cold. "She mentioned she might make a trip out here in a couple of weeks. I'd hoped she was kidding."

"She's flying in a week from Monday."

"Oh." And just like that, I'm fighting those feelings again. I don't want Mom here. I don't want to share this same space of air, or even the same state of Maine, as her. I don't want her hurting Nana more than she has already.

"She asked to stay here."

I'm on my feet, ready to run all the way back to California to give my mother a piece of my mind. "What? You can't be serious."

"I admit, I was surprised too. But I have the space and she is my daughter, so I agreed."

"You did read the same book I did when you read *Locked Light*, didn't you?"

"Laney . . ." Nana's tone holds a small warning.

"Why does she want to stay here? She loathes the Beacon. She's turned all her fans against it and ruined your business."

"Honey, I know you're angry, but in the end, I love my daughter. No matter what. And I want a relationship with her more than I want my good name, more than I want the bed and breakfast to stay in business."

I hear, but I don't understand. Still, me fighting Nana on this won't do—I am her guest as well.

"Is Bill coming?" Not that I'm excited to see Bill, but once in a great while, he does help Mom pull out reputable behavior.

"She didn't mention it, but of course, he's welcome, too."

I rinse my plate, loading it into the dishwasher.

My forearms itch and I force myself not to cave to their pull.

"I'm sorry this is so hard for you, honey. I wish things were different."

"Me too," I whisper.

"There's something else I should probably tell you."

I brace myself.

"Your mom mentioned doing an interview while she was here. An interview with *Timeline*."

I press my fingernails into the old scars. My skin is crawling over my bones, and I long to jump out of it. This can't be happening. My grandmother can't let it be happening.

"You cannot let her stay here. *Timeline* wants to come here, you know that, right? They want Mom to take them to the lighthouse, to tell her story and break America's heart. It will *ruin* you, Nana."

"Honey, are you so sure I don't deserve to be ruined?"

She's asking me to believe the impossible. I blink back the tears blurring the corners of my eyes.

Fine, I'll say it. I'll move past my fear, get it all out in the open.

"Did you lock Mom up in the lighthouse for three months before she started her senior year?"

Pain ripples through Nana's eyes like a wave retreating into the sea. "There's more than one side to a story."

"Answer me." I've raised my voice, ignoring the guests in their rooms who are getting ready to start their day.

Her gaze meets mine, and all I see is raw hurt. She turns and starts up the stairs.

I bury my head in my hands and groan. A second later, I'm tearing out the back door and across the porch, racing toward the footbridge to the lighthouse. It's old, with chipped white paint. It leads across a rocky outcropping to a place that juts out from the mainland.

The lighthouse is tired-looking, standing atop ancient, tarnished stonework. I pull at the door and boldly duck under the yellow caution tape. The first stone step is crumbled, nonexistent. I raise my leg to reach the second step, gripping the railing in case the entire staircase decides to fall upon me.

Then, I begin to climb. Red bricks line the tower, fissures deep and obvious as the staircase spirals upward. But as I climb, I'm filled with awe.

I love the ancient sturdiness of it. The stairs generations before me have climbed. I even love the cracks, much like I love the slight lines around Nana's eyes and mouth. They indicate a weathered existence. A wisdom I haven't yet been able to glean.

As I ascend the stairs, I think of Abbie, climbing the steps of the north tower on Matinicus Rock. When I reach the top of the small lamp room, I study the hundreds of tiny light refractors that make up the light. It's beautiful. I long to see it lit, brightening the night sky. I look around the room, try to imagine my high-maintenance mother locked up here for months at a time. I try to imagine Nana being okay with that. Try even to imagine my grandfather, the smiling man in the pictures around the house, enforcing such a sentence.

I think of the hurt encompassing Nana's soulful eyes.

I'd been so certain Mom was lying. But if she's not, then that means I have to believe a horrible truth about the grandmother I'm coming to love.

I inhale a quivering breath, try to see objectively through the thick fog of family drama.

Why *would* Mom lie? Why would she make up such a horrendous untruth and release it into the world?

When I'd asked her not to include Maddie in the book, she'd been so adamant that the truth be told.

The truth. The thought pinches.

Her book is on all the bestseller lists. *Timeline*, for goodness sakes. I think of the *Hello, America*, segment. Surely, Mom wouldn't lie on national television and plan to do so again for *Timeline*, and right under her own mother's nose.

I visualize the man from the picture in the sitting room, my grandfather, dragging my young mother up these stairs and locking her in the lamp room. I envision my grandmother standing by, doing nothing.

It's incomprehensible.

Something simply didn't add up. But what was that something?

I open the door to the catwalk and slide onto it, edging my hand along the outside of the tower instead of the railing, which Nana said was not sturdy. The sun splashes down on my shoulders. Below me, waves crash onto the rocks, swirling white. Their thunder makes me shudder along with them, and while a moment ago I held an affinity for the tower, now I tremble. I'm cast back to that day six years ago when I stood above another body of water, my hand holding not a lighthouse, but that of my best friend. It seems I am falling, falling, falling, the rocks behind me becoming the cracks and fissures of the lighthouse giving way to swallow me.

I press my back against the solidity of the tower and lower myself to the planks of the catwalk. I close my eyes, force myself to think of something else.

I focus on Abbie, standing atop a catwalk of another lighthouse almost two hundred years ago in the midst of a great storm.

She is scared and the sea is swirling beneath. I rack my brain for what she does during that time. Does she cry out? Pray?

And then, it comes to me. She sings.

Voice quavering, I summon up a hum in my throat, my vocal cords shaky. "It came upon a midnight clear, that glorious song of old."

No matter that this is crazy, I continue, my voice growing stronger as I think of Abbie and how she looked to God to sustain her. "From angels bending near the earth, to touch their harps of gold." I don't know all the words, but I know the tune—the highs and the lows, the melody of hope and the triumph of peace.

Christmas songs in July. And yet by the time I finish, I can open my eyes and appreciate the view.

Perhaps, I too can be as brave as Abbie Burgess.

# Chapter Seventeen

*Mindy, could you cancel my flight home next week?*
~ Text from Jason to his secretary at Rutherford Designs

## JASON

*To: jrutherford@rutherforddesigns.com*
*From: drutherford@rutherforddesigns.com*
*Subject: Re: Miriam Jacobs' Land*

*Jason,*
*I suppose I understand your hesitation to work on the Jacobs'*
*project, but you must realize this would be a huge contract for*
*us. Please reconsider. What happened with Maddie was a*
*long time ago. We all endured some hurt around that time,*
*but why should Miriam bear the consequences of something*
*she had little to do with?*
*Well done on the Sanderson plans. Just waiting for Susan's*
*approval. I'm assuming you will be heading home soon?*

*Don Rutherford*

*CEO and Head Designer*
*Rutherford Designs, Inc.*
*www.rutherforddesigns.com*


*To: drutherford@rutherforddesigns.com*
*From: jrutherford@rutherforddesigns.com*
*Subject: Re: Miriam Jacobs' Land*

*I'm sorry to disappoint, Dad. I'm willing to look at the land while I'm out here, but I stand by my decision. I will not be able to design Miriam's home. There are extenuating reasons which I won't go into here, but I hope you will trust me.*
*I'm going to stay on the East Coast for a little longer. Don't worry, I'm getting work done. Maine agrees with me. Talk soon.*

*Jason*

I push send and listen to the satisfying swoosh of finality that indicates the email is heading into my father's inbox. I'm not ready to tell him I've found Laney. He tends to place Laney in the box of my past, tucked alongside the neat compartment where he also places my mom. He won't think it's healthy I'm seeing Laney again, falling in love again.

Of course, it's not really his concern. I'm twenty-five years old, making my way in the world and fully capable of making my own decisions, even if they might end in heartbreak.

I close my laptop and stand to stretch. Eight o'clock. With any luck, the dinner crowd at The Lobster Bar will have died down.

I decide to walk downtown. The sun is halfway below the horizon, but it's warm enough for a t-shirt. When I arrive at the restaurant, I ask to be seated outside at one of Laney's tables, if possible. The hostess accommodates. She sits me beside the water, a wooden railing bordering the table. I'm facing the sea and Bar

Island. A full moon appears in the darkening sky, and a scattering of people cross a thin strip of land revealed by the low tide.

When Laney spots me, her face lights up and my heart lurches at the dimple in her right cheek, those sparkling brown eyes, the apparent joy on her face at seeing me.

"This your new favorite hangout?" she asks.

"If you're here, it is."

Her face reddens. I enjoy every inch of the blush. "Can I get you something to drink?"

"I'll try some of that blueberry lemonade."

"It's good. Be right back."

I watch her walk away. I am such a goner. How will I ever leave this place, leave her?

When she comes back, she places the ice-cold lemonade on a thick paper coaster. "Need a few minutes to decide?"

"What would you suggest?" I rub my chin, pretending to study the menu.

She rolls her eyes. "Everything's good."

"Really? Is that what you tell your other customers when they ask for your recommendation?"

"Fine. I recommend the oysters."

I make a show of gagging. "You know I hate oysters."

She cocks her head to one side. "Do I?"

"If they weren't so slimy . . . "

"So, you need a few more minutes?"

"Yes. No. I mean, don't leave. Do you have other tables?"

"One inside happily eating their baked lobsters."

"That's it! Baked lobster, please." I grin up at her and hand her my menu. "And maybe add in a salad, too."

"Good choice."

She leaves again, comes back with my meal sooner than I expect. The lobster is bright red with generous amounts of melted butter as well as a cracker and picker tool and a side of corn on the cob. "Boss says I can leave early tonight. Guess he has too much help and we're winding down."

"Perfect. I want to take you somewhere."

She laughs. "Do you ever sit still?"

"Only when you're sitting with me. How about you have a seat?"

She looks around. "Maybe for a minute." She pulls out a chair and sits across the table. I start working on the lobster and catch her smiling.

"What?"

"You stick your tongue out the side of your mouth when you're concentrating. It's kind of cute."

"I'll concentrate more often then."

She rolls her eyes. "How was your day?"

"Finished Suse's plans."

I don't imagine the disappointment on her face. "Does that mean you'll be leaving soon?"

"No, not yet."

She clears her throat. "That's right—my mom's land."

"I told my dad I'll look at the land for the firm but that I can't be the designer on her home."

"Jason, you don't have to—"

I grab for her hand, hope she doesn't care that mine is sticky with butter. "Yes, I do. What's more, I want to."

"Thank you," she whispers.

I go back to my meal. "You eat dinner yet?"

"I usually eat when I get home."

I slide a freshly shucked lobster claw over to her, offer her my butter.

"That's the best part."

"What can I say, Laney Jacobs? A lobster for my lobster."

I'm not sure she'd get the reference, but the way her face brightens nearly the shade as the lobster on my plate, I guess she does.

"Did you hear me and Kiran talking last night?"

"No. Why?"

"No reason." She lifts the lobster to her mouth and bites into its juicy flesh. She closes her eyes and moans. "That is delicious. I haven't eaten since breakfast, although to be fair, it was a late breakfast."

I offer her my corn on the cob, but she declines. "I better finish up that last table."

She squeezes my shoulder before she walks away, and I am as high as that glorious moon in the sky. I've been hoping what happened on that granite ledge three nights ago meant something to her, because it sure did for me. I hoped I hadn't scared her away with the kiss on the cheek I'd given her when I dropped her off at her grandmother's last night.

But if I read her right, that shoulder squeeze and the look of happiness when she'd spotted me tonight means I hadn't.

My stomach lurches, a knowing lodging in my gut. There is absolutely no way in all the world I am ever going to leave her again.

# Chapter Eighteen

*Come on, you guys. It's a known fact that lobsters fall in love and mate for life. You can actually see old lobster couples walking around their tank, holding claws.*
~ Phoebe, from *Friends*

## LANEY

He'd called me his *lobster*.

Until last night, that wouldn't have meant much to me. In fact, I might have considered it an insult. But now, I could only surmise he meant it in the way Kiran had used the term last night.

He thought I was his person. His special someone.

Oh, my goodness, he thought I was his special someone. Was I ready to be anybody's special someone?

It seemed every day at Nana's proved more and more how much of a mess I really was. There was so much Jason didn't know.

*If you love him, you should let him know.*

Kiran's words cast a shadow over my mind. I didn't want to think about telling Jason of my troubled history with self-mutilation. I didn't want to think on it any more than I had to. It was why I wore long-sleeve shirts, why I avoided my scars, even in the shower.

After I collect my tips, including Jason's overly generous one, I meet him in front of the restaurant. "You always tip your wait staff that generously?"

"Only the ones I have crushes on." He holds his hand out and I slip mine into his, my heart still thrumming at the feel of our palms flush against one another, our fingers interlocking. His bare forearm brushes the inside of mine, and I try to imagine him touching my scars as Kiran had traced hers last night.

The thought causes a shiver to work through me.

"Cold?"

I shake my head. "I'm okay. Where're are we going?"

"You up for an adventure?"

"I might have had my share of adventures this week."

"Care to elaborate?"

"Well, I found an old journal in Nana's attic."

"That's cool."

"It is. It belonged to a lighthouse keeper. Or rather, her dad was the actual keeper, but she helped, and once, when he went to shore, she kept the lights burning through this crazy winter storm that lasted days."

"Sounds like an adventure if I ever heard of one."

"It is—was. I haven't finished yet, but I'm trying to figure out how my grandfather came upon it."

"He was into history?"

"According to Nana, all things history and all things light-houses." I study the slope of a descending hill in front of us that goes down to the sea. A strip of wet earth extends into the water, leading to Bar Island. "Hey, where are we going?"

"Bar Island."

I'd seen a myriad of tourists cross the sandbar that appeared during low tide, and I'd been curious to take the walk. But not at eight-thirty at night.

"It's getting dark."

"Not anytime soon."

I bite my lip. "What if the tide rises fast and we get trapped on the island?"

"I guess we'll have to hunt wild boar, make a shelter out of tree branches, and sleep cuddled up to keep warm until we're rescued by the next low tide."

I slap him on his bicep. "Jason Rutherford, so help me."

"Don't worry. We have another three to four hours before the bar is covered. Although how romantic would it be to be stranded on the island, just the two of us?"

"It might be easier to see it during the day."

"You want to come back tomorrow?"

I shake my head. "Probably shouldn't. I still haven't finished cleaning Mom's room."

I lean back as we descend the hill towards the sandbar. Several people are making their way back from the island.

"She's coming in another week or so," I say.

"Who?"

"My mom." I glance sideways at him. "Did you know that?"

He shakes his head. "Dad didn't mention anything."

Am I a brat for not being able to handle a visit from my own mother? Have I matured at all in the last six years?

"Was your dad angry when you told him you couldn't work on my mom's house?"

"I think the word he used was *disappointed*."

If I cared for him, maybe I would encourage him to continue with his work on Mom's house. But the thought of him pouring his talent and creativity into a home that Mom is only building to make a point is enough to keep me from rushing to assure him.

We've reached the sand now. The path in the middle is

smoother than the edges rolling down to the water, which hold tiny bits of shell and rock.

"My dad's getting married," Jason says.

"Really?"

"Yeah. Her name's Eva. They've been dating a while. I guess it's not really a surprise."

I squeeze his hand. "You okay?"

He nods, but then shrugs. "Crazy that it should bother me all these years later, right? I mean, Mom left more than twelve years ago. She's been dead half that time. I should want my dad to be happy. It doesn't make sense."

I snort. "You're talking to the girl who can't handle the thought of her boyfriend working on her mom's house."

"Boyfriend, huh?" He stops walking, pulls me close. His breath smells of blueberries and lemons and melted butter. His thumb moves in circles at my waist.

"I don't know . . . you called me your lobster, didn't you? Shouldn't boyfriend stage come before lobsterhood?"

"Probably. And believe me, there's nothing I want more than to be your boyfriend." He sighs.

"But . . ."

"But I'll have to leave here at some point . . . what are your plans?"

I bite my lip. "At first, I only thought as far as the end of summer. Now, I can't imagine leaving Nana."

"Whether you stay or leave, I want to make this work."

I pull away, feeling the presence of the many passersby traveling away from the island. "You think this is moving a little too fast?" Just a few weeks ago I was leaving California, partly to escape Jason. Now, the last thing I want to do is never see him again. Am I weak? Or is he where I belonged all this time?

I start walking again, but don't release his hand.

"Do you?"

"You can't answer my question with a question."

"Can't I?"

I release his hand to give him a flirty shove. He laughs but instantly reclaims my hand. "It's not like we met three days ago. You're a part of my history, Laney. A part of me."

*Stop melting my heart, Jason Rutherford.*

We're silent, and I feel like he's expecting me to return the sentiment. But I can't. I won't. Because there's so much he doesn't know. While I want to forgive him for encouraging me and Maddie to jump that day, there's a part of me that wonders if I'll battle my guilt forever with him at my side.

"Are you thinking you'll end up staying with your Nana for a while?"

I hear what he's really asking. What are our next steps? What would a future together look like?

"I feel at home here. I don't want to go back to California, at least for now."

"Would you entertain a visit, at least? Say in November for my dad's wedding?"

"I might. And I guess since we're on the topic of weddings, I should let you know that Nana and I are going to one next Saturday. Nana thought you might want to come." I wince as I say this.

"Come on, if I'm going to be your boyfriend, you gotta do better than that."

I laugh. "What do you mean?"

He stops walking again. We are almost to the island and the crowd has fizzled out. "I mean, 'Jason, I'm going to a wedding next Saturday, and I would love the pleasure of your company.'"

I roll my eyes, shake my head. "Jason, I'm going to a wedding next Saturday and *Nana and* I would love the pleasure of your company."

"Well, since you're begging . . ."

We laugh.

"I'll go anywhere with you, Laney Jacobs." Our gazes lock. The last of the sun makes his eyes shimmer with both light and depth. "Come on." He tugs me onto the island where we enter a path upward. "Watch your step. I don't think the path to the overlook is that far."

It's not. And the chill in the air has kept away the mosquitoes. Or maybe they spray the path. Either way, I'm thankful.

It does feel like we're on a deserted island as we travel up the wide dirt path. Jason never lets go of my hand, and when we finally break into a small clearing, my breath catches in my throat.

"It's beautiful."

The glimmering lights of Bar Harbor stand before us, nestled in between the surrounding hills and peaks. The moon glows bright above Cadillac Mountain. The Terrace Grille and Bar Harbor Hotel twinkle in front of us. The ferries and the *Margaret Todd*, her grand sails down for the night, along with a slew of other boats, are tucked into their homes, bobbing gently in the water. Jason's hotel is across the bay on the right and the last of the sun's rays are touching the hills beyond.

"It's almost as if I'm looking at a painting. Like we're a part of it but away from it."

"I know what you mean." He traces his thumb over the back of my hand. "Want to sit?"

"Sure." We lower ourselves to a slab of granite and stare at the moon. It splashes its light on Frenchman's Bay and Bar Harbor. We're quiet, lost in our own thoughts, neither of us daring to mar the moment.

Until he does. "Do you think you'll ever forgive me, Laney? Like really forgive me?"

I don't bother to pretend I don't know what he's talking about—I know all too well. But how can we move deeper into lobsterhood if we don't have some hard conversations? I clear my throat. "Do you know I've spent hours in therapy trying to forgive not only you, but myself?"

"I—I didn't know. But I want to. Will you tell me?"

"There's nothing to tell . . . maybe that's a lie. There's nothing I want to tell." I drag in a spacious breath. "It felt like I was crawling inside myself, searching for a key to unlock the missing piece to the puzzle. The puzzle of why I couldn't move on, why I couldn't be normal."

"Laney—"

"I want to forgive you, Jason. And part of me does, I think. Mostly because I'm tired of being angry, of clutching for something that I'll never get back."

He bites his lip and swats at a stray mosquito. "If I could go back and do that day over again, I would. A thousand times I have."

"Me too."

We're quiet, and I glimpse the Milky Way galaxy to our right. It's massive and awe-inspiring and, though it must be my crazy imagination, I feel that in that moment, maybe it's Maddie's window from heaven. Could she be smiling down at us? Maybe even laughing at how torn up we still are about her death when she's having the time of her life doing whatever people do in heaven?

"I don't want to hold this inside myself anymore," I whisper.

He drapes one arm around me and pulls me close but doesn't offer any words. Just offers himself.

I lean into him, cradling my head in the crook of his neck. My body picks up the rhythm of his heartbeat, and it seems for a moment, we are synchronized. He smells of Ivory soap and that old familiar cologne. My chest aches for a thousand different reasons.

"Do you think if I say I forgive you and that I forgive myself, that it counts even if I don't feel it deep inside?"

He sighs and my body follows the up and down movement of his breaths. "I heard once forgiveness is a choice. I don't know . . . we'll never forget what happened that day. There'll always be feelings and memories that will make anger and sadness crop up. Does that mean we don't try to move forward?"

I mull over his words as I stare at the sparkling lights of the Bar Harbor Inn. I think about Abbie, who'd been so mad at her mother for leaving her little brother behind and then for being weak on the Rock, but how she seemed to put so much of that aside. Even chose to admire her mother for her attitude of thankfulness. Did Abbie ever consciously make that choice of forgiveness, or did it spill out of her as part of her faith?

I prayed sporadically. The only scripture I knew was from Nana's cards. Perhaps, if I looked to God, I'd be able to find faith. I'd be able to find forgiveness.

I study the smattering of pink, blue, white, and purple stars that cluster in a luminous band above the hills of Acadia. Surely, Whoever created that beauty is also big enough to teach my heart to forgive, to handle my fledgling faith.

"I forgive you," I say. "You never meant for Maddie to die, I know that. I don't want to waste my time on earth with guilt and doubt. I want to trust again. Trust you, trust myself . . . maybe even trust God."

He pulls me closer and strokes my face with the back of his knuckles. I smell his woodsy aftershave, the faint spice of his deodorant. "Thank you. I'm not ashamed to admit I've hoped for this for a long time." He shifts me off his chest until I'm looking at him. My heart beats a frantic tune against my ribcage, and I know what will happen next.

He lowers his head to mine and brushes his lips against my own, ever so soft, as if asking for permission to go deeper.

I give it to him as I move closer, my hands on his arms, keeping me steady.

We shared a lot more than kisses in high school, but I don't remember any of it being this powerful. His mouth works to undo me, moving along my own in a gesture that seems to only touch the surface of what he feels.

And that shakes me to the core.

I draw back, wanting more and scared for more all at once. I swallow down my doubts. "There's so much you don't know about these past years. About me, about . . ." I can't say it. I can't tell him of my struggles in rehab, of my struggles of hurting myself. Of the handful of times I thought about ending it all.

But how can we begin a relationship without him seeing my scars? Those both inside and out?

"It's okay," he whispers. "We don't have to figure it all out now. We have time. Let's take it slow, okay?" His thumb caresses my jawline, and I lean into it. "And whatever it is, Laney, I promise you, I can take it. I'm all in."

His words cause a frenzy of anticipation in my belly. "I want to tell you." And I'm relieved at the fact that I very much do. I take this as a sign that I'm ready to trust myself with him. And I find myself believing that he won't turn me away.

He's the only man who has ever truly known me. I want to say he's the only man who has ever seen my scars and still loved me.

I take a breath, ready to bare my soul. Ready to find out if I'm still enough for him.

# Chapter Nineteen

*I hate that you died, Mads. I know Laney blames me. I blame myself.*
~ Letter from Jason to Maddie found in a bottle washed up onshore two years after her death

## JASON

I wait for Laney to tell me whatever she feels she needs to. I can't imagine it changing the way I feel about her. But still, she doesn't speak. She opens her mouth, then closes it.

"How about if I guess?" I ask.

She blows out the breath she's apparently been holding, laughs in a small puff of wind. "Yeah. Give it your best shot."

"Okay . . . you worked in a brothel and took up a pseudonym of Sexy Sue. Now you're afraid I won't love you because of all the guys you sold yourself to."

"Not funny," she says. "I haven't been with any guy since . . ."

"Since me?"

She hugs her knees to her chest. "Yeah."

I wish I could say the same. "Laney, I haven't exactly been a saint these last several years. Less saintly in those early years of college, after my mom died." I shake my head. "No, forget that. I can't blame my mother's death on my poor choices." I breathe deep. How did this turn into my confession? Hadn't she just forgiven me? Was I crazy to volunteer more to forgive?

"Okay . . . anyone serious?"

Ouch. "One."

"Tell me."

"Her name was Trisha. We started dating junior year of college." I suck in a breath before diving in. "I bought her a ring."

"And she turned you down?"

"No. I never gave it to her. Carried it in my pocket for weeks. One night, I took her to this fancy restaurant where I planned to ask her. She went to the restroom, but when I reached for the ring all I could think about was a dream I'd had the night before."

Vividly, I remember trying to talk myself out of being thrown off course by a mere dream, but in the end, it mattered. A lot.

"What'd you dream?" Laney's voice is small and breathy in the night air.

"I dreamt I was asking you to marry me instead of Trisha."

"You aren't serious."

"Dead serious. When she came back from the restroom, I didn't think. I broke up with her on the spot. The next day I started my search for you."

She straightens, pulling away from me. "What?"

"I showed up at your house, Laney. Your mom told me you'd gone to Maine."

"But—but, Susan Sanderson . . ."

"I was planning a trip out here when Dad got word on that project and decided to let me try it out on my own. I think he was looking forward to time alone in the house with Eva. He proposed a couple of days after I left."

"You should have told me."

"I didn't want you to think I was stalking you or something. Showing up clear across the country to tell you I'm still in love with you. I didn't want to freak you out."

She stills. "How can you be in love with me when two months ago you were ready to propose to another woman?"

I place my hands on either side of her arms and massage gently, willing her to believe my words. "I was trying to move forward. Force myself forward. Only, it wasn't working. Because half of me was stuck in high school."

Her eyes shine with the moon and I try to convey all I'm not saying, hoping she understands what she means to me. I grapple for words. "All of my heart was—is—yours."

My gaze drops to her lips. And then, she's the one closing the gap between us. She's kissing me and I'm kissing her back. It's hot and intense and I can't get enough of her. We slide closer and my arms move over her body and she's kissing me like I'm water and oxygen and life, and I'm doing the same to her. She tastes of mint and summer. She smells of good food and salty sea. Our limbs are tangled until I can't tell where I begin and she ends. I've never wanted anyone more than I want her, but I've also never loved anyone more than I love her and so, painstakingly, I pull away.

I swallow. "I don't want to screw this up. I want to do it right, you know? If only I had a clue what that looks like."

She smiles, and the moonlight pools on the dimple in her right cheek. "You're telling me." She bites her lip. "I still need to tell you something."

I shake out my hands, as if that will dispel the attraction coursing through my body like the rapids of a white river. "Okay."

"I—I think it might be easier to show you." She grips the cuff of her right sleeve and hesitates. Her hands are shaking, and at first, I think it's from our lingering passion. But then I realize she's trying to share something with me that frightens her.

So slow I can barely tell she's moving, she inches up her sleeve. Her pale skin glows by the light of the moon.

And then, I see them.

The scars are plentiful, horizontal crests along otherwise flawless skin. At first, I can't make sense of them. What happened to her? A car accident? Something else? But as I study the uniformity of the scars and their placement, I understand.

I choke on my emotions. "Laney." To think of her in so much pain that she saw no other way out of it makes my insides shake. She takes her other sleeve and rolls that one up, bares them in the moonlight for me to see, to assess, to judge.

But if she's looking for judgment, she won't find it here.

"I'm so sorry," I whisper.

"Please." She scrunches her eyes shut. "I *don't* want your pity. As much as I'd like to blame somebody, these are all on me."

I clear my throat, fighting with myself over what to say, how to say it. "I'm sorry that I played a part in your pain. I'm sorry you felt you had nowhere to turn. Most of all, I'm sorry I wasn't there for you."

She pulls down her sleeves and locks them closed by curling her fingers along the edges of the fabric. "You tried, at first. I refused to see you, blocked your texts."

"I should have tried harder. I should have slept outside your door."

"I'm sorry they're so ugly. I hate them. I hate myself for doing it."

"How did you get past it?"

"Rehab. Therapy. Journaling. And that's just it. If I felt like I *was* actually past it, that might be healthy. But it weighs me down still. Like I'm in chains."

"Tell me how I can help."

She smiles at me, a small lift of her mouth that sends a burst of hope through me. "Just by doing what you're doing."

"Is it too painful to ask how it started?"

She bites her lip before answering. The words gush out of her as she tells me about the first time she cut herself in the shower, how it became a habit soon after that. A terrible habit she couldn't break.

She shakes her head. "I know it's messed up. But it's been over a year, and I'd like to think I'm in a better place. Even if I'm not completely healed."

She tells me about an inpatient rehab program she participated in last summer. She tells me about therapy, about writing in her journal. When she seems to have nothing else to say, I finally speak. "I hope you know this doesn't change how I feel about you. If anything, it makes me love you more."

"Pity me more, you mean."

"No. That you shared your pain with me makes me love you more." I take her hand and lay it on my lap. When I slide the fabric of her sleeve up, she resists, starts to pull away. "Shhh." Though she lets me continue, her muscles strain beneath my fingers.

When the cuff is at her elbow, I raise her arm to my mouth and, beginning at her wrist, I kiss her scars. They are slightly rough beneath my lips, but because it's her roughness and her skin, I love them. I allow my mouth to travel over her marred skin, taking my time on each scar, wishing my lips could take away the pain she once felt in that spot—not only on her skin, but in her heart. When I reach the curve of the inside of her elbow, I give one last lingering kiss to her skin.

When I look at her face, tears are coursing down her cheeks. I don't release her hand, but instead trace my finger over the marks, still damp from my mouth. "You know what these are, right?"

"No," she whispers.

"They're marks of your pain, but they're also signs of survival. They closed up. They healed. They didn't end in the draining of your life."

She leans into me and sobs until my t-shirt is drenched with her tears. I hold her close and tuck my chin over her head, protecting, hovering, caring, vowing to never let her go. Never let her walk through such pain alone ever again.

When her tears finally subside and we fear we will indeed miss our opportunity to walk the sandbar back, we head down the gentle hill to the ocean. We walk the very top of the sandbar, the water lapping lightly on either side of us, the moon and the Milky Way giving off enough light to guide us home.

# Chapter Twenty

*If the lights stood, we were saved, otherwise our fate was only too
certain.*
~ Letter from Abbie Burgess to her friend Dorothy, 1856

## LANEY

I'm beyond exhausted by the time I take a shower and fall
into bed. With the lamp still on, I close my eyes. All I can
think about is Jason's lips on my scars. As if his love is
powerful enough to seal them up once and for all.

Never, in all the times I imagined telling him about my past,
did I imagine his response, his words.

*They're marks of your pain, but they're also signs of survival.
They closed up. They healed. They didn't end in the draining of
your life.*

Who talks like that? Who pulls such a beautiful metaphor out
of the wreck of what I've done?

I love Jason Rutherford. My only regret is having to wait until
tomorrow to tell him.

My phone dings and I scoop it up.

> JASON: Sweet dreams.

> LANEY: Thank you for tonight. I will never forget it.

> JASON: When can I see you again?

> LANEY: I have to work tomorrow night. Do you want to come over and look at the lighthouse before my shift?

> JASON: Um . . . YES.

> LANEY: 🩶

A contented sigh shudders through me—the shuddering, no doubt a leftover remnant of all my tears. I am drained, empty. And full all at once.

I put my phone on the nightstand and glimpse Abbie's journal beside it, a Post-It note on top with Nana's familiar scrawl.

*I am enjoying this! I think you're right, this really IS Abbie Burgess's journal.*
*Can't wait to talk to you in the morning but couldn't keep my eyes open any longer.*
*XOXO*
*Nana*

My heart warms at the thought of sharing this with Nana.

I'm torn between reading Abbie's journal and simply shutting off the light to replay Jason's kisses in my mind until I fall asleep. But tomorrow will be busy. My next chance to read Abbie's words won't be until tomorrow night. I can't wait that long to find out if Abbie's father will return after the violent storm.

With care, I pick up the leather-bound book and open it to find where I left off, settling in to read more of Abbie's thoughts.

*January 29, 1856*

> *Still no sign of Papa, but thankfully, the storm has finally ebbed, though the ocean still breaks fiercely against the Rock. I am not sure the oil will last for the lamps. I am not sure Papa will come. I am not sure if a ship with supplies will come and aid us in our hungry state.*
>
> *Lydia cooks, although she chastises me for my hovering, as I fear she will be too extravagant with our rations. As if that were possible! We are reduced to corn meal mush and one egg each a day. Mama spends much of her time in bed, although I am convinced it is the doldrums and not simply physical ailments that keep her there.*
>
> *She is worried that Papa was caught in the storm and that the mighty sea has swallowed him up forever.*
>
> *I am frightened of the same. But I push on to keep the lamps burning, to oversee our meals and Bible readings, to care for my four remaining hens.*

*February 4, 1856*

> *We saw sunshine today! The sea has at last calmed. We opened the shutters and enjoyed beautiful daylight in our home. Surely, Papa will come soon. We pray it is so.*

*February 7, 1856*

> *The Lord has at last answered our prayers.*
>
> *I was tending the lamps at dusk, fretting over the last of the oil I poured into the holders when I spotted a small light offshore. I finished my duties in the tower, lighting all the lamps whilst my heart kicked up a frantic rhythm at the*

*thought that the light could be Papa. I prayed with all my might, "Oh, please Lord, let it be Papa!"*

*The sun hovered just above the horizon, ready to say its final farewell for the night as I ran toward the ledge, watching with bated breath as the light drew closer and closer.*

*I felt it must be Papa.*

*"Ahoy!" a familiar bellowing voice sounded over the waters.*

*"Papa!" I jumped up and down on the ledge like a silly schoolgirl, joy filling my being. My sisters' squeals sounded behind me as they raced down the stairs, smiles wreathing their faces.*

*"Girls! Oh, my girls!" Papa called as he drew closer. He threw me a rope and I towed the boat up, my muscles strong from the hard work on the Rock the last two years.*

*When the dory hit shore, he hopped up, scooping all of us into his arms in one fell swoop. We buried our faces in the wool of his coat. Tears chased down my cheeks and Papa's voice wobbled with emotion when he spoke. "Oh, I feared for your lives, my girls. I have never felt so helpless to know I could do nothing, and with that storm battering this rock and you all. Tell me, how is your mother?"*

*"She's well, Papa!" Esther called, jumping up and down in place.*

*"Thank the good Lord." He turned to me, placed his hands on either side of my arms. His eyes shone. "Abbie, my girl. You kept the lights burning. There isn't a better sight, save for my family safe and sound. Well done, dear girl. Well done."*

*He hugged me again, and this time his embrace was all for me. "They never went out, Papa. God's strength did not fail me."*

*He kissed the top of my head before turning to Lydia, Esther, and Mahala. "How about you all help me bring this bounty into the house?"*

HEIDI CHIAVAROLI

*We cheered, rolling hogsheads of salt pork and salt beef, flour and whale oil, as well as coffee, brown sugar, rice, tea, peas, beans, fresh milk and fruit, all to the house.*

*When Papa was almost to the house, the door burst open and Mama flung herself at him, tears wetting her face. He kissed her good, then, and my face heated for I had never seen them act so.*

*But something about it was quite lovely too, as I glimpsed the affection they held for one another and how all their fears were now relieved. It made me ache for something, and yet I can't be certain of what.*

*Later that night, curled by the cozy fire and with the lights burning brightly with fresh oil, we regaled Papa with our adventures—the great billow that washed away the wooden chamber, how scary it was to scrape the windows on the catwalk, the rescuing of the hens, and the sleeping in the tower. After we finished, Papa told us that the old men in town said it was the worst storm they could remember. The Rockland waterfront was ruined and many ships had been lost at sea.*

*Mama's face paled. "Benji," she whispered.*

*Papa took her hand. "I saw him in Rockland after the storm. He is okay, Thankful."*

*We all held hands then and bowed our heads to give thanks to the Lord Almighty for sparing our family in the midst of the tempest.*

*April 4, 1856*

*The supply boat has come, and I am not certain what to make of the pile of mail addressed to me. Kindly notes and letters from not only Dorothy and other school friends, but from strangers as far as New York, all extolling me for keeping the lights burning during the January storm. A reporter had come to visit us last month and news clippings sit alongside the letters. A group of ship captains, their vessels guided by*

*Matinicus Light during the storm, sent me a silver bowl made by the Revere Silversmiths in Boston as an expression of their gratitude.*

*It is all quite humbling, and yet I only performed my work. The good work of keeping the lights. That is what I told the reporter, crediting God with seeing me through.*

*But it does not deter the letters from coming. I have even received a marriage proposal, of all things!*

*Lydia tittered at that. Mama beamed. Papa's face grew quite red, and he advised that I not bother sending a reply to my would-be suitor.*

*Last month, the Lighthouse Board came to the Rock. They plan to build new towers and install Fresnel lenses, which would make the lights brighter, so as to be visible as far as fifteen miles. They also spoke of an engine house and a steam fog whistle. I am happy the lights will serve sailors better, but I will miss the old towers and lamps.*

*June 9, 1856*

*A crew of men has come to stay on the Rock to build the new engine house. It is nice to have visitors and to keep them fed as best we can. They ask of our adventures this past January, and more than one of the younger men give me admiring looks.*

*Papa does not seem overly pleased, but Mama continues working on rugs and dishcloths for my hope chest. Though I cannot ignore the pleasant rush that fills me at the attentions of the men, it also alarms me. Is this why Dorothy is drawn to her parties? Do men look at her as some of these young men do me?*

*I am not certain if I want to grow up. Part of me wishes to tend the lights forever, to be Papa's assistant forever, and yet I fear—and partly hope—life may hold more for me.*

*October 12, 1856*

*Benji has come home! We are happy to have him as he has matured greatly these last two years. So much so, Papa has applied to the Lighthouse Board, requesting that Benji be appointed assistant keeper. They have accepted him, which gives him three hundred dollars a year in addition to more rations.*

*Though Benji is the assistant, he still allows me to light the lamps. I do not know what I would do without them. Part of me is covetous of Benji's position, though I realize it is not one given to a woman. And yet, why not? I have kept the light in one of the greatest storms this island has seen, and I have done it well.*

*Oh bother, I've half a mind to cross out those prideful last two sentences, Lord forgive me. I am grateful Benji is home and it is handy to have him run to the mainland for us instead of Papa.*

*August 17, 1858*

*I have been terrible about writing, but the completion of the towers is cause enough to write! The two towers are connected with a covered walk along with a frame house for any future assistants with families of their own. We all wonder if the house will prompt Benji to court a girl in town.*

*The brighter lamps are a blessing, but oh, how my heart quivered when the work crew cut down the old towers to the roof. They are now much-appreciated storerooms, but I cannot help but lament their loss.*

*September 28, 1860*

*Today, Lydia boldly stated that she hoped Lincoln wins the election. Our family belongs to the Democratic party, so a* win for Lincoln would result in us leaving the Rock, as a Republican would need to be appointed as the next Keeper.

My younger sisters, and even Mama, are ready for our time on the Rock to end. But I don't know that I could bear it. Papa says we could move to Vinalhaven. Benji talks of joining the Union Navy if war breaks out. I cannot bear to think of being separated. I cannot bear to think of leaving the lights.

*November 6, 1860*

Today, our fates will be decided. Papa said that a few fishermen in town would sail out within distance of the Rock after the returns are in. A white flag will indicate Lincoln won, a yellow for Douglas.

And so, we wait.

*November 13, 1860*

Today, we spotted a white flag offshore. In some ways, it does feel like one of surrender. Our time on the Rock will expire in March.

The girls are quite happy and even Papa seems quietly resigned. I try to be content.

Last night, while I lit the lamps, Papa accompanied me.

"I know you feel badly to leave this place, Abbie-girl."

I blinked away tears as I lugged a hogshead of fresh whale oil from the corner.

"Vinalhaven is beautiful. It might be nice to live on a small farm, to grow food out of the soil, to tend all the hens you'd like to your heart's content."

"I suppose so." But my words are not convincing. After scolding myself, I tried on a smile, for Papa's sake. "Yes, Papa. It will be lovely."

"You are apt to meet a fine young man in Vinalhaven. One you can build a life with. One who cares about you, and not only your heroic deeds of the past."

"Oh, Papa. I'm not sure I am made to be a housewife if there is no looking forward to lighting the lamps every morning and night."

He chuckled. "You are my daughter, through and through, dear girl. The lamps are in our blood."

But I am not certain even Papa understands me. This place is home. It is where my heart is. It will break me to leave it.

And yet, leave it I must.

*February 2, 1861*

My family is set to leave the Rock next month. But I will not be going with them quite yet.

On one of his trips into town, Papa met with the new appointed keeper. His name is Captain Grant and he has a brood of young sons ready to help him take over the light.

"I spoke with him about you, Abbie. Asked him if you might stay on for a bit until they become accustomed to the routine of things. Mrs. Grant will be happy to have your help, and you will be valuable in teaching them the ways of the lamps, and of the Rock."

I threw my arms around Papa. It would be bittersweet bidding my family farewell. But to see another springtime on the Rock eases the pain in my heart of leaving it forever.

*March 7, 1861*

I am alone on the island. It is a strange state of affairs. Papa, Mama, Benji, and the girls left for Vinalhaven yesterday and the Grants are due to arrive tonight.

Last night, I crept out onto the catwalk and allowed my tiny shadow to block one of the lamps. I listened to the waves lapping at the ledge. I breathed in the salty air and gazed on the waning crescent of the moon. I am glad to stay longer and

*yet it will be strange having another family live in our home.*
*It will be strange teaching them to tend the lights.*
*I wonder about Mrs. Grant and her sons. Will they think*
*me strange for doing the work of a man? I hardly care. My*
*duty is to the Light. I will teach them the best I can in hopes*
*that Matinicus Light will be well tended for many years to*
*come.*

# Chapter Twenty-One

*But if we hope for what we do not yet have, we wait for it patiently.*
*In the same way, the Spirit helps us in our weakness.*
*Romans 8:25-26*
~ Verse on Laney's birthday card from Nana,
Age 12

## LANEY

Jason's finishing off one of Nana's scones when the doorbell rings. Nana goes to answer it, and as soon as she's out of the room, Jason's wrapping his arms around me, nuzzling my ear.

"I missed you."

I giggle. "I missed you, too. Thanks for coming over." I pull back and strain to listen to the voices in the front room. "That sounds like Zack. I think he's here to finish the repairs."

Footsteps approach the kitchen and Jason rinses his plate and loads it in the dishwasher.

"I was just about to show these two down to the light." Nana says as she enters the room. "This is Zack, my honorary grandson."

Jason holds his hand out to Zack. "Nice to meet you, Zack. I'm Jason, Laney's boyfriend."

Zack grins good-naturedly. "Nice to meet you."

Nana squeezes Zack's arm. "This place would be in shambles if it weren't for Zack."

"Maybe you want to take a look at the light with us, then?" Jason says. "Charlotte says it needs repairs."

"Oh no, we've bothered Zack enough." Nana's mouth pulls downward.

"Actually, I'd love to check out the old light. It's been too long." Zack winks at Nana. "You know, as honorary grandson and talented carpenter, and all."

Nana shakes her head. "If only it didn't feel so hopeless."

Moments later, we're outside, walking over the pedestrian ramp. "I don't want anyone getting hurt." Nana wrings her hands as we approach the lighthouse.

I consider telling her I climbed to the top of the lighthouse the other day, and aside from my overactive imagination, it didn't seem all that unsafe to me, but I abstain.

"We'll be careful, Charlotte. We're professionals, after all," Zack assures her.

We reach the whitewashed light. Zack opens the door and Nana rips down the caution tape. "Be careful now." She allows the tape to fall, part of it still sticking to the threshold.

We enter the tower. The light from the door illuminates the red bricks surrounding us. A splash of daylight from the lamp room and the tiny window halfway up the tower casts itself downward brightening the stairs as our eyes adjust to the lack of light.

Nana points at the crumbled part of the stairs. "I honestly don't know what it would take to fix all of this, but I know it can't be cheap." She points at the large cracks along the red bricks. "The catwalk railing is also in need of repair."

Soon Jason and Zack are probing around every inch, talking

shop, using terms that I'm not entirely familiar with but that do indeed sound expensive.

When I move to follow them up the stairs, Nana grips my arm. "Please, Laney. Don't go up there."

I've never seen my grandmother this consumed by fear.

I place my hand on hers. "I won't go, okay, Nana?"

She relaxes. "Will you take me back to the house?"

She's not fooling me. My grandmother is fiercely independent and doesn't need anyone to take her anywhere.

She doesn't want me in this lighthouse. But whether it's due to the structural damage or something more, I can't be sure. "Of course."

I peer up the base of the stairs, where Jason and Zack have gone. "Nana and I are heading back, okay?" Zack has the flashlight of his phone out, shining it on the fissures along the tower.

Jason gives me a thumbs-up and a wink. "We'll be over soon."

When Nana and I exit the tower, her shoulders relax. "Your grandfather and I used to go up to the light every day. He'd be so disappointed to see how bad I've allowed it to get."

Huh. I thought maybe she didn't want to spend time in the lighthouse because of Mom or Mom's book or the disrepair of the structure, but maybe it's more than that. Maybe she doesn't want to spend time with bittersweet memories.

"That's not your fault, Nana. I can't imagine the upkeep of a lighthouse. And with business suffering, how can you expect to afford it all?"

"You know, I was holding my own before the pandemic. But that, coupled with the negative publicity, has just about drained me dry."

My mind spins. "Didn't the government give aid to small businesses affected by COVID?"

She nods. "I applied for some, but those applications were never my thing. You don't want to take a look at my paperwork, do you? Another set of eyes might do me good."

A nervous edge clings to my laugh. "I don't know if *these* eyes will do you any good." Especially at this point, so far removed from any such possible funding. But Nana's defeated look causes me to reconsider. "But I'd love to take a peek if you think it might be helpful."

And if for no other reason than letting Nana know she's not alone in this.

Once we're settled in the kitchen, Nana disappears into her office and returns with a file. After looking it over, I see she applied for an Economic Injury Disaster Loan but was denied. Possibilities peck at my thoughts, likely taking advantage of the desperation I feel on my grandmother's behalf.

Could I try to reapply for her, perhaps submit better documentation? And what about the town? This is private property, and yet visitors come every day to look at the lighthouse, placing wear and tear not only on the beautiful grounds of the inn, but on the pedestrian ramp and the lighthouse itself. Surely, there's a case to be made for the town taking on and preserving the historical role the lighthouse has to offer, Miriam Jacobs' memoir or not. Would enough people in the town—people Nana has known all her life, people who can vouch for her character—get behind such a proposition?

There must be a way to save the bed and breakfast, and the lighthouse.

"Nana, I have some ideas."

"I'm all ears, honey."

I tell her my scattered thoughts about approaching the town, about resubmitting an application for a loan.

"That all sounds lovely. I simply don't know where to begin. And I hate to put anyone out, especially you."

"I want to do this, Nana. Please, let me."

She stares at me a long time, those ocean-deep eyes piercing me, studying me. "If you can, I'd be grateful, honey. But if you can't, I understand. I don't know what to do, either."

"I think it's worth a shot. I'm not saying it will help any, but it's better than standing by and doing nothing."

Jason and Zack enter through the back door and join us at the kitchen island.

"Did you put the caution tape back up?" Nana asks.

Zack nods. "We did. And I'm wondering if I shouldn't put up something more deterring, more permanent, until the work can be done. Maybe a temporary fence at the footbridge. You're right, Charlotte. It's not up to code. I don't think anyone would get hurt, but it's not worth the risk."

"That's what I was afraid of."

"It can be fixed, though. Jason and I were talking, and we'd both like to donate our time in whatever way we can."

"Now, I can't let you do that. You know I can't, Zack. As much as I appreciate the gesture, I refuse."

"We're only estimating, but the materials alone will be well over one hundred fifty thousand. Never mind all the permits." Jason worries his bottom lip between his teeth.

"He's right." Zack takes the cup of coffee Nana offers him. "The stairs and the catwalk ramp need to be rebuilt. The interior and exterior masonry need repairing and repointing. That pedestrian ramp needs reinforcing. Some of the structural steel has to be replaced. Not to mention refurbishing the lantern room. I have no idea how much automating the light would cost. But Charlotte, it could be a real beauty."

Nana rubs her temples, sighs. "While I'd like nothing more than to make the Beacon shine again, even if I did accept the donation of your services—which I won't—the price of the materials is more than the Beacon can handle, particularly with business as bad as it is."

"I want to approach the town." My voice is confident, and I barely recognize it. "The Beacon has been a public attraction for as long as Nana's owned it and she's been bearing the cost of it all these years. I can't imagine the town wouldn't want to keep the light and take responsibility for it. That is history out there, and it's so much bigger than *Locked Light*."

Nana's bottom lip quivers. "It's not that I don't believe you're one hundred percent right, dear, but to go before the town, to humble myself by begging them to take the Beacon off my hands after they've read what Miriam wrote . . . I'm not sure I can bear it."

"This town loves you, Charlotte." Zack places a calloused hand on Nana's weathered one. "They know you. Whatever Miriam wrote, it doesn't matter as much as what you've already written on their lives by being the neighbor you are."

Aw, I really do like this guy.

"Zack's right. I read *Locked Light*, the author is my mother, and I still love you. I still believe in you. Whatever story there is, I trust there's more to it than what's told in that book."

Nana's eyes shimmer. "I don't deserve any of you." She grips my fingers. "But I'm so grateful the Lord has blessed me with each of you." One more squeeze before she releases and claps her hands together on the butcher block. "Okay then, what's our first step?"

"I'm going to look into this loan a bit further and see if there's any additional COVID funding that might still be available." I lift the file and tap it on the butcher block of the island, shifting all the papers into a single neat line.

Jason nods. "I can draw up plans for rebuilding the footbridge fairly quickly."

"And I can get an estimate drawn up for the rest of the work. I'll see what prices I can find for automating the light. And I'll talk to Mom"—Zack turns to me and Jason—"she works at the selectmen's office. I'll ask her what the process is to get a hearing before the town."

"I can't tell you how much this means to me." Nana's voice trembles with emotion.

"Sorry, I'm lost. Selectmen?" I ask.

"You know, government officers of a town?" Zack's brow furrows.

"Yeah, we don't have those out west. Guess it's a small New England town thing," Jason says.

"Whatever government officials we need to go through, we

will." I glance around the table at Jason and Zack who both nod, silent acknowledgments that they'll do everything in their power to save the Beacon as well. "We're not going to let you lose this place if we can help it, Nana."

WE'VE JUST ABOUT FINISHED our Save-the-Beacon meeting when Zack takes his leave. I glance at the clock on the wall and wince. "I have to head to work."

"I can give you a ride." Jason closes out the Notes app on his phone where he has a list of lighthouse repairs.

"Great. I'll go get changed." I scurry up the stairs and change into black pants and my standard long-sleeve white t-shirt. I look longingly at Abbie's journal on my nightstand. If I'm going to continue helping Nana serve breakfast in the morning to the few guests we do have, as well as help her apply for loans and other funding for the Beacon, I might not finish Abbie's journal anytime soon.

I sigh, then head back down the stairs. I give Nana a kiss on the cheek. Jason surprises me by enveloping Nana in a hug that dwarfs her with his tall frame. "Thanks for the scone, Charlotte."

Her eyes dance. "Boyfriend, huh?"

He's immediately flabbergasted. "Um, yeah, if that's okay. Should I have asked you first?"

She chuckles. "No siree. Our Laney knows her own mind, I should say."

We bid goodbye and walk into the heat of the afternoon. Jason starts the car and unrolls the windows. I fasten my seatbelt. "I'm excited about this. You think it will work?"

"I think we'd be fools not to give it a shot."

I grin at him. "Thanks."

He glances at me, his gaze caught on my own for a millisecond before he drags it back to the road. "For what?"

"For being in on this. For offering to draw up plans free of charge."

"How often does an architect get to work on something having to do with a lighthouse? Should be fun."

We drive in silence before the restaurant comes into sight. Jason taps his hands on the steering wheel. "So . . . Zack. He's a pretty good guy, huh?"

"He's amazing. Charlotte is lucky to have—" I catch Jason's crestfallen expression. "Wait. Are you . . . jealous of Zack?"

Jason clears his throat and straightens as he pulls in front of the restaurant. "No way. Just because he's good looking, owns a successful business, is the grandson your grandmother never had, and you look at him like he's the greatest thing since sliced bread . . . no, I see absolutely no reason why I should be jealous."

I unbuckle my seatbelt, lean over, and kiss him on the cheek. "I love you." I freeze as soon as the words are there, lingering in the air between us.

Slowly, as if stuck in tar, Jason turns to me. "You love me, as in I'm-cute-for-being-jealous-of-super-hot-contractor-dude, or you love me, as in I'm-the-guy-of-your-dreams-that-you-can't-imagine-living-without-and-you-want-to-be-with-me-forever?"

"Wow. As tempting as both of those far-reaching conclusions are, I'd have to say you land somewhere in the middle." I give him another kiss on the cheek, maybe to cement the fact that I really do love him, and then I open the door and walk toward The Lobster Bar.

"I love you too, Laney Jacobs!"

My skin prickles with pleasure while my face burns. I turn to see Jason, incredibly handsome in his light blue polo, a goofy grin on his face, standing outside his BMW, one arm resting on the roof of his car.

I can't help it. I run lightly back toward him and throw myself in his arms, kissing him soundly. A strident wolf whistle pierces the air and I pull away, but Jason's hands are firm on my waist.

"Could I interest you in another stroll to Bar Island tonight?"

I groan. "As much as I would love that, I don't think the boss will let me cut out early tonight. And if I don't get some sleep, I'll never be any use to Nana."

"What about tomorrow? Need help wading through potential funding for the Beacon?"

My skin warms. "Not quite romantic, but I'd love your help."

He runs a finger over my jaw. "If it means being with you, it's romantic enough for me."

# Chapter Twenty-Two

*But for some reason, I know not why, I had no misgivings, and went
on with my work as usual. For four weeks, owing to rough weather,
no landing could be effected on the rock.*
~ Letter from Abbie Burgess to her friend Dorothy, 1856

*March 8, 1861*

*The new Keeper and his family have arrived!*

*Last night, I had just finished lighting the lamps when I
spotted a tiny light offshore. Carrying my lantern, I went to
meet the Grants and their dory.*

*"Ahoy!"*

*"Welcome!" I called. Captain Grant used the force of a
great breaker to ease the boat close to land. He threw me the
rope and I tugged the five of them onto shore.*

*The oldest of the three boys hopped out, dark hair messed
from the wind of the sea, face red from the cold. But his brown
eyes sparkled. "I'm guessing you're the famous Abbie Burgess?"*

*My skin heated and I tugged harder on the rope, bringing*

*the dory onto the ledge with the next breaker. I hadn't expected the Grant boys to be men. I'm not certain Papa had either, or I wonder if he would have let me remain on the island. "I'm not apt to think of myself as famous."*

*He took the rope from me. "Allow me."*

*Though part of me thought to insist that I could do my duties as I always have, the more sensible part allowed him to haul his family with their heavy load of trunks and provisions closer to shore.*

*The remaining two young men hopped out, assisting their mother. Lastly came Captain Grant, tall and burly as a bear. He held a warm glove out to me. "And I reckon you're Abbie Burgess."*

*Mrs. Grant swept in. "It is so lovely to meet you. I cannot tell you how glad I am to have a woman's company here for the summer. And for you to show us around is truly generous."*

*One of the other boys about my age gave me a dashing grin. "Aren't you the girl who made the papers during that winter nor'easter several years ago?"*

*"That she is!" Mrs. Grant said. I couldn't help but stare at her—at her bubbly energy and enthusiasm, so unlike Mama's. But even as I managed the thought, it felt traitorous. Mama tried her best. What was more, she counted her blessings even though she often felt so poorly. "We can hardly wait to hear of your adventures firsthand." Mrs. Grant turned to her husband. "This is Captain John Grant and my sons. Our oldest, William." She pointed to the boy I had assumed to be my age. "And John Francis." A tall, husky young man with dark blond hair and a shy smile nodded his head at me. "And our youngest, Isaac."*

*The boy who'd first jumped out of the boat and who I had assumed to be the oldest was actually the youngest. While I had pictured a brood the same age as me and my sisters when we came to the island, it might make keeping up with the light easier to have four capable men on the Rock.*

"*Pleasure to meet you all.*"

"*Well, I dare say my wife is anxious to see our quarters. Would you be so kind as to show us to the house, Miss Abbie?*" Captain Grant and William heaved the first trunk out of the boat.

*After we had emptied the dory and settled the family, we sat down to a meal I prepared before their arrival. Fried potatoes and cod, roast mutton, biscuits, pudding, and two pies. I watched as the young men polished off every crumb of the food I prepared.*

"*Goodness. I hope you all survive with the rations allotted you.*"

*Captain Grant chuckled.* "*If there's one thing the Grants can do, it is eat. I don't discourage it since my boys work hard.*"

"*They have certainly grown in the right direction.*" *Mrs. Grant smiled at each of her sons.*

*Truth be told, it wasn't hard to settle into the warmth of the family. The Grants were much bigger people than me and my sisters. They were hearty and, I suspected, would fare well on the island. While I always felt a bit big and plain around my younger sisters and mother, I was dwarfed by the Grant family, even Mrs. Grant, who was tall and sturdy.*

*Mrs. Grant insisted I allow her to clean up after dinner. Unwilling to sit idle, I took my coat from the rack.* "*I best tend the lights.*"

*Captain Grant and the youngest son named Isaac stood.* "*Please, allow us to accompany you,*" *the Captain said.*

*I nodded and after they donned their warm wool coats, we climbed the north tower together.* "*The new towers are twice as tall as the old ones.*" *I was used to climbing the stairs by now and no longer felt the pleasant burn in my legs as I did when they were first installed. When we reached the top, Captain Grant bent over, huffing slightly. Isaac, however, lit with excitement as his gaze took in the lamp room.*

*It was a wonder to look anew at the familiar sight through* his eyes. I explained to them how the new first-order lamps cast a brighter light than the third-order we had used during the great storm five years back. I showed the Grants how I cleaned the lamps and filled them with oil, how I scraped the windows outside the catwalk so the beams might shine unimpeded by fog and haze. They accompanied me onto the catwalk and Captain Grant stared out to sea, breathing in the briny wind. I pictured him at the helm of one of his boats, alive with the surrounding sea.

When I demonstrated how to scrape the windows, I caught Isaac staring—not at the task at hand, but at me. I smiled and my face flamed as I cast my attention to the chore at hand. But I could scrape the windows without thought. And Isaac staring at me, the lights playing over his handsome features, caused a whirlwind of pleasant jitters to scurry inside my belly, where they spread throughout the rest of me.

What was happening? I was twenty-one years old. Now would I decide to be so desperate for attention that I became flustered at the first smile of a handsome young man?

I finished showing Captain Grant and his son the rest of my duties, explaining the new improvements that had been recently made and my schedule for lighting the lamps. When we reached the kitchen once again, we found Mrs. Grant drying the mutton pan. Captain Grant kissed his wife on the cheek, and I turned away, blushing at their display of affection.

"Well, Mother," Mr. Grant said, "it appears we're in good hands with Abbie here to teach us the ropes."

"I am happy to do it, sir." I bid them goodnight, sequestering myself in the smaller bedroom. Mr. and Mrs. Grant would take the larger one and the three sons would stay in the wooden building.

When I snuggled deep into the covers, I could not think of anything but Isaac Grant's well-formed face by the light of my beloved lamps.

*June 2, 1861*

    *Something has happened and I do not know what to make of it.*

    *I have spent the last month with each member of the Grant family. I cook and sew with Mrs. Grant, I have shown each of the Grant sons how to care for the lamps and the steam whistle. But it is Isaac who takes the most interest in the lights. It is Isaac, it seems, who has taken the most interest in me.*

    *Last week, we held a grand lobster bake after Mr. Grant and William hauled in a lovely catch. Isaac used driftwood to build a fire and I covered it with seaweed. Mr. Grant laid clams and lobsters on top and we added more seaweed before spreading a piece of old canvas sail over the entire thing, bringing forth a most lovely smell. Sitting there with all of them, something warm and cozy nestled deep in my belly.*

    *I do miss my family and find myself wishing we could all enjoy some time together on the island. Papa and Captain Grant would get on splendidly. Still, right then, I thought there was nowhere else I might like to be than here, with these people.*

    *The weather has turned, and the days grow longer, if not quite warm. I find myself by the shore at low tide, searching out shells and bits of glass, wondering of their origins. A fortnight ago, Isaac joined me.*

    *"What are you looking for?" He stood with his hands in the pockets of his coat, looking tall and strong with the south tower behind him.*

    *"An interesting story," I answered.*

    *His mouth twitched at my remark, and I wondered if he enjoyed my company as much as I did his.*

    *"Do you mind if I join you?"*

    *"Not at all."*

    *We searched the bits of rock and sand in silence, though my blood pumped wildly in my veins whenever Isaac searched the shoreline nearest me. He bent and picked up a pebble, bouncing it in his palm for a moment. "Do you think this has an interesting story?"*

*I leaned toward him to peer into his hand. There, a small white stone, nearly translucent, shone in the folds of his palm. It was pretty, although in truth, I had seen many like it over my years on the island.*

*"It could. What do you think its story is?"*

*Those brown eyes danced like one of Dorothy's twirling friends at a party. I would miss those eyes when it was time for me to leave come the end of summer.*

*But then those sparkling orbs became serious. "I think its most interesting story is yet to be told."*

*I tilted my head to the side, puzzled. "And how is that?"*

*"It is my hope that I can say I gave this small rock to Abbie Burgess the moment before I asked her permission to kiss her."*

*My heart pounded against my ribcage as I pieced together his words within my scattered thoughts, trying to fix them straight.*

*He held the rock out to me, dipped his head with questioning eyes. I nodded, my legs as sturdy as custard. He took my hand. With his other, he allowed the rock to slide from his palm to mine. Then, in the most tender of gestures, he closed my fingers around it.*

*Heat spread through me. Keeping hold of my hand, he lowered his lips to mine until their moist warmth touched my own in a brief but confident kiss that caused a foreign tingling sensation to take hold of my body.*

*When we parted, I felt both full and empty. And yet something else was on my mind and if I did not speak of it in this moment, I feared it would be forever lost.*

*"I do not wish to be loved for my name alone."*

*It was a bold statement, for Isaac did not state he loved me. And I perhaps shouldn't presume that my name alone meant all that much to him. Yet, I could not help but think of the proposal I had received by letter after reports of my adventures during the winter storm of '56. Did Isaac care for me because of my famous name or did he care for me because of me?*

*"Abbie," he breathed. "The moment I heard of your heroic adventures, I knew you were a special lady. But it was not until I met you, until I witnessed your tender and steadfast care of these lights, until I witnessed your radiant smile at the simple pleasures of life, until I heard your laugh at one of my dim-witted musings, that I came to care for you. It is not your name, dear Abbie, that has drawn me. It is your character. Your strength. The light inside you."*

*I could not suppress a smile as I released a pent-up breath. When he kissed me again, this time a second longer and, if possible, more enticing, I gave myself over to it, and to him.*

*What does this mean for my future? I am torn. I am to go to my family on Vinalhaven in two short months. And yet how can I bear to leave Isaac?*

*At one time it was the lights I found myself missing upon this Rock. Now, I find I will miss Isaac just as much.*

*June 10, 1861*

*It surprises me how, in this most trying and exciting time of my life, I long for Mama. We have had our differences. At times, I begrudged her for her weakness and fearfulness. And yet now, I long for her wisdom.*

*I have written her a letter and pray for a speedy response.*

*June 17, 1861*

*I am sure there has never been a girl more confused than I. Isaac has not kissed me again, although he has taken to joining me for walks on the shoreline when the weather is fair, which is often of late. We talk of Fort Sumter being fired upon, he tosses around the idea of enlisting and, inwardly, I beg him not to.*

*Outwardly, I state he is serving his country right fine where he is.*

*He also joins me in the lighting of the lamps. One time, Captain Grant assured me I need not worry any longer about the task of the lamps. I near burst into tears at the implication that I should not look after my beloved lights. I do not think Captain Grant noticed, but Isaac most certainly did.*

*I wonder, if when I leave, it will feel like leaving little Rufus all over again. For yes, I have come to think of the lights as my children. Fanciful, perhaps, but they have been in my charge for eight years—longer than even Rufus—and I feel a responsibility to them.*

*Yet I have known for some time that I must hand over their guardianship to Captain Grant and his sons.*

*Just yesterday morning, Isaac and I were up in the lamp room after we extinguished the lights for the day. I was wiping down one of the refractors when I noticed him studying me. Seemed he knew how to make me blush on a whim of late, and yet he had not spoken any more romantic language between us or tried to steal a kiss, which I very much hoped he would do.*

*"I find it hard to believe you haven't done this enough that you must watch me so closely." Lest the words sounded harsh, I tempered them with a smile. I was not a pretty flirt, but perhaps I could learn.*

*"I was thinking . . ." He bit his lip, an altogether endearing trait that caused me to imagine things I should not. "I was thinking that you love these lights."*

*"I do." For how could I deny it?*

*"You love them above all else, I dare say."*

*I cleared my throat, not liking in the least where this conversation may turn. My care for the lights was a good and worthy thing—was it not? Why would he imply it was anything but?*

*I stiffened my spine. "What are you implying?"*

He shook his head. *"I am only trying to puzzle you out, Abbie Burgess."*

*But while I am flattered he spends so much time pondering me, I am not altogether certain I will like the solution to his puzzle.*

*July 9, 1861*

*The supply boat has come, bringing with it a letter from Mama. Although I normally share such correspondence with Mrs. Grant, I slid away to the safekeeping of my bedroom.*

*Dearest Abbie,*

*I can scarce believe it has been four months since we left you on Matinicus. Child, my heart aches for missing you and yet I hope this time will ease the burden of leaving your lamps.*

*Papa has taken to farm life rather well, as have I. Regular walks into town seem to have improved my constitution. It appears the Lord is not done with me yet.*

*Lydia attends many parties and I suppose with how many suitors she has, she'll pick one soon enough.*

*Isaac sounds like a dashing fellow. My child, this life is but a breath in the grand scheme of eternity. God is working now and in all to come. I wish I could give you beautiful words of wisdom as you struggle for your place in this world, but it is all a matter of growing up and finding your own way. I will say this—love is never a waste. If you care for young Isaac, and he for you, then explore what that might bring to your future. Though selfishly I want you back with us, I know you may never be content without your lights.*

*Papa sends his love, as do Esther and Mahala, Miranda and Rufus, whom we saw last month. We are making plans for*

*Rufus to come be with us and look forward to you reuniting with him as well. Send word when you know your plans.*

*Love, Mama*

*I ran a finger over the slightly damp edges of the letter, wet from the sea air, aching for my mother's arms. Strange that I should feel so now that we are apart. Perhaps it is in parting that we understand our true feelings.*

*In parting . . .*

*I allow my gaze to wander over the line that haunts me with its truth.*

*I know you may never be content without your lights.*

*Was Isaac correct in saying I love these lights above all else? Was he correct in seeing that as a hindrance?*

*And yet, what was the setback about me loving this island, particularly if Isaac loves it as I do?*

*I fell to my knees by my bedside, the braided rug rough even through my petticoats and dress. I prayed. Prayed for the Lord's wisdom, that He might show me any error in my ways. I prayed that He search my heart, that He help me put Him above all else.*

*After a long time, I stood. And I knew what I must do.*

# Chapter Twenty-Three

*I screamed as loud as I could up in that tower, but no one heard me.*
~ *Locked Light* by Miriam Jacobs

## LANEY

I close Abbie's journal, wanting to read more but also wanting to pause and soak in this moment. Her struggle is not one I can understand, and yet, it is. Abbie loved the lights and the protection and safety they offered travelers, yes, but she also loved the purpose they gave her.

I try to think what I love that has given me purpose. But nothing comes to mind. I'm a wanderer. I went to college because I didn't know what else to do. I waitressed. Since reading Abbie's diary, I've toyed with the idea of journaling more seriously. But it hasn't gone much past that—toying.

The only real passion I had now was saving the Beacon and, perhaps, building a future with Jason.

Then it hits me. My purpose for the last six years has been to mourn my friend. It has been to punish myself for the part I played in her death.

Is that the purpose I wish to cling to for the rest of my life? Was that a purpose worthy of Maddie's memory? A purpose worthy of the gift of life?

I glance at the clock. One-fifteen in the morning. I am tired, half-asleep even. But in this hazy space, I see clearly.

Like Abbie, I slide to my knees by my own bedside and pour my heart out to God. The God whose presence I know through my grandmother's cards. The God who led me to this place in time.

The God who, I was quite certain, had not abandoned me after all.

The release is swift and sure. An emptying of myself that makes way for unfamiliar comfort and freedom. A long time later, after simply kneeling in the quiet, I climb back into bed, my cheeks wet with tears. There is a lot I do not know, but one thing I very much do: I never want to be without this feeling again.

THE BACK of Beyond Bookstore sign is turned to *Closed*, but I push open the door and it gives way, the familiar jingle of the merry bell announcing my arrival.

I almost didn't come. I am still tired from staying up late the night before with Abbie's journal. I spent the morning helping Nana with breakfast and chores, the afternoon tackling funding possibilities for the Beacon with Jason.

He stayed for dinner and although there was nothing I wanted more than to spend my precious night off with him and Nana, I'd told Kiran I'd be at writing group.

Now, I shift the bag on my shoulder. A bag that contains a new writing journal I'd purchased at Sherman's down the street, along with an assortment of colorful gel pens. More for inspiration than getting any practical writing done, I admit. "Hello?"

A creaking sound from the back of the shop precedes Kiran. She jumps the last step of a flight of stairs. "You came!" She's in a pair of overalls with a light blue t-shirt underneath. She throws her arms around me as if we're lifelong friends, and I make a conscious decision not to pull away.

"I told you I would."

She smiles at me, dimples accenting her pretty face. "We're upstairs. I think you're the last one, so I'm going to lock up quick." She walks to the door, turning the lock and shutting off the lights. Still, the midsummer sun illuminates the store. I catch a generous display of *Locked Light* on an end-cap.

"Ready?"

I force my gaze away from the blue and black cover of Mom's memoir before following Kiran upstairs to a decent-sized room with windows along the street. In the distance, I catch the shimmer of Frenchman's Bay. A rectangular table sits in the middle of the room. An elderly gentleman with a bowler cap presides at one end. Accompanying him is a middle-aged woman, a young woman who must be about my age, and a forty-something-year-old man with a laptop open and a pile of pages alongside it.

He must be the showoff, I decide.

Kiran introduces me to the group, and although I try to memorize names, I'm too nervous to do more than smile and sit, perched in a corner. The middle-aged woman whose name I think is Emily pushes a plate of cookies in my direction. "Help yourself. Banana oatmeal."

I thank her and place a cookie on a napkin beside me. She hands me a bottle of water.

"Okay, update time." Kiran turns to me. "We start by telling one another what we've written since we last met. It's a good way of keeping accountable."

I nod.

"John, why don't you go first?" Kiran turns to the older gentleman.

He waves a dismissive hand through the air. "Oh, you know me. I come for the social time and the cookies. I wrote an article, but it's going to need a lot more work before I submit it anywhere."

"You want to give it to us for next time?"

"I'm still editing. Maybe next month."

Kiran nods. "Okay. Emily?" She turns to the woman who offered me a cookie.

"I'm afraid Penelope didn't take any naps this week, so I've only managed a thousand words."

Kiran smiles. "A thousand words is great."

"Better than nothing." Emily shrugs. "Before you know it, she'll be in school and I'll have more writing time, but right now I'm just trying to enjoy motherhood—and trying not to be dead-on-my-feet exhausted while doing it."

"I'm off on Tuesday. You want me to come over and babysit for a couple of hours so you can get some writing in?"

Emily shakes her head. "Kiran, you are the sweetest thing. But it's not like I'm under contract or anything. Writing can wait."

"You're not under contract *yet*, but your book is good and if you start taking yourself seriously, you can really get somewhere."

Emily titters. "Well, maybe just an hour? Penelope would love to see you again. And I'll give you lunch?"

"Deal!" Kiran bounces from Emily to the young woman whose name is Myra. Myra says she's written a chapter in her romance novel. The man with the stack of papers said he wrote twenty thousand words.

Yup, I was right. He is the showoff.

"Well, you all know I write my stuff out by hand before I put it on the computer, so I'm not sure how many words I have, but"—Kiran places a filled yellow legal pad on the table—"I've been busy."

"Wow, Kiran, you must have written half a book this week. Are you almost done?" Myra flips through the filled pages.

"That's the thing about epic fantasies. They run long and I

never feel like I'm done." She shrugs and turns to me. "Laney, do you want to tell us what you're writing?"

I swallow down my anxiety, find myself focusing on Kiran's arms without realizing it. "I don't know yet. So far all I've done is a lot of journaling. I think I'd like to write about . . . a lighthouse."

"So, like a nonfiction project?" the man with the bowler hat —John—asks.

"Um, I don't know." Then I remember Mom's memoir, sitting on the bookshelf downstairs. Mom's memoir on all the bestseller lists. Mom on *Hello, America*.

What am I thinking? I can't write about a *lighthouse*.

I clear my throat. "Actually, it's probably a stupid idea."

Emily places her hand on my arm. "No idea is stupid. Right, Kiran?"

It strikes me how Kiran might be the youngest person here, but she is clearly the leader. She has confidence, a sort of peaceful knowing about her that I envy.

"That's right," Kiran says with a firmness that brooks no room for argument. "You want to hash it out here? We're great at brainstorming."

The man with the stack of papers nods. "That's right. This group is the reason I have any ideas to begin with."

Okay, maybe I jumped to conclusions about him. Apparently, he can be humble.

But I'm already shaking my head. There's no way I can spill the hazy pittance of ideas I do have onto these near strangers. "Thank you. Maybe next time?"

"Okay, does anyone else want help brainstorming?" Kiran looks around the group but they all shake their heads. "Okey dokey, then. We'll share our critiques about Myra's chapter and then get to writing."

I listen as the group gives positive and constructive feedback on Myra's chapter—a chapter with a lot of steamy romance. She takes their comments well, making notes and thanking all of them for their time.

Kiran takes out a fresh legal pad as she speaks to me. "Now, we usually spend the next hour writing. It's the only time some of us get. We're flexible of course, but the general rule is no cell phones, no talking, no distractions. We just work."

"Okay. Great."

The room settles in silence and I open my brand new journal.

I have a weakness for beautiful writing journals. In fact, I have a small pile of them in one of the drawers back at Nana's.

But because of their unmarred beauty, part of me fears whatever I write in them won't be good enough.

I pick up my pen, my gaze landing on the crisp sleeve of my thin, long-sleeve t-shirt. It hits me then that my creative thoughts aren't the only thing I'm hiding.

My scars itch and I scratch at them above my shirt, longing to push up my sleeves or wear a loose-fitting t-shirt like the one Kiran wears. These people obviously see her scars. And yet, they respect her as their fearless writing leader. I wonder if they even see her scars anymore.

Could the same one day be true for me?

I open the journal to the first page, knowing what I will write. It will be fiction, but maybe too, it will be a way of healing.

I put my pen to paper and write the first line, more journal entry than fiction. I don't care. I simply write.

*They are with me wherever I go, but I'm trying not to be defined by them. I hope that I am more than the story they tell. I pray I am more than my scars.*

"YOU WERE PRODUCTIVE TONIGHT." Kiran stuffs her yellow legal pad in a bag that sits on the chair she occupied. Everyone is gone, save Emily who packs up the remaining cookies.

I slip my bag onto my shoulder. "I think I did get some inspiration."

"Good. So, does that mean you'll be back?"

"I think so."

"Yay!" Emily cheers. "Another writing person to add to our little society."

I laugh. "You guys make it difficult for me to think writing isn't a good idea."

"Writing is always a good idea." Kiran zips the bag and gives Emily a hug goodbye, confirming the time they'll meet the next day.

After Emily goes downstairs, Kiran shuts off the lights and we follow. Just as we hit the landing, the bell above the door jingles with Emily's departure.

"You're a natural at this, huh?" I ask.

"What?"

"Being in charge, leading, writing." Everything, it seems.

"Not that I'm critiquing your word choice, but . . . I'm critiquing your word choice." We laugh. "Natural is not at all what I am. More like I faked it until it felt natural." She points to two chairs not far from the large window in front of the store. Outside, the sun has slipped below the horizon, but light still fills the sky, coloring the dusky evening with oranges, pinks, and purples.

Maybe it's the beauty of the colors or maybe it's the flow of thoughts still lingering in my head, but I remember a random moment with my mom. A good moment. I had been eight or nine and we'd been laying on the hammock on the back porch of our rundown apartment. No guys came that night. Mom was relaxed, or maybe drugged, but I didn't understand any of that and neither did I care about anything but my head in the crook of Mom's shoulder, staring at the setting sun.

"It's going away," I said.

Mom stroked my arm with her fingertips. "It's not going anywhere, baby. We're the ones who are turning. The sun always stays in one place."

I remembered how at school I learned that the earth moves

around the sun, and the moon around the earth. She's right.

"I wonder how come we always say, 'The sun is rising' or 'The sun is setting' then?"

Mom smiled, and I noticed how pretty she was without all the makeup she usually wore. "Because we're human and we think everything revolves around us."

Kiran's voice breaks into my thoughts. "You want to sit a few minutes?"

I nod. Once we sit, Kiran brings her legs up beneath her and snuggles into the overstuffed armchair. I cross my legs at the ankles.

"So, did you tell him?"

She could use a lesson in subtlety, but I'm not about to be the one to give it to her. "You mean Jason? About . . . " I gesture vaguely at my arms.

"Yes, Jason. Your *lobster*. Did you tell him?"

Now, I know what she's talking about, at least I think I do. But I want to be sure.

"Can we just back up a little here? How did *you* know, again?"

"I told you, pain spots pain. And why else would you be wearing long-sleeve shirts when it's hot as Hades outside? Never mind running in and out of that restaurant. I know how sizzling it can get in those kitchens."

I wonder if what I've been hiding all this time hasn't been so hidden after all.

"I told him."

She raises an eyebrow at me. "You did? Wow. Have to admit, wasn't sure you would, at least not so quickly."

I shake my head. "You act like you know me. I don't get it."

She shrugs. "I see myself in you, I guess."

But I could never be so carefree and confident as the woman in front of me. Could I?

"When did you . . . start cutting?" I force out.

"Sophomore year in high school. My dad left me and my mom. I felt different from all the other girls in school. Weird, I guess. I liked to write and be in my own world. I wasn't athletic, I didn't understand boys. One night my mom got in a car accident. She had major swelling in her brain. They didn't think she'd make it. I called my dad, but he never came home."

She shifts in her seat. Though she appears comfortable with the telling of her story, I don't miss the faraway look in her eyes. "She was in the hospital, unstable, for weeks. I'd never felt more alone in my life. I didn't have family I was close with. Not many friends. I felt like God had given up on me. *I* gave up on me. One night, I took a razor blade and just started cutting. I have no idea how it happened. I don't think I'd ever even heard of anyone doing that. It was just a crazy kind of instinct, I guess. And you know what? It helped. It took my mind off everything around me. Made me numb."

I blink back tears. "I—I understand."

"Eventually my mom did come home from the hospital, and after physical therapy, she got better. But I didn't stop cutting and she didn't notice, which made me feel even worse. My mom had been out of the hospital for a couple of months when my aunt and cousin came to visit. My cousin's the one who saw what I was doing. She told my mom and my aunt, and they got me help." She gestures to herself, up and down. "You may not be able to tell by looking at me, but this here required a hefty investment in rehab and therapy sessions."

I laugh. "I don't know that I'd put it that way, but aside from your scars, I'd never be able to tell you've been through so much."

A soft smile curves her lips. "It's a never-ending journey. How about you? What happened?"

I tell her about Maddie. A little bit about my sordid history with my mother, Nana's cards, my breakup with Jason. My struggle to get through college, my time in rehab and therapy, my trip to Maine. "Only, I'm not healed yet. Not like you."

She shakes her head. "There will always be a part of me that hurts. But I have to choose to move forward each day, to believe God is not finished with me, that the best is yet to come."

The best is yet to come. I like that. In fact, wasn't that the sense I'd gotten last night as I knelt at my bedside and prayed?

"Thank you," I whisper.

She leans forward. "Can I ask you something?"

I shrug. "Sure." She's a near stranger, but there're few people I've been more open with.

"Why do you hide your arms?"

I shift in my seat, feeling her probing dark gaze drilling into me. Seeing everything I've been trying hard to hide for so long.

"Isn't it obvious?" How can she sit there and judge me? Just because she's gotten past her scars doesn't mean I have, or ever will.

"You're embarrassed. Ashamed by them."

"Yeah, of course I am. Not to mention the fact that they're ugly."

Kiran presses her lips together. "I guess it's all in how we see ourselves. How we define ugly."

"Okay . . ."

"So, when I started thinking of my scars not as a symbol of how broken I was but as a symbol of all I'd conquered, I started seeing them differently."

A symbol of healing. Hadn't Jason said something similar?

"I believe a God who heals sees our scars differently than we do. He's got a few of His own, after all. And they're not signs of pain and death, they're signs of victory."

Part of me wants to argue. One can't compare the scars of Christ to my own self-inflicted wounds. But another part—the part that knelt at my bedside last night and handed over everything to a God bigger than me—wants to search out the meaning behind Kiran's words.

Could my painful past be the very thing to open up a new way forward for me?

It's impossible. It's improbable.

And it's causing a wellspring of hope to burst up within me.

# Chapter Twenty-Four

*During this time we were without the assistance of any male member of our family.*
~ Letter from Abbie Burgess to her friend Dorothy, 1856

*July 11, 1861*

*I have shared my plans with Captain and Mrs. Grant. I dare say I have broken Mrs. Grant's heart, as she has greatly appreciated my company and had hope all would turn out differently.*

*My own heart is also breaking. But deep down, I know I cannot stay. I will leave for Vinalhaven. I will leave my beloved lamps to see if I can find who I am without them.*

*I try not to think of Isaac, of what could have been. I never assured him I could care for him more than the lights. I cannot say it until I am sure it is true.*

*Tonight, I found myself up in the lamp room at twilight, lighting the wicks. I can perform the task without thinking and it's comforting, a ritual. Removing the glass chimneys from the lamps, lighting a candle and holding it to each of the fourteen wicks until a soft flame rises up. Sometimes, I light each lamp with a prayer.*

*One for the sailors who pass its light.*

*One for Papa, then for Mama, and for each member of my family.*

*For Captain Grant and Mrs. Grant and their sons.*

*I always allow Isaac his own light.*

*It satisfies something within my soul.*

*I was praying for Isaac, for wherever the Lord should place him, when I heard the footsteps. At first, I resented them. This was to be my last time lighting the lamps. I looked forward to the sacred time.*

*But then the object of my prayers appeared at the doorway and I fumbled with the matches. "Isaac."*

*His face was red and his fists bunched at his side. "Mother says you plan to leave tomorrow."*

*I nodded. "Yes. I think it time I join my family at Vinalhaven."*

*His mouth grew firm. It was difficult to reconcile with the softness of his kiss only a few months before.*

*"I will take you tomorrow."*

*I swallowed. "I thought your father—"*

*"I'm perfectly capable of sailing a dory to Vinalhaven."*

*"I believe you are. I only thought . . ."*

*"What did you think, Abbie? That I wouldn't want to spend every minute I can with you?"*

*I gulped down my emotion. And then he was gone.*

*We leave tomorrow morning. I'm not certain my heart will pass the test, either of leaving Matinicus or of leaving Isaac.*

*July 13, 1861*

*My spirit was sodden with grief yesterday morning as I*

watched the twin towers on the Rock fade into the horizon. I would likely never see Matinicus Rock again, unless I made a visit to the Grants, which Mrs. Grant begged me to do. But I am certain it would prove too painful, on more than one account.

Yes, I will miss the lights. More so, I ached at the thought of saying goodbye to the man beside me. As difficult as it was to bid Mrs. Grant farewell, as difficult as it was to watch my beloved lights disappear into the sea, it would be one hundred times more difficult to stand on the shores of Vinalhaven and watch the ocean swallow up Isaac and the dory.

The realization provided a measure of relief. How foolish that I should find it so, and yet all this time I wondered if my mad obsession with the lamps had rendered me incapable of real love. And here, now, what a liberation to find it not so.

Yet, what would I do? Throw myself upon the mercy of Isaac? Tell him I loved him more than the lamps?

"I'm sorry, Abbie." Isaac searched the far horizon where the twin towers had melted into the sky. "I know you will miss them." He checked the compass and the bearings he had been given for Vinalhaven.

"I will. But I will miss your family more."

He raised an eyebrow, a sad grin pulling at the corners of his mouth. "My mother, you mean, I suppose."

"I mean you." The words came out bashful and soft, were likely swallowed by the wind. Yet if I could be brave in the face of the fiercest storms, if I could keep the lights burning in the towers, I could be brave now, in love. In illuminating my feelings toward Isaac. "I can live without the lights if I must. I'm not sure I can live without you."

The moment the words passed my lips, I doubted the speaking of them. Was I foolish to declare such things when I was trapped on this boat with him, unable to escape and still a good two hours away from Vinalhaven?

Isaac's face twisted, and for a horrifying moment I

*thought he might cry. "I think the wind must be playing tricks on my ears. I thought I just heard you say you love me."*

*I released a pent-up breath. He did still care for me! I gave him a small smile. "Not in so many words, but yes, Isaac. I do love you."*

*"Then why, Abbie Burgess, are you leaving?"*

*"I could not think of another way to show you that I could say farewell to my lights."*

*"And farewell to me also?"*

*"I hoped to write you when I reached Vinalhaven. I thought some distance and time might prove my sincerity toward you."*

*He slid across from me in the boat, scooping my hands into his own. The sun shone bright on the water and I squinted to see his handsome face.*

*"Last month, I planned to travel to Vinalhaven to speak with your father." He grimaced. "But doubt consumed me. I wondered if you tricked yourself into caring for me. If I was only a means for you to stay with the lights. If one of my other brothers had shown interest, then perhaps you would settle for him."*

*"Oh, Isaac!" I could not help myself. I threw my arms around him, nearly rocking the boat. Slowly, his arms came around me. "The last thing I am doing is settling for you. I love you. I love how you take your work seriously yet make time to notice the beauty of your surroundings. I love how you help your mother and how you speak of God as if He were right in the room. And yes, I love that you love the lights, that we have that in common. It is not something many share, but I am grateful to share it with you."*

*He pulled back from me, lowering his lips to mine in a kiss as sweet as honey and as promising as rainclouds on the horizon during a long drought. I sank into him and boldly deepened the kiss, thrilling at his eager response, at his hands moving up and down my arms.*

*We did not do much talking the remainder of the boat ride, but when the shores of Vinalhaven appeared, we parted and giggled like schoolchildren. "I take it you have no objections to me speaking to your father this very day to ask for your hand in marriage?"*

*I smiled, my insides alight with joy that could rival the most powerful Fresnel lens. "No objections at all."*

I pause after reading Abbie's entry, for it seems a fitting way to honor the couple's happy reunion. I am glad Abbie found love, that she could visit her family and yet ultimately go back to her beloved lights on Matinicus Rock.

I flip to the next entry, disappointed that it's dated an entire five years later.

*July 9, 1866*

*I can hardly believe it has been so long since I have written. I am quite ashamed. But the years have been full and busy, and with the war finally ending, I wish to record the gratitude I feel on this day.*

*Isaac and I were married five years ago next month. We still make our home on Matinicus with his parents. We are blessed to do so. Can you believe I have two children with a third on the way? Little Francis is the spitting image of his father, so tall and sure of himself. Malvina takes after me for how petite she is. We wonder what the Lord will bless us with in this next babe.*

*Though Isaac insists Malvina is still too young, I took her up to the lights last night. Her eyes grew wide as we climbed the stairs. When she saw the brightness of the lights, she put her hands out as if to shield her eyes. I wonder if she will take after Lydia in her distaste for life on the Rock, but secretly, I hope she takes after her mother and falls in love with the lights.*

*And yet time has proven that while I love the lights, my*

*heart is capable of loving those precious to me all the more. I*
*am content in my husband's arms each night and write often*
*to Mama of her grandchildren. Strange that I should miss her*
*so, but falling in love and becoming a mother myself, I hold a*
*new appreciation for Mama. Not that I must agree with all*
*her choices, but I cannot help but think of how she struggled,*
*how she clung to the Lord in her wrestling. She still battles her*
*worries and physical ailments. I trust that if God does not free*
*her of her infirmities in this life, He will in the next.*

*I must get dinner on the table.*

Again, the entries are sparse, and I read through them quickly.
I read of Abbie's third and fourth children, Miranda and Harris. I
read of Abbie faithfully tending the lights of Matinicus for nearly
ten more years until finally, in 1875, she became Isaac's assistant at
Whitehead Light in Spruce Head, Maine.

*April 15, 1875*

*I cannot pretend it is a joyful occasion to bid my lights a*
*last farewell. After twenty-two years with them, they are a part*
*of me. I don't know how to start my mornings without extin-*
*guishing their brightness or how to end the evening without*
*willing them to life.*

*Yet, we have a new adventure ahead of us at Whitehead*
*Light, where I will, for the first time, be appointed Assistant*
*Keeper alongside my Isaac as Keeper. It is an honor. And I*
*trust that the Lord is not finished with us. Perhaps even the*
*greatest adventures are still in the making.*

*May 27, 1875*

*Word has come that Papa has died. My heart grieves,*
*compounded by memories of him on Matinicus and the loss of*
*my lights there. I try not to mourn too much, to put a smile on*
*for my children and husband, but I long for bed in a way that*

*reminds me of Mama when fear and anxiety took over her spirit.*

*I pray to the Lord, trusting for Him to give me strength as He has done all my life. When I climbed the stairs of the old north tower during that gusty storm, when I slid out onto that catwalk. When I told Isaac of my love.*

*In these hardest of times, when my husband pulls me close to comfort me, I ask myself what is the brave thing to do? It is to move forward and lean on His strength, and not my own.*

*August 8, 1881*

*My husband is a good and proper hero! I have always known it, but now it seems the world will know it as well.*

*Yesterday morning, I was sick in bed with the summer influenza. Isaac reported a dense fog had lifted when he spotted some men being swept out to sea, their overturned yawl not far from them. The violent waves seemed more than they could handle. Isaac sent Malvina with the alarm to the keeper of the life-saving station, but though the girl can run like the wind, the station is a mile away, so Isaac and thirteen-year-old Frank launched their own rescue boat.*

*To think on it now gives me chills for the danger they took upon themselves in the saving of those souls.*

*So fierce was the sea past the lee of the light that my husband threw over both sail and ballast simply to keep the boat from swamping. The nearest way to the drowning men was across a dangerous shoal, but witnessing the men's struggles, his heart prodded him through it. When he reached the sufferers clinging to their capsized boat, he and Frank, spent from rowing, lifted the near unconscious men into their own boat. The poor men were exhausted and numb with cold, their trousers chafed off and their skin shredded with ghastly wounds by the abrasions of their struggles in keeping hold of the boat's bottom.*

*Isaac steered his boat back while Frank tried to calm the
men. I am most beholden and grateful to the Lord for sparing
my husband and son, and for allowing them to help the men.
Had it ended differently, I am not sure what I would do.*

*At the same time, I am angered to have been helpless in
bed with all the commotion. I wonder if Mama felt this way
during the great storm in '56. As a young girl full of energy, I
sometimes thought she wanted to be ill. But yesterday, that was
the farthest from the truth for me. I wonder, now that I am
getting on in years and a mother myself, did I really understand my mother at all?*

*Now that I am feeling better, I told my handsome
husband I would fix up a feast for him tonight. He is merci-
lessly teasing me that there's more than one hero in the family,
now. I should say so! He and Frank deserve every morsel of the
turkey I will fix.*

I turn the page to find a printed paper from a book, although
the copy does not show the title. Still, it is a photocopy, something
modern. Did my grandfather place it here when doing his own
reading of the journal?

I unfold it, creased and slightly yellow from being pressed
within the book for all these years.

*The Grants lived on Whitehead Island for fifteen years,
during which time Keeper Grant served as a teacher for the
children on the island besides performing his light-keeping
duties. Clara Norton, the daughter of the keeper of the life-
saving station, which had been established on the island in
1874, later wrote about the island school.*
*"In the winter months we had school for about six or eight
weeks, taught by Captain Isaac Grant at the lighthouse. He
was a wonderful man. He used the very finest language and
taught us so many things that aren't usually taught in school.
It was understood that we were never to show up for school on*

*inspection days, as Captain Grant was supposed to always be
busy with his work and was not supposed to teach school."
Keeper Grant received a silver lifesaving medal and some
notoriety, though not as much as his wife received, when he
rescued two men on the morning of August 7, 1881.
https://www.lighthousefriends.com/light.asp?ID=778*

It warms my heart to know that Abbie had chosen such a kind and worthy man. I think of Jason, of how he's grown in the last six years. Of his encouraging words on Bar Island, of his desire to help Nana, of his refusal to work on Mom's home because he knew it didn't sit right with me.

I place the journal on my nightstand and shut off the light. No matter how much I want to keep reading, my eyes are heavy and I have more loan applications to sort through the next day, not to mention paperwork to file at the selectmen's office. I'm going to need all of my strength to continue facing the daunting task of helping Nana save the bed and breakfast.

I snuggle into my covers. Jason will be by my side. That fact alone makes me a bit less fearful to take on the job.

# Chapter Twenty-Five

*Maybe everyone I love will end up leaving. I wish you were here to talk some sense into Laney. I miss her so much it hurts.*
~ Letter from Jason to Maddie found in a bottle washed up onshore two years after her death

## JASON

I save the document on my laptop and sit back, rolling my shoulders and neck. I've spent most of the day drafting plans for the Beacon footbridge. I'll email them to Zack, who will use them to get a final estimate for the work to be done on the lighthouse.

My time with Laney this past week has been spent filling out forms for loans and COVID grants. We have helped Charlotte submit a proposal to the town. Zack has been by the bed and breakfast several times, taking measurements and calculating materials. We will be ready for the town meeting that takes place in another week.

I hope, for both Charlotte's sake and Laney's, that we can convince the town to take over the care of the lighthouse.

My phone rings. I glance at it as I scoop it up, seeing my Dad's name light up the screen. He's been strangely silent since I refused to work on Miriam Jacobs' home, and although I've been busy, I can't pretend that silence hasn't bothered me.

"Hey, Dad."

"Jason. Good to hear your voice, son."

"You too, Dad. How's California? How's Eva?"

"She's deep into wedding planning." He chuckles, but it comes out strained.

"I'm happy for you guys." I am surprised to find I almost mean the words.

"Thank you." A moment of awkward silence fills the line before he speaks again. "I have to admit, son, I'm beginning to wonder if you've run away for good."

My turn to laugh. "Not for good, although this trip is giving me a lot to think about."

"You found her, then."

"I did."

"How is she?"

"She's . . . different." And yet that was an entirely inadequate way to describe Laney. For yes, she was different. But she was also more authentic, more deep-thinking, more vulnerable and caring. If possible, I love her even more knowing these new parts of her. "I love her, Dad."

"Wow."

"Listen, I know you must be worried I'm gone so long, but I'll be back soon. By August, anyway. There's a town meeting a week from Monday that I'd like to stick around for."

"Already into town politics and everything, huh?"

I grit my teeth. He's hurt. He's scared I'm not coming back. He's scared I'm leaving him like Mom did all those years ago.

I remind myself of these things so as not to be angry. After all these years, I can honestly say that Mom leaving was not my fault.

"Dad, I don't know where the future's going to land me, but if it happens to be on the east coast, I could work remotely, right? Fly in for meetings once a month—no biggie. I might be able to build up our clientele out here."

"Unless you refuse to design the jobs when they're offered."

Ouch. Low blow.

"I'm trying here, okay? Laney and her mom have a lot of stuff to wade through, and me getting involved by building her a house that Laney feels is a jab at her grandmother is more than I'm willing to dive into right now. I don't want to hurt her. Can't Joe do it?"

"He can, but you're the guy that does our best work."

My insides stir at the compliment.

"And you're already there on the company dime, I might add."

The bile in my mouth turns sour. "I'll reimburse the company," I grind out.

He sighs, and I hope it signals the end of the conversation. "Susan's very impressed with your ideas. She loves the plans."

"Good."

"She's recommending us to one of her friends in New Hampshire."

"Nice."

"Jason—"

"Dad—"

We give stilted laughs. "You go," he says.

I suck in a breath. "I hate disappointing you. I hope you know that. Even if my future puts me out here, I'd only be a plane ride away. It's not like I'd be leaving for good. I'll never leave you, Dad."

I hear him sniff hard into the phone. "I know that, son. Thank you. I'm sorry I'm being bullheaded. You being away, me planning the wedding . . . well, it's given me some time to think. I wasn't there for you like I should have been all those years ago. I was too consumed with my own pain. I was a lousy father, Jason. I'm sorry."

His words pull at long-buried emotions. He's never addressed that time in our life so directly. Although I start to tell him I understand and that it's okay, I realize that brushing off his statement will never allow the broken parts inside me to heal, either. My scars aren't outward, like some of Laney's.

I'd told Laney her scars were a symbol of survival, of strength. But I'd never seen my inner lesions the same way. Now, Dad is tearing at them, trying to open them back up. And maybe that's what needs to happen for them to heal.

"I was twelve, Dad. And my mom had left. But you know what? I didn't feel like I just lost Mom, 'cause I lost you too. I had no one. I was so alone." I'm horrified to find unchecked emotion building in my throat. Had I ever cried, aside from the day Mom left? I'd certainly never cried over my father's inability to be a dad.

"Jason," my father chokes on my name before he curses. "If I could go back and do it all over again, I would. I was selfish, son. I was drowning in my pain so much I didn't see yours. I wish I could change things, but I—I can't. All I can do is ask for you to be patient with me going forward. I am so sorry. I'm trying to change, son. Eva, she helped me to see I need to."

Eva did? Maybe I should be thanking my future stepmom instead of growing bitter that my dad was moving on without my real mom.

"Let's move forward without all this mess hanging over our heads, okay?" I clear the remaining emotion from my throat.

"That sounds like a plan. Hey . . . you still like to fish?"

"It's been a while, but yeah, I do."

"How about if we go together when you get back? I'll charter something. Deep-sea fishing."

"Dad, I don't need a charter trip. Having you with me by the lake is enough."

I hear something muffled on the end of the line. When Dad speaks, his words are a croak. "Okay. It's a plan."

We say goodbye. When I push the red button to end the call, I flop back on the bed of the hotel room, a foreign space in my chest when I breathe. It feels . . . good, right even.

Maybe there's still hope for me and my dad after all. Maybe there's still hope for me.

# Chapter Twenty-Six

*The nature of secrets is that they long to be kept and long to be told all at the same time.*
~ Josie Martin in her debut novel, *Where Grace Appears*

## LANEY

Jason turns right off Route 1 into a long driveway with a stained-glass sign that reads *The Orchard House Bed and Breakfast*. A large but adorable old Victorian with a wide wraparound porch sits at the top of the hill, a barn-turned-gift-shop behind it.

Jason whistles long and low.

"This place is great." From the backseat, I peer around where Nana sits in the front seat.

"I met Hannah years ago when we worked at the Bar Harbor Inn together. She and her children have made quite a business out of this place. Her five-course breakfasts are an inspiration."

After we park, Jason helps Nana out of the car. My breath

catches as he stands, incredibly handsome in dress pants, a button-down shirt, and an ocean-blue tie. As Nana leads us toward the sprawling grass at the bottom of the apple orchards where white chairs have been set up before a birch arbor, Jason takes my hand and leans down to whisper in my ear.

"Did I tell you that you look gorgeous?"

I squeeze his arm. "Only about a hundred times when you picked us up. But thank you. You're not so bad yourself."

I am wearing a white and green sleeveless dress that hooks around the back of the neck and flows just below my knees. In my bedroom back at the Beacon, I'd stared at the full-length mirror, trying to imagine going to the wedding in the flattering dress. It was certainly warm enough to do so. But the mere thought made my skin clammy and sent my heart hammering. I might as well imagine showing up to the wedding naked for the amount of anxiety baring my arms cost me.

In the end, I settled on a thin, nearly shear white coverup. It flowed, opening in the front. If one were to look hard, my scars could be seen, but I figured it was a good first step toward bravery.

"Charlotte!" A pretty woman in her late twenties with long chestnut hair runs toward us, her emerald green dress swishing at her knees. She envelops Nana in a hug that nearly lifts my petite grandmother off the ground.

It strikes me then how Nana holds an entire life of which I'm unaware. These people who love her, who most certainly communicated with her over the years in more than cards and letters, have always been there for her.

I swallow, trying to keep my needless jealousy at bay, thankful for Jason, strong and steady at my side.

Finally, the woman pulls back. "How are you?" She notices me, then, holds her hand out. "You must be Laney. I'm Josie."

But before I can answer, a boy of about four with dark hair comes barreling toward Josie and throws his arms around one of her legs. "Mommy, I can't get my buttons straight."

Josie smiles, releasing my hand to tussle the boy's hair. "And this is my son, Amos." She kneels beside him, undoing the crooked buttons on his white button-down shirt. He wiggles beneath her ministrations.

"Josie is Hannah's daughter. She's the one who spearheaded this bed and breakfast idea. She runs the book shop. And she's an author herself." Nana introduces Josie to Jason and the two shake hands.

"Mom's getting ready inside. She asked me to send you up when you got here. Honorary maid-of-honor duties or something."

Nana laughs, and she looks ten years younger. It's the first time I'm forced to consider if owning the Beacon is what's best for her. Here we are, planning and plotting to save it, but what if it's weighing Nana down, causing her undue stress?

"Well, then, this old maid better hop to it. I'll catch up with you two in a bit?"

I nod, and after Nana walks away, I turn to Josie, recognition swallowing me whole. "Wait. You're not the author Josie Martin, are you?"

She grins. "That's me. You've heard of my books?"

"Heard of them? I've read them all, I think. I love your stories. Your characters jump off the page."

She smiles. "Thank you. Actually, here's my inspiration now." A tall, handsome man carrying a small boy who is the spitting image of him approaches. "This is my husband, Tripp. Tripp, this is Charlotte's granddaughter, Laney, and her boyfriend Jason."

We all shake hands and in the next few moments, I'm surrounded by more people—all Hannah's children and their spouses and children. I lose count, and I lose track of who is who, but one pretty blonde woman named Amie compliments my earrings and a rugged man in a wheelchair holding an adorable newborn in a frilly pink dress strikes up a conversation with Jason.

I hardly know these people, and yet they're welcoming me as

family, simply because I'm an extension of Nana. It's a happy swarm of smiles and small talk. Not for the first time, my heart aches as I wonder what it might have been like to grow up in a large, close-knit family like this one.

We head toward the chairs set before the birch arbor. Amie holds the hand of her husband who is also Tripp's brother, and gestures to the somewhat small wedding crowd. "Neither Mom nor Kevin wanted a big to-do. Just family and close friends. But we couldn't skimp on the food or dancing, of course. It's a celebration, after all."

We find our seats just as beautiful music sounds from the back. I glimpse Hannah, a pretty lady in her fifties with light blonde hair and a brilliant smile that resembles Amie's. She wears a simple cream dress and kisses a young man, whom I guess to be her only son, on the cheek before starting up the aisle to her soon-to-be-husband. Kevin looks at her as if she is the only one in the world, and I find my eyes smarting though I barely know these people.

A teenaged boy with long, dark hair stands beside Kevin while Nana stands beside Hannah. The reverend speaks on a passage in the Bible on love, and it's so inspiring that I promise myself I'll look it up later tonight.

After the bride and groom have kissed and walked down the aisle together, we're directed toward the barn, where tables are set up among tasteful champagne-colored decorations. I meet more of the family, including Hannah's twin grandchildren, Davey and Isaac, and a great-aunt whom I understand gifted the Victorian to Hannah. Josie also introduces me to a woman about my age named Luna, who explains she is the daughter of Hannah's late husband.

My mind is spinning when we find our seats.

"You okay?" Jason asks.

"This is a *big* family. Makes me wonder what it would be like if I grew up like this. You know, with solid parents, with brothers and sisters."

Jason leans toward me and taps my nose. "But then you might not be my Laney Jacobs, and I happen to think you're perfect just the way you are."

I roll my eyes. "You need to stop being so perfect yourself."

I know things won't always be this easy nor this carefree in our relationship. But for right now, I'm enjoying every minute of it.

Before long, Nana joins us, and the bride and groom enter the barn to a raucous round of applause.

When we sit, we find Hannah's oldest daughter Maggie at our table, along with her husband Josh and their four children. We talk about the bed and breakfast and the twins' baseball season. Josh and Jason strike up a conversation about house renovations. We're served Italian bruschetta with tomato, garlic, basil, and extra virgin olive oil followed by filet mignon and herb jumbo shrimp. The cake is light and white with a heavenly raspberry cream filling that Hannah made herself.

By the time the dancing begins, I'm stuffed and content. When the first note of Ed Sheeran's "Perfect" plays, Jason tugs my hand and leads me onto the dance floor. I place my hands on his solid shoulders. His fingers rest on my waist, tightening, bringing me closer.

The scent of his cologne drifts around me and I allow my guard to come down, begin imagining what it would be like to dance with him forever.

When the "Cupid Shuffle" comes on, we laugh at each other's missteps. Jason takes a couple of turns around the dance floor with Nana. I sit at the table as Maggie bounces her newborn son, Maverick, on her lap.

She smiles at her husband dancing with their petite daughter. When her gaze moves to Jason and Nana dancing to John Legend's "All of Me," she says, "He really likes you."

I blink. "Jason?"

"I can tell by the way he looks at you—he's all in."

"We've been through a lot. We used to date in high school but just reconnected. It's . . . kind of complicated."

"Oh, I know about complicated."

I cock my head, waiting for more but not wanting to voice my question lest she think me nosy.

Maggie lowers her gaze. "Josh's late wife, Davey and Isaac's mother, was an addict. We've had our own share of wading through the difficult."

"Oh, wow. How'd you get through it all?"

She tilts her head, her sparkling earrings framing her pretty face. For the first time, I glimpse her resemblance to Hannah. "Lots of grace, being quick to forgive, praying like crazy."

I nod. "Sage advice."

Maggie bites her lip. "How is Charlotte? You know, with everything going on with your mom and all?" As soon as her words are out, she winces. "Not that it's any of my business, but Mom's been worried. I guess we all have."

"It's okay. You guys are like family to her."

"We love Charlotte."

"She's . . . strong. I admire her for that." How else to answer Maggie's question? "She hasn't said a whole lot about it. I think she's trying not to speak poorly of my mother, but something tells me there's more to Mom's memoir than she's written. I just don't know what." I pause. "Did you read it? *Locked Light?*"

Unlike me, this family has known Nana all their lives. Surely, they can share in some righteous anger on my grandmother's behalf over what Mom has written.

Maggie shakes her head. "I haven't, but Josie has. She had a few choice words about it." She cranes her neck to where Josie is giving her younger son—Eddie, I believe—a drink of water at the next table. Maggie calls for her, and Josie walks over as she watches her son run onto the dance floor, jumping like a kangaroo around the dancing couples.

"What's up?" she asks.

"Laney was asking if I read *Locked Light.*"

"That garbage? Not that I'm into burning books, mind you, but when it comes to our Charlotte's well-being, her daughter can take her pack of lies and shove it—"

Maggie places a calming hand on Josie's arm. Shakes her head.

Josie's face turns the color of the red geraniums hanging on Nana's porch. She laughs, a nervous, anxious sort of laugh that doesn't jive with what I've seen from her so far. "Oops. That's your mother I'm talking about, isn't it, Laney? I tend to get carried away. Forgive me."

I force a strained smile. "I have my own struggles when it comes to the woman who raised me, but I was curious about your reaction to Mom's memoir. I appreciate you not holding back." I laugh nervously before continuing. "So . . . I mean, none of it can be . . ."

I'm at a loss for words. I feel like an ungrateful and undeserving grandchild to even ask the question. But Nana hasn't outright denied Mom's claims. She even hinted she'd made mistakes in the past. What did that mean? Mistakes in parenting?

"True?" Josie shakes her head. "Absolutely not. Charlotte is the most caring, just woman I know. I nearly threw up when I read what *Locked Light* accused her and your grandfather of doing." On the dance floor, Josie's youngest son falls and is stepped on by a guest's high heel. He begins wailing. "Excuse me. Mama duty calls." And even though Tripp is already scooping their son off the floor, Josie stays her course, wrapping her arms around both her husband and son as they all dance together, little Eddie's tears fast disappearing.

"My sister is loyal to a fault." Maggie looks after her younger sister.

"To a fault?"

The oldest Martin sibling presses her lips together. "I mean, once she loves someone, she has trouble entertaining the possibility that they might be human. That they've likely made mistakes, too."

"So, you think my grandmother could have locked my mother in a lighthouse?"

Maggie's mouth pulls downward. "No. No, of course not. Forget I said anything. I haven't even read the book. I have no idea what I'm talking about. Just know this—we love Charlotte. We'll do anything at all to help her."

# Chapter Twenty-Seven

*Then he got up and rebuked the wind and the waves, and it was completely calm.*

Matthew 8:26
~ Verse on Nana's birthday card to Laney,
Age 16

## LANEY

The ride home is a silent one. It was after ten when we started out, and although Hannah insisted we stay the night, Nana was equally adamant that we return home. She had one couple booked at the inn, and she needed to be sure to be back to serve breakfast the next morning.

When we drive onto Mount Desert Island, I peer at Nana sitting in the backseat. "You awake, Nana?"

"Mmm-hmm."

"Did you have fun at the wedding?"

"I did. Nothing makes me happier than seeing my very best friend happy."

"Do you wish you lived closer to Hannah and her family?"

"No, honey. I wish to live right where I do."

"Okay." I look out the window at the dark night, at the street-lights illuminating paved road ahead.

"I love Hannah and her family, but the Beacon and Acadia, are my home. You, Laney, are also my home."

I sink deeper into the passenger's seat of Jason's BMW. "You're my home, too, Nana."

And I mean it. I can't imagine going back to California. I can't imagine leaving Nana. This place, this woman, have become my home.

I glance at Jason. He returns the look, winking at me in the near dark. I'm filled with relief. He understands. He gets me. We'll figure this out—our future, however it might look.

Ten minutes later, we turn into the driveway of the Beacon. "What in the world . . . ?" Flashing lights of two police cars sit in the drive, sirens silent.

I crane my head to glimpse the house, a million possibilities floating through my mind. A fire. Did I leave the stove on? Or perhaps a break-in. Maybe one of our guests had a heart attack.

"Oh my." Nana's voice wobbles from the backseat where she takes up praying aloud in fast mutterings.

Jason pushes down on the gas pedal, pulling into a spot close to the house and beside one of the police cars. We open our doors, and Jason helps Nana out of the backseat. "Don't worry, Char-lotte. The house is still standing. We'll figure this out."

The glow of a large flashlight in the back of the property catches my eye. Two policemen stand before the yellow caution tape of the footbridge, shining their lights on our beautiful lighthouse.

Red graffiti letters remind me of fresh blood on pale skin. The Beacon is bleeding and tarnished with ugly words and my heart aches to see her so.

A strangled cry rises within me at the same time Nana must

also see the ugly words, for a gasp of horror escapes her own throat.

The first letter, an F, is the darkest of red, spelling out the most horrid of words, followed by a myriad of cruel names, some having to do with someone who abuses children, and some that do not.

Beside me, Nana crumples to the dewy grass. Jason and I rush to either side of her. My heart seizes, both with fear for Nana's health and anger over whoever would commit such a heinous crime.

"Nana, it's okay. It's going to be okay." My words are as much for my grandmother as for myself.

"Let's get her inside." Jason takes the bulk of Nana's weight. She nods, walking on unstable legs with us to the side door of the house where two more police officers shine flashlights on a broken window.

Jason takes over, introducing himself, shaking their hands. "What happened?"

"Vandalism on the lighthouse and a brick thrown into this window. It doesn't appear that anyone entered the house."

"No one's hurt?"

"No, sir."

"Can we go inside?"

One of the officers, a short, stocky man, nods. "We'll be in momentarily to speak with Ms. Jacobs."

Once inside, we flip on additional lights and lead Nana to her favorite chair in the sitting room. "I'm okay," she keeps saying. "It was just a fright is all, I'm okay. I'd like to speak to the officers."

"They're coming inside in a moment. Can I get you some tea?" I force strength I don't feel into my words, saying my syllables fast to hide my own trembling emotion.

She shakes her head. "Can you check on the Lavaliers, honey? I'm sure they must have been frightened."

Two officers enter the sitting room, standing a few paces in front of Nana. "The Lavaliers were your guests staying here, is that right?" the stocky officer asks.

Nana nods. "Bob and Nan Lavalier, that's right."

"I'm afraid they felt compelled to leave. They were the ones who reported the crime."

Nana closes her eyes in defeat. "Of course. I'm just glad they weren't hurt."

I'm glad too, although I can't help but see Nana's ledgers in my mind's eye. She will reimburse the Lavaliers for their stay tonight, of course, and no doubt the remaining two nights they'd booked for tomorrow and Monday.

She will need to replace the window, paint the lighthouse.

But all that is the least of our problems. For who will want to stay here after word gets out?

"Do you have any idea who is behind this?" Jason stands with his hands on his hips, facing the officers, and I've never been more grateful for his presence.

"I'm afraid not. Ms. Jacobs, do you have any cameras on the premises? Any other guests staying here who might have seen something?"

Nana shakes her head. "No."

"Well, we're doing all we can. Unfortunately, finding our perpetrator might be a shot in the dark without cameras or witnesses."

"I understand." Nana's voice is tinny and small, not like her own at all.

"We'd like you to walk through the rooms before we leave. Just make sure anything isn't out of sorts."

"I thought you said they didn't enter the house?" I take a step closer to Nana, as if to protect her from all this.

"We don't believe they did. But better to get your feel for it as well." This time, it's the other officer who speaks. He's younger than the first, tall and lean with thick-framed glasses.

I think of my room and the few belongings I've brought to

Nana's. I have nothing of value. My waitressing tips in a jar. The journal.

Crazy to think anyone would bother with either, but still, I turn and jog up the stairs.

I push the door open and scan my room, my gaze falling on the jar of tip money, seemingly untouched. I look to my night-stand. When I see the leather-bound journal as I've left it, my muscles wilt into a puddle of relief.

"Laney, what is—" Jason stops at my threshold.

"Just had a moment of panic." I caress the cover of Abbie's journal. "Of course, it's still here."

He swallows, nods. "I'm going to look in the shed or maybe the guest house for something to board up that window until Zack can replace it. In the morning, I'll head to the hardware store for some paint and see what I can do for the lighthouse. I hate to think of you both having to look at that for even a day."

"Thank you," I whisper.

"I think I should stay for the night, if it's okay with Charlotte."

"That might be a good idea." Yes, I'm a woman of the twenty-first century. Strong, capable, and all that. But I can't deny how having him here will make the rest of the dark night more bearable.

After we walk through the remaining rooms and the police officers ask us a few more questions before taking their leave, Nana agrees that Jason should stay the night. He finds a sturdy piece of plywood in the shed and does his best to board up the window. Although Nana encourages him to take one of the guest bedrooms, he insists on staying downstairs in case the perpetrators dare return. Nana makes up the couch for him and fetches an extra pillow and quilt. After assuring us for the tenth time that she's okay, she claims she needs a good night's rest and heads up to bed.

Alone in the sitting room, I softly kiss Jason goodnight,

allowing his steady arms to wrap around me. After a long while, I finally tear myself away and climb the stairs to my room.

Once I close the door behind me, I peel off my dress, take off my makeup, brush my teeth, and slip into a tank top and shorts. I fall into my bed, listening to the now familiar sound of the waves coming through the screened window. I inhale the faint scent of the sea, brewing and swirling beneath me, ever constant.

I think of the lighthouse, as bruised and bloodied as my own arms had once been. Its beauty has been stolen. I can only blame my mother.

I pick up Abbie's journal with a determination I haven't known since before Maddie's death. I'd almost forgotten what a fighter I used to be. How else had I grown up under Miriam Jacobs' roof?

But all the fire went out of me after Maddie died. I turned inward, like a shriveled insect, dry of passion and joy and hope and all things that made life worth living.

Not anymore.

Nana needs me. She needs me to fight for the Beacon, to stand in the place of a daughter who has betrayed her in the worst way.

I will not cower in fear. I will seek out hope and good. I will refuse to let my grandmother down.

# Chapter Twenty-Eight

*Though at times greatly exhausted with my labors, not once did the lights fail. Under God I was able to perform all my accustomed duties as well as my father's.*
~ Letter from Abbie Burgess to her friend Dorothy, 1856

*June 5, 1890*

*It seems life, like the shore, and like the waves, is ever shifting. Ever changing. I would like to think at the age of fifty that I have learned to accept that, but I'm not certain I always do.*

*We are leaving Whitehead. Frank is to be married next month, and for this I rejoice as June is a lovely girl. The younger children are readying to make their way in the world as well, and Isaac is prepared for a change. A change that is a bit too far away for my liking, but one that I have agreed to, on the condition that we take my eighty-four-year-old mother.*

*Now, this is one adventure the Lord will surely have to give me strength for! Miranda feels ill of late and Lydia is too far away to care for Mama. I have volunteered the duty.*

*Esther and Mahala still have children underfoot and the fact remains that something of an unfinished quality still stands between me and Mama. I long to spend her last days with her.*

*The Beacon Lighthouse is north of here, and yet Isaac tells me its rooms are many with plenty of space for all of us to live in comfort.*

*My mother is not long for this world and the ache in my lungs tells me that perhaps I am not, either. Perhaps this will be our last lighthouse stop on our way to the One true and eternal light.*

I stop my gaze from moving farther down the page. Instead, I pause at this most wondrous discovery, this piece of history leaping out from the pages of this old journal.

Abbie came to this place. She lived here, could have slept in these very rooms. I blink, determined to read on.

*June 28, 1890*

*We are settled on a piece of land known as Mount Desert Island, in a town called Eden. It is on a beautiful coastal stretch of land and mountains. I did not expect such beauty. It is the first time we are to be keepers on the mainland, and I quite think my aching legs are content with it.*

*Mama has made the adjustment well, although she has made me promise that she should be buried alongside Papa in Vinalhaven after she meets her Maker.*

*Isaac has taken to lighting the lamps at night and I rise to extinguish them. After all these years, we work well together, and sometimes, when we sorely need alone time, we meet one another up in the lamp room. I find it romantic and a comfort to discover that I am not too old for such things after all.*

*I also find it fitting that I should again turn to my journal after so many years of neglecting it. With the changes in both our travels and the children growing as they are, I want to turn back and puzzle together my life and the meaning of it.*

*Mama was having a good day yesterday and I sat with her for a spell. I asked her about Rufus. To my surprise, she shed tears. Although she insisted she made the right decision, she grieves that time. She'd felt certain something horrid would have happened to my little brother had he gone to Matinicus.*

*I am beginning to understand that my mother grieves a lot.*

*"I spent too much of my life trying to hide my fears and wounds in the comfort of tonics and the solace of my bed. I should have lived better, Abbie. And yet, I did one thing right —for look at you, my dear girl. You are everything I wish I could be."*

*I cried horrid tears at that, shaking my head and protesting that I was not as good or brave or full of faith as she thought. I struggle often. Even now, I doubt God's goodness, that He will allow me to see my children grown, that He will allow me to love my husband into an age as old as Mama's.*

*"Remember, my Abbie. This is not all there is. The Lord, as old as I am, is not finished with me. He will continue the good He began. I am a small part in the redeeming of His creation, but a part nonetheless. There is more to come. The most breathtaking part is yet to come."*

*I lean into her words and I seek the scriptures all the more until they fill me with a light as brilliant as the one that shines out my bedroom window and splashes onto the ever-changing seas.*

I want to know more. But Abbie's words are more rushed than in her youth, as if she's sensing she does not have a long stretch of time. I finger the few pages left in the journal, coming to terms with the fact that one way or another, my time with Abbie will also end soon.

But, she was here, in this house, in the light outside my window.

I wonder if Abbie and Isaac shared a bed in this very room, or perhaps in the Lavender Room, which has a fireplace. It gives me chills to think of it. To think that right now, with the loss of the Beacon's keeper's logs, I am the only one who possesses this piece of good news. I can hardly wait to tell Nana and Jason in the morning.

I continue reading. I see a quiet contentment in Abbie's life as she works alongside Isaac to care for the Beacon and care for her mother. She seems to find the faith of her youth after the heart-to-heart with her mother. I drink in the passages about everyday life filled with joyful contentment.

It isn't until August of the following year, 1891, that Abbie's mother dies. Abbie writes:

*Mama has moved on. And yet, I find myself happy for her. She awaits a new and perfect body with our Lord and I cannot help but remember her oft-spoken words about the hope of eternity, of a better life. I have shared my thoughts with Isaac and we have spoken to the monument mason near Vinalhaven, preparing a fitting headstone.*

I remember the picture of a gravestone I first found in the box alongside Abbie's journal. Throwing off my covers, I creep as quietly as I can out of my bedroom and up the attic stairs, the old bound book in hand. I hesitate. Did the police check the attic?

I remember Abbie climbing the stairs of the old north tower in the midst of the great nor'easter. I cling tighter to her journal, pushing myself upward. I climb the stairs and switch on the lights, slipping into my mother's old room, where I last stored the box of memorabilia.

I sit cross-legged on the floor and dig past the multiple books to the photocopied page of Thankful Burgess's gravestone.

At first, I can't see anything unusual about it aside from the comma I first noticed. The headstone is shaped like an arrowhead with decorative markings on top and reads simply

THANKFUL,

It states she was the wife of Samuel Burgess. That she died on August 24, 1891 at the age of eighty-five.

I note again the comma after her name, how it struck me as peculiar the first time I saw the picture.

"Laney?" A loud whisper comes from below.

"Up here," I whisper back. I must have woken Jason with my middle-of-the-night sleuthing.

Creaking footsteps chase themselves to the top of the stairs. When Jason appears at the threshold of Mom's bedroom, I wave, scrunching my neck into my shoulders. "Sorry. I thought I was being quiet."

"I'm sleeping light tonight, I guess."

He wears the same pants he wore to the wedding, sans his belt, and a white undershirt that defines the muscles in his arms and chest. I swallow down the pull of attraction that comes with knowing he was sleeping only feet below me.

I cross my arms in front of myself, hiding my forearms and covering my chest, allowing the picture of Thankful's headstone to fall between us. Jason lowers himself beside me, legs crossed before him. "So, what's up?" He looks around the room at Mom's old bed, at the bookshelf now empty save for the V.C. Andrews novels.

"This was Mom's old room. I was reading Abbie's journal, and I remembered something from this box."

"Your mom's box?"

I shake my head. "My grandfather's, I think. It was in the attic."

He leans over and peers at the photograph. "A gravestone?"

"Abbie's mother's. I just read about her mother dying. It was . . . touching. Abbie had a lot of pent-up feelings toward her mother, but I think she forgave her by the end. Here—" I start to reach for the journal but tuck my hands back in front of myself.

"Laney . . ." My name is soft on Jason's tongue. He allows it to linger between us until I lift my gaze.

"What?" I ask, even as I realize all we're not saying. Even as I realize that the one word is almost a dare. Will he ask me to bare my arms to him? To bare my entire self, scars and all, beneath this fluorescent light? Will he ask something of me I am not ready to give?

"Do you want me to grab you a sweatshirt? Not that—I mean, you're beautiful. Hear me? You're beautiful, every inch of you." He's taking in my face, my neck. His eyes are traveling downward and I quiver beneath his gaze. But not from fear. This time, with desire.

Slowly, I unfold my arms and hold them out for him to see. There is no hiding them by darkness and moonlight this time. The revealing lights overhead leave nothing to the imagination regarding the mutilation of my skin.

"I stand by what I said. I'm telling you, woman, nothing will change my mind."

I lean forward to kiss him. He pulls me close. Every nerve ending within me is tingling. I wrap my arms around him, drawing him closer until I'm drowning in how good he feels. Just when I think there's no stopping, though, he pulls away with a groan.

"I have a feeling this isn't what your grandmother had in mind when she agreed I could stay the night."

I blow out a long breath. Of course. To think I could forget myself so entirely in Mom's old bedroom only hours after those ugly words were painted on Nana's lighthouse . . .

"You're right. Besides, I came up here for answers."

He nods his head at the journal. "What were you going to show me?"

This time, I pick up Abbie's diary, trying to see my scars as Jason might, but only cringing at how boldly and unapologetically they plaster themselves across my arms. Every time I seem to make progress in how I view them, I'm forced further out of my comfort zone, forced to face the fact that I'm not as far along as I thought in my healing.

"Look." I point to the last entry and read Abbie's words aloud.

"'Mama has moved on. And yet, I find myself happy for her. She awaits a new and perfect body with our Lord and I can't help but remember her oft-spoken words about the hope of eternity, of a better life. I have shared my thoughts with Isaac and we have spoken to the monument mason near Vinalhaven, preparing a fitting headstone for her.'" I look to Jason. "Doesn't that sound like there should be something special about Thankful's gravestone?" I turn to the picture. "But although it seems beautiful, I'm not sure I see anything unusual."

"Can I take a look?" Jason holds his hand out for the photograph. I give it to him. He leans away from me to better capture the light as he squints at the photograph. "Her name was Thankful, huh? That's pretty neat."

"I agree. From what Abbie writes, she did try to cling to gratitude, despite the struggles she went through. I feel like my grandfather must have had a special interest in her grave if he had the picture."

He taps the old photograph. "You know, I can't believe it, but I think my archeological studies are finally about to prove their worth."

I tilt my head to the side. "What do you mean?"

"I used to study gravestones. I guess I was obsessed with what people long ago might have been buried with, how they died, how they lived, what—and who—they left behind."

"Okay."

"I did some research because I remembered seeing a lot of periods after the end of surnames on headstones."

"What'd you find?"

"Nothing definite. Seems, depending on where you are in the

country or the world, it could mean several things. Sometimes it was a symbol that marked the end of a family line. The end of a lineage. So, if the last male patriarch died, they might put a period at the end of his surname on his gravestone."

"That makes sense, I guess."

"But sometimes it was put after females, so that *wouldn't* make sense. Another explanation I found was simply that a period showed a great loss to the family. The finality of death."

"Sad." Sadder still to think of burying my own mother, how I wouldn't feel the need to put a period at the end of her name. I wince at the unnecessary thought. Nana, on the other hand . . . but I don't finish that consideration for the mere imagining of Nana's headstone has me swallowing back emotion. "Did you learn anything about commas?"

"Yeah, actually. But first, did you notice the spacing in the letters of her name?" He points to the banner with Thankful's name, his finger falling on the *T* and tracing to the right until he reaches the *L* at the end of her name. The *T* and the *H* are quite close, the *T* tucked up close to the beginning of the banner. Gradually though, the letters gain space between one another until the *L* and the comma are visibly farther apart than the letters at the beginning of Thankful's name.

"Seems the mason didn't figure out his spacing very well."

Jason chuckles. "Not a chance. Maine has the most abundant granite quarries this side of the Atlantic. These guys were the finest stone carvers around. Also, they used stencils to ensure accuracy. I believe the spacing is on purpose. In fact, I've seen it before."

"Okay, Smarty Pants. What does it mean, then?" I lean closer, genuinely curious as to what explanation he might give.

He again points to the beginning of Thankful's name. "The closeness at the beginning of the name with a gradual stretching out tends to denote a message. A message that says, in the grand scheme of all eternity, life on earth is but a brief passing, spanning out as we enter old age into a boundless eternity. The comma is a symbol of death, but not a death without hope. No doubt, Thankful was a believer in God and of the afterlife. Because of that, death is not a period—it's a comma. A breath, a waiting, a symbol of more to come. God's work continues."

I'm enraptured by his words. Not only by the intellect and surety of them, but by Jason speaking about things of faith that meant so much to Abbie, mean so much to Nana, and are coming to mean very much to me also. I stare at the comma. "God's work continues," I whisper, remembering Thankful's words to Abbie.

*There is more to come—the most breathtaking part is yet to come.*

Then Kiran's words about the scars of Jesus.

*They're not signs of pain and death, they're signs of victory.*

Not a period, but a comma.

Goosebumps travel over my skin. It's almost otherworldly, as if the God of the universe is trying to get *my* attention with Abbie's words. With Jason's acceptance. With Nana's love, starting all those years ago with the cards she sent me.

Could my past, my scars, be the beginning of something more and not the horrible end I've been drowning beneath for so long?

"It's pretty cool, actually." He places the picture in front of us.

"It's *really* cool. Thank you, Jason."

"My pleasure."

"You regret not going into archaeology?"

He shrugs. "Sometimes, but you know, drafting the Beacon footbridge, trying to keep true to its history and structure, that's almost as satisfying as researching gravestone iconography. Maybe I ended up where I'm supposed to be, after all."

I can't stop staring at him. Funny how love has helped me forgive all that was harbored between us. Do I wish that long ago day ended differently? With everything in my being. But this summer has convinced me that holding onto pain doesn't honor Maddie, either in her life or in her death. What honors my friend is love, hope, peace, and forgiveness.

For the first time, I don't think of Maddie as a fallen sparrow. I think of her as one caught by the Light. And now, that Light is helping me to look forward.

Jason points to Abbie's journal. "Looks like you're almost done."

I open the page to where I stuck my grandfather's photocopies. There's one entry left. "Will you read it with me?"

"I'd be honored."

I open the journal to the last entry and begin to read aloud.

*June 2, 1892*

> *Isaac has been offered a position at Portland in the Engineers Department of the First Lighthouse District. I'm so proud of him, even as I wonder if I will be able to accompany him on our next adventure.*
>
> *And yet, maybe my next journey is one I must take alone. Sometimes, I think the time is not far distant when I shall climb these lighthouse stairs no more. It has almost seemed to me that the light was part of myself. When we had care of the old lard oil lamps on Matinicus Rock, they were more difficult to tend than these lamps are, and sometimes they would not burn so well when first lighted, especially in cold weather when the oil got cold. Then, some nights, I could not sleep a wink all night though I knew the keeper himself was watching. And many nights I have watched the light my part of the night, thinking nervously of what might happen should the light fail.*
>
> *In all these years I always put the lamps in order and I lit them at sunset. Those old lamps—as they were when my father lived on Matinicus Rock—are so thoroughly impressed in my memory that even now I often dream of them. There were fourteen lamps and fourteen reflectors. When I dream of them it always seems as though I had been away a long while, and I am trying to get back in time to light the lamps before sunset. Sometimes I walk on the water, sometimes I am in a*

*boat, and sometimes I seem to be going through the air—I must always see the light burning in both places before I wake. I always go through the same scenes in cleaning the lamps and lighting them, and I feel a great deal more worried in my dreams than I do when I am awake.*

*I wonder if the care of the lighthouse will follow my soul after it has left this worn-out body. If I ever have a gravestone, I would like it to be in the form of a lighthouse or beacon, a reminder perhaps that my soul is in the care of the greatest Keeper of all. He never sleeps but always tends to the small lights inside of us. He is watching, so that I may finally rest.*

I blink back tears as I turn the page, willing there to be another entry from Abbie. But the remaining pages are blank.

"That's it. She . . . she must have died."

"Did you Google her?"

I shake my head. "At first I did, but I don't remember the year she died and I didn't read much. I wanted to finish her journal first, find out about her before I researched." Now, I'm not sure if it would have been better to read the facts of Abbie's life on an impersonal Wikipedia page or historical blog.

"You want me to look?" Jason's voice is tender, soft.

"Yes."

He takes out his phone and after a few minutes, shows me a picture of Abbie's gravestone. An aluminum scale replica lighthouse separate from the headstone is placed over her resting place. Her death, June 16, 1892, less than a year after her own mother's death and two weeks after this last entry.

"Looks like she got her wish, though."

Although a nice gesture, the lighthouse is small—too small to represent such a dynamic woman. And yet it calls to mind Abbie's words, that she is in the care of a great Keeper.

I bite my lip, allowing sadness to wash over me like one of the billowing waves that washed over Matinicus Rock when Abbie manned the lighthouse without the help of her father. There is sadness and loss here, and that's okay. But I can't forget the victory, either. Abbie's story is a great one. Could it renew the interest of the town? Cause them to think more favorably on the historical significance of this place and the precious landmark it is for future generations?

"She and her husband tended the Beacon when she wrote this."

Jason's mouth falls open. "No way."

"Amazing, right?"

When Jason and I finally rise from our spot on the floor, the sun is beginning to crest over the horizon, illuminating the light and the horrid accusation of those bloody words on the face of the lighthouse.

"I'm going to head to the store and get some paint."

I nod, taking Abbie's journal and the photograph of her mother's grave, appreciating the comma as I think of Abbie's death. Of Maddie's. Of my own time in darkness, battling for light. "I think I'll go start breakfast. I have a lot to talk over with Nana when she wakes."

Jason kisses me gently. I sink into him, tired but content.

"Thank you for not giving up on me," I say.

"Thank you for not giving up on yourself." He smiles at me, gives me one more lingering kiss, and then starts down the stairs.

I run my fingers over Abbie's journal and take in a cleansing breath, exhaling a prayer for direction and strength to navigate this next week, to help save the Beacon.

And all beneath the watchful eye of my mother.

# Chapter Twenty-Nine

*Though the doors were locked, Jesus came and stood among them*
*and said, "Peace be with you!"*
*John 20:26*
~ Verse on Nana's birthday card to Laney,
Age 19

## LANEY

When the clock strikes nine and Nana is still not up, I place the waffle batter I prepared in the fridge and head upstairs to change into jeans and a painting shirt that can get dirty. Jason has been at the lighthouse, painting as best he can with a rickety ladder he found in the old guest house. I've watched from the kitchen window. The process looks painful—the white paint not nearly enough to cover the angry red marks.

"Good morning, dear." Nana meets me at the top of the stairs.

"Good morning. I made waffles."

"I can't imagine anything better."

I do an about-face and walk down the stairs. Once in the kitchen, I plug in the waffle iron and pull the batter from the fridge.

"My, it felt good to sleep in." Nana pours herself a cup of coffee from the pot I started hours ago.

"Did you sleep okay?"

"Would you believe I did? Last night's events have cleared up a few things for me." She doesn't elaborate. I don't ask, anxious to share my news about Abbie.

She walks to the window and stares at Jason stretching to cover the red marks on the side of the lighthouse. "Oh, that dear boy."

"Jason said the officers took pictures last night, and we took more this morning, in case you need them for insurance purposes. But we both agreed we couldn't bear to look at those words any longer than we had to."

She nods. "I agree." She stares out the window another moment before speaking. "You know, the last time I had a Sunday morning without guests was in January. I think I'll head to church. Do you feel like joining me?"

"Oh. Um, I've never been to church. Well, except after Maddie . . ." I allow my words to trail off. Maddie's memorial service had been at a church. I'd attended, of course. Not that I remembered much about it.

"There's no requirement for prior experience." Nana's eyes twinkle.

"I'd love to come."

"Wonderful. Jason's welcome too, of course."

"He might be ready for a break."

Jason does indeed accept the invitation, and although I worry we both might nod off during the service due to our lack of sleep, we once again pile into Jason's rental. Nana directs us into town to an old white church that's as full of welcome as it is of history.

"You okay with this?" I whisper to Jason as Nana greets a woman in high heels and a short-sleeve sundress.

He winks at me. "I think I can handle it. I at least got a couple hours of sleep last night."

"Laney!"

I turn just in time to see Kiran before she throws her arms around me. "I'm so glad you're here!" She's wearing jeans with a gaping hole in one knee and a loose-fitting green t-shirt. "And you brought the lobster."

I rub my forehead to try and hide my burning face. "Jason."

He gives me a puzzled look, but a smile plays on his lips. "Nice to see you again, Kiran."

"I sit in the back if you want to join me."

"Thanks, but we're here with my grandmother. Actually, we better go find her. I don't want her to think we've abandoned her."

We bid Kiran goodbye and search out Nana.

I shouldn't have worried she'd be alone. My grandmother is talking with a small group of women in the foyer. When she sees me, she gestures me over.

"Laney, this is Alexis, Zack's mother. And Tina and Vicki and Nora. Ladies, I apologize for getting behind on our get-togethers, but things have been crazy."

The woman named Tina lays a hand on my grandmother's arm. "Charlotte, why don't you let me take over scheduling the women's brunches? There's no shame in passing the torch."

Nana nods, her shoulders relaxing. "That would actually be a bit of a relief. Thank you, Tina."

Jason spots Zack and goes over to greet him. By the time we're seated in the sanctuary, I feel content and cozy tucked in the old wooden pew between Nana and Jason. The songs are a mix of slower, meditative songs and some upbeat music. One of the ladies Nana introduced me to—Vicki or Nora, I can't remember —reads a story about the risen Christ appearing to Thomas.

There's a lot that strikes me about the story. That Jesus says,

"Peace be with you," to Thomas, who doubts him. That He invites Thomas to touch His scars.

I realize not everything is about me. And if I did have any allusions of that, they were cured the day Maddie died. But sitting here in this worn wooden pew, bright light pouring through the tall windows on the side of us, it's not lost on me that my first time in church is a story about scars. It's not lost on me how Abbie's words about entrusting her soul to God are still fresh in my mind, how I'm getting emotional thinking about them now. How lack of sleep and worry over the Beacon and Nana and whoever wrote those horrid words are all tugging on the frayed edges of my emotions.

And yet, what stands out to me are the words, "Peace be with you."

When the pastor speaks, he tells of hope in those scars of Jesus, of triumph. Something slides in place in my spirit. This is what Kiran was talking about. Of the beginning of heaven coming to earth, restoring not only the bodies of God's children, but restoring everything. Of a holy meeting between God's dwelling place and the dwelling place of humanity.

It's all a bit beyond me, and at the same time, it isn't. For it's the hope I saw in Nana's cards during those growing-up years. It's the hope I see in her now, the hope I saw in Abbie's words, in Kiran sharing about her own pain, the hope I glimpsed when Jason explained to me the significance of the comma on Thankful's gravestone.

We close with a song that holds a gorgeous tune and begins with, "Be Thou My Vision." It sounds as if it were penned back in medieval times and a stirring sweeps through my spirit and I want these words for myself. I want to claim them as my own and chase God for the rest of my living days. Am I tired? Yes. Am I overwhelmed? Yes. Am I looking for sense and purpose in the broken parts of my life and could this be a convenient crutch? Maybe. But something tells me it's more than that—that I'm beginning to glimpse what it means to be human, to hold my scars lightly and hold hope tightly.

I might doubt, but I don't doubt that something new is being born this day. And it begins here, in the scars of a Savior.

WE'RE quiet on the way home, and when Jason pulls into the drive, he yawns. "Thanks, Charlotte. I'm glad you invited me."

"Anytime, honey. Thanks for all your painting. You can hardly tell."

Not exactly true. Faint red lines still show beneath the white paint.

"Needs a few more coats. But I'm going to catch a nap at the hotel before Zack stops by to measure the windows later. I don't want to miss him."

"You guys are becoming quite the chums, aren't you?" Nana observes.

"What can I say? He's a cool guy."

I squeeze Jason's hand and lean over to give him a kiss on the cheek. "Thank you for everything."

Nana and I climb out of the car and wave goodbye. Jason gives a friendly beep before pulling out of the driveway.

When I head towards the door, Nana places a gentle hand on my arm. "Could you sit with me a few minutes?" She points to two Adirondack chairs off to the side of the yard. Towering pines give them a sense of privacy from lighthouse tourists, and yet through the trees, the Beacon is still visible.

"Yes. Actually, I was hoping to talk to you, too."

"Perfect." She ushers me to the chairs and we sit. "Perhaps I should have prepared us some lemonade or iced tea?"

"Nana, this is lovely. We can have tea after." I lean my head back on the chair, listening to the sounds of gulls overhead. I breathe air into my lungs, filling every cavity of space with the breath of life. I wonder at the peace I have. Mom is coming tomorrow. The future of the Beacon is still in limbo. It doesn't make sense. "I really enjoyed that service."

"Hmmm. Me too. I feel I have some clarity."

I smile. "Me too."

She gives my fingers a brief squeeze. "I think I'm done, Laney."

Something about the finality of her tone makes my chest squeeze, tightness replacing the airy lightness of a moment earlier.

"Done with . . ."

"I think it's time I face the fact that the Beacon's time as a bed and breakfast, at least under my care, is coming to an end."

I swallow down the hot lava of emotion bubbling up inside of me. "What? Nana, no. You've worked so hard. You said last night that the Beacon is your home. You can't give up now."

"I'm not giving up, honey. I'm trying to protect what's left of this place. To be wise with its gifts. It's not safe here anymore. Not safe for my granddaughter. Not safe for my guests. Last night proved that. It's an uphill battle, I'm afraid, and I'm not sure it's one I have the strength to fight any longer."

"But we're fighting alongside you, Nana! Me, Jason, Zack. We can be strong together."

"Oh, my darling girl. Sometimes being strong isn't feeling strong. Sometimes being strong is admitting your faults and weaknesses. I know you want to believe I was a perfect parent to your mother, but the reality is, I wasn't. And although the last thing I want to do is disappoint you, keeping this place open feels too much like I'm battling my daughter. I'm done."

I move my tongue around in my mouth, searching for words to change her mind, to convince her. "Abbie." The name comes out as a croak. "Abbie lived here. She tended this lighthouse."

Nana raises her eyebrows. "Abbie Burgess?"

"Abbie Burgess Grant by that time, but yes. Nana, you have to read the rest of her journal. It was beyond touching. And there's this comma on her mother's grave. And she lived here with her husband Isaac and her children. Don't you think that makes all the difference?"

"It's remarkable, that's for sure. But at this point, I doubt one inspiring historical story is enough to wipe out the anger that some feel toward the Beacon and its more modern-day story. I don't know that it will make a difference to your mother."

My mind is whirling. "But don't you think finding Abbie's journal after all this time . . . means something?" Maybe I'm grasping, using anything to try and convince my grandmother that when it comes to the Beacon, all is not lost.

"Honey, I very much look forward to reading Abbie's journal, and I can't wait to share the findings with whomever is interested. But as far as me keeping the bed and breakfast open . . . my season of tending it is coming to an end, I think."

"I'll take it over, then, Nana. I know I have a lot to learn, but you could help me, couldn't you? We can stay here together and keep it running. No one would mess with Miriam Jacobs' daughter, would they? And we can share the history of it. Abbie's history, my grandfather's history—"

"Your mother's history?"

"Who cares about her and her stupid book?" My words come out angry and forceful, and I immediately temper my tone. "I'm sorry."

She sighs long and deep. "We can't ignore the part your mother plays in all of this. Believe me when I say it touches my heart to hear you say you want to be involved in the running of the Beacon. When Miriam left, I never would have imagined her little girl would one day return and offer such a thing . . ." Nana chokes on her words and massages her throat, eyes shining. "But in the end, I need to see how this visit with my daughter plays out. I want peace, Laney. Can you understand that?"

"Yes," I whisper. "I really do."

"I love you, dear girl. You will never know what a blessing you've been to me."

"I love you too, Nana. And even though I don't want to see

243

you lose this place, I'll respect whatever you decide. No matter what, I'm glad I found you, and I'm sorry it took so long."

"Oh, honey." She pulls me into her arms with a strength that surprises me. When we part, she drags in a gusty breath. "Now, how about you fetch that journal for me? Seems I have some catching up to do, and I have nothing on my agenda save for sitting on the porch and reading."

# Chapter Thirty

*I cannot think you would enjoy remaining here any great length of time for the sea is never still, and when agitated, its roar shuts out every other sound, even drowning our voices.*
~ Letter from Abbie Burgess to her friend Dorothy, 1856

## LANEY

"Hello!" The upbeat, merry voice of my mother rings through Nana's house. Its familiar, high pitch enters my ears where it ping-pongs down my throat, through my chest and into my stomach, where it finally settles.

Bitter bile sours the back of my throat. I don't like that I feel so unkindly toward her. Yet, no amount of wishing will change it. It's clear she hasn't come here to reconcile with Nana. She's come for her *Timeline* interview. She's come, perhaps, to cement her house plans. She's come to rub all her good fortune in Nana's face. I don't know how I'm going to be able to stand by and allow it. At the very least, I might be able to serve as some sort of buffer.

In my bedroom, I take one last look in the mirror. I clip the sparrow necklace I haven't worn since Maddie's death to my neck. I've decided on a yellow sleeveless sundress and today, I won't be using a coverup. I'd like to think it's because I'm healing—that with everything that happened this summer, I'm learning to accept my past and my pain, learning to find victory over and through. And while all that might be true, I'm also certain that I want to present something to my mother that I never have in my life: strength.

I open the door, the slight breeze in the action caressing my bare arms. It's foreign and I whisper a prayer for strength, that I won't quake in my mother's presence. I head down the stairs to where Mom and Nana are embracing. When I catch a glimpse of Mom's face, eyes closed and mouth tight as if she's trying to stop herself from crying, I can't help my surprise. Is she happy to see Nana, or is it all an elaborate show?

I've never seen them together, and I'm not sure what I expected.

I firm my jaw and straighten. When Mom opens her eyes, her face lights up. "Elaine. Aren't you a vision?" She reaches for me, placing cold hands on my upper arms and holding me back a space to study me. "Seems Maine agrees with you more than it did me."

I allow her to hug me, and I pat her back lightly, my gaze resting on Nana, standing before us, looking as if she's trying to savor the moment.

"Would you like some iced tea, Miriam? Or lemonade? Coffee?"

"Lemonade would be divine." Mom sets her purse on a worn stuffed chair and glances around. "I see this place hasn't changed much. Except for the plywood. What happened?" She nods toward the boarded-up window. After looking at it yesterday,

Zack said he'd have to special order the replacement. He didn't expect it in for at least a few weeks.

"Oh, we had some shenanigans here while we were at Hannah's wedding Saturday night." Nana starts toward the kitchen.

Why is she protecting my mom from the consequences of her actions when Nana herself hasn't been protected from them? And although it's on my tongue to set the facts straight, I clamp my lips shut. I don't want to cause more trouble for my grandmother.

Mom and I follow Nana into the kitchen. "It will be fixed by Wednesday, won't it? That's when the crew will be here for the interview."

Okay, I tried.

"Seriously, Mom?" I reach into the hutch for three glasses and drop ice into each of them. They land with an angry, satisfying plop.

"What?" Her dark eyes are wide and doe-like. They don't fool me.

"Don't tell me you're oblivious to what's been going on here."

"Laney . . ." Nana's voice is pained, begging me to keep the peace.

"No, Nana. She doesn't get to waltz in here and criticize your home because it doesn't measure up to what she wants the Beacon to be for her silly interview."

Mom tosses her hair over her shoulder and straightens. "Really, Elaine. I know they're a bit rough and tumble out here in Maine country, but you needn't speak to your mother like that."

"You are unbelievable. You must know what hardship your *memoir* has cost Nana. Not to mention, the bed and breakfast. You've caused a lot of hurt."

She lets out a derisive laugh. "*I've* caused a lot of hurt? Don't speak of things which you don't know, daughter. You're apt to make a fool of yourself."

"What don't I know? Tell me. Because I read your book, and I'm still not connecting the dots."

"Oh, so if I locked you up in a lighthouse when you were seventeen, you'd be all hunky dory with it? You think I should hide the truth? Hide the pain of my childhood just to make this place look good?" She glances at my arms. "You know, honey, I'm glad to see you're not hiding anymore. I'd think you wouldn't expect your mother to hide, either."

I look at Nana, but she's clutching the pitcher of lemonade, her knuckles white, staring at my mother. Frustration builds within me. Why won't she defend herself?

Mom crosses her arms in front of her chest. "You know, it took a lot for me to come back here."

"It didn't take anything besides a national interview. You coming back home is not some altruistic endeavor to make things right with Nana, and you know it." I'm seething now. I'm unhinged. Any progress I've made in healing this summer seems to have flown out the window.

"Laney, please . . ." It's Nana's pleading that finally breaks through to me. But my anger rises, this time toward her. I want to ask Nana what hold my mother has over her, but I know. Because no matter what, Mom is her daughter. No matter what, my grandmother loves her. She wants Mom in her life.

"I can't do this." The words come out soft. I leave the kitchen and head up the stairs. Once in my room, I close the door behind me and search for a long-sleeve t-shirt. I'd been wrong to think Nana needs me.

I pull on the shirt, catching a glimpse of the lighthouse out my window. I think of Abbie and her mother, of the rift Abbie felt between them up until the end. But that is not the same as what's wrong with me and Mom. My problem with my mother is much more clear-cut and harsh.

Mom is a liar.

How can she walk around, preparing for national interviews

and signing a host of books, knowing she's written a lie? It simply doesn't make sense.

I think of Nana, holding that lemonade pitcher tightly, not speaking. Why won't she defend herself?

What am I missing?

# Chapter Thirty-One

*I don't have answers to where you are, or even where Laney is. So, I'm throwing this letter into the ocean, hoping somehow, God will catch it.*
~ Letter from Jason to Maddie found in a bottle washed up onshore two years after her death

## JASON

My phone rings just as I finish sending an email to Susan Sanderson's contractor. When I see Laney's name, my heartbeat picks up a notch. I swipe to answer. "Hey, didn't think I'd hear from you this afternoon."

"You around?" Her voice is wobbly and tense. I know in an instant that it didn't go well with her mom.

"Yeah. Need me to come pick you up?" I'm grabbing my keys, my wallet.

"I could meet you somewhere."

"I'm already on my way. We'll go wherever you want."

"I'll meet you at the end of the driveway."

In four minutes, I'm pulling into Charlotte's drive and Laney's sliding into the front seat. She has a long-sleeve t-shirt on over a dress.

"I'm losing it, Jason."

I place a hand on her arm. "You're not. You're upset. Talk to me."

She cranes her head toward the bed and breakfast, as if checking to make sure no one is coming out of the house. "Can you drive?"

"Any place in particular?"

"Can you take me to my mom's land?"

I groan. "You sure that's a good idea?"

"You said you'd take me whenever I wanted to go. I want to go now." The anger flowing out of her is nearly palpable, as if she's looking for a target.

I put the car in drive. "Yeah, sure. I'll take you. But are you going to tell me what happened?"

She nods. I turn the car to head in the direction of Northeast Harbor.

"I vowed I'd handle her being here okay, and I didn't. I'm a horrible person. I thought after this summer, after reconnecting with you, after getting to know Nana, after reading Abbie's journal, even after that church service yesterday . . . I thought I was healing. That maybe she couldn't get under my skin so much. But I was dead wrong."

"This isn't an easy situation. It's not just you she's hurting now. You're worried about your grandmother."

"The worst part is that Nana won't even defend herself. Why won't she speak up? I don't understand."

"Charlotte isn't a weak woman."

We drive in silence for several minutes as I turn onto Route 3 and make my way into the quaint town of Northeast Harbor. It's a small seaside town that's quieter than Bar Harbor with quaint shops and abundant boats. When I reach a tall and majestic piece of land overlooking the water with a *Sale Pending* sign at the end of the dirt drive, I pull in.

Laney releases a humorless laugh. "Perfect place for an ugly mansion."

I pull as far as I can into the lot before turning to her. "You want to get out?"

She answers by pushing open the car door. We walk toward the ocean.

"I suppose she's going to build a super fancy house?"

I shove my hands in my pockets. "I wouldn't know, remember? I told my dad I wouldn't be designing it."

She blinks, seems to see me for the first time since I picked her up. "I'm sorry. I've been so preoccupied I didn't even ask. How are things with you and your dad?"

I nod. "We had a heart-to-heart. I told him how I felt neglected after Mom died. He told me he was sorry. It felt . . . healthy."

"I'm glad for you." A hint of sadness marks her words, as if she covets the reconciliation I've reached with my dad.

She sits on a slab of rock beneath towering pines. Ahead of us lies the shimmering waters of the Gulf of Maine.

I sit beside her. "Thanks." I waver, suspending the conversation, feeling I should say something meaningful and wise but also not wanting to upset her. "Did you talk to your mom?"

"I talked to her, all right. Right after she made an issue over the broken window. Not up to par for *Timeline*, I guess."

I lean back on my hands. Ahead of us, a loon ducks beneath the water. A minute later it comes back up several feet away. "I mean really talk to her, Laney. About everything you felt growing up, about how it's killing you that her book is hurting your grandmother. How it hurt you."

"Why doesn't Nana talk to her? Why won't she stand up for the Beacon?" Laney reaches down and grabs a fistful of earth and loose rocks. She stands, poising herself above the ocean, and hurls the soil into the abyss below.

I stand and wrap my arms around her. She turns into the crook of my neck, and I tuck my chin against her hair. She smells of lavender and sea salt.

"She's never been there for me." She's talking about her mother, now. Quiet sobs shake her body and I tighten my grip on her. "I practically raised myself, you know? And after Maddie died, she couldn't even be bothered to go to her funeral. But she was all too willing to put my best friend in her stupid book. She's so selfish. And I'm terrified I'm just like her, or at least that I will be if I don't set all this straight."

I rub her back in slow, smooth strokes. "Laney . . . I didn't read her book, but if your grandmother hasn't outright denied what she wrote, did you ever stop to think it might be . . . true?"

She thrusts me away from her. "How can you say that? You've spent time with my grandmother. You've sat at her dinner table. How can you accuse her of—of locking her daughter away in a lighthouse?" She storms toward the edge of the cliff. For one horrible second, my chest lurches and I think she'll jump. But no, of course not. It's only the memories of that day haunting me.

She stands above the water, hair flying off her shoulders. I come beside her, shoving my hands in my pockets. "I love your grandmother. You know that. But people change. Sometimes what we think we'd never do confronts us. I'm not saying your grandmother is a bad person. I'm saying maybe you don't know the whole story. Talk to your mom. Really talk to her. Talk to your grandmother. Have some real conversations."

She shakes her head and walks with fierce steps back to the car. "I can't do this right now."

"Talk to me, Laney. Tell me what you're thinking."

She whirls around. "And what if it's true, Jason? What if my grandparents did lock my mother up in the lighthouse? Where does that leave me? Where does that leave me and Nana? The Beacon? All the good things that have brought us together this summer? How could a woman who sends birthday cards and letters like the ones I've received all my life possibly commit such a horrid act?"

"*Talk* to her."

She walks down the drive, her steps hurried.

"Where are you going?"

"On a hike. I need to clear my head."

"Laney, come back." Has there ever been a more frustrating woman on the face of this earth?

She keeps walking. I run after her until I fall into step beside her.

"You don't need to follow me. I'll call an Uber after I'm done. I'm sorry I wasted your time. I just—I need to think, and I can't go back to the Beacon yet."

"Okay." I continue walking by her side.

She stops. "Jason, I'm serious. You don't need to follow me."

"I'm not following you. I'm walking beside you."

She shakes her head. "You're a mule-headed man."

"You tried to push me away once before, remember? And I let you. I didn't see you for six years. You better bet your life I'm not going anywhere this time. So yeah, I'll walk with you from here to the top of Cadillac Mountain if I have to."

She continues walking for another minute but her bottom lip trembles. Without warning, she stops and throws her arms around me, her body shuddering in loud sobs.

I cling to her tight, rubbing her shoulder blades, the tiny bones that make up her spine. "I'm not leaving. We're in this together," I whisper into her hair. "I'm here to stay."

# Chapter Thirty-Two

*I think this place might be helping me. As much as I didn't want to come, maybe this is the one good thing Mom has ever done for me— send me away.*
~ Laney Jacobs' rehab journal

### LANEY

By the time Jason drops me off at the Beacon, it's dark. Beneath the moonlight, the white of the lighthouse shines bright. I turn the key in the side door and slide in. A single lamp brightens the empty sitting room.

I'm relieved no one is here, relieved I won't have to face either Nana or Mom until tomorrow. What will I say to them? Jason's prompting echoes in my head. Have an authentic conversation with both members of my family. Deep down, I know it's what I should do. But having never had much of a genuine relationship with Mom, I'm not sure how to go about it. And Nana . . . what if I don't want to hear what she has to say?

I turn on the lights in the kitchen. Fill the kettle with water. I find a bag of chamomile and lavender tea, place it in a handmade ceramic mug. When I hear footsteps on the stairs, I hold my breath, not sure who will come around the corner.

Nana. I breathe a sigh of relief.

"Hello," she says softly, placing Abbie's journal on the butcher block of the island.

"Hello." I can't meet her gaze. "I'm sorry I ran off earlier." Apparently, I tend to do this—run. I'm realizing that about myself.

Nana lowers herself to a seat on the other side of the island. She taps Abbie's journal. "I finished."

"What did you think?"

"I'm glad I read it. I think your grandfather wanted to take me to Thankful's grave. Maybe Abbie's too. I wish he had shared his findings with me while he was still alive."

"Maybe we could go. Together."

"I'd very much like that."

The kettle whistles. I take my time pouring the steaming water into my mug. "Jason told me about the comma after Thankful's name and the spacing of the letters. It symbolizes that death is just a comma, a pause or a doorway, before an eternity with God."

A smile softens the corners of Nana's mouth, creating a deep chasm of wrinkles on either side of her face. "I like that. Appropriate for Thankful and Abbie, I should think."

I nod, at a loss for what to say. I lift the kettle. "Would you like a cup?"

Nana shakes her head. "No, thank you. I'll be up for the bathroom all night."

My turn to smile.

"I've been thinking." Nana's gaze settles on Abbie's journal. "I can relate to Thankful."

"How so?"

"She fought her battles. She questioned her decision to leave her son, to support her husband and go to Matinicus with the rest

256

of her children." She shrugs. "Or perhaps I'm reading too much into what Abbie wrote and projecting my own experiences onto Thankful."

I swallow, the steam from my mug rising to meet me. "Nana, please, tell me what I'm missing. Don't you think I deserve to know?"

She breathes in and then exhales a wobbly gust of air. "I think perhaps you do. Although some of it is not mine to tell."

I glance upward toward a slight creaking of movement. Mom, walking around in one of the guest bedrooms. "Will you tell me what you can?"

"I've prayed long and hard about that. Lord help me, I haven't received a clear answer. But now, with your mother here and with this interview . . ."

I don't speak. I don't want to break the rhythm of what she is about to tell me.

"Miriam always knew her own mind. She had such a strong spirit—a good thing, really. But when you're a parent, sometimes it's also a scary thing."

I'm holding my breath, preparing myself for whatever Nana is about to reveal.

"She was seventeen when she first brought Vincent home to us." Her gaze flicks to me before finding rest on my mug of tea. "Your grandfather was not fond of the young man, and truth be told, neither was I. He was a smooth talker. Handsome as all get-out. We had him for dinner one night and Jack asked him about his folks, about his plans after high school. He fed us a bunch of lies about his mom being a famous actress on set in Hollywood and his father being her manager."

"How did you know he was lying?"

Nana shifts in her seat, looking uneasy. "Jack saw him sleeping behind the market. He asked around and heard from the police chief that Vincent was in and out of group homes and juvenile detention for theft and drugs. When we confronted Miriam about it, she was furious. She said maybe Vincent did lie, but it was only because he loved her and wanted to impress us. She said if we were really interested in helping the poor and extending hospitality to the stranger like Jesus preached, we'd help Vincent."

A lump catches in my throat.

"She was right, you know. We were hypocrites. Here we were, going to church every week and running a bed and breakfast with plenty of rooms, but we couldn't bother with one troubled kid. Jack and I talked about becoming foster parents to help Vincent, but in the end, we didn't think it wise. Besides, our motivation for doing so wouldn't have been love, it would have been proving to our daughter we weren't hypocrites. That boy had such a hold over her. We couldn't imagine him living beneath our roof."

I think of the picture I found in Mom's nightstand, of the pearls at her neck, sitting on a boy's lap. Vincent? I feel a tug of pity for the kid and wonder where he is now.

"One night, Jack came home and said he didn't think we'd be seeing Vincent anymore. He said he'd had a talk with the boy, had given him a thousand dollars to take a bus back out west and start over. I couldn't believe he'd bribed him. I couldn't believe it, and yet a part of me was grateful he was gone. Or so we thought."

I wrap my fingers around the handle of my mug but don't make a move to sip it, frightened any movement will disrupt Nana's memories, or that she will realize all she's telling me and change her mind.

"Miriam was heartbroken for a couple of weeks, but she didn't say anything about Vincent. And then, we noticed a change in her. She was . . . off. We received a call from the police one night that she'd been arrested for—for—prostitution."

"What?"

"They'd found her downtown late at night trying to sell her virginity to the highest bidder. She said she needed money to find Vincent. A drug test revealed heroin in her system." Nana chokes on her words. "My baby . . . heroin.

"We sent her to rehab and it helped for a while, but when the same thing happened four months later and there was no rehab facility available to take her immediately, Jack grounded her. Said she was to stay in her room and come downstairs only for meals. It was tough then, trying to manage a bed and breakfast with all the family dynamics. And Miriam never came into a room without making an entrance—and making our guests uncomfortable." Nana traces a dark crack along the top of the butcher block. "We were just so helpless. All we could think to do was keep her safe until we could get her into rehab again."

My mind spins. I knew Mom dabbled in drugs before Bill. I knew she slept with a slew of men, but prostitution and heroin at the age of seventeen?

Nana inhales a shaky breath. "Looking back now, I admit we handled the situation poorly. Not a day goes by that I don't wish we hadn't closed down the Beacon, searched the world for the best facility for her, really tried to help her through everything. Even if it was just the three of us.

"One night, Jack and I woke to screaming coming from the lighthouse. We ran out with our flashlights, not knowing what we'd find. Part of me thought Miriam had climbed to the catwalk and thrown herself into the sea. But when we reached the footbridge, Miriam came running out, her tank top and skirt ripped, her chest and face bloodied." Nana's crying now, trying to speak through her tears. "I squeezed my baby so tight, felt certain she battled an inner demon or some other mental illness that made her hurt herself." Nana glances at me and her mouth turns tight.

"It's okay, Nana. Go on."

She brings her hand to her mouth, shakes her head. "She was screaming so loud. I can still hear her as clear as if it happened yesterday. She said, 'He raped me!' I was certain she must be hallucinating. Who could be up in our lighthouse? We asked her, but she didn't tell us. Just said she was able to get away, that she locked him up there.

"Jack went to investigate. I don't think either of us thought he'd find anything. But we were wrong. Vincent was in the lamp room, visible signs there'd been a tussle. Jack yelled down for me to call the police, and I did. They took Miriam in for questioning, but she wouldn't speak a word to them. The next day, she accused us of sending Vincent away again, that if we hadn't locked her in the lighthouse it would have never happened."

Nana ends her story and we sit in silence.

"I don't understand." I shake my head.

"I've said too much already. It's your mother's story to tell, only it is not the one she chooses to remember."

"Nana, are you saying Mom talked herself into believing you locked her in the lighthouse?" I know the brain can do strange things, but this is absurd, even for my mother.

"We spoke to many psychiatrists who work with teenagers, tried to make sense of why Miriam put together the story she did. The best answer we received was that the trauma of the rape cemented a more bearable scenario in her mind. One where her parents, and not the boy she loved, were the enemy. And let's face it, Jack and I were far from perfect. We made so many mistakes, handled her behavior and addiction so badly."

"Didn't you talk to her, try to jog her memory?"

"Perhaps not as much as we should have. The therapists insisted her memory would come back in time, when she was ready to heal. Things quieted after that. Miriam went back to school, came home at a decent time. No more drugs, no more wild nights with boys. We thought we were getting past it, and although it pained me to know my daughter believed we were capable of such cruelty, I accepted it as the punishment I was to bear for my part in it all."

I remember the V.C. Andrews books upstairs. *Flowers in the Attic.* A grandmother who locks her grandchildren in an attic. Did Mom fabricate getting locked in a lighthouse after reading those books, or maybe while reading them? Is that what her brain did—make up a story born of her reading material?

"One day after her eighteenth birthday, she left home. I only saw her once in all these years, though the Lord knows I've tried to connect with her."

I can't measure all my feelings in the moment, but the possibility that Mom really believes the story she's written in *Locked Light* strangely comforts. That she may not be intentionally lying to harm my grandmother shines a ray of hope through me. A small ray, granted, but a ray, nonetheless. For the first time in maybe ever, I feel a speck of pity for the woman who birthed me.

"So, her memory never came back?"

"No. And now that she's finally here, I'm not sure bringing it up again won't do more harm than good. Whenever I've stood by the truth in the past, she's accused me of lying. There's nothing more disheartening than your daughter believing you're a liar."

"But Nana. This has gone on too long. Whether or not Mom believes it, it's still not the truth. And it's ruining you. It's ruining your business. Isn't there anyone who can prove what happened that night? The police conducted an investigation, didn't they?"

"They did. But your mom refused to talk, she refused to be examined. The only time she accused Vincent is when we first saw her at the bottom of the lighthouse."

"What happened to him? Vincent?"

"He went to juvenile prison for a while. That's all I know."

"Do you think he's . . . " But I can't finish the thought.

Nana shakes her head. "He's not your father, Laney. Don't think that."

"Not the time up in the lighthouse, but do you think she reconnected with him after she left? If she didn't believe he raped her, or . . ." My brain hurts. What if he hadn't raped her? What if Mom made that up, too? No doubt mental instability played a factor in all of this. How to begin sorting it all out?

Nana places a hand on mine. "You didn't hear her that night. You didn't see her. She wasn't imagining things, Laney. And up until then, she'd never lied. Even when she went against our wishes, she did it brazenly. Even now, honey, I'm sure your mother feels she's telling the truth."

# Chapter Thirty-Three

*Sometimes the weeks I spent locked in the lighthouse take on a hazy quality. Black-and-white instead of color. I think this is my mind's way of trying to block out the pain.*
*~ Locked Light by Miriam Jacobs*

## LANEY

I slept fitfully that night, dreams of my mother running out of the lighthouse with torn clothes haunting me alongside visions of Abbie Burgess standing atop the catwalk of the Beacon, content and grateful for the life she's made with her husband in tending the lights. I dream of the boy in the photograph. I hate that he tarnished our beloved Beacon. I'm left to wonder if the good of the lighthouse—of the souls who cared for it, the sailors it ushered home, the love Abbie, Isaac, and their family found through it, and the love my grandparents found in tending it—could be swept aside by one evil act?

For the first time, I'm realizing that maybe I never properly understood my mother.

I scratch at my scars as I walk toward the lighthouse. The caution tape sways in the wind, and I'm grateful there are no tourists. I pick my way down the rocks beneath the footbridge. The boulders are large and gray. Closer to the shore, the waterline stains the rocks dark. I sit on a boulder and look up at the stone pilings, at the footbridge that connects to the door of the lighthouse. My gaze follows the whitewashed stones up to the black catwalk and the glass windows of the lamp room, where the lights once shone.

I imagine everything I saw in my dreams—Abbie working tirelessly to light the path for the sailors, Abbie and Isaac sneaking off to be together in the lamp room, my grandfather falling in love with this light, and my grandmother helping him run the bed and breakfast to keep his dream alive. When I think of Vincent and my mother, I squeeze my eyes shut.

"Laney, I didn't see you there."

I open my eyes and turn to see the object of my thoughts, perched precariously on a rock several yards from me. "Hey."

"I wanted to go up, but it looks like it might not be safe?"

"It needs work. We're trying to get the town to take it over."

Mom sits beside me, her ballet flats not at all practical for the rugged terrain. She brings her skinny-jean-clad legs up to her chest and hooks her arms around her knees. The skin of her hands is still young and smooth and slightly tan from playing tennis.

"We?"

I nod.

"You've become quite attached to your grandmother this summer, haven't you?"

"It's been good getting to know her."

Mom cranes her neck to peer at the lighthouse. "You know, I didn't keep you away to spite her. I thought it was best. It was . . . painful to see her."

How is it possible to tackle hard conversations when two people are standing on entirely different truths? And yet, wasn't that the challenge of being human, of empathizing with those who didn't see the same as we do?

"Because you believe she locked you in the lighthouse."

She blows a breath of air out, fanning her bangs. "No. I *know* she locked me in the lighthouse. But it's not just that. You read my memoir. There was a lot they should have done differently."

"And because you were a perfect parent, you feel they should have been too."

"That's not fair, Laney. I didn't lock you in a lighthouse."

"I asked you not to write about Maddie in your book. You betrayed me."

"I never agreed to that. I wish it didn't hurt you, but Maddie's death affected me more than you know. That could have been you. It was the wake-up call I needed."

"So glad my best friend's death could be *your* wake-up call."

"That's not what I meant." Mom inhales a sharp breath. "She's a part of my story, too. If you had asked me not to write about her from the beginning, it might have been doable. But by the time you found out, we were already going over galleys—"

"How could I have known you were going to write about her?"

"I told you tons of times how her death affected me."

I roll my eyes. "Sorry if I wasn't listening. Turns out I was preoccupied with my own grief."

Mom bites her lip. "I'm sorry I hurt you, honey."

"How come you didn't write about Vincent in the memoir?"

She pales. "I don't like to talk about him."

"But I thought your memoir was about healing. About releasing all the wounds of your past and baring all. Isn't he part of that?"

"Your grandmother shouldn't have told you about him. It's not her burden to share."

"Then you tell me, Mom. What happened?"

She blinks, fast. "I loved him. I loved him and they tried to keep us apart."

I want to ask her about the night they were in the lighthouse, but I don't want to poke her into silence.

She continues. "He was rough around the edges. Charming. Always on the outskirts of trouble."

"Did you see him after you left Bar Harbor? Did you find him?"

"Honestly, I don't know why you're asking about him—"

"Because I want to know. I'm trying to understand why you . . ." *Are the way you are.*

"He's not your father, Laney, if that's what you're getting at."

"Who is my father?" I whisper the words. I've asked them before. I don't know why I think this time will be different, why she will give me an answer.

"I told you before, honey. I'm sorry, but I don't know. That was a hazy time in my life. I was irresponsible—"

"On drugs?"

She presses her lips together, drags in a great breath. The waves splash against the rocks below us. The tide is coming in. "Yes, I did use then. But I got clean when I found out I was pregnant, I swear it, Laney. You were my motivation. You saved me."

She's never told me that before. Something in me wants to believe the words, but I'm too raw, the wounds she's inflicted over the years too scabbed and scarred to allow her entrance. Is she trying to earn her way into my good graces? Or is she trying to give something of herself to me?

We're quiet for several long moments, studying the ocean. It's ever changing, ever new, and yet as old as time. It's the same ocean that was here when the lighthouse was built. The same ocean Abbie surveyed for distressed ships. The same ocean that looked on as my mother climbed those lighthouse stairs to be with Vincent.

"Why did you go up into the lighthouse with him?" I try the question on, wondering if Mom will slip with the truth, or if something within her will become dislodged.

But she looks genuinely confused. "With who?"

"With Vincent."

"I didn't . . ." Hurt crosses her pretty features. "That's right. You've been talking with your grandmother. Well, I'm sorry to disappoint you, Elaine, but my mother's the one who has her facts wrong. Hey, I'd want to block out the fact that I locked my daughter in a lighthouse, too."

How ironic that both women seem so certain of what they believe.

"So, you remember Grandpa bringing you up to the lighthouse and locking you inside."

"Vividly."

I bite my bottom lip, stare up at the white beast.

"Your grandmother said you two found an old journal about a female light keeper who lived here over a century ago."

I look up, unsure whether to feel betrayed or touched that Nana would share Abbie's story with Mom. I nod.

"Will you come to the interview with me? Share what you found?"

My throat tightens. "What?"

"It sounds like an interesting story, and from what I understand, this woman is a Maine historical heroine."

I don't rush to answer, instead try to dissect my mother's motivations for asking. Is she trying to align herself with brave Abbie? Create a story to which I don't want to contribute? Or is she simply trying to rope me into being part of this publicity stunt? Her readers are curious about her life. They're curious about me. It's why she likes to put pictures of me on social media. But would agreeing to this be betraying Nana and the Beacon, or would it be helping my grandmother and the bed and breakfast?

"Um, can I think about that?"

"Of course."

I tap the toes of my sneakers on the rock. "I have to get ready for my shift at work."

"I'd love to visit. Perhaps I'll take your grandmother out to dinner tonight."

I shake my head. "Mom, you've got to see how messed up this is, right? You've ruined Nana. Now, you want to visit her and take her out for dinner?"

"Despite what you think, I do have a heart. Don't you think I want to be right with your grandmother? Don't you think I hate that my father died before I could make amends with him?"

"If it pained you so much, why didn't you make more of an effort back then?"

She stares off into the swirling sea. The water moves up and down as one swollen body. In the distance, a sailboat glides by. The sailor waves, but neither I nor my mom raise our hands to return the gesture.

"It's complicated."

I stand. "You wrote a whole book about it. You're conducting national interviews. I think you'd somehow find the words to explain it to your daughter."

"Can you try not to think the worst of me for once in your life?"

I squeeze my eyes shut. How can I when my entire life has been filled with dashed hopes every time I've expected something from my mother? "I have to go."

"Maybe we'll see you tonight?"

I want to tell her no, for Nana's sake. But maybe my septuagenarian grandmother doesn't need my protection. "Okay." Maybe my lack of enthusiasm will be enough to dissuade her.

"Have a good night, honey. I love you."

I bite my tongue while giving her a halfhearted wave and heading back toward the bed and breakfast. I've heard confessions of love from my mother before, but they seldom were backed up with any action that proved the words.

# Chapter Thirty-Four

*There's something freeing about writing in these pages. On some days, I even imagine I'll read them in a different time, a different place. A time when I'm well.*

~ Laney Jacobs' rehab journal

## LANEY

Mom and Nana don't show up to dinner that night, and for that, I'm thankful. Someone else does, though. Kiran. She flops down at a table outside with her yellow legal pad and begins writing before she even looks at the menu.

"Hey." I greet her after Natasha seats her.

"Oh, hey, Laney. Missed you at writing group last night."

"Yeah, my mom came into town." I don't elaborate.

"Oh, that's nice."

"Yeah, I suppose. What can I get you to drink?"

She orders a ginger ale, and I bring it back to her after ringing up the one other table I'm serving. I take out my notepad to jot down her order. "Have you decided yet?"

She orders a Cobb salad with lobster and gives me a brilliant grin. "I'm celebrating tonight."

I lower my notepad. "What are you celebrating?'

"I finished my book!"

"No way. Congratulations. That's huge."

"Yeah, it's a pretty great feeling."

"I bet. What's your next step?"

"Editing." She might as well have told me she's won the lottery for how excited she seems.

I laugh. "So, do you hire an editor or something?"

"I might. But I'm going to self-edit first. Read through it, study some craft books, see what I can pick up that needs fixing,"

"And you'll be able to tell what that is?"

"I think so. At least, in part. It's kind of like life. Like sometimes we get a sense that something needs fixing, even if we don't know what it is." She shakes her head. "I don't know, maybe I'm just expecting it to be some kind of intuitive experience."

"Or what if you know it needs fixing, but you don't know how to go about fixing it?" I think of my convoluted relationship with my mother, with how Nana is entwined in it all.

Kiran gazes out at the water, darker with the approaching night. "I suppose I might have to ask someone else, then. Maybe a person farther along on the journey than I am."

I bite my lip. Without much thought, I plop down across from her. "I don't know if you remember that my mom and I don't have the best relationship," I blurt out.

She blinks. "I remember."

I sigh, long and deep. "I'm sorry. It's just, my relationship with her is part of my life that needs fixing and I don't know how to go about it. Maybe you could be my editor?"

My skin grows clammy as I voice the words. How desperate am I to foist such a personal request on a near-stranger? A near-stranger who is trying to eat a celebratory dinner without having to deal with her waitress's problems.

Yet, Kiran doesn't *feel* like a stranger. She feels like a fellow human who understands me.

A soft smile forms on her lips. "I don't think I can edit your life. But I'm a pretty good listener."

I tap my order pad. "Let me put this in for you and make sure no one else needs me. I'll be right back."

I give the kitchen Kiran's order, check in with Natasha to make sure everything's under control, then head back to her table. I'm apologizing before I even reach her.

"You know what? I'm a nutcase. Can we please forget everything I just said? It was way out of line and I don't need to be spilling my—"

"Laney." Her voice brooks no room for noncompliance. "Spill it. I'm a great friend and I want to be yours. Friends try to help each other through their problems. They listen, right?"

*Friend.*

I realize then that, since Maddie died, I haven't had many friends. Okay, that's putting it mildly. I haven't had *any* friends. Sure, there were the occasional school acquaintances on social media, but as far as real-life, lasting friendships? I've been too scared. Too frightened to open myself up to anyone like I had Maddie all those years ago. Too frightened to do something to ruin another person I cared about.

"Thanks," I whisper. And then I let it flow. I tell Kiran about growing up with my mom, how I never knew what I was going to get on any given day, how she brought men and drugs and volatility into our home. I told her how Maddie and her parents had been more family to me than Mom, but how her death had changed all of that. I told her about Jason. About rehab. About how Mom changed after meeting Bill, but it was into someone unrecognizable, someone I felt certain was playing a part in a play in which I didn't want to partake. I told her about Nana's cards and deciding to come to Maine, about reading Abbie's story, about the upcoming *Timeline* interview. I end with Mom's request that I talk about the journal on live television.

Somewhere in the middle of my story, I get her food. I also take another table and by the time I make it back to her, she's finished her salad. "Thanks for listening," I say.

"That's what friends do." She smiles. "I wish I had answers or advice for you, Laney. All I can say is you have to be able to live with yourself and what you do—or don't—say during that interview. Is that something you're willing to do?"

"If it's the truth, I am."

"And what if the truth isn't what you want to believe it is?"

"You think Nana's the one not telling the truth?"

"I didn't say that. I just mean, maybe no one will ever get to the bottom of what happened all those years ago. Are you ready to die on one hill or the other?"

"I'm not sure. If it could help the bed and breakfast . . . if it could help Nana, I think I might."

"Well, there you go. But I would talk to your mom, tell her you're not compromising what you believe is the truth to make her look good. Maybe she'll rescind her offer."

I nod. "That makes sense."

"In the end, you're the one who has to walk around in your skin. We've both been hurt by people who were supposed to love us. I only found healing when I found forgiveness."

"It'd be easier to forgive my mother if it were all in the past. If she didn't continue hurting my grandmother with her actions."

"You're right. That's not an easy kind of forgiving to do. But it doesn't mean you forget what she's doing or turn a blind eye to it." Kiran licks her lips. "I think forgiving is more about taking ourselves out of the equation altogether."

"I don't get it."

"Like, maybe it isn't for you to take sides when it comes to what's between your mom and grandmother. Maybe you love them both but stay out of their history and find your own."

"But how do I do that?"

"I'm not sure. I only know that in my own past, forgiveness was possible when I've looked to God for peace. Not sought retribution or the need to feel I'm right. It's a tough road. But we don't have to walk it alone."

"Thanks, Kiran."

"Anytime. I'll be praying for you."

I give her a hug, instruct her in no uncertain terms not to tip me as she's already given me more than enough, and bid her goodbye.

"You think we'll see you next Monday?" she asks on the way out.

"Definitely. I can't wait—" I slap my forehead. "I completely forgot. It's the town meeting. I can't miss it."

"Oh, that's right. Okay, no worries. We'll see you when we see you. And if you're ever up for a writing session, feel free to stop by the bookstore at one—that's when I take my lunch."

"Awesome." We plan for Thursday, which will give me an opportunity to update Kiran on however the interview goes, with or without me.

When I get home, no one is up. I take a shower and slide into bed, mulling over my friend's words.

I pray.

It feels stilted and awkward at first, but then as I settle in, remember the story of Thomas, of Jesus bestowing peace on him, inviting him to come near to the scars of his resurrected body. I sink in. I pour out my troubled heart. And in the moment right before I drift off to sleep, I know what I will do.

# Chapter Thirty-Five

*I make it my business to get to the bottom of the truth.*
~ Tim Johnson, *Timeline* host

## LANEY

Tim Johnson looks a lot older in person than on camera. As I sit across from him in the living room of the Beacon, the lighthouse in the backdrop of the window behind me, I notice the makeup caked on his face. For a moment, I pity him for how much time he must spend cleaning makeup from his pores. Then I remember that I will have to do the same tonight, as my face is thick with makeup in preparation for the interview.

Lights and cameras are pointed at me. I'm facing the boarded-up broken window, which doesn't do much for my mental state. Now that I'm in the hot seat, I'm already doubting agreeing to the interview.

After a long talk with Nana, in which she encouraged me to "follow my gut and she would support me wholeheartedly whatever I decided," and a very different talk with Mom, which involved an exchange with her publicist and marketing manager and *Timeline*, they agreed that Tim would ask me only questions related to my personal relationship with Mom and the story I found this summer from Abbie Burgess.

Yesterday, I'd nearly chickened out, going to Mom with my doubts. I'd found her in her old bedroom, staring at the picture of her and Vincent. "Mom?"

It took her a minute to tear herself from the photo. "Oh, hey, honey."

"I'm thinking about backing out of the interview."

Her mouth pulled downward. "The *Timeline* staff is all prepared for you. It really would be unprofessional to pull out now."

"I'm not trying to be professional. In a twisted way, I'm trying to protect you."

"They agreed not to ask you any questions about what happened between me and your grandmother all those years ago."

"But what about what happened between us?"

She stared at me, a familiar blankness to her brown eyes that threatened to swallow me whole. It confirmed the worst. She did not understand the gravity of how she'd hurt me.

She straightened, placing the picture facedown on a pile of her other belongings. "We've talked about this before. I realize I couldn't possibly win any Mother-of-the-Year Awards, but I've apologized for that. I was mentally unwell. I had addiction problems. Being locked in a lighthouse would cause mental instability in the best of us. Despite all that, I did do my best."

Tears prick the corners of my eyes, but I force them back. I try to remember her apologizing for how unavailable she was during my childhood, but I can't. And I know one thing for certain—I would have remembered an apology. I would have clung to it. Something else illuminates itself in that moment, though. Mom needs the story that her parents locked her in a lighthouse to be true. Because if it's not, she has no excuse for her addictions. For her neglect of me as a child. For the many men she's invited into her bed.

I'm not claiming my grandparents were perfect, Nana herself has admitted they weren't. Maybe they were too strict, too fearful their daughter would ruin her life with Vincent or another boy like him. Maybe they did play a part in her depression and illness. But I know one thing for certain: they did not lock her in the lighthouse.

"Mom, if I go on this show and they ask me about you when I was growing up, I can't lie. I don't want to hurt you." I'm surprised that this statement, is in fact, true. I've prayed for the strength to forgive my mother, to separate myself from the history surrounding her and Nana. It's not so easy, however, to separate myself from my own history.

Still, I can only see this interview playing out one way: with me hurting Mom.

"I have nothing to hide, Laney. Even your grandmother agreed to an interview. I wrote about my shortcomings as a mother in the book. My readers know this. They identify with it, I'd say. They just want to see the real you."

I could give them that, at least.

So, here I am, sitting across from Tim Johnson, who has interviewed hundreds of people more interesting than I am. This is not live. They will edit and cut and mold the interviews together into the story they want to tell. They're interviewing Nana right after me before ending with Mom.

My great fear is that it will go down like some tasteless Jerry Springer episode. I seek out Jason, the only person I agreed to have in this room, aside from the lights and camera crew. He gives me a smile. I can't wait until it's over and I can run into his arms.

"Are you ready, Laney?" Tim pats his brow with a handkerchief. His hairline is beginning to recede into an extreme widow's peak, and I wonder if they put makeup on the high rise of his head as well.

"Yes." I fold my hands in my lap. The dress I'm wearing is

short sleeves with a muted gray and blue flowered print. My arms are bare, and although I doubt the camera will catch the insides of my forearms, leaving my coverup behind is a reminder to myself that I'm no longer hiding my past, my doubts, my wounds. I'm trying to begin anew, to walk in light and truth.

A cameraman counts down to record and Tim rolls his neck and winks at me. "We'll try to make this as painless as possible."

I swallow. Tim leans back in one of Nana's overstuffed chairs and pastes on a serious expression. *Timeline* is all serious—the mellow, somber tones, the lighting.

"Laney, I understand this is the first time you've visited the place where your mother grew up. Tell me, what has your experience been like?"

Immediately, I feel unease. This guy is fishing for something. He doesn't care about me, or my mom. He cares about a good story.

I glance at Jason and he nods, one corner of his mouth lifting. I breathe deep and let my answer come unrushed. "I've really enjoyed coming to the Beacon, getting to know my grandmother and the people in this town, learning the ins and outs of the bed and breakfast." I give myself a mental pat on the back for mentioning the bed and breakfast. That's why I'm here, after all. To help Nana and the Beacon.

"Have you and your grandmother talked about your mom?"

This is teetering dangerously close to territory that, from my understanding, we were not going to talk about. But it's not quite there, I suppose, as Tim doesn't ask about what happened all those years ago. Hmm. This guy isn't one of America's top reporters for nothing.

"Not much," I decide is the safest answer. I'll wrestle with whether that is a lie later. "At first, I asked Nana about my mother a lot, but she didn't feel it was right to speak about what happened so long ago without my mother being present."

"And now that she's here and your family is together? Have you spoken about what happened in the past?"

I no longer feel pity for Tim over his makeup. In fact, I hope it takes hours to scrub out of his pores.

I grit my teeth before answering. "It was my understanding you were saving those questions for my mom."

Tim blinks, as if remembering. "Of course. Laney, you only need answer the questions you feel compelled to answer. This isn't a courtroom after all."

Ha. I hadn't thought of it that way, but now that he says it, I find it easy to compare this interview with taking the witness stand.

"Let's go in a different direction, shall we? Tell me what life growing up with your mother was like?"

I swallow. This question, I've agreed to. I only need to tell the truth. But at that moment, the scars on my arms start itching and I can't resist rubbing them on my lap to quell the sensation. "Um, it was . . . I guess, difficult, is a good word." I laugh nervously, my gaze running to Jason as my legs very much want to do.

"How so?"

"Mom battled depression and addiction. Children growing up in those circumstances never have it easy." Is it evident how intentionally hazy I'm being?

Tim's gaze falls to my arms which I'm desperately trying to press into my thighs to quell the itching. "Did your mother ever hurt you, Laney? Physically?"

I pause, maybe too long. I try to think. She grabbed me hard a few times, but she never beat me. "N-No. No."

"Your mother has become an overnight success, her story built on the negative happenings in her own childhood and how she overcame her addictions. How do you feel about the success she's experiencing?"

"Conflicted."

"Conflicted?" Tim presses.

"I wish she were not experiencing it at the expense of my grandmother and her business."

"How has her book hurt your grandmother?"

I don't bother hiding my eye roll. "If you'd read it, you'd know, Tim."

He's cool as a cucumber, unruffled by my disrespectful and sarcastic tone. I look at Jason, who is miming something that looks like, *Breathe.*

I do.

Tim shifts in his seat, leans back, and crosses one leg over the other. "How has your mother's memoir hurt your grandmother's business?"

"My grandparents have run the Beacon Bed and Breakfast for almost thirty years. When Mom's book released, many of her fans chose to ostracize the Beacon, going so far as to shame some of its guests for staying here. This place is special, one of the most beautiful inns on this side of the country, in my opinion. It holds a lot of history. A lot of good history. But now, my grandmother, a woman I believe is innocent of the crimes she's been accused, has to live in fear. Someone threw a brick through her window last week. The lighthouse was vandalized."

I'm saying too much, perhaps. I just insinuated that my mother's memoir is not true, something I didn't intend to outright say.

Tim's eyebrows raise, as if he's not aware of the recent attacks on the Beacon. "Are you saying your grandmother's life is in danger because of *Locked Light*?"

"I—I don't know if I'd put it that strongly. But if she or one of her guests were standing where that brick hit, they'd certainly be severely injured."

"Laney, would you tell us the story behind your arms?"

"M-my arms?"

I see one of the cameras zoom to my hands, folded and clenched in my lap. Jason takes a few steps in my direction, as if to shield me. But I'm the one who insisted on not hiding. I'm the one who chose to bare my arms for all of America to see.

"I see some scars," Tim says, although I wonder if my mother, or even my mother's publicist, gave him a head's up. Mom had hinted at my time in rehab in the book, but as far as I know she'd never gone into details.

My hands begin to shake. Jason takes another step forward. "I thought this interview was supposed to be about Laney's mother?"

The producer, a stocky man with thick glasses named Dave who has a penchant for rolling back and forth on his heels like a pendulum, holds his hands out to Jason. "I'm sorry, sir, but if you're going to be a distraction, we'll have to ask you to leave."

Tim and Dave exchange a look. Tim uncrosses his legs, leans toward me. "Perhaps we take a quick break?"

I nod and, on wobbly legs, allow Jason to pull me from the chair and outside onto the porch where I breathe in cleansing sea air.

"You don't have to finish in there, Laney."

"I know. I want to. Am I doing horribly?"

"Are you kidding me? You're killing it. But if that guy has the gall to ask about"—he gestures to my arms—"I hate to think what else he might ask."

"I could refuse to answer, but . . . Jason, what if there's another teenage girl out there who needs to know she's not alone? I didn't expect it, but maybe this is something good that will come out of this mess."

He stares toward the lighthouse, jaw firm. Finally, he nods. "I'm behind whatever you decide."

When I sit down again with Tim ten minutes later, he asks me off camera if I'd like to continue with the question. I nod and when the cameras show a red recording light, he asks again if I'd tell him the story behind my arms.

"I lost my best friend in a horrible accident when I was seventeen. I didn't know how to deal with the pain. I started cutting myself."

"Did you talk to your mom about how you felt?"

I shake my head. "No."

"She was clean by that time, I understand? Newly married to a reputable businessman?"

"They were dating, I believe. But we didn't have much of a relationship by that point. I didn't feel the need to go to her."

The words hurt to say, and I wonder if they will hurt my mom when she hears them. But they are the truth.

Tim grows even more serious. "Do you think your mother's neglect played into your self-harm?"

My chest grows tight. I don't think I've ever asked myself this question, at least not this directly. I seek out an honest answer, searching the crevices of my past to come up with the truth.

"I'm not sure," I finally say, unwilling to cast blame on my mother. But the damage is done. Tim has planted the question in the minds of *Timeline*'s audience. He's planted it in my own mind. "All I can say is I'm grateful for people who didn't give up on me when I couldn't find my way forward. I'm grateful I wasn't alone—that's the message I want others out there to hear. If you are hurting, you are not alone."

I remember the sense of an otherworldly presence as I knelt by my bed, as I sat in the old wooden pew of that church, as I read of Abbie's faith and the message behind that small but significant comma.

I was not alone. God had not abandoned me.

Suddenly, nothing else seemed important. It was as if I'd discovered the main idea of my life—God was *with* me.

And with the light of that knowledge, clutching my pain and unforgiveness seemed glaringly unimportant.

"I understand you made a fascinating discovery while at your grandmother's this summer? Could you tell us about it?"

I blink, trying to focus my thoughts, a lightness filling my chest. This was my chance to talk about Abbie's journal. Still a bit shaken by the revelation I just had, I latch onto my reason for doing the interview in the first place.

Nana. The Beacon. Abbie's story.

*Timeline* has called in several historians to authenticate the journal, and this morning, we heard back what I already knew—this is the journal of the real Abbie Burgess.

I tell Tim how I found Abbie's journal in a box in the attic, how I wasn't sure it was related to the Beacon at all until I neared the end.

"Abbie's a bit of a local heroine in these parts, isn't she?" Tim asks.

I nod. "She's well known for tending the lights on Matinicus Rock during a great nor'easter in January, 1856. Though her father was the official lighthouse keeper, he was forced to take a trip to the mainland when they were low on supplies. The storm washed away part of the house and was one of the fiercest recorded during the century. Yet, Abbie kept the lights burning the entire time her father was gone, which ended up being weeks. Not only that, but she took care of her sickly mother and younger siblings. She was sixteen years old."

"And what connection did you find to the Beacon?"

It almost feels grievous to skip ahead to the end of Abbie's life when the middle is equally fascinating, but I understand this interview isn't about Abbie—it's about Mom and Nana and the Beacon, and I suppose in some ways, me.

"The Beacon's lighthouse logs disappeared in the 80's, before my grandparents bought the lighthouse and keeper's house and turned it into an inn. As far as I know, there was no other record of Abbie and her husband, Isaac, tending this light. But she wrote of it clearly in her journal."

"And I understand that only you and your grandmother have read the journal thus far?"

"That's right—other than the historians who've authenticated it."

"What did you take away from Abbie and this piece of history?"

I suck in a deep breath. "That, to Abbie, being brave meant doing hard things. Tending the lighthouse during a storm, learning to be content in her circumstances, learning to forgive."

"Who did Abbie have to forgive?"

"Her mother." My voice comes out in a squeak.

Tim's eyes widen so slightly that I'm sure only I—and not the cameras—will notice. "What did Abbie have to forgive her mother for?"

I wet my lips. "They left behind Abbie's little brother when they came to the island. Her mother was often sick and full of anxiety. I think Abbie sometimes thought of her as weak."

Even as I speak, I can see Tim connecting the dots to a bigger story. I see the story for myself.

"And did Abbie forgive her mother?"

"Yes. Abbie's mother, Thankful, lived with her and Isaac at the Beacon. That's where they fully reconciled."

Tim shifts in his seat, trying to phrase his next question. "And do you see reconciliation for you and your mother in your future, Laney? Another Beacon resolution, perhaps? Do you forgive your mother?"

"I'm trying," is all I can say. When the cameras finally shut off, I swipe at the tears at the corners of my eyes. Tim shakes my hand and says I did a marvelous job. I manage a shaky nod and scurry from the room.

# Chapter Thirty-Six

*If you hold to my teaching, you are really my disciples. Then you will know the truth, and the truth will set you free.*
*John 8:31-32*
~ Verse on Laney's birthday card from Nana, Age 18

## LANEY

The crew takes a break for lunch. When they return, it's Nana in the hot seat with Tim Johnson, both me and Mom looking on.

I can't possibly see how this can play out well for anyone. In the kitchen just a few minutes before, Nana wrung her hands and tried to back out. "Miriam, I can't do this. I can't tell a story I don't believe."

"Tell the story you believe, then, Mom. Let the viewers decide for themselves."

"But how can this be good for your reputation? Won't it create controversy for you?"

"I outlined all the dynamics with my publicist. She assured me there's no such thing as bad publicity. Just be honest, Mom. Really, it's okay."

I can't understand why Nana is doing this. She doesn't seem to care much about setting her good name to rights. She's even accepted that the bed and breakfast may not make it. The only reason that remains is that Mom has asked her to be a part of this circus. This interview is why Mom has come home, and perhaps Nana feels it will break open doors for them.

I don't see how, but love isn't always rational, particularly a mother's love.

It's hard to watch Nana answer Tim's questions. She's clearly uncomfortable, a prisoner in her own home. And yet I admire the straightness of her back, the lift of her chin as she braces herself for the queries.

"Your daughter hasn't been home in twenty-seven years. How does it feel to have her back?"

"I love my daughter and I hope having her home can be the beginning of healing for us."

"Your husband has since passed, I understand?"

"Yes."

"I'm sorry to hear that."

Nana nods.

"Do you think Miriam has come home because she only has you to come home to now?"

Nana blinks. Beside me, Jason holds my hand, runs small circles on my knuckles.

"My husband has been dead for ten years. I hardly think that played a part in Miriam's decision to come home, but I'm sure you can ask her yourself."

Go, Nana.

Tim Johnson doesn't miss a beat, though. "Was your husband a difficult man?"

"My husband was a wonderful man and a wonderful father. Not perfect, mind you. But I don't think anyone who knew him would describe him as difficult."

"Did he ever lay a hand on you or your daughter in an unkind way?"

"Absolutely not."

"Charlotte, did your husband lock Miriam in the lighthouse?"

The small silence that follows engulfs the room. "No. He grounded her to her room until we could find a rehab facility in which to place her."

"Miriam was troubled and perhaps a risk to herself, so you locked her away?"

I clench my hands into fists, mindless of Jason's hand in mine.

"She never gave us reason to think she'd hurt herself. It was when she was on the streets, able to obtain drugs, that we feared for her. That's why we grounded her."

Tim goes on to question Nana until the story my grandmother told me a couple nights ago comes out. She is careful with her words. She doesn't share as much as she shared with me, but the story is believable, plausible, even. She begins to cry when she speaks of Mom running out of the lighthouse with torn clothes. It's easy to see, at least to me, that Nana absolutely believes this version to be true.

I don't wish ill upon my mother, but what if the truth is revealed and set straight? What if Mom's readers glimpse another side to this story? What if the work of Nana's life might be saved after all?

When I glance at Mom, she is chewing on a fingernail, blinking quickly. I haven't seen these gestures in a long time, and I recognize the anxiety building. She's concealed it for so long, been in control for so long. But looking at her now, I see a woman coming unhinged.

I wonder then why we weren't interviewed together. Or at least why Mom and Nana weren't. And then it occurs to me that *Timeline* is perhaps looking to pit us against one another. It won't take much editing to show the complicated family dynamics. The lines between us are already clearly drawn. Now, listening to Nana, I can imagine what *Timeline* has in store.

Would putting us together have been any better, though? Yes, I decide. Nana would not have allowed a volatile confrontation. Even Mom, who has built her brand around a sort of transcendent tranquility that rises above the bad done to her, would probably not have allowed any disagreements to become explosive on camera.

Tim finishes Nana's interview and Dave calls for a fifteen-minute break before Mom's interview.

Although Mom insists, I'm not sure I can stick around to watch her. And yet, Nana agrees to be there, and I don't want her to be alone. Besides, it may be better to see it now than during the highly edited primetime television show.

By the time Mom takes the chair, she is completely together. But as she sits, a knock comes at the door. I rush to answer it, grateful for the delay.

"Zack. Things are kind of crazy around here right now."

But Mom's calling from her seat in the sitting room. "Is that little Zack Garrison? Come on in, Zack. It's okay, Laney. I asked him to come today."

I look between my mother and Zack. "What? Why?"

Beside me, Nana's brow is also furrowed in confusion.

But despite Dave's obvious frustration at the delay, Mom is rushing over to us. "I found his number in your address book in the hutch, Mom. The producer wasn't comfortable with recording in the lighthouse unless we had the contractor who assessed the repairs on site."

Zack gives Nana a sheepish grin. "I hope it's okay I'm here, Charlotte. From the sounds of it, they were considering going up anyway. Thought it'd be safer if I stopped by."

Nana shakes her head. "No, it's fine. But I don't want anyone to get hurt."

"Yeah, I'm not saying it's a great idea." Zack shoves his hands in his pockets.

Dave, Tim, and Mom meander over. Dave is rolling back and forth on his feet again. "Well, it's not going to collapse, is it?"

"That's highly unlikely," Zack admits. "Most of the damages have been caught in plenty of time and I did put a temporary reinforcement on the footbridge yesterday, but the catwalk is unsafe. No one should go out there. You'll have to be careful of the bottom step up to the lamp room as well."

Dave claps his hands together. "That's good enough for me. The waivers are already signed. Let's get this going. Tim and Miriam, why don't you take your seats? We'll record the visit to the lighthouse after we finish with the interview."

We all watch as Mom and Tim sit down. Zack slings an arm around Nana's shoulders. I'm glad he's here.

Dave counts down and then Tim is asking Mom questions about her book. Did it surprise her with its success? Is she glad she wrote it?

"Why do you think so many people are connecting with your story?" he asks.

"Readers tell me they resonate with my story. Not all of us have had addiction problems. Not all of us have been locked away in a scary place. But we all have been trapped by the expectations of others. Most of us have had to work to separate ourselves from toxic relationships."

Oh, this is painful. More painful than I imagined. I squeeze Nana's hand. Zack looks like he's about ready to fly across the room and strangle my mother. Nana gives him a small smile and a nod, as if to say, "It's okay. I'm okay. I can handle this."

Tim leans back, propping one hand against his chin. "Your mother has a very different story about what happened during that time."

Mom nods. "I know."

"And yet you still visit her. You still have open communication with her."

"It's been a long time. But I love my mother. I love both my parents. I've forgiven them."

287

I almost vomit in my mouth. This is so twisted on a million levels. Why did Nana ever agree to this interview, and in her own home? Why did I agree to it?

I grasp for the knowledge I knew during my interview. Even in this, God is with me. No matter what.

"Why do you think your mother clings to a different version of the story you tell?"

Mom laughs, but it's not a laugh filled with humor. "Isn't it obvious? It's too painful for her. She's made up something more bearable in her mind."

"And who's to say you haven't done the same?"

Silence cloaks the room. I hold my breath.

Mom titters, the top foot of her crossed legs swinging back and forth in a nervous tick. "Because I *remember*."

"Would you take us up to the lighthouse and tell us your story, Miriam?" Tim asks in a dramatic end to the sitting room interview.

WE TAKE down the caution tape. It seems absurd that we are collaborating with all of this. That we're enabling Mom to tell this story. And yet, when I voice this aloud to Nana on the short walk to the lighthouse, she simply squeezes my arm. "I'm trying to meet your mother where she's at. She feels she needs to do this, and I'm trying to support her, Lord help me. I'm praying this might be the beginning of restoration for us."

I didn't see how, and secretly, I thought Nana was overly desperate to believe so herself. But here I am, winding up caution tape while Zack shows the camera crew, the producer, and Tim around the lighthouse. They have asked Mom to wait back at the house. This is the first time since she was a teenager that she'll visit the light, and Dave insists it will be more wowing for viewers if it's authentic.

When they're ready to tape, Nana, Jason, and I perch on one

of the large boulders at the beginning of the footbridge, out of sight of the camera. One cameraman wheels his camera backward along the bridge. Tim and Mom walk slowly toward the lighthouse.

"This will be your first time back in the lighthouse since you were eighteen."

"Seventeen." Mom grabs the railing of the footbridge, walks slowly toward the light. "I didn't return to the lighthouse after my parents locked me in the lamp room."

"How do you feel right now, Miriam? Being back here after all these years?"

"It doesn't feel real," she whispers.

"Are you ready to go inside?"

Mom peers into the door, swallows, and nods. It's all very dramatic, very made-for-television. And yet Mom is all into it. Indeed, she does look like she's in another time, another place.

We watch them go in. We can't follow, and in some ways, it will be better not to know. Zack is with them. If Nana really wants the lowdown, she can ask him.

It seems they've been in there an awful long time, fifteen minutes at least, when I hear an ear-curdling scream. A loud bang comes from the top of the lighthouse.

"No! Get off me!"

I am on my feet, running. Up, up, the lighthouse stairs. Pushing past the camera crews and Dave to see Mom against the railing of the catwalk, arms braced behind her on the metal, hair messed in the wind, eyes wild. Zack stands before her, holding out a hand and inching forward as if to calm her.

"Miriam, that railing is not safe. You need to come inside."

"Get away from me!"

I don't recognize my mother. She is not calm and collected, she is the mother of my childhood. Desperate, strung out, searching for more.

"Turn off the cameras," I order. They don't listen, and I hate them. I hate myself for going along with this.

"Mom."

She blinks, and when she sees me, her face crumples. "My baby. My baby."

Zack backs around the refractors in the center of the lamp room to make room for me.

"It's okay, Mom." I hold my hand out. The railing Mom clings to trembles and I have a horrible vision of her toppling from the catwalk to the rocks and waters below. Flashes of me and Maddie falling toward water linger in my mind's eye. Me coming up. Maddie never knowing the light of life again.

My breaths come fast and in the space of a second, I realize I *love* my mother. I care for her. I don't want this. Of course, I don't want this. "Please, Mom, come to me."

And then I'm grabbing her hand, pulling her off the catwalk and into the lamp room. She's clinging to me and sobbing, shaking her head.

"I didn't know," she's saying. "I—I couldn't remember."

I want to ask what she couldn't remember, but more importantly, we need to get her down, away from the lighthouse.

"Interview's over," I tell Dave before ushering Mom inch by painful inch back to the house.

# Chapter Thirty-Seven

*It has almost seemed to me that the light was part of myself.*
~ Final letter of Abbie Burgess Grant

## LANEY

The *Timeline* crew is gone. Mom is upstairs in her bedroom. I've gotten her settled, and after she'd rummaged in her medicine bag for two orange prescription bottles and chugged the pair of pills down with half a glass of water, she falls on her bed, fully clothed, and enters a deep sleep.

When I'm sure she's resting, I close her door and tiptoe down the hallway into the kitchen, grateful our only guests checked out earlier in the day.

Nana hands me a cup of tea and sits at the island with Jason and Zack. "How is she?"

"Sleeping." I turn to Zack. "What happened?"

Zack rakes a hand through his dirty blond hair. "Not sure I know. Tim was asking her about being locked in the lighthouse. She started stumbling over her words, kept looking around the lamp room like a monster was going to jump out at us. At first, I thought it was for show because she was very convincing. Then I felt bad for her, could see something up there haunted her."

He taps his hand on the butcher-block counter. "I don't know if it was to calm her or not, but Tim asked about Abbie Burgess. He asked if knowing Abbie tended those very lights helped her identify with her, with the bravery needed to endure what they'd both been through. Miriam seemed to gather herself at the question, but she stepped out onto the catwalk when she talked about Abbie. I tried to get the producer's attention, but he waved me off. Miriam said she imagined Abbie searching these very waters for the lost. She leaned on the rail, and I could see it bend. It all happened so fast, but I called for her and grabbed her away. When I did, she lost it, Charlotte."

Nana's mouth turns into a firm line. "Lost it?"

"She pushed me back, told me to get off her, called me Vinny. I fell against the lamps and she went berserk, running back onto the catwalk. That's about when Laney came up. Good thing she did, too."

"She remembers," I whisper.

"She remembered something, all right." Zack turns to Nana. "Charlotte, I'm sorry. I should have put my foot down about anyone going up there. But I didn't think—I mean, I told them not to go on the catwalk."

Nana grabs for his hand. "It's not your fault. You couldn't have known. I'm only glad they're gone."

"Hate to tell you, but I'm thinking they'll be back." A tick starts in Jason's cheek. "They don't have a full story."

"Well, they can get it somewhere else." Nana throws back her tea as if it's a shot of whiskey and slams it back on the counter. "This is my home, and enough is enough. God forgive me for thinking this was a good idea." She reaches for another tea bag.

"But, Nana, maybe Mom remembers. Wouldn't that be a blessing?"

Nana sighs. "We'll see, I suppose. We'll see."

Zack and Jason go outside to secure the lighthouse and rehang the caution tape. When it's just me and Nana, I wrap her in a hug. "You know, Nana. I think you might be the strongest woman I know."

She laughs. "It's the Lord's strength, honey. Not mine."

We pull apart and go back to sipping our tea. "I don't know . . ." I swirl the dregs in my cup. "I can't stop thinking that if it weren't for the mention of Abbie during Mom's interview, she wouldn't have gone on the catwalk. Zack wouldn't have grabbed her. She wouldn't have been forced to face the truth of the past."

A sad smile forms on Nana's mouth. "Maybe the Lord is still using Abbie to help the Beacon. To help us heal."

"I pray you're right."

THE NEXT MORNING, Mom appears for breakfast as cool and collected as I've ever seen her. My heart sinks. Nothing has changed after all, then. If Mom did remember what happened with Vincent in the lighthouse, she has chosen to cover up her memories. Either that, or the part of her brain that blocked them out in the first place has again taken over.

She pours herself a mug of coffee and leans against the counter.

"How are you feeling, dear?" Caution laces Nana's tone.

"Better."

No. Nothing has changed. Mom will fly back to California. She will build her dream house here in Maine. Perhaps she will invite Nana over to dinner when it's finished, but it won't be because she wants to spend time with her. It won't be out of love. It will be to show off how far she's come without Nana's help. Mom will continue promoting her book. The *Timeline* episode will air, and Mom is right—whether it's good or bad publicity, it will no doubt create more sales, all while potentially continuing to harm Nana's business.

Mom shifts where she stands, then slumps against the counter. "I'm better. And worse, all at once."

I swallow.

"I've asked the crew to come back today."

I close my eyes. "Mom—"

She puts up a hand to stop me. "I've asked them to come back because I need to tell them the truth." She looks at Nana, her brown eyes swimming. "Mom, I—I honestly did not remember until yesterday." Her voice is shaking and when Nana stumbles forward, she inches away, shaking her head fiercely. "No, wait. Let me finish."

Nana stops. The paper napkin in my hand is disintegrating beneath my wringing.

"I don't know how I convinced myself . . ." She swallows and I hear the lump in her throat. "One of my doctors thought I was bipolar. Who knows, maybe I'm reaching for excuses. But I want you to know I did not remember what Vincent did up in the lighthouse until yesterday. Something clicked in my brain when Zack grabbed me. You have to believe me. I—I can't believe this myself." Mom's face crumples.

Nana goes to her. Mom doesn't push her away. They are both sobbing, and so am I. After a long while, Nana steps back. "Do you remember your father grounding you?" she asks softly.

Mom nods, her hands shaking. "And I really thought I remembered him locking me up in the lighthouse. But ever since last night . . . I'm not sure if . . . if a part of my brain didn't make up a less painful memory to replace Vincent's betrayal. He was so nasty that night, I hardly recognized him. Couldn't believe he was the boy I fell in love with. I—I think I may have been wrong." She removes her hand from her mouth, her voice quivering, her eyes wide with fear. "What an absolute mess. Mom, I'm so sorry."

Nana grabs Mom's hand.

Mom bites her lip. "I want you to know I'm ready to own up to it. To tell the world."

"Miriam, you don't have to do that. Let it rest. You don't have anything to prove. Not to me."

Mom straightens. "I have to prove this to myself." She looks at me. "And prove it to my daughter. This will be the hardest thing I've ever done, but I want to do the right thing. I want to be brave, Laney, just like your Abbie."

She holds her hands out, but I can't make myself go into them. There's simply too much past hurt and distrust between us.

Mom's expression sags and she glances at Nana, arms falling to her sides. Nana moves to hug her and something snags in my chest.

Yes, Nana's her mother. But if she can move toward forgiveness, then maybe, just maybe, I can too.

Cautiously and a bit awkwardly, I step into the circle of their embrace.

This will be messy. It will be far from perfect and take tons of work—work I don't know that I have the energy to commit. But I also know it can't be done without seeking God's grace and peace and forgiveness in the midst of it all.

Maybe, after all this time, it will look like finding our way back. Our way back home. Our way back to one another.

# Chapter Thirty-Eight

*I wonder if the care of the lighthouse will follow my soul after it has left this worn-out body.*
~ Final letter of Abbie Burgess Grant

## LANEY

The town meeting is packed. Despite the air conditioning, the place smells of too much perfume and body odor, and we are the last item on the docket.

I'm sitting with Jason and Nana and Zack. It's heartening to see all of Nana and Zack's friends greet them. There's no denying they are both well-liked in this town. Surely, that can only help our case.

We listen with eager ears about a plan for a new library, followed by much discussion and debate. Then a complaint about a dog's repeated violence, a fire and police soccer game fundraiser, and a zoning dispute.

Finally, the moderator comes to our topic. He is wearing a

coat jacket and a button-down shirt, and his forehead glows from the fluorescent lights. "I have a proposal from Charlotte Jacobs of 52 Beacon Way regarding the historic Beacon Lighthouse. Charlotte states that while she is saddened to make this request, in recent years the lighthouse has become a hardship for her. Repairs, estimated at two hundred fifty thousand dollars and confirmed by the town, are too much for her to handle, and the lighthouse is no longer safe for visitors until the repairs can be completed. Charlotte states that tourists cross her property all year long and she is left to care for the cleanup and wear and tear that results. Of recent interest is the authenticated discovery of the journal of Abbie Burgess, famed nineteenth-century lighthouse keeper of Matinicus Rock, discovered at the Beacon's keeper's house. It proves that Abbie and her husband Isaac did tend the Beacon for a short time before Abbie's death. Charlotte beseeches the town to consider taking over the care and maintenance of this historic lighthouse. She hopes to remain at the inn, running her business there."

I let out a breath as the moderator finishes. He peers above his reading glasses, taking in the crowd. "I'd like to open this up for discussion. Please come to the microphone, state your name and address, and your comments."

The first one up is a woman I recognize from the restaurant. I think she works at the library. She has a long gray braid and wears a floral dress. Her name is Lori.

"I think it would be a shame if the town doesn't take over the lighthouse. Frankly, I was surprised to learn it isn't already owned by the town. It's our duty and responsibility to keep history alive. And with all the publicity it's been getting lately . . . and now with Abbie Burgess's journal discovered there, I don't see how we can possibly allow Charlotte to struggle alone with it. Better to take it over now before it deteriorates to an extent where it cannot be fixed."

Most of the audience applauds when she finishes, and I take

that as a good sign. Two others address the crowd, in favor of the town taking over the lighthouse. Then a skinny, curmudgeonly man takes the microphone and he begins by jabbing his finger in the air.

"We don't need our taxes any higher. Especially for a building that has brought the negative attention the Beacon has. Bar Harbor is a peaceful town, one that makes most of its wages during the short summer tourist months. We don't need the kind of bad publicity it's brought."

A couple of townsfolk nod and applaud his words. I bite my lip.

"Anyone else?"

We simply can't end on that note. I'm not sure if residing in the town for three months gives me a right to speak, but I stand anyway and move to the microphone, feeling the weight of hundreds of pairs of eyes on me.

I'm not wearing long sleeves, and for once I don't think about what they might think of me. *I* know what I think of me. I know what God thinks of me. That is enough.

I state my name and Nana's address, my voice coming out louder in the mike than I anticipated. I back away from it an inch or two. "Charlotte Jacobs is my grandmother. And, yes, Miriam Jacobs is my mother. I know the Beacon has been surrounded by a lot of negative attention of late, but I think that's about to change." Mom has already made a public statement on her social media accounts, and once the *Timeline* interview airs, it will be well-known that Nana is innocent. "My mother is rescinding her accusations against my grandmother. In fact, she is encouraging patrons to support the Beacon. My grandmother is not asking for any compensation. She is willing to donate the lighthouse to the town."

I catch a small group standing in the back, and I almost choke on my emotion. Kiran. And beside her, the entire writing group. John. Emily. Myra. The proficient writing man whose name I can't remember. They've skipped their meeting to come and support me, likely at Kiran's prompting.

I swallow, trying to focus as I continue. "I was the one to discover Abbie's journal. If she taught me one thing, it's that, although we're sometimes forced into hardships we didn't think we could ever endure, we are never alone. Abbie looked to her faith for strength. She loved her family and she loved giving light to those wandering on the cold, dark seas. I propose that we continue her legacy in the keeping and maintaining of this light. Not just for my grandmother's sake, or even for the sake of all of us in this room, but for the sake of generations to come. When Abbie found herself on Matinicus Rock in the greatest storm of the century while her father was stuck on the mainland, she remembered his charge to her. To keep the lights burning. Town of Bar Harbor, I think, if Abbie lived today, she would give us that same charge—to shine light upon the history of this place, both the good and the bad, to keep the Beacon as a symbol of hope and faith. To keep the lights burning."

When I move away from the microphone, a rush of applause meets my ears. I can't help it, my face crumples and tears flow as I make my way back to my seat. Jason hugs me, as does Nana.

The moderator bangs his gavel. "I would need a motion for the town to accept Charlotte Jacob's donation of the Beacon Lighthouse and to agree to taking on the repairs and ongoing maintenance and care of it."

The woman in the floral dress makes the motion. Several around the room second it. My heart hammers against my chest.

"All in favor of the town taking over the care and ongoing maintenance and repairs for the Beacon Lighthouse at 52 Beacon Way?"

An overwhelming chorus of "Aye's" echo through the room, and then Nana is the one in tears.

"Those opposed?"

A few piddly "Nay's" reach our ears.

"It carries. More on this next meeting."

The moderator bangs his gavel and Nana squeezes my hand. "You did it, my girl."

"We did it." I wink at her. "Abbie would approve, I think."

Nana laughs. "That she would, my girl. That she would."

# Epilogue

*She claims she was locked in a lighthouse by her parents, but a revelation in that lighthouse twenty-seven years later casts light on what may have really happened all those years ago. Will finding answers once and for all reunite or destroy the Jacobs family?*
~ *Timeline* Preview

## LANEY

*Three Months Later*

On the couch in Nana's sitting room, I snuggle deeper into the crook of Jason's arm. Beside me, Mom and Bill share a bowl of popcorn. Nana and Zack sit on separate chairs, a roaring fire warming the chill in the early fall air.

Nana has tried to warn me about the desolate winters in Acadia. About the cold, the dark, the snow. And yet, I can't be dissuaded. This is my home. And now, thanks to the Economic Injury Disaster Loan that came through for the bed and breakfast, there is no shortage of work to be done.

The town showed great interest in Abbie's journal, and so Nana lent it to the historical society. Last month, however, she sold the rights to print it to Mom's publisher. Soon, all will be able to experience the firsthand accounts of Abbie's heroism and faith.

Zack has already begun the lighthouse repairs and hopes to be finished by next summer. Using some of the money from the loan, Nana is also hiring him to renovate three of the guest bathrooms and the rundown guest house on the property that she's used as a shed in recent years.

Between Mom's reversal on her story and public apology to Nana, not to mention the *Timeline* interview that airs in three minutes, we are booking like crazy, next spring and summer already completely full.

Mom clinks a spoon against her glass of sparkling water. "Can I have your attention?"

We all quiet, looking at her. She has a rosy hue to her cheeks these days. For the first time since I've known her, she seems happy. Bill has agreed to cut his hours at work and they are planning a trip to Italy in the spring. She has decided a small cottage on her Maine land would be more appropriate and economically friendly. She's giving the money she would have spent on her dream house to the Joyful Heart Foundation, an organization focused on helping victims of sexual assault, domestic violence, and child abuse.

She's come a long way. We still have our moments. She doesn't always understand why I want to stay in Maine year-round, but we are moving forward in forgiveness.

"No matter what this episode looks like, I want to thank each one of you, especially my mother and my daughter. You have stuck by me when I didn't deserve it. I've put you through hell. And I can only pray that this interview will tell our story in the way it deserves to be told. But if it doesn't—don't fret, they will most certainly be hearing from my lawyer."

I roll my eyes but laugh. She's still Miriam Jacobs, after all.

As the music for *Timeline* begins to play and the narrator for the preview speaks over haunting shots of the Beacon, Jason squeezes my hand. In two weeks, we'll be traveling back to California for his father's wedding. And although I've come to feel safe here on the east coast, the west coast doesn't scare me like it did five months earlier. I'm healing. I'm talking a lot to Kiran. I'm writing. I'm praying. I'm learning to see my scars not as a reminder of my brokenness, but as a reminder of a God who came to a doubting disciple with a "Peace be with you." A God who covers over scars with promises.

We watch the hour-long show together. It's difficult to watch. To relive, to see Nana so vulnerable before all of America, to see myself through the eyes of viewers, scratching at my scars. The producers have included Mom's breakdown up in the lighthouse and seeing it for myself for the first time brings tears coursing down my cheeks. I grab for her hand and she raises my fingers to her lips and kisses them. "It's okay," she whispers. "I can live with myself this way."

Even Mom's confession after the lighthouse incident is painful to watch. Tim probes, questioning her hard, trying to find holes in her argument that she had truly believed her parents had locked her up in the lighthouse. He interviews mental health doctors who have recorded similar circumstances in their own patients. It's all very illuminating, all very sad, and yet all very redeeming.

When it ends, and the credits roll, Mom switches the television off. "So, what do you think?"

Bill kisses Mom on the cheek. "I'm proud of you, honey."

"I second that," I say.

Nana looks at Mom with such love in her eyes, I feel like I'm glimpsing how the father in the prodigal son parable looked at his son when he finally returned home. "That took a lot of courage, Miriam."

She smiles. "Let the social backlash begin." Though she's already made a public statement on all her social media channels, no doubt there will be fresh criticism from her fans after the airing of tonight's show.

"Well, I think it's safe to say we've answered the *Timeline* question." I sit up in my chair. "Our family is, no doubt, stronger for all we've gone through these last few months."

"Amen to that," Nana says, and Mom nods.

"You want to take a walk?" Jason whispers a few minutes later.

I agree, and we don our coats and slip outside after promising to be back for Nana's famous chocolate cake.

We walk toward the lighthouse. The moon reflects against its white body, and I anticipate the glow of the automated lights shining on the water by next summer. I wonder what Abbie would think of such lights. Here and now, I appreciate her efforts anew, both at the Beacon and on Matinicus.

"What'd you think?" Jason grasps my hand in his.

"I'm happy with it. More so, I'm happy with Mom. You know, for the first time I feel like there's hope for us to be a real family."

"Speaking of family . . . " He turns to me, running his thumb over my knuckles. "I'm not sure I'm so crazy about a long-distance relationship."

"Okay." I swallow. "We've always agreed to take things slow." I'm panicking. Is he breaking up with me? But we'd been so good. Like, *so* good. We'd been through so much. How will I ever live without him?

"I know. But I'm wondering if you might want to speed things up."

My heartbeat slows and then picks up speed, like a chugging train bound for its destination. "What?"

"I put a down payment on a small house two miles up the road. You can see the ocean. There are windows and tons of natural light. An office above a garage where you could write. I realize you want to be close to your grandmother, and I don't want to take you away. But there's nothing else I'd like than to share this new home with you."

I'm not thinking straight. He wants to move in together? Call me old-fashioned, but—

And then he kneels on the dewy grass, taking out a single solitaire diamond that sparkles against the moon. "I don't want to be apart from you ever again. You've taught me so much, Laney, about myself, about who I want to be. Will you do me the honor of becoming my wife?"

I can't breathe. I can't speak. All I can do is stare at Jason's shining eyes, and then at that shimmering diamond that represents not only his love, but all we've been through.

He shifts. "I know we've established how special commas are, but this is an awful long pause. You're killing me here, Laney."

I laugh, the gesture dispelling any of the tension left in the air. "Yes. Of course, yes!"

I kneel before him, sinking into his warm embrace and the heat of his kiss, remembering all the commas of my life. The waiting. The struggles. The hope. The growing.

And God's answer—He's not yet finished. His good work is continuing. The story is just beginning.

The best is yet to come.

# Author's Note

I have always been fascinated by lighthouses, and so it was with great enthusiasm I researched Abbie Burgess and her work as lighthouse keeper at Matinicus Rock. I came to admire her heroic efforts through the great storm of 1856 and I longed to write of her story in the background of a fictional setting.

Though the evidence does point to the fact that Abbie's parents likely left their *two* younger children with their *two* oldest daughters, who remained on the mainland, this was also hard to track down as there is nothing written during Abbie's time on Matinicus Rock of her four siblings who stayed on the mainland. For fictional purposes, I changed this number to two siblings, one older and one younger. There is also no reason to believe Abbie would have been unusually distressed by this, but for the sake of creativity, I have imagined that she harbors some resentment toward her mother for leaving a little brother behind. Again, this is not due to anything I read but all due to my imagination. I read nothing to indicate that Abbie and Thankful had anything but a wonderful relationship.

The Beacon Lighthouse is purely fictional, as is Abbie's time in it. She did tend Matinicus Rock with her husband, Isaac, after their marriage, followed by Whitehead Light before retiring in

1890 and moving to Portland, Maine, where Isaac was appointed to the Engineers Department of the First Lighthouse District. Abbie died at the age of 52, in 1892, a year after her mother, Thankful.

A huge thank you to Diana Grady for pointing me to the story behind the comma of Thankful Burgess's grave by means of Peter at Ralston Gallery in Rockport, Maine. Thank you, Peter, for hunting down this story! (Check out Peter's amazing coastal Maine-inspired photos, including a photo of Thankful's grave at https://www.ralstongallery.com)

Another huge thank you to the research work of Dorothy Holder Jones and Ruth Sexton Sargent, whose writings in *The Original Biography of Abbie Burgess, Lighthouse Heroine*, played an instrumental part in my understanding of what Abbie's life on Matinicus was like. And a beautiful thank you to N.T. Wright for his thoughts on scars which I have paraphrased in this story.

Thank you to Hannah Linder for the beautiful cover, to Sandra Ardoin for being a faithful critique partner for the last fifteen years (how can that be, Sandy?!), to Melissa Jagears for her editing help, and to Donna Anuszczyk, Erin Laramore, and Priscilla Nix for their sharp proofreading eyes. I couldn't do this alone, and I'm so thankful for each of you.

This was the first time I offered preorder book bundles on my website to help support this project months in advance of release. Thank you to all the readers who preordered from me, and especially to those who went above and beyond in their support by purchasing book bundles—Kelly Cabral, Lisa Larsen Hill, Jessica Miranda, and Ann Valentine. I so appreciate each of you ladies!

A huge thank you to my ever-supportive family—Daniel, James, and Noah. I love you guys so much.

Last of all, a heartfelt thank you to the Author of Life. You inspire me with stories to tell when I walk in the woods, gaze at the ocean, spend time with loved ones, or read your Word. Thank you for breathing life into all you touch.

Did you catch Heidi's Orchard House Bed and Breakfast Series, featuring Charlotte's friend Hannah and the Martin clan? Read on for a sample from the first book in the series, Where Grace Appears.

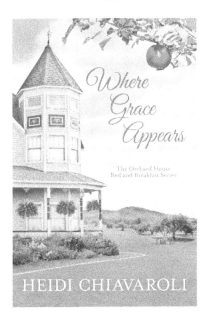

# Where Grace Appears

The nature of secrets is that they long to be kept and long to be told all at the same time.

At least that's the conclusion I came to as I stared at the solid wood door of my childhood home. Only a year away from my master's in clinical psychology at NYU, and the one thing threatening success...the secret lodged in my belly.

I knew all about the psychology of secrets—our need for self-preservation, why we held our confidences close to our hearts, the proven healing of mind and body that often comes with their release. And so I had followed James Pennebaker's advice and written my secret on a torn page of my journal. Then I burned it with a match over my sink, watched my words dissolve into ash, and convinced myself that it had been freed from my conscience.

I would put Pennebaker's theory to the test over the next several weeks. For yes, I had known all about the psychology of secrets from my textbooks.

And now, I would know about them firsthand.

I pushed open the door, remembering the many times I'd crossed this threshold to find Mom pulling a batch of oatmeal cookies out of the oven for the latest PTO fundraiser. Maggie would be pacing before the kitchen bar, fretting over an upcoming date, while Lizzie sprawled on the floor patting Scrabble's furry belly. Bronson would be laboring over an algebra problem at the dining room table, while Amie pasted wildflower petals onto cardstock beside him.

And Dad...Dad would be holed up in his office, of course, or out at the mission, saving the world.

"Hello?" I wrestled my suitcase through the doorway, filled with more books and notebooks than clothes and accessories. "I'm home!"

The rooms echoed back uncharacteristically silent despite the scent of freshly-baked brownies. I passed Dad's office and a pang started in my breastbone. I forced my gaze away from the partially open door, not yet ready to see what I knew was there—the hollow curve of his chair, the dust thick on his dear books. I'd crack at least one open in his honor this summer. Maybe a Bertrand Russell book, or Aristotle, maybe *Fate* by Ralph Waldo Emerson. It wouldn't be easy, but I'd pull on my big girl pants and do it, if not for Dad's sake this time, then as a sort of toast to his memory.

The roar of a compressor came from the back of the house and I left my suitcase to search out its owner. Where was everyone? While I wasn't vain enough to expect a welcome home party, I did think at least Lizzie would have ensured I didn't return home to an empty house. It had been five months since I'd seen them, after all. Five months, and in some ways, a lifetime.

"Hello?" I entered the dining room to see a familiar form standing on a small ladder, holding a nail gun to freshly-painted crown molding.

He turned, and my heart gave an unexpected lurch.

Tripp Colton was the last person I needed to see right now. I still couldn't think of that day last summer without a flush of embarrassment creeping over me. He should have never said those words. And he definitely shouldn't have kissed me like that. He had ruined our perfectly lovely, comfortable relationship in one stormy, steamy afternoon.

We'd never be the same again.

"Josie." His voice possessed a warmth I didn't expect. Maybe there was still hope for us to reclaim what we'd once had. Maybe there was still hope for our friendship.

These past silent months had been torture but now, glimpsing a promise of goodwill, I longed to fight for the old order of things. To not lose Tripp's friendship no matter how we got to this place. No matter the regret tied to that summer day. No matter the secret singeing my chest.

He stepped off the ladder and gave me a hug, eliciting a lurch of longing. I wanted to sink into those strong arms, into the spicy aroma of cologne and wood shavings and sea. So familiar. So achingly comforting. So unlike Finn's book and leather scent.

I shook my head free of the forbidden thoughts, glanced at Tripp's khakis and polo shirt, searched for solid ground between us.

"Grandpop didn't up the dress code for his best project manager again, did he?"

Tripp smiled that delicious smile, the one that drove all the girls in high school crazy. Curly black hair matched his deep eyes, the faintest five o'clock shadow making his mysterious dark looks and white teeth all that more alluring.

Not that I'd ever been one of the crazy high school girls, of course. I'd just been Josie, his best friend.

Tripp shrugged. "The old boy has high standards, what can I say?" His smile spread wider. "I'm kidding. I was on the way to the library but had a half-hour to spare. Figured I could put this up for your mother—I caught her with power tools last week."

I groaned. Ever since Mom had taken off a piece of her thumb with a belt sander when I was twelve, we'd tried to keep her away from the power tools. It had become a running joke in the family that she stick with what suited her best—books and good home cooking. "Then consider the Martin children—and Mom's fingers—forever in your debt." We laughed, and it felt good. Like the old us, instead of the after-that-summer-day us.

I headed to the adjoining kitchen and took a glass from the corner cupboard. I pushed it against the water dispenser on the refrigerator, noting the dispenser light was out. My thoughts turned to Dad again, just as hopeless as Mom when it came to handy house fixes. Poor Dad had always been too caught up in the mentally constructive to have anything to do with the physical improvement of anything. Lucky for us, Tripp didn't mind trading handyman services for dibs on whatever came out of Mom's kitchen.

I turned from the fridge, catching sight of a neatly folded sheet and pillow on the corner of the living room sofa. I wondered who Mom had allowed to crash on our couch this week. "So, a library visit, huh? They get in a new Calvin and Hobbes or something?" Despite my best efforts, I never could get Tripp to crack much more than an occasional graphic novel.

"Ha, ha." He shook his head, picked up a smaller molding, climbed the ladder, and fit it in the corner like a perfect puzzle piece before nailing it in place. He smoothed his hand along the wood, testing it out, searching for a bump or imperfection—something to fix. Because that's what Tripp did. Fix things.

Too bad he couldn't fix what happened between us just as easily.

"I'm going to the library for your mother." He climbed down the ladder and our gazes caught. For a terrible moment, I felt the awkwardness I feared would be ours from here on out. He shifted his attention back to the molding above.

I cleared my throat, grasped for words and understanding. Mom was one of the librarians. "Why does she need you to get something for her? She's working today, isn't she?"

"Her retirement party? At three o'clock?" Tripp rolled up the hose of the nail gun.

"R-retirement?" Surely, I hadn't missed that piece of information. Yes, I'd been distracted of late, but not so distracted I'd miss such big news.

And a party? I'd received a text from Maggie last week, something about the twins' Little League tournament. Nothing mentioning retirement. Lizzie called a few days ago to play me a new song she'd written. Had she said anything?

Tripp squeezed my shoulder. "Hey, you okay? No one has to know you forgot. It hasn't even started yet. We'll head over together...if you want."

His hand landed steady on me, solid if not a bit hesitant. I so needed firm ground right now.

But no, arriving at Mom's party together would never do. I needed to create clear boundaries between us. No mixed signals, especially now.

I pulled away from his warm hand. "I didn't forget. No one told me."

Right. That was it, wasn't it? I pulled out a chair and sat heavily. "Mom's really retiring?"

"That's the word."

We'd always been tight on money, and Mom was still young—too young to think about retiring. Unless...I gasped for sudden breath, chest tight. "Is she okay?"

"She's fine, Josie. Better than fine, I think. She's just ready for a change, you know? Even talked about renting some space over on Main Street, opening up a bookstore."

I stared, mouth agape.

Tripp's face reddened. "Amie talks too much sometimes."

"Apparently," I muttered. Still, it annoyed me that Tripp knew more than I did about what went on with my own family. I mean, a bookshop? That was *huge*. And no one thought to tell me?

An unpleasant twinge of guilt came as I recalled the many phone calls and text messages—especially the ones from Mom—that I'd either ignored or acknowledged with simple "likes" or smiley-faced emojis. I had my reasons, of course. Not particularly good ones, but reasons nonetheless.

Finn *had* been a distraction. One I'd kept to myself, hadn't even shared with Maggie, never mind Mom. He'd been from

Dad's world, after all. It would be too much for Mom, especially not even a year after Dad's death.

Not to mention that my obsession with Finn was such an incredibly un-Josielike thing to do. Yes, I'd always been the wild Martin. The impulsive, blunt, opinionated, passionate Martin. But I'd never lost my head around a man and I certainly never let anything get in the way of my big career plans. Not until Professor Finn Becker came along, anyway.

My face burned as I remembered the moments we shared, how the alluring power of him had been enough to swallow me up, to create oblivion in all other areas of my life.

I'd forgotten the careful outline I'd sketched out for my life. I'd forgotten respectability and reason. I'd thrown myself into the dangerous. Played with fire. It shouldn't be a surprise I'd gotten burned. Torched.

Now, I had nothing but sizzling shame in the depths of my spirit. Too bad it wasn't enough to undo all that had been done.

I sighed. None of those memories deserved a place here, on my homecoming day. Mom's retirement day. Just think...a *bookshop*. How many times had Dad sat at this very dining room table talking about this long-held dream?

Tripp waved a hand in front of my face, and I blinked to see something like disappointment marring his features.

"I'm sorry. I'm more distracted than usual, I guess."

"Planning that next book in your head?"

I averted my gaze. "I haven't written since high school, and you know it."

"That's right. Too busy strapping all those letters to the end of your name in the Big Apple to consider silly things like stories, is that it?"

His scoffing tone rubbed me the wrong way. I breathed deep, pressed my lips together, and attempted to reign in that old temper. "Because you're such a huge proponent of deep, well-told stories, I suppose? Don't worry, Colton. I could never match the likes of Captain Underpants, anyway."

"Hey, that is a brilliant series concept." He grew serious, studied me without cracking a smile, a thousand unspoken words in his gaze. "You do know I would have gobbled up anything you'd written, Jo."

I bristled at his nickname for me. It was bad enough Mom and Dad had the entire *Little Women* thing going on with our names, but sometimes I wondered if our association with the March family hadn't cursed us in some ways. Mom had been so thrilled when I wrote my first story in elementary school. *I'd Cross the Desert for Milk.* It was awful. But you wouldn't have known it by Mom's enthusiasm.

Over the years, as Amie gravitated to art and Lizzie to music, as I bucked against the urge to write, and even last year as Maggie threw away her marketing career to be a wife and mother, I wondered if we'd inadvertently formed some sort of name-fulfilling prophecy. Had knowing Mom and Dad named us after the March family led us to mirror them in some ways? Many times, in ways we didn't even want?

Over time, I'd pulled away from creative writing and moved toward philosophy and psychology. Towards Dad's dreams for me. For who was I to compete with Jo March?

I shook my head, forcing myself back to the present. Back to Tripp stating he wanted to read my stories. Back to that horrid nickname he had for me. "Don't call me 'Jo.' Besides, we both know you never had the attention span for anything more than a graphic novel."

He leaned forward. "Remember *Noah and the Seed*? That was a brilliant story."

A grin tugged at the corners of my mouth. "It had pictures. That's why you liked it."

Amie had drawn the pictures, and we'd presented it at story time at the children's hospital a month after Lizzie's thyroid surgery. There'd been nothing better than seeing those little faces light up as they transported from the bright playroom corner of a hospital to a world I'd created with words.

Enthralled by my story and Amie's pictures, the uncertainty etched on their small faces had disappeared, replaced by a look of wonder.

I pushed the memory away. I'd decided on a different route to help people now. Dad would have been proud of all I'd accomplished so far in making a name for myself in the field of psychology at NYU.

I sniffed, not quite able to push away the full memories of those times in the hospital—with Tripp leaning against a wall enjoying the stories as much as the children.

He pulled out a chair and sat beside me. "I loved all your stories, even the ones without pictures. Still love them." His gaze held mine, and something about it brought me to the edge of longing, so much so it was devastating.

I shot to my feet, familiar panic working its way to my chest. "Why don't you head on over to the library? I have to put some things away. I'll see you there?"

He swallowed, the thick bob of his Adam's apple moving along his smooth neck. "Yeah, sure. Whatever you want."

"Thanks." This was what I wanted. It was. To be left alone.

He gathered up his tools and ladder, seemed prepared to leave in silence.

"Tripp." I caught him before he headed out the back door to his truck. "It's good to see you."

His smile, etched with a sadness I'd expected to have disappeared by now, didn't quite reach the edges of his mouth. "You too, Josie."

I didn't breathe until the sound of his truck was an echo down our quiet street.

We would clear the air between us sometime soon. But it didn't have to be the very afternoon I came home.

TRIPP STARTED up his work truck and leaned back against the headrest, his thoughts filled with his encounter with Josie. She joked he wasn't much of a reader, and that might be true, but he read one thing very well, even if she'd never admit it—her.

That sad, desperate look in her sharp gray eyes, hidden beneath that mass of wild chestnut hair, covered something she didn't want him to see. It didn't matter that it'd been five months —five long months—since they'd seen one another. He knew.

Something was wrong. Was it just being home again, realizing the loss of her father anew? She used to confide in him, but those days vanished faster than coffees on a construction site.

Seeing her was like reopening an old wound. With much pain, he realized he still held out hope for them to be together someday. His best friend. The girl he'd loved all his life.

But she'd rejected him, tore his heart to shreds like one would an old bank statement. He'd convinced himself he was getting over her, even went on a date or two, but always found the poor girl, who sat across from him at dinner, lacking. Not with any kind of blatant physical or character flaw, but with the simple fact that she wasn't Josie, the girl who took up every inch and corner of his heart.

He put his truck in drive and sent up a quick prayer for whatever the future brought for them. How would he even survive this retirement party? Josie'd want to catch up with her siblings no doubt. Would she even acknowledge his presence?

But he wasn't going for Josie, he was going for Hannah. The woman had been like a mother to him all these years. He couldn't miss her big day. Seeing Josie again—even if she didn't give him the time of day—was just an added benefit.

His phone rang out over his Bluetooth and he turned left on Bay View Street toward the library, the sparkling Maine coast on his right. He picked up. "Hey, Pedro. What's up?"

"You at the office, Boss Man?"

"I can be." His best foreman didn't ask for much, so when he did, Tripp tried to accommodate.

"I gotta talk to you before I lose my cool."

Pedro didn't lose his cool often. Not over receiving the wrong materials on a job-site. Not over a picky homeowner who changed their mind a hundred times over tile backsplash choices. Not even over a four-hundred-dollar table saw gone bust.

An unpleasant knowing settled in Tripp's stomach. "I'll be there in five minutes." He'd have to be late to the library. Keeping his foreman happy trumped being on time for a retirement party. Better to keep Grandpop out of it all if possible. Especially if... "This doesn't have anything to do with a certain blond-haired college kid who'd rather be surfing than building houses, does it?"

"You called it, Boss."

Tripp groaned and hung up with Pedro, his fingers tight on the wheel. He probably should have fired that kid a week ago. Probably should have sent him packing, told him to get a job at a beach club where he could have smiled pretty for tips all summer long. If only it wasn't so complicated.

If only the lazy laborer was someone other than his own brother.

Visit Heidi's website to sign up for her newsletter to be the first to know about new releases, book deals, and fun writing updates! www.heidichiavaroli.com

# About the Author

Heidi Chiavaroli (pronounced shev-uh-roli...sort of like *Chevrolet* and *ravioli* mushed together!) wrote her first story in third grade, titled *I'd Cross the Desert for Milk*. Years later, she revisited writing, using her two small boys' nap times to pursue what she thought at the time was a foolish dream.

Heidi's debut novel, *Freedom's Ring*, was a Carol Award winner and a Christy Award finalist, a *Romantic Times* Top Pick and a *Booklist* Top Ten Romance Debut. Her latest Carol Award-winning dual timeline novel, *The Orchard House*, is inspired by the lesser-known events in Louisa May Alcott's life and compelled her to create The Orchard House Bed and Breakfast series. Heidi makes her home in Massachusetts with her husband and two sons. Visit her online at heidichiavaroli.com

Milton Keynes UK
Ingram Content Group UK Ltd.
UKHW011824140624
444031UK00016B/191/J

9 781957 663111